WHISPERS IN THE DARK

WHISPERS IN THE DARK

Allison Gunn

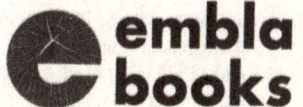

First published in the UK in 2025 by

An imprint of Bonnier Books UK
5th Floor, HYLO, 105 Bunhill Row,
London, EC1Y 8LZ

Copyright © Allison Gunn, 2025
Originally published in the USA by Simon & Schuster under
the title 'Nowhere'. Copyright © Allison Gunn, 2024.

All rights reserved.
No part of this publication may be reproduced, stored or transmitted in any form
or by any means, electronic, mechanical, photocopying or otherwise, without
the prior written permission of the publisher.

The right of Allison Gunn to be identified as Author of this work has been asserted by
them in accordance with the Copyright, Designs and Patents Act, 1988.

This is a work of fiction. Names, places, events and incidents are either the products
of the author's imagination or used fictitiously. Any resemblance to actual
persons, living or dead, or actual events is purely coincidental.

A CIP catalogue record for this book is available from the British Library.

ISBN: 978-1-47142-071-9

Also available as an ebook

Typeset by IDSUK (Data Connection) Ltd
Printed and bound in Great Britain by Clays Ltd, Elcograf S.p.A.

The authorised representative in the EEA is Bonnier Books
UK (Ireland) Limited.
Registered office address: Floor 3, Block 3, Miesian Plaza,
Dublin 2, D02 Y754, Ireland
compliance@bonnierbooks.ie
www.bonnierbooks.co.uk

For Carys and Lennon—always remember who you are.

Prologue

"I'm sorry, Officer. Can you repeat that?"

Officer Danny Boyd would have preferred not to answer the dispatcher. No matter how hard he tried to shake the feeling, Danny knew someone, or something, was watching him from the trees encircling the tiny Virginia town. To speak would draw attention, alerting the predator to his presence just as a deer's rustling in the forest guided his rifle's aim. Danny was perfectly aware of what it was like to be the hunter, but never before had he known what it felt like to be hunted . . . until now.

His gut churned. He had already gambled with the last thirty minutes, spending more time in Dahlmouth than he'd ever wanted to, even before the chilling silence he found today.

"You heard what I said!" Danny barked into the radio as he brought the patrol car's engine to life. "They're gone."

His eyes darted back and forth over the pavement and weeds sticking out of the broken sidewalk along Dahlmouth's Main Street. Suddenly, Danny caught movement out of the corner of his left eye. He jerked in that direction, his hand gripping the butt of his gun in the leather holster. Danny tried not to exhale directly into the radio as he saw Officer Jack Carlyle, his partner, emerging from Dahlmouth's police station, shaking his head as he walked back to the patrol car. Danny didn't need to ask why Jack looked so befuddled. He had already accepted what his partner simply could not.

Danny knew they had a duty to explore further—to follow the obvious lead and start a sweep of the woods. Yet, an alarm bell was screeching in his ears. There was something very wrong with this call, those trees, this place. The moment he saw the carvings on the trees, a strange and primal terror shot through him.

The markings were unavoidable—a circular symbol punctured by a large V. The symbol was everywhere, and the image of some faceless creep wandering from trunk to trunk, methodically carving the sigil for hours on end, was the stuff of nightmares. But in his gut Danny knew something much more disturbing lurked in the shadows.

"Officer, *who* is gone?" The dispatcher's nasally voice crackled over the receiver and startled Danny.

Sweat soaked the back of his neck. Jack ignored him as he swung into the passenger side of the car, and Danny took this as his cue to make one last sweep of the scene. Even if Dahlmouth's entire population popped up now, it would take a hell of a lot to make him stay one second longer.

"All of them. Everyone is just . . . gone."

One

"Uh, guess again, Charlie." Rachel glanced in the rearview mirror at her two girls. The keys in the ignition swung to and fro. Her dark aviator sunglasses hid her disapproval; nevertheless, she was sure Charlie knew *exactly* how Rachel felt about her going out for an evening ride to Roanoke with Gemma Thompson while the girl's teenage brother—Alex—served as the sole chaperone for the outing.

"But, Mama," Charlie implored, "it's just to see the lights and drive right back. I'll only be gone a couple hours." She leaned forward to put her hands on Rachel's shoulders. Her voice was sweet and high, not so different from the one she'd had when she was eight or nine—the days when Charlie still seemed to like Rachel no matter how headstrong she had always been. Rachel had been proud of her daughter's feisty nature back then. It was a commonality the two shared, and perhaps the only quality Charlie possessed in which Rachel could see herself. Now, it was quickly becoming the very thing driving them apart.

"Why can't Mrs. Thompson take you, then? Why does it have to be Alex?"

"Because the PTA meeting is on Thursday night. You know that. Mrs. Thompson has to be there; she's president."

Rachel couldn't keep the damn meetings straight, even though they were held with religious regularity. None of them were particularly useful. Thus far, the only one Rachel had found enlightening was when Mrs. Janet Jamerson showed up to give Principal Gary a talking-to in front of the middle-school gym regarding the number of times he'd given her girl detention for dress code transgressions. This was injustice at its finest when, per Mrs. Jamerson, everybody knew Alice Henn wore shorter skirts with bright lacy undies underneath for god and everyone to see. Naturally, Mrs. Kimmy Henn had a few words to say to Janet.

Before anyone knew it, Rachel was serving as a human wall between two women in their late forties who swung their fists like bikers and pulled hair like they were teenagers all over again. Kimmy busted Rachel's lip and should have had charges filed against her for assaulting an officer. However, seeing as Rachel was Dahlmouth's police chief, it would make for awkward future encounters. Besides, it was good for a belly laugh later that evening when she and her husband, Finn, were on the back porch with two beers.

The happy memory quickly soured in Rachel's mind. She didn't even recognize the people she and Finn had been before. Where once the echo of Finn's laughter in her thoughts brought a smile to her face, Rachel now felt nothing but disdain.

"Daddy said she could go," Lucy piped up dreamily. Rachel looked back to see her six-year-old drawing faces in the condensation on the window with her pudgy little fingers. The morning sun lit up Lucy's light blonde hair so that she glowed like a pint-sized saint.

"Absolutely not," Rachel said.

"Lucy!" Charlie shrieked and brought her fist down into the seat between the two girls. "Thanks a lot!"

"Lucy doesn't have anything to do with it. You're not going because it's a stupid idea," Rachel boomed and prepared to put the van in reverse. She pretended to focus on safe Safe Driving Skills™ like she lectured the kids at Dahlmouth High about every spring, just before half of them flooded the country roads with shiny new IDs and bottles of Miller High Life hidden in the trunk.

"I'm lucky anyone wants to take me out at all anymore!" Charlie's vitriol turned toward Rachel. "Thanks to you and—"

"Daddy could take us," Lucy suggested, face still hidden by the holy light around her head.

"SHUT UP!" Charlie shrieked and once more slammed down her fist, this time dangerously close to her little sister's thigh.

"ENOUGH!" Charlie and Lucy froze mid-breath. "We're done with suggestions for the day, ladies. How 'bout we focus on the scenery in silence while we drive to school, yeah?"

Rachel hit the gas hard, wheels spinning before they caught on the gravel and the car screeched out of the Kennan family's driveway.

* * *

"So, did you hear old Bobblehead Melanie is coming back to town?" Deputy Jeremy Whitman cackled as he spun half circles in his swivel chair.

As Rachel watched him spin, his usual shit-eating grin spread wide across his face, she still marveled at how the hell Jeremy was the most capable officer at her disposal—the second-in-command over what was otherwise a nearly comical ragtag police force. With a perpetual fondness for gossip, Grey Goose, and girls, Jeremy had yet to fully understand the responsibility resting on his broad shoulders. Though only two years younger than her, his brown puppy-dog eyes and immaturity kept him pegged at twenty-five rather than thirty-five in Rachel's mind. While Jeremy's small belly bulge had recently turned into a full beer gut and his dark hair had started to thin, her deputy would forever be an incurable man-child.

"You're worse than the goddamn hens at church." Rachel brought her coffee cup down harder than intended and sent brown sludge dribbling onto her desk where there were already hundreds, maybe thousands, of other coffee stains and cigarette burns covering the wooden relic. Most had been imprinted there years before she was born.

"How much time do you think will pass before we get another old biddy calling about a parked car with the windows fogged up?" Jeremy proceeded to make an offensive gesture to mimic Melanie's well-known oral talents.

"I'll make sure I send you out on that call since you're so happy to see Melanie coming back to town." Rachel rolled her eyes and checked her cell phone. She still had fifteen more minutes before she could justify a smoke break in secret.

"Rachel. Rachel!" Officer Marcus Blevins, a kid better suited for pizza delivery than the police force, shouted for her at the station's front door. His usually spiked, light blond hair was flattened against his head, dark hollows cradling his eyeballs. "AJ Johnson's flipping shit again."

"What's wrong now?"

"He's on his CB going on about something he and Tommy Wise found in the woods off Route 6." Marcus sounded as if each word pained him, not out of concern but annoyance. "Sounds like one of us should go out."

"I can already tell you the kid's blitzed out of his mind, 'specially if he's out there with one of the Wises again," Jeremy said, and suddenly became interested in sorting through the months-old citations scattered across his desk.

"It's nine o'clock in the morning," Marcus stated, as if it made a difference.

"You think that matters?" Rachel grunted. "The Wises shoot up their breakfast."

"Thanks for explaining that, Chief," Marcus scoffed. "Like I didn't grow up with these pricks."

"Anywhere else, they'd kick your ass for talking to your superiors that way." Rachel took another sip of her coffee. One of these days, she would go ahead and follow through with her threats. After three years, she was almost there. She'd start with this cartoon character first.

Marcus Blevins could have gone into IT or graphic design or even the circus, but under no circumstances should he have gone into criminal justice. That was his parents' doing. Marcus was hired a week before Rachel, a parting gift from the bitter old man who was her predecessor. Ever since then, she had tolerated the *golly gee whiz* veneer Marcus offered strangers, the cocky retorts he shot at anyone who challenged him, and the utter incompetence that would have prevented him from getting a job anywhere other than the tiny town he'd never left. Marcus believed Dahlmouth owed him respect as a birthright. Only outsiders like Rachel needed to work for the locals' approval.

"Look, he's hysterical." Marcus shrugged. "I can't even tell what he's talking about." He took another step backward. Jeremy kept wheeling around in the chair as it screeched its disapproval.

"You'd better be backing your ass out of that door to go check in on him, then." Rachel offered him a cheers with her coffee cup.

"Oh, come on, guys. Please! Jennifer's been up all night with Maisie. Jenn thinks she's cutting teeth, but it's fuckin' miserable. Nobody in the house has slept for days."

"Cry me a river, Marky boy," Jeremy began in his usual machismo tone. "We all got kids here."

"Yeah, but I actually see mine, dipshit," Marcus sneered.

"Hey, fuck you!" Jeremy brought his fist down on his desk and sent notices flying in every direction. "I'll kick your ass, you—"

"So you want one of us to go out there so you can head home?" Rachel had very little time for puffed chests and red faces.

"Jenn really needs—I mean, she hasn't slept—and I think Maisie might need the doctor at some point. And we don't have any more baby Tylenol in the house, so . . ." The kid shifted awkwardly in the doorway. His abrupt absences always seemed to correspond with the days when they received any kind of call that would require actual assistance. Now that his daughter had arrived, Marcus just had a better excuse.

"Fine," Rachel snapped. "But you owe me personally."

"You know she hates dealing with that stretch of road, dickhead." Jeremy glared over his shoulder. "Imagine how you'd feel if somebody made you go stomping around where your kid—"

"That's not why, asshole." Rachel softly kicked the edge of his desk with her boot to cut the conversation off.

Her son was not a topic she cared to discuss with anyone, not even when combating her officers' nonsense. Jeremy knew that better than most. The pair spent nearly every day together as is, but in the weeks following the accident, the man didn't leave her side. He'd continued searching the riverbanks along with Rachel well after everyone else had abandoned the task. Not once had they talked about those days in the entire year that had passed since.

"None of us wants to deal with the Wises' bullshit anymore, myself included. But as far as I can tell, you're not really giving me an op—"

"Thanks a ton, Rachel." Marcus sighed and disappeared in the same breath.

"Dick," Jeremy said and rapped his knuckles on the desk.

"Get your shit." Rachel gently nudged Jeremy's boot this time as she pushed herself away from the desk.

"What?"

"You're coming with me."

"No. Do I have to?" Jeremy groaned. "Why would you do this to me, Rach?"

"I'm not dealing with those hopped-up bastards alone. If you'll recall, the last time we had to clean up after the Wises, the fuckers took a baseball bat to the county deputy and our cruiser."

Jeremy snorted. "That was a hell of a lot of fun, though."

"I'm putting an end to one of them if they pull that shit again today."

"No, you ain't." Jeremy smiled broadly and winked. "You're too much of a bleeding-heart, finely trained city cop to do that. I don't think you could put a bullet in 'em if they charged at you with rifles."

"Get your ass in gear. Let's go!" Rachel fought to dismiss the burning in her cheeks, already halfway out the door with the cruiser keys jingling between her fingers.

Two

Driving along Route 6 twisted Rachel's guts up these days, especially rumbling over the small bridge at mile-marker ten. Today, Rachel chose to believe it had more to do with the call about AJ Johnson and Tommy Wise than anything to do with the waters flowing beneath that damn bridge. Less than three years in the position, and Rachel was already tired of wrestling with big ol' country meth boys and their mamas with missing teeth and leather skin, but she'd be damned if she ran home to Richmond and a demotion.

The Wises were the top meth cooks in a fifteen-mile radius, and that meant a hell of a lot of business streamed through their trembling fingers. Lately, it seemed kids either left Dahlmouth upon graduation or ran off into the woods to stick a needle in their arms. Just before the car crash that claimed her son, Rachel had called in the state troopers to raid the Wise family's nearby trailers and wipe out their meth lab. It had been a blow to the family business, but Rachel had no doubt they were building it back up, this time with more guns and angry dogs.

They arrived at mile-marker thirteen, both bracing themselves. She worried they would waste half the day tripping around the woods, trying to track down AJ and Tommy to make sure they didn't do something violently stupid. But there was no need to scour the trees; Tommy's beat-up Ford flatback was pulled over into a ditch, leaning at an angle that suggested one big gust might flip it over.

Tommy was nowhere to be found. However, a twitching AJ was pacing at the Ford's tailgate, chewing at his fingernails with wide eyes as the cruiser rumbled up behind him. Unlike the wraithlike Wise family, AJ was a hulk of a guy with a massive, tangled brown beard and shaggy hair that stuck out from under his John Deere cap. Today he wore a long-sleeve green flannel shirt with the buttons undone, exposing a ratty Insane Clown Posse T-shirt. His ripped-up jeans were sagging and the black waistband of his boxers peeked out. He shook his head and shuddered, engaged in a robust conversation with himself.

"Oh, boy." Jeremy grabbed the walkie from the center console as they pulled up. "This should be fun."

Rachel still remembered the day AJ had tossed his graduation cap into the air in Dahlmouth High's auditorium. His parents had been the first to show up on the Kennans' doorstep when they moved in, tuna casserole in hand. She hadn't seen them in a long time now but didn't have to question why. Their boy had changed into something they never imagined, their hopes and dreams for him dying as meth consumed his light. Rachel understood that loss all too well even if the circumstances varied. She blinked away the memory and refocused.

Rachel knew better than to charge up on the kid. She stepped out of the car and heard him whimpering as he paced, bouncing on the balls of his feet whenever he turned. Jeremy swung out of the passenger side with his signature swagger and started toward AJ. The image of AJ jabbing Jeremy in the belly with a fishing knife played through Rachel's mind like a movie preview.

"Jeremy, hold up one goddamn second," Rachel said. "AJ, what's your problem today, son? Heard you on the radio talking about some pretty gnarly stuff. Sounds like you're having a rough go of it. Where's Tommy?" Rachel's eyes flickered toward the trees, waiting for the Wise kid to come charging out, guns blazing.

"It can't be real," AJ muttered and looked up at her. Tears were brimming in his eyes and his face had splotchy red patches underneath the mass of hair. "Mama Wise always warned us, but ..." He ran two shaky hands over his kelly-green baseball hat. "I just ... y'all go take a look. An' then I'll come with you, 'kay? I'll turn myself right over with no fuss. I swear. Jus', p-please."

"Why don't you get in the cruiser first, and then we'll talk about whatever—?"

"NO!" AJ cut Jeremy off with a deranged cry. Spit flew from his lips in strings. "I ain't no fool! I step in there, and y'all won't even take a look at all."

"Well, that's not very trusting, friend." Jeremy smiled and cocked his head.

"Fine. That's fine, AJ." Rachel nodded. "Can you tell me where Tommy went? He leave you here on your own?"

AJ's lips trembled as he covered his ears. "He weren't gonna stick around ... not after that." The boy gestured toward the woods before pulling back into himself like a frightened child.

Jeremy smacked his gum. "Can't imagine the cops comin' made him want to stay either."

Rachel exhaled, resisting the urge to put her hand on AJ's shoulder. "Deputy Whitman is going to wait here with you while I go take a look. Just tell me where I'm headed."

"You should both go." AJ whimpered again and pressed his palms against his face. "You should both see it."

"Ain't gonna happen." Jeremy folded his arms across his chest. "One of us needs to stay with you to make sure you don't hurt yourself or anybody else, son."

"I ain't gonna hurt anybody!" AJ barked and sprayed more saliva.

"Okay, tell me where to go, then." Rachel borrowed the voice she used when she soothed the kids back to sleep after a bad dream.

AJ shook his head, clutched himself, and swung from side to side. Slowly, he pointed off into the tree line.

"It's in there." Another whimper.

"Tommy in there, too?" Jeremy muttered, his gaze following the direction of AJ's finger.

In all likelihood, Tommy Wise had been so spooked by AJ's call to the cops that he'd taken off for the compound. Still, Rachel popped open the strap of her holster in case she was walking into an ill-planned trap. It was more likely she'd be going up against a bear or a mountain lion. Just because AJ saw shit in Technicolor didn't mean there wasn't some hint of truth at its core.

"What am I looking for?" Rachel pressed on.

"Just look at the trees," AJ squealed and backed away from the tree line, nearly colliding with Jeremy, who had edged his way behind him. "If it's real, it'll be there. Ain't no mistakin' it."

Rachel threw a wary look Jeremy's way. He nodded at her with his brows raised, and grinned as if it were all delightfully funny. Rachel turned and started down the embankment at a trot, the tread of her boots slipping in the wet grass and red mud.

AJ's hysteria grew louder as she entered the woods, and she hoped Jeremy could handle him without popping off. For all his unnecessary machismo, Jeremy typically kept a cool head with Dahlmouth's citizens even at their rowdiest. He'd known most of them his entire life and, much to Rachel's chagrin, was far more successful than her in talking them down from going nuclear.

When the Kennan family moved to Dahlmouth three years ago, Rachel had liked how remote and wooded it was. In the beginning, she would go hiking at least once a week, even in the dead of winter. It gave her a place to escape, to decompress without a couple hundred sets of eyes sizing her up. It was a world away from the cities she and Finn grew up in, and certainly a change of pace from where they began their lives together.

But she had come to mistrust the woods in time. Rachel had seen too much gory mischief there, most of it related to people acting like the Lord above found fit to grant them access to "hunting" rifles that could leave exit wounds the size of grapefruits in their fellow man.

She especially hated *this* stretch of woods, though. Not far from where Rachel wandered, the James River cut its wide path through the forest. Small bits of shredded metal and glass were still embedded in its sandy shore. Dark water rushed over a detached bumper no one had ever bothered to remove. High above at the edge of the small Route 6 bridge, a tiny wooden cross sat by the side of the road, white paint chipped nearly all the way off now, a tiny stuffed bear buried in the mud around it.

Roadside memorials never actually slowed anyone's speed or made them sober up any faster, but some people insisted on that sort of thing. Folks told her it was necessary for healing, though she wasn't sure for whom. It certainly wasn't for Rachel's sake. Every time she drove past the memorial the church had thrown together at that bridge—without the Kennans' consent—something between hate and horror flared in her chest. Aidan had been eight years old when he died—he hadn't played with teddy bears anymore, but that was cuter for the church folks to lay there than water guns and baseballs.

Water guns and baseballs ... summers before the world ended: Aidan running through the backyard in his bare feet as Charlie nailed him with a volley from her Super Soaker; Lucy's gleeful squealing a constant undercurrent as Finn chased after her with the water hose. Rachel's brain snagged on Finn's smile, and the scene faded to black. That smile now seemed to taint every warm memory of the life they'd once lived.

Fifty feet into the woods, Rachel couldn't hear AJ whining anymore or Jeremy growling for the kid to get ahold of himself. The wind rustling through leaves replaced any noise that might have come off Route 6. But there was something more; she could feel the pangs of it in her gut. It was fear, a stranger to Rachel these days, since fear was only felt by those who wish very much to continue breathing. Rachel was long past that now. Or so she thought.

She strained to hear any sound of a branch breaking or underbrush shaking. There was nothing at all. Rachel sensed *nothing*. The woods should have been alive with activity, winter melting away and spring waking lurking creatures. Rachel should have been able to hear the roaring of that god-awful river. But all that remained was the wind overhead and her boots crunching on dead leaves.

Suddenly, the hair on the back of Rachel's neck rose despite the scarf she wore and the day's mild temperature. Her heart picked up its pace while her palms grew slick. Perhaps someone was watching her—her body instinctively reacting to the threat of being hunted. That's not what it felt like, though. She wasn't being stalked; Rachel was being called.

From the woods, where the trees grew denser and the sunlight struggled to reach the underbrush, something beckoned her. Those woods ... they wanted her attention, wanted to absorb her into the darkness until the world forgot her name. Wanted to steal her breath and return the forest to complete stillness. Tiny, warm fingers crept up and closed around her wrist—

Rachel jumped and swatted at her hand. No, she was just imagining things. There was nothing there—not even a beetle. Her mind was being a nasty little prick again. She shook her head and took a deep breath. She needed more sleep, more exercise, less nicotine, less caffeine, and it'd probably do her a lot of good to get laid. None of those things were likely to change soon, however, so all she could do was continue taking the meds the good doc gave her and quiet her brain when it played its dirty tricks.

She was about to give up on AJ's hysteria when, as if the wind caught her chin and turned her face just so, she saw the thing a few feet to her right. Rachel wondered how she had ever missed it at all.

The human wreckage pinned to the tree before her may have been a man, considering its build. Yet, Rachel couldn't be 100 percent certain. As Rachel neared it, she saw the poor fucker had a railroad spike driven through its gut. Its feet dangled against the ground uselessly with steel-toed hiking boots still attached. Its left arm was suspended and tacked to a tree branch through the soft space between its delicate wrist bones.

A perverse imitation of the Scarecrow from *The Wizard of Oz*.

Her pulse quickened, immediately wondering if this was indeed where Tommy Wise had gotten off to. She didn't want to be the one to notify the Wises that yet another member had fallen; they wouldn't believe Rachel didn't do it herself, and she'd be facing down several Glocks in her face.

Rachel clawed at her brown wool scarf from underneath her jacket's collar. It tightened like a noose before giving way, and she quickly covered her mouth and nose. The body didn't smell, but something about the grotesque figure felt infectious. Nevertheless, she drew closer to gaze into what used to be a human face. The eyes were gone—not mashed in or poked out; those eyeballs were completely removed, leaving nothing but empty sockets, nerves coiled and drying inside. Its mouth hung agape, the jaw skewed to the left, and one glance into the cavity confirmed what Rachel already suspected to be true. Amidst broken teeth and rotting gums, this unfortunate soul was missing their tongue.

She was still more troubled by what little was left of the victim's face. The top layer of flesh had been peeled away, exposing what was now dark muscle and yellowing bone. A small army of red ants zigzagged their way through the stringy ligaments. The scalp remained unscathed, not a strand out of place in the short dark ponytail.

Rachel's eyes then dropped to the corpse's limp right hand before following the trail down to the ground. She flinched, immediately grateful no one was around to witness it. Crouching low, she pressed her scarf even tighter to her nose. She found a jagged hunting knife, small ribbons of skin still snagged in its grooves. A mass of shriveling flesh, unmistakably the missing front of the victim's face, laid at its side. Like a discarded Halloween mask, the face revealed brown leaves on the forest floor through its now-abandoned eyeholes.

This corpse and its disconnected face didn't appear to be Tommy Wise's, though that didn't make her feel much better. Rachel had seen plenty of dead bodies in her time, but she had to admit she'd never stared down anything like this. It wasn't just the brutality of the murder. This thing was mocking her—like it was promising that things in Dahlmouth would never be peaceful under her watch.

Rachel rose again and took a few steps backward, her eyes trained on the mutilated body before she realized she was frightened to turn away from it. At this, she scoffed while silently chiding herself. Dead men didn't move, and this one certainly wasn't going anywhere. She forced herself to spin around even as the sweat on her neck turned cold and goosebumps spread across her forearms beneath a thick coat.

Walk; don't run. Walk; don't you dare run, Rachel coached herself with a clenched jaw.

But she didn't have to lecture herself for long. Midstep, she came to a halt as her ears perked. She held her breath to listen once more. Between each stride, amid the dead leaves crunching under her boots, she heard something that was unmistakable despite being improbable.

She pressed her lips together and closed her eyes. Hoped to be wrong. She'd rather do anything else besides chase after the pitiful wail of a small child, echoing off the broken trunks and bare branches from god only knew how far away. The longer she stood there in the restored quiet, the more humiliated she felt. Yes, her brain was playing dirty tricks today, and it was very much winning.

The same silence that had unnerved her when she entered the woods comforted her now. There was no child, no cries, no rustling from her dead man pinned to the oak. Of course there wasn't. Rachel muttered a curse under her breath, shook her head, and resumed her march back to the road. She'd win the battle with her own mind even if it meant shutting out everything else around her. After all, Rachel had become very good at that.

* * *

"We're going to need to call the sheriff," Rachel boomed, emerging from the woods at a brisk walk, though her instincts still screamed at her to run.

"You spotted Bigfoot, too, eh?" Jeremy smirked and hooked his thumbs into the belt loops below his broad belly. Rachel charged up the embankment without the slightest hint of amusement.

"It *is* real, isn't it? Oh shit." AJ fell down on his ass at the side of the road, cradling his head in his hands. "She knew it. Jesus Christ, Mama Wise knew it all along."

Reading her expression, Jeremy's face suddenly shifted from amused to concerned. "What is it, Rach?"

"Chief," Rachel muttered as she swung open the cruiser's door to grab the police radio.

"What?" Jeremy narrowed his eyes and raised his voice over AJ's growing mania.

"It's *chief* to you, Jeremy. Christ, at least *pretend* to use protocol when I'm having to call in the goddamn sheriff."

"What the hell is in there?" Jeremy looked up at the tree line, his gun unholstered and gripped in his hands, although it remained lowered.

"You're not going to need that."

"Then why you acting like it's some big deal? I like to have my gun ready if it's a big fuckin' deal."

"Because the fucked-up thing in the forest is dead already. You scared of dead men?" Rachel swung herself inside the car.

"*I* am," AJ whispered miserably and hugged his knees to his chest.

As Rachel gripped the handheld radio, the hint of a chorus floated on the breeze—soft, sweet, nearly imperceptible. A slight prickle crawled along her neck as young voices swirled together and dispersed. But as quickly as it came, the whisper of a song was gone, swept away by the wind through bare tree branches.

She held still for a moment. Through the windshield, as if drawn by a magnet, her gaze met AJ's. His eyes were wild and desperate; the young man sought reassurance. She wanted to believe the fear reflected back at her was just that of a high gone terribly wrong—an unfortunate mix of meth and murder. The longer their eyes remained locked, however, the more certain Rachel became: AJ had heard the children's song, too—even if Jeremy appeared to be oblivious—and all the weaponry and bravado AJ gained around the Wises was not enough to quell his panic in the wake of that melody.

His face fell, his gaze souring until all Rachel saw was resentment and unspoken accusations. He glared right through her as if her own skin had been peeled away to expose her inner workings. AJ knew Rachel would be of no help at all . . . that she'd chalk this all up to drugs run amuck, that she—Chief Rachel Kennan of Dahlmouth, Virginia—was a goddamn liar who'd run from the truth until she had nowhere else to hide. And the thing was, AJ wasn't entirely wrong.

Three

It was nine a.m. Finn Kennan was in a staring contest with the laptop screen and losing.

Writer's block is a myth, his older brother Caleb always said. *You gotta keep on going, man.*

That was, of course, easy to say when you had managed to sell three passable scripts to two popular studios for two six-figure checks and one for seven figures. That wasn't even taking into consideration the mountain of cocaine that fueled Caleb's prolific writing. It had a way of making the muse sing.

As it was, Finn had never seen six figures on a check—and the closest thing he had to cocaine these days was the collection of Pixy Stix he had snatched out of Lucy's Halloween candy. They were hidden in the deepest drawer of his writing desk alongside the cigarettes he "gave up." He glared bitterly at the e-cigarette that sat above the top keys on his laptop. One day soon, he would crack out a razor, line up a couple rows of purple-flavored Pixy dust, and snort, just to see what would happen. Then he would light up every last damn cigarette in that crinkled pack and puff away while laying down America's greatest novel. Yeah, it would work just like that.

Finn used to be an actual writer. Back in the good old days of his angst-ridden youth, he had written no less than three novels. Each one was terrible, and his professors at William & Mary had done him the favor of destroying them in a few short semesters. Since then, though, he had cranked out some respectable short stories that had seen the light of day in a couple magazines. He also maintained one exceptionally witty blog about the sociopolitical landscape of America. That had spawned an active social media feed where he lamented, to exactly 2,904 followers, about the clowns who ran society. It was no small feat given that he lived in the middle of bumfuck nowhere with no real friends and an internet connection that was never guaranteed on even the clearest of days.

He wasn't just some bitter, middle-aged basement blogger, though, no matter how it looked. Once upon a time, Finn had penned a highly celebrated exposé on the contradictory ideology of Appalachia for a big-time magazine. Per the talking heads that mattered, it was the "prescient and desperately needed light shone on America's drug-riddled rural underbelly." It had even won awards. While he couldn't maintain the momentum behind his first major piece, Finn had at least been a real journalist in Richmond covering crime for the *Sentinel*, specifically homicides. That was how he had met Rachel. Only now did he know that was the moment when shit went off track.

Fourteen years later, he'd found himself writing puff pieces for the ten-page flyer they called a newspaper in Dahlmouth—a bad rip-off of Mayberry that he'd only reluctantly agreed to move to for his currently estranged wife's career advancement in law enforcement. The irony of Finn surrendering his dreams for a now-failed marriage and a brutal institution he had recently come to advocate dismantling was not lost on him.

Currently, Finn was on unpaid "medical leave," but he couldn't envision ever actually returning to the paper's newsroom, which inexplicably smelled like mushrooms 24/7. Though it had been nearly a year now, no one had asked him whether he was coming back or not. Finn knew why; after what had happened, he would forevermore be a slobbering, drunken son of a bitch in the hearts and minds of Dahlmouth's pious residents. There was no redemption for a sinner like him.

Then again, even before the accident, precisely no one in Dahlmouth had been a fan of Finn. From day one, their closest neighbors—the Tuckers—had been sure to glare from their driveway each time Finn dared to leave the house. After the Kennans's Ford Escape picked up a nail on the road, he made the tragic mistake of admitting to big ol' Darryl Tucker that he didn't know how to change a tire. Darryl returned with a bag of tools and a magical spare tire from his garage, wordlessly switched the tires out, and huffed back to his house. Since then, Finn had often heard a well-defined set of slurs muttered in his direction from across the lawn.

Finn was certain the rest of Dahlmouth's residents felt the exact same way. He never even had a chance here, though Finn wasn't sure he'd ever really wanted one.

These were the moments when, if he let his mind stew on it too much, he thought, *Fuck it all*, and would grab the car keys to head to the liquor store two towns over. Then he would remember

Lucy—her screams being choked off as water filled the car; her tiny fingers nearly slipping from his grasp as the current tried to tear her away; the crushing panic that he'd lose not one but two of his children that night. That's when he'd start puffing away on his e-cigarette instead, the bright blue light on the end flashing to life and making him look like a forty-five-year-old moron at a rave.

Finn dropped his head to the desk and beat it slowly on the black pressed wood, inches from the laptop. He was surrounded by an absolute mess. Chaos and filth. No wonder his muse seemed to have packed up and left.

Besides an empty teacup with the kids' faces on it and a stained inspirational tag ("Reach for the moon, and you'll always be amongst the stars") stuck on the side of his desk, the basement couldn't be called his alone. Sure, he slept on the lumpy sectional couch on the other end, and yes, he spent the vast majority of his time lingering down there, but it was everyone else's dump, really.

The washing machine and dryer were technically in a room all their own, but the mountains of laundry had grown so high, he could no longer close the door to drown out the rattling of the machines. That was his fault, he supposed. The least Finn could do was fifty loads of laundry a week, right? He just didn't think he could face the lace and cut-away hearts that had begun creeping their way into Charlie's undie supply these days.

Lucy had made her mark on the basement in much more pronounced ways. There were Disney stickers the size of Finn's head up and down the stairway. Once, he'd tried ripping off a particularly offensive one—the blue Genie from *Aladdin* with a dumb-ass smile plastered across his face—but it left a massive white ghost of goo behind. His cherubic monster never failed to leave handprints in glitter glue on the walls and couch, which inevitably rubbed off on the vintage T-shirts Finn still wore to salvage his youth.

He turned back to his blank laptop screen. *Fuck. It. All.*

Finn snatched the battered pack of Camel Lights out of the desk drawer and charged up the basement stairs, passing Mickey's Hall of Fame and Lucy's latest addition: puffy stickers of Princesses Anna and Elsa and their "hilarious" snowman. As he crested the staircase and padded into the living room, it was almost as if he didn't live there anymore. In fact, it looked much as if no one else lived there either. It had been abandoned since the night Aidan left—all nice and neat without a single pillow out of place. Their family pictures were still on the wall and all the furniture had been left right where it had always been, but Finn couldn't remember the last time he saw anyone take a seat there. The essential puzzle piece that had made them a family was gone.

Aidan had been a gift. Yes, people say that about every child, but Finn could have told them that was bullshit. Charlie had been a hell of a surprise, so much so that Rachel had wanted to end the pregnancy. They had never so much as theorized about a baby together. They were barely even romantic—just frequently drunk and even more often desperate for distractions from life. Rachel was still living with her girlfriend at the time, a pickle neither of them had any motivation to rectify until two blue lines on a plastic stick kicked them in the ass. Finn begged

Rachel to give it a go and, six months into the pregnancy, Rachel had reluctantly moved into Finn's studio apartment.

By then, Finn was head over heels in love with the expectant mother of his child. He'd never given much thought to having children or getting hitched, let alone to a cop with a stereotypical bad attitude and *fuck off* veneer. Finn fell for her all the same, and soon, marrying Rachel was all he thought about. He could kick himself for being such a goddamned fool. Now, he knew Rachel didn't fall in love—was perhaps incapable of such a thing. She'd humored him, though, which only deepened his humiliation when Finn discovered Rachel's affairs following Aidan's death. Finn wanted to believe what she had said hundreds of times before: he was her companion; she couldn't imagine a world without him; she didn't want anyone else to be the father of her children. But Rachel had said a lot of things before the crash that simply didn't stand the test of time.

Their children, however, made the hell between them worth something. Charlie was a beautiful yet challenging baby, and Finn was terrified every moment of every day and night for the first few years of her life. Nothing could soothe her crying; no discipline could convince toddler Charlie to keep her hands off the stove or in her parents' grip when crossing the street. Wrestling with their tempestuous firstborn, Finn had never felt more helpless.

It was much the same with Lucy. Having made her grand entrance two months early, Finn and Rachel became well acquainted with fear yet again, taking shifts by her incubator in the NICU for weeks. Even after they left the hospital, Rachel was so paranoid about Lucy's health she barely let Finn touch her until she grew too tired to take care of Lucy alone.

But Aidan, born smack in between Charlie and Lucy, was nothing but joy. Finn and Rachel had carefully planned his creation and every aspect of what his little world would be. They spent months configuring his nursery to be perfect in shades of burgundy and cream. His name had gone onto a nursery school waiting list before he was born. Rachel had even consented to Aidan being baptized to help Finn's painfully pious mother sleep better at night.

They had done everything right preparing for their son, and he didn't disappoint. Aidan was perfect, from his thick mop of blond curls and the gray eyes that so perfectly matched Finn's to his tiny little fingers and toes. He didn't fuss much, and when he did, all Finn had to do was scoop him up and hum a little Radiohead, and the kid was at peace once more.

Aidan grew sweeter with each month of his life. He lived for story time with Daddy and the playground with Mommy. Aidan knew precisely what jokes to crack to make Charlie smile even at her feistiest. When Lucy was sick, Aidan would snuggle her and help his parents tend to her. He was terrible at keeping things clean, especially his room, where he frequently hid muddy socks and rotten snacks he had snuck up there in the middle of the night. He was light and love and silliness and magic, and then he had been snuffed out at eight years old for nothing—erased by Dahlmouth's fucked-up god as though mocking Finn and Rachel for their devotion.

Finn tried to shake off the memories and the thick blanket of rage that accompanied them. He couldn't fall into despair again. As his therapist frequently reminded him, his girls still needed their dad even if Rachel decided she did not.

Finn made a sharp turn and slid a little on the kitchen tile in his socks, the only place in the house where he was still somewhat appreciated. Every evening, Finn became a ninja master in that kitchen, shoving sandwiches, fruit, and juice into lunchboxes while simultaneously tending to a dinner that would inevitably piss off one of his daughters, but would be eaten nonetheless. Each morning, Finn made sure the girls had a full belly before walking out the door—be it with the assistance of Count Chocula or *Teen People*'s newest protein-packed wheatgrass smoothie recipe provided via text from Charlie with zero explanation. Rachel didn't ask, but he set out coffee in a stainless-steel travel mug for her every morning as well. She grabbed it on her way out with the girls without ever acknowledging his presence, always finding something to say to the kids at the exact moment when he opened his mouth to say goodbye.

Finn flew past the coffee pot that was still half-full from the seven o'clock brew, yanked open the back door, and stepped out onto their high wooden porch. He plopped down in an oversized wicker chair no one used anymore before lighting up the first cigarette he'd had in two weeks. Officially, he had quit when Lucy was born. That, however, had only really held true when he was sober. Rachel and Finn had spent many a night post-Lucy out on that porch with old-fashioneds in hand and a pack of Camels that would be gone by morning. That was why Finn couldn't smoke anymore. Rachel had come to equate his smoking with his drinking since the one usually followed the other.

Finn didn't like thinking about it, and by "it," he meant quite a lot: the year leading up to the present; the fake-out living room; Aidan's untouched bedroom between Lucy's and the one he and Rachel once shared; the backwater town she'd dragged him to when she had the chance at a fancy title; his failed career at Bumfuck, Nowhere's rag, as his father would have said; the unmasked looks of despisement and judgment he got damn near everywhere he went—really anything about the life he currently found himself wedged in was an unpleasant trail he'd rather not travel. Instead, watching the clouds of smoke unfurl and float away toward the trees, he tried to empty his mind of the junk like his tea bags advised. He might smoke the whole pack. That just might be his entire day. He sank cozily into the wicker chair, insulating himself from the morning mountain air.

It was quiet out here; Finn would give it that. It was one of the only things about Dahlmouth he didn't mind. Finn tended to side more and more with Thoreau and Emerson as he aged, preferring the simplicity of nature over man's shitty way of running the world.

A couple of squirrels tumbled out of the tree line and chased after one another. Everybody was starting to wake up for spring in that forest, all skinny, hungry, and ready for trouble. Finn was still watching smoke twist in the air when he saw a flicker of white move between two trees, far off in the woods. It looked taller than a fox but thinner than a bear. Finn couldn't think of any creature in those woods that would match its pale, almost glowing, shade. He sat staring at the spot where the movement had been for several moments, the cigarette burning low between his fingers.

When nothing stirred again, Finn chalked it up to his old-man eyes. Sucking at the cigarette, Finn was happy to wipe the little pale flicker from his memories entirely, but something about it made him feel uncharacteristically anxious. It was more than the movement. Finn had the unshakable feeling that he was not only being watched from the same cluster of trees, but that he was being *assessed*. Not studied, not observed—appraised, weighed, and tried. Judged.

That was when he knew Rachel's ire and this entire Bible-thumping town was way too fucking deep in his head. Finn couldn't even enjoy a cigarette anymore without feeling the wrath of a god he'd canned long ago. He flicked the forbidden cig off the porch and stood up to go back inside. At the same time, his cell phone vibrated on the kitchen counter. Tripping over the door's threshold, Finn caught himself from whacking into the counter just in time, grabbed the cell phone, and answered, out of breath.

"Rachel?" he panted.

"I need you to go pick up the kids." Her voice was firm and steady like she had stubbornly trained it to be. This was her police-lady voice, and it was the only one she had been using with Finn for quite a while now. This time, however, there was a note of urgency behind it.

"But it's only nine thirty in the morning—"

"Just go and get them. Pick them up and take them straight home. No stopping for sodas and chocolate or whatever you usually buy Lucy off with."

Finn ran his tongue over his front teeth and ignored the jab. "Are they okay?"

"They're fine. Everything is fine." Her voice tightened slightly on the *fine*. He was the only one who would have picked up on the anxiety buried in her tone, though that special ability failed to bring a smile to his face anymore. "I just need you to get them right now. If anybody asks, tell them the dentist in Salisbury had to move their appointments up or some shit."

"Or some shit?" Finn repeated dryly.

"Make something up," Rachel barked. "Something that doesn't sound stupid."

"I'll go with the dentist story, then. You know how to tell a convincing lie better than me."

"Fuck off, Finn," Rachel spat like she had the words ready to fly before they had even begun chatting.

"Rach, tell me what's going on."

"Jesus Christ—just go grab the kids!" She hung up the phone before Finn could get another word out.

Four

"We ask parents to let teachers know in advance of appointments."

"I know." Finn held up both hands as if to surrender before Lee-Jackson Middle School's administrative assistant, Mrs. Elaine Brady, could reach across the desk and grab him by the neck. "Last-minute schedule change."

Finn tried to smile beneath Mrs. Brady's stern glare, but his charm never made headway in Dahlmouth. Instead, the aging woman with tight brown ringlets and growing jowls continued dissecting him with her dark eyes. A not-so-small part of him felt like turning tail and running, but he could only imagine trying to explain that to Lucy, who clung to his hand. She swayed gently, rocking his arm back and forth as they stood before the front desk where Mrs. Brady presided.

"Where's Charlie?" Lucy bubbled up at Mrs. Brady, wrenching the woman's stare away from Finn. Lucy couldn't quite see over the top of the counter, so Mrs. Brady leaned over to look the girl in the eyes. As she did, Finn could see the school librarian, Mrs. Simmons, farther back in the office, as well as Miss Kneely, the other office administrator who must have been working there since 1945. More cold, unblinking eyes.

"It takes big kids a little longer to get their things, you know," Mrs. Brady said sweetly to Lucy. "They have so many books to carry and assignments to pull together, especially when they weren't planning on leaving so soon." The woman's eyes were back on Finn with renewed distaste, the two biddies behind her fading into the background once more.

"I'll be sure to remind Rachel that appointment changes are most unwelcome." Finn winked at her and summoned a wider smile.

"There she is, Daddy!" Lucy interrupted, pointing out the large windows of the fishbowl office. Charlie was marching over with a sour expression that warned Finn a storm was brewing. Her dirty-blonde hair with hot-pink tips was pulled into a loose ponytail that swung with every huffy stomp she made.

"Well, then, thank you for your help, Mrs. Brady!" Finn spun around, delighted to be on his way, even if he was reaching his hand into the hornet's nest that was Charlie's mood.

"Mr. Kennan?"

Finn's smile faltered slightly as Mrs. Brady arched a brow. "Ma'am?"

"You make sure to tell the chief we appreciate everything she does enforcing the law, but she's not above the school's rules, yes?"

"Yes, ma'am." Finn winked again and took off with huge strides, pulling Lucy along like an oversized baby doll. They slipped out into the hall, Finn's sneakers making a high-pitched squeak as though he had reversed course on a basketball court. Charlie nearly ran right into him. This was the only spark needed to set off the bomb.

"What's gone wrong this time?" Charlie's brow was twisted with rage, her words coming out through gritted teeth. "You pulled me out of third period, Dad. That's the only class I have with Kendall this semester!"

"Class with who?" Finn tried to sort out Charlie's wrath in his head, but he couldn't quite fit the scattered pieces together.

"Kendall, Daddy." Lucy still swung his arm while her gaze wandered out the school's glass front doors.

Charlie's eyes narrowed, resembling Rachel's so much that Finn momentarily felt his insides squirm. "You two are really on a roll today ... out to destroy my *entire* life." She pushed past him.

"Excuse me?" Finn blinked hard, his voice sharper than he intended.

"Mom won't let me go to Roanoke!" Charlie belted out as she whirled around, clutching a textbook against her chest. Her pale, pointed face was unevenly covered with red splotches as tears began working their way into her eyes. "She won't let me go to Roanoke with Gemma. Now you won't let me spend time with Kendall in school. So, I guess we're just cutting me off from all my friends now." Charlie suddenly burst into sobs, her shoulders heaving as teardrops shimmered on her cheeks.

Finn's eyes darted around the hall to see if anyone would come running toward his thirteen-year-old's cries. They weren't moving, but sure enough Finn caught Mrs. Brady, Mrs. Simmons, and Miss Kneely gathered around the front desk, three pairs of suspicious, disapproving eyes fixed on him. "What about Roanoke?"

Whispers in the Dark

At this, Charlie glared through her tears and huffed. She shook her head at Finn, seemingly disgusted, then turned and charged through the doors.

"You said she could go with Gemma to Roanoke, 'member?" Lucy looked up at Finn.

Finn didn't remember anything about Charlie and Gemma and Roanoke, but if Rachel thought he'd given Charlie permission to do anything, his wife would have shut it down in a heartbeat. Now Charlie's meltdown made sense. He bent down and scooped up Lucy with one arm before heading out into the morning sunlight after his distraught teen.

* * *

"Dad, you have just as much say as Mom does. She can't just overrule you." Charlie tapped on the dashboard with her flat palm as if to better illustrate how serious she was. Finn wanted to laugh, both at how Charlie was trying to sell her allegiance now and at the notion he and Rachel were equal in the family's hierarchy. Instead, he narrowed his eyes to focus on the road and clenched his jaw.

"Mommy said we can go later," Lucy chimed in from behind Charlie's seat.

"She didn't say anything about *you* going." Charlie sent darts from her eyes flying back toward Lucy. "Daddy, it's not like we're doing anything crazy. We just want to drive to Roanoke to see the Mill Mountain Star. It's not a big deal. We've done it a thousand times."

"Maybe your mom and I can—"

"Daddy, why are we going home early?" Lucy was in the process of cranking down the backseat window of Finn's 1992 Dodge Spirit. It was his first car, his only car, his good luck charm. Finn refused to drive Rachel's new Jeep Cherokee. It reminded him too much of the twisted-up SUV that had been sitting in a junkyard somewhere for the past year.

"Your mom—"

"Dad! I'm serious! You can't let her boss you around like this!" Charlie hit the dashboard again with more force.

"It was s'posed to be my turn to play the triangle in music today," Lucy said airily as she stuck her little hand out into the wind currents.

"No one cares, Luce!" Charlie turned halfway in her seat. "It's not fair, Dad! She never lets me out of the house! Not since—"

"Charlie, she's not going to budge just because I say something to her. You know that. Lucy-Loo, hon, I'm sorry you're missing out on the triangle. I know you've been waiting to play it. I don't know why, but your mom said you both needed to come home."

"So, she says 'Jump,' and you ask 'How high?' now?"

Finn dared to take his eyes off the road for one moment to glare at his oldest rather than use his words, for Lucy's sake. He had gotten very good at that. It didn't matter, though. Charlie looked away out the passenger-side window, hugging herself.

"It must be something scary," Lucy whispered. "Mommy doesn't like us missing school."

Finn looked at his little girl in the rearview mirror for a few quiet moments. "I don't think it's anything scary, Loo-Hoo. Your mom didn't say anything was wrong."

But Rachel didn't have to say anything was wrong for Finn to know that something most definitely was, and Lucy didn't need Finn lying to her to know that adults were full of baloney when scared.

Five

"Naturally, the coroner's report is going to take a bit of time." Sheriff Odell sniffed hard and glanced up with a knowing look at Rachel from the photos splayed out on the desk in front of him. "But I have to tell you, Chief Kennan, I don't think you have anything to worry about."

"What do you mean?" Rachel noticed her hand was trembling slightly as she lifted her double espresso to her lips. She pulled her arm in close to her chest to steady the quake.

He chuckled and shook his head. "I'm saying, I don't think you have a psychotic killer on the loose in Dahlmouth."

"You think it was limited to our fine fellow here?" Rachel nodded to the photo of the faceless man.

"I'm saying that I don't think it was murder."

"Are you kidding me?"

"Chief, based on the position of the weapon and the physical remains, it looks like your victim took a knife to his *own* face."

Rachel cleared her throat, set down her coffee cup, and leaned forward. "I understand self-mutilation may have been involved, but he was nailed to a goddamn tree. If that doesn't scream *foul play*, I don't know what else would. You actually think the guy was capable of doing all that to himself?"

Whispers in the Dark

Odell sat far back in his seat, tilting the wooden four-legged chair onto two legs. Rachel imagined him leaning into his confidence a tad too far and crashing to the ground, smacking his thick skull against the tile floor.

"How many addicts you got running around out there, Chief? Hell, wasn't it one of your notorious Wise boys that found this guy?"

Rachel inhaled deeply. "Sheriff, just because we have a narcotics problem—"

"Drug use in that area of the county has increased threefold since you came wandering into Dahlmouth, and that makes for some strange trouble. If memory serves me correctly, there was a whole string of incidents with druggies mutilating livestock out your way last year. Am I remembering that wrong, Chief? Maybe you don't recall since it was 'round the time your boy—"

"Meth does not account for every crime in Dahlmouth." Rachel barely contained the snarl in her throat as she pushed ahead. "And I certainly don't think you can jump to that conclusion without a full investigation."

"But I wouldn't rule it out." Sheriff Odell flashed her a wide, toothy smile.

"Of course not." Rachel fought to swallow the swell of anger. The asshole knew he was getting a rise out of her. She could already hear him bragging about riling up the hot-headed bull dyke to the boys later. "I'm not ruling out drug involvement. I just don't think you can assume the guy injected some bad batch and sawed his own face off. Seems like a bit of a stretch to—"

"Did I ever tell you about the time I had a fella burn down his own mama's house because he was hopped up and convinced there were eyeballs in her walls?"

"This fucker was *nailed* to a *tree*." Rachel clenched her jaw until her back teeth hurt.

"Halfway, as you wrote in the report. Funny thing, right? Why would a killer only pin half of the guy to a tree?" The sheriff crossed his burly arms. "And how'd a killer take off the victim's face if the guy could still swing at him with an unrestrained arm?" Sheriff Odell cocked his head to the side, his lip curling.

"He could have been sedated. He could have already been unconscious from prior trauma. There are a million ways—"

"See, I think you're still adjusting." Sheriff Odell laced his fingers together and leaned forward with a twinkle in his eye. "You ain't in the big city anymore. How many times do I have to remind you?"

"Don't you start this patronizing bullshit again." Rachel's spine stiffened as she hid her balled fists under the table. She had come to expect the good ol' boy to take every shot at her possible, but Rachel hadn't anticipated the sheriff would fight her on such a grisly crime just to knock her down a peg.

Odell scrubbed at his nose and sighed. "Look, if I wanted to kill somebody out here, I'd grab me a rifle and go hunting with the guy. There ain't no sense in going through some elaborate plan to off a guy when there's a perfectly good store of firearms in every home for a fifty-mile radius."

Rachel rolled her eyes. "Maybe the killer isn't from here. I don't think the victim is local. Nobody has filed a missing persons report with us or with you, or at least that's what your new little bitch boy at the front desk said.

"So, it would make equal sense if the killer was an outsider, too. Maybe they assumed Dahlmouth is so remote and backward, their police department would bumble over themselves, chalk it up to some meth heads, and call it a day."

Sheriff Odell chuckled and shook his head. Rachel smiled tightly and narrowed her eyes, but dutifully listened. "The odds of somebody tranquilizing some unlucky son of a bitch, cruising through Dahlmouth, and carrying the guy off into the woods to torture him is a wild fantasy your brain cooked up to keep you preoccupied."

Sheriff Odell's eyebrows arched high as he looked her up and down.

"Well, I guess we won't know until toxicology comes back," Rachel said.

"Oh, that's gonna take a while, I'm afraid," Odell said. "Lab's real backed up lately."

Rachel smirked at the man's words and threw a funny little stare at the ceiling that Odell wouldn't understand.

"I'm telling you, Chief," he said, "it's gonna show your victim was as high as a—"

"Until then, I'm setting a curfew," Rachel cut him off. "And I'm setting up a police presence around those woods as well as regular patrols through town."

The sheriff sneered. "Yeah? How are you planning on doing that with five officers on your force, Chief?"

"Well, I was hoping to get a little extra help from the county, sir." The words stuck in Rachel's throat like she had swallowed glass shards.

"I seem to recall that the last time my boys helped you folks out, my deputy took a baseball bat to the face."

"Bless his heart. Maybe your deputy should learn to duck?" There was no point in hiding her vitriol now. Clearly Odell had made up his mind to refuse her request for assistance.

"I just don't know that I can afford to get additional resources out to you, especially given what we know about the deceased." Odell began gathering the photos before him into a neat stack.

"We don't know *anything* about the deceased." Rachel raised her voice as she watched the man sweep the case into a file to be tossed into a cabinet for the rest of time. "That's why I'm clamping down. If it turns out to be a murder, the individual that perpetrated this is one sick mother—"

"Why don't we wait for the coroner's report?" Odell held up his palm as if he were a crossing guard, and Rachel knew she had run into a full stop. "Ain't nobody in Dahlmouth gonna appreciate you or us issuing a curfew. I don't think they'd even abide by it, honestly."

"And what happens when I've got another mutilated body on my hands? Will you explain to my citizens that you wanted to wait for a report to come through before you'd send a couple guys over to help us patrol?"

"I'm sure you've got the situation under control. If the incident is as bad as you think, you have the training in this very area under your belt. Hell, Chief, maybe this is finally when all those years investigating homicides in Richmond will pay off."

Rachel felt like reaching over and bashing a couple of the bastard's teeth out. Instead, she nodded and looked away toward the door of the examination room.

"I guess I better be getting down the road, then," she muttered and tapped her palms flat upon the table before her.

"Sounds good, Chief. It's a long drive back, and I'm sure your helpless citizens are desperate to know where their white knight has gone." Rachel opened her mouth to unleash hell, but he pushed right on without pause. "I'll give you a buzz when the report comes back in. And, hey, look, I know you're pissed at me. That's all right. You're looking out for your people like you're supposed to. I get that. You let me know if anything else funny happens, all right?"

"Right. Then you'll send your boys out just as fast as lightning, won't ya?"

"If you want my help, Chief, I'd start practicing some manners." Odell's smirk turned wicked as his voice dipped low. "And maybe try smiling more often, sweetie."

Six

Rachel hit the round bell atop the counter four times before the familiar face she'd hoped to see peeked around the corner. Michelle's green eyes flashed with panic, and Rachel knew the woman was contemplating running away into her lab. There wasn't a point to that, though, and Michelle was smart enough to know it. Rachel would only follow her back there, and boy, oh boy, was that likely to cause a world of problems.

"What do you want?" The thin woman pressed her lips together and swept silky blonde strands behind both her ears.

"How've you been?" Rachel smiled brightly and chewed her gum a little faster. Michelle was flustered just by the sight of her, as usual, which only encouraged Rachel more.

"Fine. What do you want?" Michelle crossed her arms over her green scrubs.

"Heard you got engaged."

"I did." Michelle barely managed to choke the words out as her face grew markedly flushed.

"Congratulations." Rachel continued to smile brightly even as she felt bitterness swell in her chest. "How's Bible college treating him? Still going well?"

"I asked what you wanted!" Michelle broke character and screamed outright before Rachel could push further.

"I need a favor." Rachel dropped her smile and took a deep inhale.

"I don't have time for favors right now." Michelle shook her head and took a step back. "We're up to our eyeballs in cases."

"Oh." Rachel puffed out her bottom lip ever so slightly and leaned forward on the morgue's reception window. "Geez, I meant to ask you . . . Look, I've been thinking a lot about some counseling lately, but I think maybe Jesus could help out, too." Rachel nodded sincerely as Michelle's eyes widened. "I don't really think it'd be appropriate for me to mix religion with my duties in Dahlmouth, so I was thinking about maybe visiting some of the churches around here in Roanoke." Rachel waved her pointer finger in the air, a smirk returning to her face. "Like, what's it called? Bethany Baptist? Is that right?"

"What kind of favor?" Michelle spat out quickly.

"Wait . . . oh, my god!" Rachel gasped in fake alarm just to get a rise out of the woman she'd spent the better part of a year "corrupting," as Michelle put it. "Is that your boyfriend—I mean, fiancé's—church?"

"Rachel, tell me what you want!" Michelle practically shook with rage and panic.

"I need a case expedited." Rachel's voice returned to normal, though the nasty smirk lingered.

"Do you have any idea how many times I'm told that in a day?"

"Sure." Rachel nodded. "But not by me."

Michelle's nostrils flared as she robotically approached the window. "The last time I did you a favor, I said it was the very last time," she spoke in a low, warning tone.

"I know." Rachel licked her lips and looked down at the scuffs on the counter.

"Do you have any idea how much I risked for you?"

"Yeah, I do." Rachel nodded curtly before looking up into the other woman's gaze. "But this favor isn't like the last one. I'm not asking you to do anything . . ." Rachel shrugged as she searched for the right words. All of the accurate ones sounded wrong because, in fact, what she'd had Michelle do before was wrong by anyone's standards. Rachel cleared her throat before dropping to a whisper: "I'm not asking you to do anything crazy."

"I'm not bailing you *or* him out again. Do you understand me?" Rachel knew Michelle would've raised her forefinger to wag it in her face if there hadn't been security cameras to capture it. That's what Michelle did whenever she was pretending she didn't want to do something that flirted or even catapulted over the edges of her morality—she feigned outrage.

"I'm not asking you to bail anyone out," Rachel continued to whisper. "I'm only asking that my victim's report gets processed a little faster than the bullshit ones. There's something really fucked up about this one, Chelle. I can feel it in my gut. You know I'm the one cop out in those fuckin' woods with any instincts whatsoever, which means I'm the sole person keeping them safe—"

"God help them if you're the only one standing between them and damnation," Michelle muttered and tightened her grip on her arms.

Rachel paused before the smile returned to her face. She leaned forward again with a gleam in her eye. Michelle backed up one pace, but Rachel didn't miss the way the woman's breath picked up.

"The point is, I'm trying to do the right thing here, and those people need me. I can't help them until I have those lab results because Odell won't give me shit until I can prove my victim wasn't just a druggie—"

"And what if he was a druggie?"

"Oh, I have very little doubt you'll find something in the guy's system, but I said *just* a druggie. There's something very wrong going on here; I know it."

"How?" Michelle tried and failed to look bored by the case.

"Just a feeling." Rachel shrugged. "Have you seen the body yet?"

"You'll have to be more specific," Michelle said.

"I'm pretty sure if you'd seen it, you'd remember." The corners of her mouth twitched. "He's a memorable kinda guy."

Michelle swiped at the clipboard on the desk in front of her, and Rachel watched her scan for the names of drop-offs. "So, not even an ID on the victim?"

Rachel shook her head. "It'd be much appreciated if you could help us with that little detail as well." Michelle's body tensed much the way Rachel had seen it tighten a dozen times before under far more exciting circumstances.

"Rach." Michelle sighed as her eyes bored a hole through the clipboard. "I've got tons of cases just as urgent—"

"Bullshit," Rachel muttered. "Chelle, give me a break here, please."

"You can't keep doing this." Michelle looked up, and to Rachel's surprise, she saw tears shimmering in her eyes. "How many times will you ask me for another favor?"

Rage surged within Rachel, and she clenched her back teeth for a moment. The gathering tears Michelle displayed didn't elicit sympathy. Rather, the vague accusation that Rachel was doing something predatory, something dangerous, sparked malice. She should've been used to the veiled judgment, and indeed anyone else could've thrown their holy disdain Rachel's way without her giving it a second thought. But not Michelle. What happened between them wouldn't be rewritten to alleviate Michelle's guilt. Rachel wouldn't take the blame for Michelle's self-hatred courtesy of a bigoted god. If Michelle couldn't fight her way through the lies she'd accepted for herself, Rachel had no time to waste on what could've been.

"Michelle"—Rachel's tone grew sharp, dripping with venom that had long been brewing toward the woman standing before her—"I've only ever asked you for one fucking thing. Everything else you wanted to do even if you're now trying to pray the gay away. I never fuckin' forced anything on you."

"I don't—" Michelle slammed the clipboard down on the counter and leaned closer. "I never said you forced me to do any of . . . *that* stuff, but what you asked me to do for Finn—changing those numbers on his blood alcohol level that night—Rachel, I don't think I can ever forgive myself for that. I lose sleep because of what I did for you."

Rachel drew a deep breath before she leaned further across the counter. "What you did wasn't for me, and it wasn't for Finn,"

Rachel murmured. "It was for my daughters. Finn can rot in hell, but my kids need their father sober and in one piece. That wasn't going to happen behind bars."

"You enable him." Michelle hurled the accusation at Rachel at a volume just below a whisper.

Rachel locked fiery eyes with her. "You are the last person who should lecture me seeing how you smile and play nice for your fiancé every Sunday even while he condemns the rest of us queers from the pulpit. Seems like you're awfully content to enable assholes as long as they do it in the name of god."

Immediately, the woman shrank back. She never went to war for what she believed in, and for that, Rachel didn't think she'd ever respect her again.

Michelle bit her bottom lip hard, dropping her gaze to the floor. Slowly, she nodded before running her fingers through the pieces of hair she'd already tucked behind her ears. "I'll run the labs tonight, but there's no promise a comprehensive panel will come back quickly."

"I don't need a comprehensive to get what I need." Rachel exhaled and straightened her spine. When Michelle nodded again, Rachel remembered some of what her mother taught her. "Thank you, Chelle. I really appreciate it ... sincerely."

"Yeah," Michelle muttered and began to turn away. "I'll fax it over to the station as soon as I have preliminary results."

"Thanks," Rachel repeated as she caught sight of the diamond glittering on Michelle's ring finger. Another white-hot pang of resentment shot through Rachel. "Hey, Chelle?"

Michelle paused to look at Rachel, her unease visible to even the most oblivious observer.

"What happened to the cute little promise ring business?" Rachel sloppily gestured toward Michelle's left hand. In response, Michelle slowly raised her right hand to reveal the reassignment of the chastity ring her father had gifted her.

"Ah." Rachel scrunched her nose. Once again, she lowered her voice for privacy as well as for sinking invisible knives. "So, the reverend-in-training still thinks you're a virgin, then? Or does it not count if it's with a woman?"

"Fuck you," Michelle hissed before storming away.

"Looking forward to that report!" Rachel called after her.

A door slammed somewhere in the morgue as a shit-eating grin spread across Rachel's face. It never hurt to have friends in all kinds of places, no matter how much they wished it wasn't so.

Seven

Hours passed before Finn heard anything else from Rachel. On any other day, this would be normal. Most of the time, Finn wouldn't know anything, hear anything, or see anything of Rachel until she returned home in the late evening after work. Even then, he mostly navigated around her in the kitchen as she picked at whatever he had made hours before. Sometimes she briefed him on the bills; occasionally, he would update her on the girls' schoolwork. Most of the time, he just watched her and sipped tea before they put Lucy to bed. That day, however, he waited for her messages the same way Charlie hung on every word her friends posted to social media.

Charlie blared her own mix of angry, sad, and empowered poplets from her closed room throughout the day. Finn suspected she was furiously texting anyone and everyone who would listen to her about how unfair life really was: what a wicked witch her mother was; what a spineless sack her father was. That was the only reason he could imagine his brother would text him out of the blue:

Gotta grow a pair, Finn. Don't let Rach
keep your balls locked up forever.

Meanwhile, Lucy merrily built and smashed Play-Doh castles on the kitchen table before moving on to bathing all her baby dolls in the tub. Finn eventually coaxed her into snuggling on the basement couch with a bowl of popcorn and the newest *Star Wars* movie. Lucy couldn't seem to stay awake long enough to get through the originals, a deep disappointment to Finn, though he did his best to keep that to himself.

The whole time, Finn checked his phone. There were social media updates, an occasional *Politico* alert, but no messages from Rachel. The untamed, fun parts of Finn's brain wondered if this was how the zombie apocalypse began: a cryptic phone call from the police chief, a hustled retreat to the house, then utter silence while the world outside ate itself alive. By three thirty, this thought no longer made him smirk. He broke down and texted Rachel:

Any updates?

Nothing.

Around four or so, Finn heard Charlie's music die down from overhead and the loud trot of her footsteps coming down the stairs. He steeled himself for another tirade, but when her tennis shoes hit the basement floor, she wore a sly smile. Craning his head over Lucy's, Finn noticed Charlie had changed from her school outfit into skinny jeans and a baby-blue zip-up hoodie, looking older than he cared to believe.

"Daddy," she began in a singsong voice. "Any word from Mom?" Finn shook his head and sighed before kissing the top of Lucy's blonde head. "Oh no. I hope everything is all right."

Charlie pretended to be troubled, hand on her hip and lips hitched to the side, though she didn't pull it off very well. She then stuck her hands into her hoodie pockets and walked toward the back of the couch.

"I'm sure it's fine," Finn mumbled. "She'd get in touch if anything were—"

"Gem says they found a dead body in the woods. Says her mom heard Jeremy over the scanner sayin' it's definitely murder." Finn looked over at Charlie's face to read if there was anything funny about the way she spat out the news. While an odd smirk remained fixed there, nothing about her expression appeared to be joking around. Lucy broke her gaze from Chewbacca to look up at Finn with a creased brow.

"Well, that explains why your mother has been occupied. Guess we should start planning to settle in for the evening without her. Hey, I know you were rocking your own concert with the T-Swift up there, but did you manage to get anything actually useful done? Homework, for instance?"

"Everything's finished, yeah." Her eyes fell on the television for a few moments as she pressed her lips together. Finn raised his brows; it was clear Charlie was selecting the best moment to press him.

"Good. That's great, kiddo."

"But I could really use someone's help reviewing the stuff." Charlie looked into Finn's face, blue eyes glittering.

"Cool. Let me finish this up with Luce, and I'll take a loo—"

"Dad, it's pre-algebra!" Charlie exclaimed, the smile on her face instantly replaced with panic. "You won't understand."

"Charlie, how stupid do you think I am? Believe it or not, I, too, got through eighth grade."

Charlie arched an eyebrow, and much to Finn's displeasure, it wasn't without cause. There was a reason he had veered in the direction of the creative arts. Even if he had full command of middle-school math (which he didn't), Finn couldn't make heads or tails of the fancy new techniques the teachers were showing the kids to solve time-tested problems.

"I was hoping I could meet up with some of my classmates to review what the teacher went over in class today—"

"Here it is." Finn chuckled. "Knew you were angling for something."

"Daddy, *please!*" Suddenly Charlie was Lucy's age again, ready to fall on the ground and hold on to his ankles until she got what she wanted. "*Please*, Daddy! I just want to go study with my friends. *Please!*"

"Studying . . . right. Again, how dumb do you think I am?" Finn winked at her and turned back toward the television. "Please don't answer that. You're not going."

"We aren't going to get into any trouble. I swear!"

"You're staying home, Charlie."

"Daddy!" Her voice was souring from the sugary-sweet nectar it had been, inching closer to her mother's tone. "It's healthy to spend time with friends!"

"And you do all the time, kid. You spend more time with Gemma and Sarah and Kendra—"

"Kendall."

"Yeah, her, too. You spend more time with them than you do here." Finn couldn't help himself as he forced a yawn to push Charlie's buttons. It was too easy now that she'd acquired Rachel's short fuse with the onset of puberty.

"That's not true!"

"I would know; I'm the one keeping tabs on everybody, remember? Mr. Mom and all." Finn threw another look over his shoulder at Charlie, whose face was turning a brilliant shade of red. "Listen, your mom said we should sit tight. That's what we're doing."

"I want to be normal again," Charlie spoke through gritted teeth. "This isn't about a dead body, and you know it. This is about Aidan." Finn's jaw clenched as the name left Charlie's mouth, though she didn't seem to notice. "But what happened to Aidan doesn't have anything to do with me and my friends hanging out. I don't even have many friends anymore because you and Mom—"

Finn cut Charlie off with a sharp glare that would've sent his daughter running to her room only a few months prior. He already spent his days carrying the guilt that he'd forever warped Lucy's childhood. The last thing he needed was to be condemned for interfering with Charlie's social life in this backwater town. It was better she didn't get too close to these people anyway. Finn couldn't swallow Charlie becoming a holy roller so she could collect more pals at the church's youth group. Let them all reject the wicked Kennan family. Finn preferred it that way, and one day when his daughter headed out into the real world, he was certain Charlie would agree.

"Look." Charlie swallowed, redirected, and softened her voice. "Mom dealt with dead people all the time in Richmond, and that never stopped us from going out."

Finn couldn't argue with her on that one. Rachel would come home from a crime scene, change clothes, and round the kids up to go get ice cream without thinking twice. Things were different in Dahlmouth, however. Even before the accident, Rachel displayed a paranoia here that Finn had never previously seen in her. Now, Rachel took crime as a personal offense.

Following the crash, this new approach to her job evolved further, and Rachel seemed to think all criminal activity posed an immediate threat to their family. Lucy was pulled from swimming lessons because the instructor had once been in a domestic dispute. Charlie couldn't go to Friday-night games anymore because, according to Rachel, that's when the entire student body became raging drunks. This version of Rachel was only satisfied when she held complete control—no one else had proved themselves worthy, least of all Finn.

"What's the point of staying here locked up and paranoid because Mom says so?" Charlie knocked Finn out of his brooding.

"Who's paranoid?" He smiled. "I'm not paranoid. Lucy's not paranoid, are you, Luce?" Finn glanced down at Lucy, whose eyes had returned to the lightsaber duel on the television. Without looking away, she shook her head very slowly. "See? No one is paranoid here except you, m'dear."

"So we're stuck here waiting indefinitely for Mom even though she hasn't texted you once? She's probably forgotten all about us."

"Mommy hasn't forgotten about us!" Lucy spun around to stand on her knees and look over the couch at her older sister.

"Calm down, Lucy." Finn rolled his eyes and snatched up the remote, hitting pause. "Charlie means Mom forgot to text us what's happen—"

"I don't know, Luce." Charlie's tone suddenly dripped with venom. "I think Mommy might have forgotten all about you and me, and she's *definitely* forgotten about Daddy."

"Charlie! What's wrong with you?" Finn threw a hand up in the air, tempted for a brief second to flip off his own kid. "Can't you watch TV or something? Surf the interwebs and make the TikToks. Be *normal*, as you said."

"I'll make a deal with you." Charlie crossed her arms, a single eyebrow arched high.

"No deal, Daddy!" Lucy roared, glaring at her sister.

"Shut up, Lucy!"

"Hey! Don't tell your sister to shut up," Finn yelled over the growing din.

"I'll make you a deal," Charlie repeated as her eyes bored into Finn. "I'll go out just for a little bit, and I'll come home before dinner. I'll even take the back way so no one will see me. Mom will never know, and in return, I won't tell her you were smoking this morning." Finn's jaw dropped as a wide smile graced Charlie's bubblegum-pink lips.

"Joke's on you, Charlie! Daddy doesn't smoke anymore!" Lucy pointed directly at Charlie and cackled.

"Mom would find it pretty funny, too, Luce!" Charlie opened her mouth wide and mimicked a silent guffaw, leaning over and clutching her belly to mock both Finn and Lucy.

Finn suddenly felt as though he had been kneed in the groin. Earlier today Rachel had interrupted his forbidden cigarette with her cryptic phone call; he'd forgotten all about the lone butt he'd tossed onto the lawn. *Goddammit.*

Sparring with Rachel was a pastime he was thankful to have left behind, but it always loomed in the background. He didn't mind the pissy phone calls and passive-aggressive texts so much anymore, but Finn avoided Rachel's in-person showdowns like the plague. Rachel knew how to push his buttons better than anyone. She now also knew what happened if she pushed him too far. Rachel would love nothing more than to see Finn twist back into the version of himself he'd allowed to emerge only once and had quickly buried. He refused to follow in the footsteps of his abusive father ever again, but he didn't want to be tested too much either.

"I want you home by six sharp," Finn muttered quickly.

"*What?!*" Lucy exclaimed.

"But under no circumstances do I want you walking alone. Do you understand?" Finn tried to push the image of a furious Rachel grabbing his laptop and smashing it against the wall out of his head. "And I want you to text me every half hour. Got that?"

Charlie was eagerly nodding, her shit-eating smile swallowing most of her face. "Kendall is riding her bike there with me and back, and I *promise* I will text you. I'm not Mom."

"Watch it," Finn warned while Lucy let out an outraged squeak.

"Thanks, Daddy! You're the best!" Charlie ran over and pecked him on the cheek, almost shaking with excitement. She'd won, and Finn's heart sank a little as he realized Charlie now knew exactly how to manipulate her schmuck of a father when needed. Every day, she became a little more like Rachel. He should've seen that coming.

"That's not right, Daddy!" Lucy glared at him as Charlie ruffled the little girl's hair and ran toward the stairs.

"Text me as soon as you get to Gemma's!" Finn called after her.

"Okay!" Charlie was already at the top of the steps.

"And I swear to god, if you get a text from me saying your mother is on the way, you'd better haul ass back to this house!"

"Daddy!" Lucy gasped.

"Do you hear me?" Finn yelled louder.

"Thanks, Dad!" The next thing Finn heard was the front door slamming.

"You cussed." Lucy flopped down on her bottom.

"That I did. Apologies, Luce." Finn settled back down next to her and hit the pause button again to return to galactic battles.

"*And* you smoked."

Finn sighed and stared into the accusing eyes of his little buttercup.

"I did that, too. Caught me red-handed." He touched the tip of her nose with his pointer finger. "Can you do me a favor and not mention that to your mom?"

"Charlie got to go out when she promised. What do I get?"

"Yeowch. I have to bribe you, too, Lucy-Loo?" She nodded vigorously. "Fine. Whatever your heart desires. Go ahead and take Daddy for all he's worth."

Finn spent the next two hours portraying every character that wasn't Anna in the *Frozen* sing-along DVD—Lucy's prized possession and Finn's mortal enemy.

Eight

The forest surrounding Dahlmouth took on a lovely, albeit strange, blue-green tinge when the afternoons grew long. Today was no different. As Charlie pedaled faster, her battered ten-speed bike whirring loud enough to drown out the tree frogs nestled in the woods, she couldn't help but feel a little calmer than she had the entire afternoon at home. Her father had made it nearly impossible to say anything positive about the place, but when Charlie was on her own, she found enough things to like about Dahlmouth. Maybe it was nature and fresh air and all that, but Charlie suspected it had more to do with her friends.

In Richmond, Charlie'd had plenty of friends at the pricey Montessori school her grandmother paid for so that all the Kennan children could attend. They were the right kind of friends, too—the kind with parents who only drank their lattes from indie coffee shops and could rattle off the latest legislation Representative Doesn't-Actually-Care introduced that day. Those parents fell into the appropriate income bracket—the one her father came from and was supposed to have maintained had he not married down. Her former friends ate organic fruit snacks and danced ballet and rode to school in electric cars.

But Charlie had never given a shit about those friends. It was here in what her father deemed a backwater, hillbilly town that Charlie found her real friends—ones who accepted her no matter what. As Kendall swooped in from the right on her sticker-covered bike, a wide grin appeared on Charlie's face. Soon, Sarah sped in beside them and the trio were racing toward Gemma's.

Kendall, Sarah, Gem—the best friends she could have ever dreamed up—had been with her every step of the way since the night the wheels flew off her father's crazy train. They could've left her like everyone else. Charlie was certain Sarah's parents would have preferred that, in fact. Yet, they refused to cast her off, even if Charlie didn't quite understand why.

They knew everything about her and the godforsaken Kennan family, and they still closed ranks when prying eyes fell on Charlie. The girls covered for Charlie when she cried in the bathroom, standing outside of the stall and sneering at anyone who dared linger too long. When Charlie refused to put on a bathing suit at the end-of-the-year party, Kendall and Sarah also sat on the edge of the pool in jeans and T-shirts without a single question. Any time Pastor Paul popped up and tried to pull Charlie aside for a heart-to-heart, Gemma managed to distract him with her newly plunging neckline. Charlie came to realize the family members she chose for herself were far more precious than the ones assigned to her at birth. Somehow, that eased the loss of Aidan slightly.

That thought, that *name*, wiped the smile right off Charlie's face as the girls zoomed past the tiny field where her little brother played T-ball not so long ago. Suddenly, she was swept up by memories yet again. Aidan's slate-gray eyes, his scrunched nose, the silly little dance he used to do whenever the family ordered pizza—all of it swirled around Charlie's brain as if she'd just left him playing in the lawn . . . as if he'd be right there with his Tonka trucks when she got home.

The night her father had drunkenly veered off the road to avoid a deer, Charlie had been practicing at the school for the spring concert. As Gemma and Charlie climbed into the Thompsons' Dodge Caravan for a ride home, Mrs. Thompson answered her cell phone and Charlie knew from the way her face fell that something was terribly wrong. She spent the next several days at the Thompsons' while her father sobbed in a corner somewhere and her mother obsessively reviewed every piece of evidence related to Aidan's death, desperate to find his drowned body so the family could bury something.

No one called to check on Charlie. Neither parent apologized when they finally did pick her up. When Mrs. Thompson moved in to give the chief a sympathetic hug, her mother maneuvered away in time to avoid it.

Charlie understood then that she should not mention Aidan to her mother, and never ever should she cry about him in front of her. And mourning Aidan around her father only resulted in him falling apart. His grief overwhelmed everyone else's, and Charlie quickly learned it was better not to feed that operatic tragedy. He had always been dramatic, but Charlie had never held it against him until then. Her father couldn't even see past himself long enough to let Charlie feel something, the selfish bastard. She would have preferred it if her dad was still drinking, if only to make him funny again.

And then there was Lucy. *Poor*, damaged, perversely lucky little Lucy became the center of her parents' world after Aidan died. She was the one they'd almost lost in the same accident, which made her special and sacred. Her little sister had witnessed their dad's unforgivable fuckup and lived to never tell anyone the whole tale. They said Lucy was the last person who saw Aidan, the one who had watched the James River rip him out of the SUV's shattered window to an unknown watery grave. She'd seen unfiltered death before she could even read.

Charlie tried accepting that it made sense for her parents to coddle Lucy and rush her off to the child psychologist whenever something seemed off. No matter how hard Charlie wanted to understand, however, she couldn't let go of the bitterness that had taken root inside her. Rage and grief bubbled up through her veins to crawl under her skin morning, day, and night. So, while precious little Lucy drew fucked-up pictures of their brother's bloated corpse dancing along the riverbank for the adults to fret over, Charlie hid away in the bathroom with a disposable razor and slashed at her thighs. No one noticed because no one thought to ask. As her parents began to shut down entirely and Lucy's memory started to seal away the images from that night, Charlie continued to mourn in her own way, in her own time.

She had argued with Aidan over toothpaste on the bathroom counter that last morning. Charlie had called him a *little shit* when her parents were too far away to hear her. Aidan had looked at her with hurt puppy-dog eyes, but he didn't fight back. The little shit hadn't fought back that *one* time. That was what

Charlie couldn't forget. She didn't think she would ever be able to stop replaying the moment in her head.

"Charlie!" Kendall called as she playfully swiped at Charlie's handlebars. Just like that, Charlie broke free of the past. Aidan's wounded expression evaporated, replaced by the grin on Kendall's face that gave Charlie unwanted butterflies. "Earth to Charlie! You all right?"

Kendall knew she wasn't. That was the point, and Charlie was thankful she didn't have to explain otherwise. Instead, she nodded and the girls soon screeched their way to a stop in Gemma's driveway. The fourth member of their squad was already standing on the porch with a smirk that promised mischief.

"Took y'all long enough!" Gemma yelled as the girls dropped their rides on the lawn.

"Jail breaks ain't easy!" Kendall gestured toward Charlie and winked.

* * *

The sky overhead was starting to cloud over, forecasting showers in the near future, when the girls set off down the footpath into the forest lining Gemma's property. The tree frogs had gone silent, and the woods that closed in on all sides stood still in the face of an oncoming storm. The girls reached their meeting place in less time than usual, each nearly out of breath when they entered the perfect, round circle braced by logs. This was where they typically congregated on carefree weekends or on the days when life had really gone to shit.

Thus far, Charlie was satisfied that she, Gemma, Sarah, and Kendall were surviving the last year of middle school. They had made a few small waves. Gemma, in particular, was fast becoming a favorite amongst the older boys who had forgotten she had been a yucky elementary schooler two years prior. She was "the pretty one"; Gemma probably would have been the popular one, too, had she not chosen such inauspicious friends.

Meanwhile, Sarah was a superstar in all things academic. Dahlmouth had never churned out an Ivy League student. Sarah could do it if she wanted to, though; that was obvious even in sixth grade. Kids said Sarah was a nerd, but Charlie thought she just might be the only person in the whole damn town with any kind of bright future on the horizon.

Then there was Kendall. Her jeans were always a little too tight and ripped up. She wore fishnets whenever someone forced her to put on a dress, even then insisting on wearing her tennis shoes with doodles sketched along the white rubber. Without a doubt, Kendall was the rebel of the group—the one who stood out and didn't care whether others liked it.

While her only friends were forging their own paths forward, Charlie supposed she was just along for the ride. She wasn't especially pretty or smart or bold. She didn't play sports or instruments, and she avoided making trouble though she was well aware Dahlmouth was waiting for her to raise some hell. It was a rebellion thing, the church ladies said—something having to do with her mom being the police chief and all that. Charlie knew it was more, though. She was a Kennan, after all.

In Dahlmouth, people had always been curious about the Kennans because... well, they "weren't from around here." But one goddamn sentence over the CB sent some folks digging into who the Kennans *really* were. The night that Aidan had been ripped from their lives, Finn's labs had all come back relatively normal, but the first responders to the crash said her dad blew three times the legal limit on the Breathalyzer. It all went to hell from there.

Her dad's articles weren't hard to find, especially the one that made a spectacle out of poor Appalachian white trash in Kentucky. His social media sealed the deal, revealing not just how much he loathed Dahlmouth, but how he'd long ago rejected his Catholic upbringing. In a town of a few hundred where the local church was the closest thing to a country club, her father was outed as the lone atheist.

And it was the whole "outing" thing that plagued the family. Charlie had always known her parents were different. They didn't look at each other quite the same way other couples did, not even when she was a little kid. Her parents laughed and drank and hung out together. They fell asleep watching TV, snuggled here and there, but they weren't what couples looked like in the movies when two people fell in love. Much to her own humiliation, Charlie had never really given it much thought until a classmate figured out how the Internet Archive works. Overnight, Dahlmouth discovered how bullshit her parents' marriage was before Charlie knew herself.

A week after Aidan died, Jeremy showed up on their doorstep with an expression too solemn for the deputy's usually irreverent disposition. The only person her mother could really call a friend hurriedly pulled her outside to chat. From the living room window, Charlie watched as Jeremy broke the news to Chief Kennan. Sure, her son was dead and all, but Dahlmouth was more riled up about Rachel's old social media profile. After all, it spilled the beans her parents had desperately tried to can.

As it turned out, Chief Kennan was a much different woman fourteen years prior—less paranoid, less bitter, less fearful of the person inside her skin. Less careful about who knew, too. The old pictures showed her mother in racy attire perpetually paired with combat boots, kissing girls in clubs and flicking off the camera at every opportunity. But they also showed her smiling and laughing in a way Charlie never knew . . . like she was genuinely happy, like Rachel was free.

Whatever dumb-ass series of events that led to Charlie's conception ruined that. *Charlie* ruined that; she'd sentenced her mother to a lifetime of silence because that's what a person did when they fucked up, right? They swallowed their feelings, their identity, and dealt with the consequences.

Well, now Charlie was dealing with the consequences, too. Everyone knew her father was a drunken prick, and now they knew Finn thought they were goddamn idiots along with their Lord and Savior. They'd discovered her mother was not just a queer, not just a fornicator, but a deceiver, and Charlie was the byproduct of her parents' lies. It wasn't long before most of her "friends" began rejecting her phone calls and ignoring her texts. Her mother may have dismissed it, but Charlie got the message loud and clear. It was the same reason Lucy only had one sniffly little playmate left. No one was bold enough to say it to their faces, but Charlie heard enough of the whispers exchanged at Dahlmouth's lone grocery store to know the remaining Kennan children were now just as unwelcome as their parents.

Perhaps *especially* Charlie, because she was the one who might show up at youth group, or stand beside their kid at the spring concert, or date their son. Charlie was infected with Finn and Rachel's sin, and who knew how far she could spread it if given the chance.

Dahlmouth had condemned Charlie for simply existing. But here in this wooded circle between these friends, Charlie belonged. Nothing mattered beyond that now, no matter what her dad tried to say.

"Charlie doesn't have long, ladies, so let's do this." Gemma winked over her shoulder as she pulled her small pink backpack up to her navel.

Charlie smiled. She was safe here. She was home here. She was with her soulmates.

"What was the deal this morning with your dad pulling you out of class?" Kendall sniffed and pulled her hair into a high ponytail, exposing her midriff and the belly piercing she'd done herself during a sleepover a few months ago. Charlie tried and failed to avert her eyes. "I thought something had to be totally fucked."

"Something *is* totally fucked." Gemma brought over the tiniest rolled cigarette Charlie had ever seen and flicked an orange lighter to test the flame. "It has something to do with the dead guy Tommy Wise and AJ Johnson found over by Route 6."

Sarah shot a worried glance at Charlie before looking down at the rolled-up paper in Gemma's hand. At this, Charlie pulled her cell halfway out of her jeans pocket to check for any texts from her dad. No news.

"Really?" Kendall looked to Charlie with those sparkling hazel eyes.

"I don't know." Charlie shrugged. "Dad doesn't know anything and the chief is MIA as usual."

"Mom heard it on the scanner this morning when she was washing dishes. Chief was calling in the county cops." Gemma locked the joint in between her lips and lit the end.

"Bet you anything Tommy's the one who killed 'em." Kendall extended her hand for the pass-off from Gemma.

"Seems fairly obvious," Sarah muttered. "Then again, Dahlmouth's finest aren't so fine. Sorry, Charlie."

Charlie shrugged again and shook her head. She would never argue that her mother was a bad detective; Rachel was simply a shitty ringleader of an even shittier circus. The only other cop in Dahlmouth that was remotely competent was Jeremy, and that was saying something. Everybody knew Jeremy was more interested in skirts than crime, which Charlie supposed endeared him to her mother. They shared a common hobby.

"Gem, that smells like shit. You sure Alex got the right stuff?" Charlie felt like plugging up her nose at the overpowering scent.

"It's the real stuff, Charlie," Kendall insisted as she exhaled a large plume. Kendall would know; her daddy had long been the biggest pothead this side of the James River. Still, Chief Mom left him alone. Dahlmouth had bigger problems than a little Mary Jane (or even a lot of it), as long as it stayed on the down-low.

Kendall passed the joint to Sarah, who immediately inhaled.

"Shit, Sarah. You look like a pro," Kendall mused with her usual deep giggle. All the girls started to laugh a moment later when Sarah started coughing violently, tears forming in her eyes. "Never mind." Kendall could barely get the words out, laughing so hard she was doubled over. Sarah wrinkled her nose and laughed with the others before handing it over to Charlie.

"So, what did I miss today?" Charlie asked before she brought the joint to her lips and sucked in a fireball.

"Jake McNeil got all butt-hurt about the soccer team." Kendall blew out her own cloud and watched it float up.

"Oh, yeah? What happened?" Charlie smiled, eyes darting back and forth between Gemma and Kendall.

"Oh, boy." Sarah chuckled softly and shook her head.

Charlie looked to Kendall to fill in the gaps, but the other girl's attention was elsewhere. Her cherry lips remained frozen in a smile, but her brows had furrowed and her eyes, focused on something far beyond Charlie's shoulder, were now flooded by maybe fear or sadness or panic—or some jumble of all those things together.

"Kendall, you okay?" Charlie began to turn to look over her shoulder as well when the girl seemed to shake off whatever had taken hold of her and grabbed at Charlie's arm. Kendall blinked and started laughing again as Charlie tried to ignore her friend's thin fingers pressing into her skin.

"I'm fine, I'm fine. I just thought I saw ... something. What were we ...? Oh yeah, Jake."

Kendall took a big breath and stretched her arm toward Sarah to pass off the cigarette again. But Sarah shook her head and waved away Kendall's arm. Sarah's eyes were now scanning the trees behind Charlie, too, her forehead creased with concern.

"So, you know how Jake thinks he is the soccer god?" Kendall held up her hands in mock adoration before stepping in closer and handing the joint to Charlie. "All because his mommy has paid for him to do regional soccer with a Roanoke team since he was like, I don't know, four or some shit."

Charlie nodded and glanced over her shoulder nervously as Sarah rose to her feet and wandered past the cluster of girls. There was nothing but more dark trees and tangled brush as far as Charlie could tell, but Sarah seemed locked in on a target. When Charlie turned back toward Kendall, she noticed Gemma was watching Sarah's trajectory as well with a strange gaze. Kendall's eyes bored into Charlie's, refusing to break away.

"Well, Coach Harris apparently failed to see what was so special about regional soccer"—Kendall raised an eyebrow and grinned—"because the team list was posted today, and Jake wasn't on it."

Gemma wandered off from their group now, too, casually walking in Sarah's footsteps. "Sarah?" Gemma called.

"All these years, the school team has never been good enough for him." Kendall's voice picked up speed as she drew closer to Charlie, the floral scent of her perfume reaching Charlie despite the marijuana smoke hanging between them. They were both shivering a little now. She hadn't even taken another inhale, but she gave the joint over to Kendall again anyway.

"Now he wants to walk up and get a spot on the team?" Kendall shook her head a little too fast. "Other boys have been playing for the school for years. Like, who does he think he is? Why should someone else lose a spot just because he decided he wanted to be one of us this year?"

Charlie could hear Gemma's footsteps crunching leaves far off now but she wasn't calling for Sarah anymore. Charlie looked over her shoulder once again and saw Sarah had come to a full stop thirty feet or so away, looking down a small dip in the forest floor. Gemma was headed that way, too, arms tightly hugging herself. Kendall's hand shot out and grabbed Charlie by the chin to turn her head back. Before Charlie could stop herself, she gasped and placed a hand on Kendall's bony wrist.

"So, Jake flipped out when he saw the list pinned up outside the cafeteria. I mean, he *really* lost his shit."

Charlie thought she could hear whimpering now, a soft and miserable cry she knew her foggy brain wasn't inventing. Her heart sped up then, her palms growing sweaty despite the cold. This time, none of it had to do with her close proximity to Kendall.

"Kendall, I think we should go see—"

But Kendall only spoke over Charlie, her voice growing faster as her grip tightened. "Jake started kicking the lockers. I mean, really kicking on them hard. He left a dent in Suellen's. Then he took his book bag and flung it at—"

"Kendall!" Charlie shouted and started to pull away from her friend's iron clasp. "We need to go check on—"

"NO!" Kendall's smile went out like a flashlight, unmasking a terrified expression. "We need to go right fucking now." Her grip tightened further, and Kendall started to pull hard at Charlie's arm.

"Kendall, we can't leave Sarah and Gem." Charlie resisted Kendall's tug and tried to pivot on her feet.

"NO! Charlie!" Kendall shrieked. "Something is *wrong* over there." Her voice cracked a little and she closed her eyes tightly.

"What did you see?" Charlie whipped around to look at Sarah and Gemma again. They were both frozen now, standing side by side like statues, though Gemma's shoulders were moving up and down as if she were sobbing noiselessly.

"I . . . It was nothing. Please, let's go, Charlie." Kendall pulled on Charlie's hand hard enough to make her stumble.

"You take off, then. I'm not leaving them."

A noise Charlie couldn't quite place ran like an undercurrent beneath the girls' argument even while Gemma and Sarah had fallen silent. As she began to pry at Kendall's fingers, the sound twisted and warped before becoming louder. Soon, Charlie was almost certain it was the sound of children singing a schoolyard tune in the distance. A shockwave of panic electrified Charlie, giving her enough strength to rip loose from the girl.

"Charlie, NO!" Kendall shrieked before hugging herself. She shivered and spun in a circle, searching for something Charlie couldn't see. The children's song grew louder as Kendall was consumed by hysterics. Terror turned wide-eyed Charlie's legs to jelly and, for a moment, she thought she might pass out as her vision blurred.

Suddenly, Kendall began swatting at her forearms and wailing, "Get away from me! I'm not going!" This was enough to break Charlie from her own paralyzing fear.

"Kendall, stop that!" Charlie yelled, her voice harsh to cover her terror. "This is just a joke, okay?" Charlie decided this on the fly. "It's probably Gemma's stupid brother and his friends." But Kendall didn't seem to hear anything as she grabbed at her hair and gasped.

"Kendall, I'm getting Sarah and Gemma, and we're all leaving *together*, okay? This stops now." Charlie turned and rushed toward Sarah and Gemma.

"Sarah? Gem?" As she drew near her two silent friends, Charlie didn't like the quiver in her own voice. It made her feel weak and small—like she was a tiny girl again, calling for her mom because she was scared of the dark. She tried clearing her throat to cover the tremor and channeled the chief's stern voice instead. "Hey, stop messing around! You're freaking Kendall out."

Behind her, Kendall began sobbing. "Don't look at it, Charlie. It's not right."

The closer Charlie came to her friends, the more her legs trembled. She knew it wasn't from the cold but refused to accept she was so easily controlled by fear. Her breath was coming out in white puffs now and the tip of her nose was numb. The merry little song of the children was close now, but Charlie couldn't make out any words. All she knew was her skin crawled as the voices multiplied and rose higher with glee.

"Guys, stop it! This isn't funny. You're scaring Kendall."

Charlie stood beside Gemma and looked at her face. Gemma didn't bother to look at Charlie. Maybe she couldn't. Maybe she hadn't heard Charlie's approach at all. The pretty girl's round face was full of despair, tears streaming down her cheeks and etching a path through a rosy blush. Charlie realized the heaving of Gemma's shoulders had not been from sobs, but from the giant gasps of air she was taking in far too fast. And her eyes . . . it was as if she had suddenly been shown all the death and tragedy visited upon humankind through time. Her mouth hung slightly askew, ready to wail but with no volume behind it.

And Sarah . . . Sarah was even worse off. Charlie could only see the profile of her face, but it was empty. Just empty, all emotion drained. The spark in her eyes was gone, snuffed out entirely and replaced by a void. Her hands hung limp at her sides, and Charlie wondered if she was still breathing at all.

"Sarah? Gem?" Charlie repeated through a tight throat.

The voices were all around her now, blending together and dropping low into indecipherable whispers. The children's melody remained in the rustle of the leaves, the croaks of tree frogs, and the river's rushing water, which should have been too distant to hear. In the midst of it all, Charlie was certain she heard Aidan playfully calling her name.

Suddenly, something compelled her to look away from her friends and toward the ground that dipped before them. In the microseconds that passed as her face turned, she realized she wasn't even putting up a fight.

Whispers in the Dark

There had never been a time when she wasn't ready to fight back. It was the one thing Charlie had inherited from her mother that still made her proud.

Her thoughts, her memories, her reason—they all ceased. All that remained was her and the darkness. A hungry darkness that coiled around her and embraced her soul. She was suspended in endless sorrow, an eternity of suffering laid out before her. Charlie didn't fight and not once did she blink, even as Kendall charged past them and into the arms of that which held them so devoutly.

Nine

"Luce, I'm gonna be honest with you—this is the most revolting thing I've ever witnessed." Finn stood on the other side of the breakfast bar, chin propped in his hand as he watched Lucy gobble cold pasta rings from a can.

"They're better this way, Daddy!" she exclaimed with a red-sauce mustache.

"There's no way that's true."

"Taste them!" Lucy held out her spoon with the gelatinous noodles and sauce quivering in a heap.

"No, thank you." Finn grimaced and pulled away from his six-year-old heathen. "I don't want to know what I've poisoned my child with."

Lucy laughed hard at this before stuffing the spoon in her mouth again.

Shaking his head, Finn pulled out his phone for the hundredth time that day to check for any sign of Rachel. As much as he hated to admit it, Finn was worried about her. She never went this long without texting back, not even when things were at their worst. He told himself dead bodies took a lot of time, and Rachel was probably somewhere pulling her hair out over paperwork and someone else's incompetence. Then again, she had texted him from grisly crime scenes in Richmond when dead bodies were the only thing she dealt with.

But it was different back then, Finn tried to remind himself. Back then, Rachel's texts made him feel warm and content. Back then, they exchanged entire conversations via off-color memes that cracked them both up. Back then, Finn couldn't wait for his wife to step through the front door, help him tuck the kids into bed, and curl up beside him to watch a scary movie. He couldn't stand the idea that even then, their life together had been a lie.

"Daddy, I don't like this song." Lucy set her spoon down into her spaghetti jelly with a grimace. Finn hadn't even realized the tiny dot of a radio had pulled up Bob Dylan's "Like a Rolling Stone." Suddenly, he couldn't hear or feel anything other than the song and the tug on his bowels it now induced.

They exchanged uncomfortable looks, and Finn knew the melody had carried Lucy right back to her booster seat as broken glass pelted her little cheeks. Only the two of them knew this was the last song Aidan ever heard. That night had created a bizarre bond between them similar to what Finn imagined soldiers who saw combat together felt. Neither of them talked much about it; they didn't have to. The crash was something Finn and Lucy would never stop reliving.

"Sorry about that, kiddo." Finn pushed away from the counter and shouted, "Off!" at the radio.

As soon as the song died away, three loud raps pounded against the front door.

One. Pause.

Two. Pause.

Three. Full stop.

For a moment, Finn stared toward the living room. The porch lights were turned on, even though dusk was only now setting in. There should be nothing dangerous about this sudden visit from a concerned citizen likely looking for Rachel to spill the tea on today's rumors, but Finn's chest tightened, nonetheless. Lucy turned around on the barstool, the can of spaghetti loops forgotten entirely as she, too, stared down the living room and into the foyer beyond. Finn shook off his silly hesitation and started across the kitchen to pass into the living room.

"Daddy!" Finn spun around as though her sharp whisper had stuck a dart in his behind. "Don't answer the door." As she fiercely shook her tiny blonde head, Finn's palms broke out into a cold sweat.

"Honey," Finn breathed out and forced a reassuring smile, "it's all right. It's just some nosy neighbor asking about your mom."

"No, it's not." Another headshake.

Her little brow was furrowed hard, and her lips quivered. Something about Lucy's terror was contagious. For a moment, Finn considered sweeping her off to the basement until Rachel returned. Another single, firm pound landed against the door, jerking Finn's attention back again. He instinctively reversed two steps.

"Don't answer it, Daddy," Lucy whispered again, her eyes growing wider.

Suddenly, his phone vibrated in his pocket. Finn whipped it out and stared at the long-awaited message from Rachel:

Hung up in Roanoke. Tell the girls I love them, and I'll be home soon.

The girls. The *GIRLS*. Finn nearly dropped the phone.

"Charlotte," he gasped. "Shit! Charlie!" He dashed toward the door without another moment's pause.

"Daddy, no!" Lucy screeched from behind him, but Finn couldn't hear a thing, thanks to the pounding inside his head.

Finn tore open the door. It crashed against the wall, rattling the front windows. Charlie stood slumped against the brick entryway, her eyes staring down unfocused toward Finn's feet. Though fully clothed, Charlie was soaked from head to toe as if she had crawled her way out of the goddamned river. Thick chunks of vomit were caught in her hair, and long strings of drool hung from her lips, pooled on the chest of her hoodie. Charlie shivered every few seconds, or was it twitching? Her mouth hung open, not as if she was ready to start explaining herself, but as if the muscles in her jaw had gone slack.

"Charlie? Charlie!" Finn's voice rose sharply as he reached out to wrap his daughter in his arms. He pulled her into his chest and looked around over her shoulder, but there was no one. Neither hide nor hair of Gemma, Sarah, or Kendra, or whatever her name was. Charlie collapsed against him, complete deadweight.

"Jesus Christ, Charlotte!"

He scooped her up like she was his wee babe again. He slammed the door shut and flipped the dead bolt. Charlie felt like a cold wet rag. He turned on his heels and ran with her up the stairs to the bathroom. Finn panted as they reached the top step. "No, no—you can't do this to me, kid."

Finn sat her down on the floor of the bathroom as gently as he could, his eyes burning with tears. His hands and arms shook violently as he reached into the shower and turned the knob on high. Finn held a hand in the water and turned back to look at his young teen. She looked more like a rag doll than a rebel. Her eyes were still eerily vacant. He looked away as a puddle of urine grew beneath her.

Finn had first pegged her state as being alcohol induced, but her pupils were three times their normal size. He had never seen anyone so drunk they looked this rough, and Finn had been a member of Beta Phi for three years in undergrad. If it wasn't a case of the Natty Light blues, Finn could only assume his girl was playing around with more nefarious things—heavier shit that Finn had never played with. It wasn't weed; it wasn't blow; it wasn't shrooms or X. He had seen and felt those effects, but Charlie didn't fit the bill for any of them.

He supposed you treated all bad trips the same way, but the fear that he was looking at an overdose nagged at him. How would he even know what an overdose looked like when he hadn't the foggiest clue what she had been up to? Then again, did it matter? Wasn't it better to play it safe rather than be sorry? Shouldn't she be evaluated regardless? For several beats, Finn tried to remember what hospital would be the closest to Dahlmouth, but it wouldn't come to him. He knew—goddammit, he knew for sure—but the memory stubbornly refused to come.

The hospital. The name might not come to him, but the sick, all-consuming panic forever associated with the place hit him like a freight train all over again. The emergency lights blurring together. The gurney's straps pressing into his chest and belly. Lucy's wailing from a year ago tore through his fog. Images flashed like lightning in the recesses of his mind, and he forgot to breathe. Aidan . . . Aidan was gone. He nearly dropped to his knees right there on the bathroom tile.

Not again. Not Charlie, too.

He should call Rachel or 911. It was one and the same, really. Rachel would know what to do—whether their eldest was overdosing, whether she needed to go to the hospital, what the name of the goddamn hospital even was, how badly Finn had fucked up this time. And then, Rachel would finally take the kids away from him forever just as she'd threatened in the weeks following Aidan's death. This would be the last straw, and Finn would be done. He had no doubt Rachel would find a way to crush even the smallest amount of visitation rights after this. In that moment, Finn couldn't have blamed her.

"Jesus," Finn whimpered, sniffed hard, and moved to where Charlie sat on the floor. "Charlie"—Finn knelt to look in her eyes—"it's really important that I know what happened. What did you take, honey? I won't be mad. I need to know so I can help you." Finn scanned her face for any sign of recognition. "I need to know if we . . . if we should go to the hospital, okay?"

Finally, Charlie's eyes blinked and she raised them to look at Finn, though her mouth still hung agape. It didn't matter. Her eye movement was all the encouragement Finn needed.

"Come on, Charlie. You gotta let me help you, kid. Your mom is not going to be as understanding, believe me. But if you tell me, I swear I won't say anything to her. I'll find a way to spin it, and this will be our little secret. I promise. I just need to know what happened, honey." Finn tapped at her cheeks, but she didn't blink again.

Finn sat back on his heels, hands on his bent knees, to survey Charlie. Her breathing was fine—steady even, no panting or interruption in its rhythm. He reached out and grabbed hold of her wrist to feel her pulse. Finn tried and failed to count her beats per minute several times. It was no use. His brain was far too loud for the careful calm required to calculate her heartbeat. One thing was sure, though: it was regular. No beats were skipped; her heart wasn't racing, nor was it slow. Just as her breathing, her pulse felt blessedly normal.

His own heart raced faster than ever as Finn fumbled for his phone in his rear pocket. Maybe Charlie wasn't a goner, but if he had an ounce of decency, Finn knew he needed to face the music and get her checked out. He swallowed against a whimper as he sorted through his most recent calls, his thumb hovering above Rachel's name.

Nodding to himself, Finn was one breath from hitting her number when Charlie's clammy hand gently landed against his cheek. He gasped, dropped his phone, and looked up into his daughter's eyes. Something flickered deep within her enlarged pupils. Though her face was still lax, the color began to return to her cheeks. She gently dragged her thin fingers down the side of his face and returned a slight nod.

Whispers in the Dark

"I'm okay, Daddy," Charlie forced out in a weak whisper. "Don't call Mother . . . *please*."

Tears flooded Finn's eyes as he clasped his hand over Charlie's. His little girl was okay—more than okay if she was conscious enough to fear Rachel's wrath. Finn would know.

"All right, Charlie." Finn exhaled. "I'm putting your ass in the shower, kid. We'll get this taken care of and chat about it later, yeah?"

Fifteen minutes later, Charlie sat with glazed eyes in the bottom of the tub, half-dressed but in the water stream nonetheless. Finn frantically rummaged around in Charlie's bedroom for pajamas that could be tossed onto his halfway conscious teen from a distance. He could feel time accelerating as if it was fused with Rachel's gas pedal.

"Daddy." A small voice floated into Charlie's room from the hall. Finn whipped around, baggy pink sweatpants dangling from his fist. Lucy sat on the top step, peeking around from the corner of the banister. She looked even more terrified than Finn felt.

"Sweetheart, I have to take care of your sister right now. She's not feeling well."

"You shouldn't have done that, Daddy." Tears were brimming in Lucy's eyes. She was gripping the banister with white knuckles.

"Shouldn't have done what, Luce?"

"You shouldn't have let it in," Lucy whispered and backed down the staircase, out of sight.

The hair on Finn's arms stood up, but he didn't have time to follow after his youngest. He swallowed hard and took a deep breath. It made sense for Lucy to craft such cryptic warnings after what she'd seen with Aidan. All her fanciful and disturbing statements over the past year . . . the shrink had told Rachel and Finn it was totally normal given the circumstances. Finn should understand better than anyone that the mind could create the most twisted of images.

If Finn could have cut out the part of his brain that forced flashbacks from that night, he gladly would have grabbed a scalpel. But there was no erasing the sight of Aidan's head lolling to the side as Finn tried to wrestle himself out of the quickly flooding front seat. There was Lucy's screaming—constant, piercing—but nothing so loud as the dead silence from Aidan. Even after Finn had freed himself and pulled Lucy from her car seat, half-drowned and looking as if she had been mauled, he couldn't manage to separate Aidan's body from the demolished Escape as it took on more water and moved faster down the river.

He must've dipped beneath the surface fifteen times, losing his grip over and over again, but it was that last time that haunted Finn, that woke him from the deepest sleep drenched in sweat, that interrupted his thoughts whenever he sat down to write.

The last time he dove down, Aidan wasn't there anymore. His therapist said that part was almost certainly true, which prompted his guilty conscience to create the following part: a pale face and wide mouth flashing before his eyes. The torn white lace of the small specter's unraveling dress twirling brightly against the black water where his son's body should have been. Eyes dark as night, long brown hair twisting around its face, a slight smirk on its lips before they opened impossibly wide—Finn didn't know it at the time, but that was the moment that would truly force him into sobriety. Whiskey had never been so cruel.

He'd instinctively reeled away, pushing himself backward from the vehicle as the irrational fear of the twisted creature grabbing him seized his common sense. Below the raging whitecaps, Finn shrieked and sucked in murky water. His chest locked, and the current tossed him around until Finn thought he might lose consciousness. Even then, he flailed his legs and arms—not to swim back to his son, but to ensure that thing couldn't drag him to the bottom of the riverbed.

And that was when he gave up, climbing onto the riverbank to vomit before wrapping Lucy in his arms as she wailed. More broken than the SUV he'd destroyed, Finn watched the wreckage helplessly as the waters swept it and Aidan away. It wasn't until the emergency lights and sirens illuminated the night and lit up Finn's hellscape in electric red and blue that he really understood Aidan was gone.

From the corner of his eye, Finn thought he saw the door to Aidan's room creak open ever so slightly on its hinges and his heart began racing. There wasn't time for his bullshit when Charlie needed him as much as she did right now. Finn shrugged off the temporary madness and dashed to the bathroom.

* * *

Another half hour passed before Finn was able to coach Charlie out of the shower and into the baggy T-shirt and sweats he'd found balled up on the floor next to her laundry bin. She collapsed onto her bedroom floor beside the bed, legs crumpled beneath her, but still sitting upright. Finn took the chance to grab a towel from the bathroom and snatch her brush up off her desk. He plopped down onto her lime-green bedspread and started furiously squeezing the water out of her hair.

"You've really gotten into it this time, kiddo. I mean, *really*. What if your mother had come back before we'd gotten you taken care of?" Finn squeezed extra hard at that, tugging her head backward, but Charlie didn't react at all. Her hands remained limp in her lap, fingers open and palms facing the ceiling. "We're going to talk about this later. Do you understand? If you think you're off the hook, you are sorely mistaken. I did some stupid stuff growing up, but whatever you got yourself into tonight takes the goddamn cake."

Ten

Daddy was busy trying to put Charlie back together again—so busy he didn't hear Lucy creep up the stairs again on her hands and knees. She didn't want anyone to know where she was anyway, at least not until Mommy came home. Daddy was fun, and Lucy generally preferred his company over Mommy's, but when things went wrong, Mommy knew exactly what to do. Mommy was calm, Mommy could think fast, Mommy had the gun.

The wooden floor at the top step was cold against her palms. The house felt all wrong now, and deep down, Lucy knew it would never feel quite right ever again. The same way the home had changed into something sad and strange the night Aidan left, this place would twist onto its side forever after this night . . . all because Daddy let it in.

A slight breeze tickled her ear. She turned to see where it had come from and immediately wished she hadn't. The door to the bedroom between hers and Mommy's was wide open. It was dark as always in there, but Lucy could see enough to know the window was gaping, cold night air blowing the curtains this way and that. That window hadn't been open for at least a year, and Lucy didn't think Mommy was likely to touch it ever again.

Mommy kept the door closed to pretend the room didn't exist because it was Aidan's.

Lucy slowly rose to her feet, looking back at Charlie's bedroom to be certain no one was watching her. She heard Daddy's low voice murmuring to Charlie. Even though she couldn't make out the words, she knew Charlie was in the biggest kind of trouble you could ever get into with Daddy. That didn't matter, though, because the Charlie that sat in a heap on the other side of the bed no longer cared about being grounded or fussed at.

The wrong Charlie was looking into the mirror on her closet door, but Lucy couldn't make out her face. She was at just the right angle to tiptoe around the banister without being seen so she could go shut the door that should never have been opened. Lucy had long been scared to get too close to Aidan's old door, but it didn't feel like something was hiding in there anymore. No, whatever had opened that window was already inside the house, just as the Charlie Thing was there plain as day. Lucy didn't like that thought at all. She ran forward, grabbed the brass doorknob, and pulled it shut as quietly as she could. Then, she held her breath, waiting for someone to come looking for her, but Daddy's voice never stopped droning on.

With the room closed up good, Lucy didn't know where to go. She thought about running into her bedroom and locking the door, but what good would locks do now? The next place she considered was Mommy's bed. Lucy could slide underneath the blankets and hold them tight until Mommy got home. Mommy would see the trouble right away, of course. She would handle it in no time flat. All Lucy had to do was wait for Mommy to come home and fix it.

But that wouldn't work either. Mommy and Daddy thought the girls didn't know Daddy hadn't slept in there since the bad night. There would be no reason for him to check Mommy's room for Lucy, and once Daddy was downstairs, there was nothing between this thing that wasn't Charlie and her. Lucy couldn't have that. No, she needed to get far away from the Charlie Thing while she waited for Mommy to make it better. Mommy would never let them take Lucy, too, even if she had ignored the pictures Lucy made.

Lucy would have to sneak down the steps again. The middle floor—the one where she had so recently been enjoying her SpaghettiOs—was lined with windows. On any other day, it made Lucy happy, with plenty of sunshine and animals to spy. But Lucy didn't want to spy anything out of those windows tonight, and when she had scuttled down there a few minutes prior, she felt them out there watching her. They wanted her, yes. She'd known that since the bad night. But now they knew the Charlie Thing would get Lucy for all of them. They were only watching to see how it happened.

Daddy's basement would be the safest. No windows, no doors. All she had to do was get there. Soon enough, Daddy would finish up with the Charlie Thing and settle downstairs for the evening. Lucy would stay there with him while Mommy made things right. Was that good enough? If they wanted Lucy bad enough, couldn't they get through Daddy? He wasn't exactly Superman, but Daddy couldn't help that. It was the best option she had. Daddy was her only chance until Mommy came home to save them all, and that was better than nothing.

Lucy's tummy turned and tightened. She knew Mommy had started keeping a gun in pieces inside her bedstand not long ago—right after Mommy and Daddy stopped screaming at each other. She thought about grabbing the pieces and running downstairs, but she would never figure out how to put them together right, and Daddy would be furious if he found her with them. She didn't want to make Daddy sad.

Then she thought of Gramma Kennan. What were the words she had always said? Lucy couldn't quite remember, but she knew Gramma said magic words while holding her long necklace that protected her from super-scary things. Gramma fussed at Daddy every time they visited because he never said those words and he never ever took Lucy to church.

Still, when Gramma passed away, Daddy took her long necklace from beside her bed and put it in his pocket. He didn't tell anybody, even when Uncle Caleb started looking for it, and Lucy hadn't tattled on Daddy because Uncle Caleb always got everything he wanted anyway. Well, right now she needed Gramma's super necklace, even if she couldn't remember the magic words that went with it. She was pretty sure the necklace would work a little on its own.

Where would Daddy have put it? He wouldn't have kept it in Mommy's room anymore, that's for sure. Lucy was pretty certain then that it had to be hiding somewhere downstairs. Daddy didn't have any other place to hide things anymore. Mommy had found all of his sneaky spots after the bad night.

Lucy decided she had no other choice but to make a break for the basement. The only trick was making it down there. She crept back from the door that should always stay closed and made the turn around the end of the banister as sneaky as she could. Daddy's voice had stopped now, but she could still hear him rummaging around in Charlie's room. Lucy peered in from a distance and saw Daddy sorting through Charlie's wet clothing, pulling pockets inside out and shaking his head. He had pulled down the lime-green covers, ready to help the Charlie Thing into bed for the night.

Just then, something caught Lucy's eye and made her freeze. Lucy had been watching Daddy in the mirror, but something else had been watching her at the same time. The Charlie Thing, sitting on the floor and acting numb, wasn't so sleepy anymore—at least not its face. Instead, it was looking directly into the mirror at Lucy standing in the hallway, and while the Charlie Thing looked the spitting image of her sister, there was something terribly wrong with it.

The Charlie Thing watched Lucy with intense, dark eyes Lucy remembered all too well from the night Aidan left. Charlie's bluebell irises had been swallowed up by a blackness that crowded out the whites of her eyes, and after staring at Lucy for several moments, the corners of the Charlie Thing's mouth tugged upward into a predatory grin. Lucy's bladder twitched and she thought she might mess on the floor. She clutched at her privates to hold it in and took off in a flash for the staircase. Lucy didn't care if Daddy heard her now. The Charlie Thing knew exactly where she was, and nothing else mattered until Mommy got home.

Eleven

Rachel sat in her unmarked SUV outside of the Roanoke Marriot until the sun sank below the building, stewing and smoking cigarette after cigarette. She glanced down at the clock on the dashboard. Six thirty p.m. Dinnertime. Finn was sure to be feeding the girls and wondering where the hell she was. She could've told him about the body, about having to run and lick the sheriff's boots like a moron, about why she was taking so damned long. But then Rachel would get stuck in an endless cycle of questions, and it was likely Finn wouldn't believe her anyway.

The hotel before her hadn't changed one bit. There was nothing special about its white, vaguely terra-cotta exterior and sliding front doors. Yet, the pesky little place had caused so many problems. Most people, she supposed, would do everything they could to avoid the place after what had happened there. Not Rachel.

She should be headed home, but somehow Michelle's same old bullshit song and dance pushed Rachel in this direction. It seemed every time Michelle chose her dogma over her, this damn place called Rachel back. After all, Michelle was the one who had set into motion the meltdown at the hotel six months before.

The moment Michelle had broken the news to Rachel about running into the arms of a goddamn minister who would save her from the gay agenda, Rachel knew she had some hell to raise. Not two hours later, Rachel had already picked up another woman at a rundown dive and checked into what would otherwise have been a meaningless hotel. It was then that Rachel decided to turn the location back on her cell phone, knowing Finn would be able to track her. That was when she sent him a particularly scathing text indicating she wouldn't be home that evening. The night Michelle threw Jesus in Rachel's face like a middle finger was the same night Rachel had very intentionally set out to die.

Memories played inside her head on loop: Finn's heavy knock at the door, the absolute rage on his face when Rachel opened it, the palpable fear that radiated off her brief lover as she shoved past Finn, pulling on her clothes as she trotted down the hall. Then, the ticking time bomb known as Finn and Rachel's marriage exploded at long last.

In that room, Rachel finally met the beast lurking in the deepest parts of Finn's brain—the one he'd hidden so well back when they'd been companions. For the first time, she'd known what it was like to fear the man Rachel had spent so much time coddling, and it had delighted her. Sure, there was panic as her vision began to fade while his grip around her neck cut off her oxygen, but it was mixed with the satisfaction of knowing she had succeeded in pushing him over the edge—of luring Finn into total self-destruction. Most of all, Rachel felt relief that her suffering was coming to an end; peace that she'd soon be with her son; a bizarre closeness with Aidan, knowing they'd both died at the hands of the same man.

But as the fight began to leave Rachel's body beneath his, Finn had let go. He'd pulled away from her, breaking down into pitiful wails on the side of the bed as Rachel coughed and wheezed to regain her breath. Her wrists and forearms were bruised, her insides battered, her neck on fire as she stared at the room's water-stained ceiling. And in that moment, Rachel hated Finn in a way she didn't know was possible—not for the way they'd beaten the shit out of each other or the pain he'd inflicted—Rachel had wanted that.

She hated him for refusing to give her the thing she wanted most: Finn denied her death.

He couldn't do it. The son of a bitch was incapable of finishing the job, and Rachel never wanted Finn to touch her again because of it. Gone were the days of playful wrestling in bed because they'd never be able to sleep beside one another without thinking of that night. There'd be no more joking to shove one another out of the way as they raced for control of the remote because they'd never find the other's force funny again. They would never manage a civil disagreement about pizza toppings or ice-cream flavors now when the words they'd exchanged that night were meant to be the last shattering ones they ever spoke.

By then, however, Rachel wasn't sure it even mattered. There would never be any joy again because Aidan was gone. Finn had done that. He'd blotted out the light forevermore.

* * *

Whispers in the Dark

It was almost eleven by the time Rachel pulled into the driveway at home. When she gripped the handle of the front door and found it unlocked, she wasn't surprised—just annoyed enough to roll her eyes. It was warm and cozy when she stepped into the hall, so much so that Rachel wondered how much the damn electric bill was going to cost next month.

The house was quiet, unusual for the time. On most nights, she would still have heard the murmur of Charlie singing along to whatever was blasting in her headphones upstairs, in addition to whatever dumb-ass movie Finn had playing in surround sound downstairs. Rachel glanced up the long staircase and saw the whole upper level was dark except the bathroom, the door of which had been left ajar, probably for Lucy to see her way through the night.

The track lights over the breakfast bar in the kitchen were still on as well, illuminating the room in a faint glow. Rachel walked over to the refrigerator to grab whatever leftovers Finn might have packed away. She couldn't remember eating anything all day other than a dry, heavy protein bar from a gas station on the way to Roanoke that morning. Then she noticed the half-eaten can of SpaghettiOs on the bar, a reddish-orange ring staining the rim. There would be no point in looking for remnants of any kind of solid meal if Finn had opted for spaghetti goo.

Rachel grabbed the can and tossed it into the sink, running water into the orange gel noodles, before looking out into the dark backyard. Their porch was dimly lit by the sliver of the moon overhead, but the rest of the world out there was an infinite black sea. Rachel's eyes hovered near where she knew the tree line would be.

For a moment, she could see her dead hiker out there, no longer pinned to a tree, but walking around in that bizarre Scarecrow stance anyway. Face torn away, innards leaking from the hole in his belly, the corpse tried to call to her . . . to tell her a dead man's tale and a warning. Even in her imagination, however, Rachel couldn't make out what story the hiker had to tell. Whatever hell he'd witnessed, she feared it would stay silent with him forever. Rachel shook her head, wiping clean the image of the mutilated man as she finished rinsing out the pasta can and tossed it into the full recycling bin.

As she raised her eyes to the window once more, Rachel startled and took a step back. The yard and the trees beyond were shrouded in night, but something out there held the faint glow of the moon and reflected it back despite the inescapable darkness. Rachel narrowed her eyes and leaned in to catch a better glimpse. As she did, the thin slice of light folded in on itself, dissolving into the tree line as if it had never existed at all. Indeed, Rachel suspected it hadn't ever truly been there. Just as the child's cry and the broken lullaby had tested her sanity earlier in the day, Rachel was still sharp enough to recognize when stress was wearing at her. Her dead man could wait, and so, too, could all of Rachel's mindfucks. It was time for meds and bed. Otherwise, Rachel feared she might finally crack. For now, she was still holding it together, even if it was by the barest thread.

Twelve

Four-year-old Abby Grayson had been lost in a dream she very much did not want to leave. A sparkling white unicorn pranced around her in a field full of wildflowers, its shimmering rainbow mane brighter than the sun itself. The sky was cloudless and blue. From a distance, Abby heard someone call her name, and when she turned, Barbie stood a few short steps from the edge of a forest. Sparkling orbs of light—neon pinks, blues, yellows, and greens—glowed as they danced through the trees behind Abby's impossibly perfect hero. Abby never went into the woods other than when her Brownie troop had to earn a badge for Earth Day; there were too many creepy-crawlies in the wild for her liking. She'd follow Barbie anywhere, though.

Just as Abby took a step toward the pretty-in-pink blonde, however, the little girl awoke. Sleep blurred her vision for a moment, but Abby's heart was pounding before she even finished rubbing her eyes. Her little bare feet felt cold and clammy against linoleum, worlds away from the lovely summer scene she'd been in moments before. In the next beat, Abby realized she stood alone in the kitchen, surrounded by darkness. Her long cotton nightgown with Barbie's face imprinted on the front was soaked in sweat.

Abby had sleepwalked once before, but her mommy had still been awake. This time, the television was silent. Mommy's gentle chuckles were absent from the living room. The lights were all off. She snapped her eyelids shut, feeling her small body begin to shake. This wasn't right. Mommy needed to come get her right now because there was no way Abby could stand the thought of running back through the long hallway and into her room. Anything could be waiting for her along the way. The ugly clown from her classmate's recent birthday party suddenly popped into her head, this time with fangs as he lurked in the shadows, ready to snatch her up.

She had just opened her mouth to scream for Mommy, eyes still clamped painfully tight, when there was a soft knock on the door. Abby gasped, her eyelids shooting open before she could help herself. Her damp feet slid as she instinctively took a step back. However, when Abby's eyes adjusted, calm washed over her.

Beyond the door, Gemma's cheerful face was illuminated by the bright floodlights that flickered on whenever a fat, silly raccoon scuttled past in the Graysons' backyard. Abby and her mommy had spent lots of evenings laughing, watching one they named Teddy waddle out of the forest to steal smelly scraps out of the trash can. The lights made the night better, less scary out there. And so did Gemma.

Gemma had babysat Abby for as long as the little girl could remember. With her pearly white teeth, sunny smile, and perfectly smooth blonde hair, Gemma reminded Abby of Barbie quite a lot. She always liked her for that. What made Gemma really special, though, was how nice and fun she was. Gemma never failed to bring her bracelet-making kit and sneak in chocolate Mommy didn't know about. The bestest babysitter loved to braid Abby's long brown hair while they watched funny videos on Gemma's phone that her parents wouldn't otherwise allow. And whenever it was time for Abby to go to bed, Gemma always left the hallway lights on and stuck close by.

Not once had Gemma tattled to Mommy, even when she drew a princess on her bedroom wall. Instead, her babysitter spent tons of time scrubbing the pink crayon off the wall, and though Abby could tell she was mad, Gemma never said a word to anyone. She wasn't ever going to let Abby get in trouble—this much the little girl was sure of.

What worried Abby this time was not that Gemma was visiting. It was that Gemma was stuck out there so late at night when the weather was still very cold. Her clothes were wet; even her beautiful hair stuck to her cheeks like she'd just gotten out of the pool. Being wet in the cold could make a person very sick—Mommy had told her so. Even though Gemma smiled brightly at her from the other side of the door, Abby wondered if she was in trouble . . . if Gemma knew how sick she could get running around like that. If she did, Gemma could use the key Mommy hid under the doormat to come inside and get warm. Mommy had shown it to Gemma a bunch of times before.

Gemma knocked again at the door before waving at Abby. Her smile broadened before she curled her finger toward herself, beckoning Abby to come over. Way down in her tummy, Abby felt something squirm. Something scary was going on. She knew as much because Gemma was never, ever this dumb.

Then again, sometimes grown-ups acted pretty stupid. Daddy and his friends had played football out there in the pouring rain several times, getting all covered in mud while taking big gulps from giant cans. Another time, Mommy and Aunt Becky had danced so silly at Nana's that they fell into the Christmas tree and spilled their grape juice everywhere. People kept saying Gemma was growing up too fast, and now Abby understood. Gemma was enough of a big kid now that she, too, was doing dumb-dumb things.

"Abby!" Gemma cocked her head to the side. Her smile still stretched wide across her face. "Come here!"

One time, Daddy came home super-duper late. He couldn't walk right; his words were all jumbled. Daddy couldn't even find his keys. Mommy flung open that back door, hands on her hips, and fussed at him to get his behind (though Mommy did *not* say "behind") in the house before he got sick. He needed to come in and lie down, and she was never letting him go out with his stupid buddies ever again. Boy, did Daddy hurry inside and go to sleep after that. So, that's what Abby decided Gemma now needed, too.

The little girl pounded toward the door, trying to make sure Gemma could hear every stomp so she'd know how serious Abby was. Like her mommy, Abby balled up her fists and planted them on both hips before rolling her eyes. The older girl didn't stop smiling. In fact, she looked happier with each step Abby took toward the door. Adults weren't very good at knowing when they were in big trouble.

Abby twisted the lock and tried to fling the door wide like Mommy, but the brass knob slipped in her sweaty hands. The back door swung open almost silently.

Whispers in the Dark

"What are you doing out here?" Abby forced her angriest voice to come out as Gemma quietly knelt down to her level. "You could get sick. You get in here and go lay down, Gemma Thompson!"

Gemma's grin was sweet as pie like always, but there was a mischievous sparkle in her eyes that Abby wasn't used to. It wasn't quite the same look Gemma gave Abby when they pinkie-promised to keep a secret, but it wasn't too different from the one Gemma wore when they were about to play hide-and-seek. A strange, sour smell hit Abby as Gemma squatted before her, and suddenly, Abby felt upset. Gemma really was sick; she'd thrown up all on her clothes.

"I'm gonna go get Mommy," Abby whimpered.

"No, no!" Gemma shook her head, still smiling despite the pinkish goo smeared all over her zip-up hoodie.

"But you're sick!"

"I'm okay," Gemma whispered, her voice turning soft and soothing like it did when Abby got scared of getting shampoo in her eyes during bath time. "I was sick before, but I'm feeling better now."

Abby leaned against the edge of the door, her small fingers still clinging to the doorknob. She didn't believe Gemma. If she was feeling better, Gemma would've taken off her smelly clothes. Abby now agreed with the ladies at church; Gemma was changing *way* too fast.

"I want to show you something." She shifted on her heels a little and leaned closer to Abby.

"What is it?"

"It's a big secret. Do you think you can keep a secret, Abby?"

Abby's brow furrowed. "You know I can! I didn't tell anybody you like Jesse Turner!"

A funny little giggle escaped Gemma's mouth. "You're right. I can trust you." She tucked her wet hair behind her ears, and her expression became a bit more serious. "I want you to come with me so I can show you the secret, but we can't tell your parents."

"Where is it?"

"Not far. Just over there." Gemma pointed over her shoulder toward the dark forest, and Abby instantly felt frightened. Monsters hung out in the woods at night.

But this was Gemma, and Gemma would never let her get into trouble.

"I . . . The woods are scary." Abby scooted a little behind the door, only part of her face exposed. "Don't make me go, Gemma. I'll go in the daytime, I promise."

Gemma's expression changed. Her smile disappeared; the happiness gone in the blink of an eye. Still, something flickered in Gemma's eyes as if things were still very funny.

"It's not scary, I swear. It's the best thing you've ever seen, darling."

Weird. Gemma had never called her *darling*. Only Nana and the old ladies in Dahlmouth said stuff like that.

"Abby." Gemma's voice grew deeper than Abby had ever heard it. She tilted her chin down to stare harder at the little girl. "You must come with me. I'm going to show you a special place. There are lots of little boys and girls there, and they want to play with you. You'll have so much fun, Abby, I promise."

"Their mommies let them play at night?" Her bedtime was eight o'clock on the dot, but Abby knew some kids got to stay up way later. It wasn't fair.

"All night, and all day." The broad smile returned to Gemma's face, more cheerful than before. "You remember when we read about Peter Pan?" Abby nodded, her face slowly re-emerging from behind the door. "Do you remember Neverland and the Lost Boys? How Wendy got to go and read them stories, and none of them ever had to grow up. They played as much as they wanted and got to stay up late and eat all the stuff they wanted, too, right?"

Abby nodded once more, this time faster. Gemma leaned forward further, her palms now pressing onto the wooden step beneath her as if getting ready to tackle Abby the way Daddy's friends did while playing ball.

"What if I told you that I found a place just like that?" Gemma whispered. "Someplace magical where you can do whatever you want, whenever you want, and you don't ever have to worry about getting in trouble with Mommy again."

That sounded good. Nothing felt worse than when Mommy was mad at her. Still, Abby knew Peter Pan was make-believe. Even Gemma had told her so. And Mommy usually didn't get mad for no reason. She almost always told Abby why she was upset, and sometimes Abby could understand why. It was dangerous to swim too far out in the river; Mommy said she could get washed away like the little Kennan boy had. Mommy yelled at her for playing with her Barbies too close to the road, and then a big old truck flew past that could've hurt Abby. Mommy said her job was to keep Abby safe, and the more Abby thought about it, the more that made sense.

"But I want Mommy to come."

"Oh." Gemma giggled lightly. "Mommy is going to come, too. But she's sleeping right now, so she'll come later. I promise."

"Really? Did Mommy say so?"

"Abby, I swear on my life, Mommy will come. I'll make sure of it. You've gotta listen to me."

That was indeed what Abby's parents had always told her. They'd even said she would get into big trouble if she didn't mind Gemma.

Abby took one long look over Gemma's shoulder toward the shadow-wreathed trees. Somewhere deep inside the woods, little neon lights flickered on and off. The wind blew, and Abby could even hear the kids Gemma promised playing. They sounded happy, like they were having the best time of their lives.

"You promise I won't get in trouble?" Abby whispered and met Gemma's stare once more.

"Cross my heart and hope to die." Gemma extended her pinkie finger. It twitched like Gemma had been hit by a lightning bolt, but Abby locked her little finger around it anyway.

Gemma rose to her feet, clasping hands with the little girl. Abby should've put on shoes. She remembered this a few steps away from the edge of the trees, when a twig snapped beneath her bare feet. The thing was, Abby didn't realize they'd walked so fast. Once she took Gemma's hand, it felt like everything sped up.

Just as Abby had walked in her sleep to the kitchen, she wondered if she was now walking toward the woods half-awake.

Whispers in the Dark

That didn't feel right. Neither did Gemma's increasingly tight grip around her hand. The children's voices didn't sound the same now either.

Rather than the playful laughter Abby had heard from the Graysons' door, they'd begun singing a tune Abby had never heard before. It was so loud, yet Abby couldn't understand what they were saying. Underneath it all, however, there were wails and frightened whispers.

A little boy was crying for his mommy.

Another was screaming—only screaming with no words at all.

For one brief moment, Abby did not want to go. No, she needed to turn back and go get her mommy. But her body wouldn't work, and in the next second, Abby didn't have thoughts at all anymore.

As she and Gemma disappeared into the thick brush, little Abby Grayson forgot all about Mommy, Barbie, and even her name. It was better that way.

Thirteen

"Finn. Finn!"

Rachel's hissing broke through Finn's sleep at the same time he realized her steel-toed boot was tapping the bottom of his socked foot. He opened his gray eyes slowly, blinking ten or fifteen times before the bright world came into focus. The basement was illuminated like a chapel, every lamp he had stuck down there switched on all around him. The TV station he had been watching had switched over to a program selling exercise balls.

Rachel stood at the end of the couch, a tall dark shape against the glow of the lamps.

"You trying to convert her now?"

His eyes adjusted to see the bemused expression on his wife's shadowed face. "What?" He inhaled and rubbed his eyes.

"Luce." Rachel crossed her arms and looked down at the floor directly beside his spot on the couch. "She's going to make a piss-poor Catholic given how much she hates incense and strange men."

Finn rolled over. On the floor, Lucy was curled up on her side with a balled-up towel under her head and one of his sweatshirts covering her as a makeshift blanket. Their youngest was fast asleep, her chubby cheeks puffed out, drool escaping from between her lips. She was clutching Finn's mother's rosary in her tiny clenched fist. Finn blinked a few more times before sitting up and running a hand through his messy hair.

"I don't know how she got that." Finn groaned. "Jesus, I don't even know where I put it."

"You don't want her breaking it," Rachel muttered.

"I didn't give—"

"Why didn't you put her to bed? She can't be up late watching TV with you. She's only six, for fuck's sake." Rachel leaned down to untangle the white-and-maroon rosary from Lucy's fingers.

"I *did* put her to bed, Rach," Finn insisted though he couldn't truly remember. His brain raced through the evening's events but kept getting stuck on Charlie. No, he'd definitely put Lucy to bed, right? Finn knew he had watched her at least go into the bedroom. "I put her in bed. I don't know how she got down here."

"Well, here you go." Rachel dropped the rosary into Finn's hand. "I'm taking Luce upstairs. Don't bother getting up."

As Rachel started to tug under Lucy's armpits to scoop her into her arms, the little girl shot upright, nearly knocking Rachel in the mouth.

"Mommy!" Lucy gasped with eyes as big as the moon. "Mommy, you're home!" She fell forward and grabbed at Rachel's pant legs. Rachel shot Finn a look that made his insides rumble.

"Luce, were you having a bad dream, sweetheart?" Finn leaned forward and brushed away strands of Lucy's light blonde hair that had stuck to her cheeks.

"Mommy, I've been waiting for you to get home!" Lucy was quivering from head to toe, wrapping her arms and legs around Rachel's calves.

"I'm sorry, baby girl. I had to take care of some stuff in town. I was gone for a long time, I know. I'm sorry."

It had always amazed Finn how soft and tender Rachel's voice could become if she had a reason. He tried to remember the last time any of that warmth had been directed his way but couldn't place it. At the time, Finn didn't know it was the last time she'd ever talk to him that way. So, as with all good things people fail to appreciate, it had gone into the trash bin of Finn's memory right along with the last time Aidan hugged him.

Rachel rubbed Lucy's arms and tried to kneel, but their daughter wouldn't loosen her hold enough for that.

"Something bad happened." Lucy wiped her nose on Rachel's tan pants.

Finn felt his heart leap into his throat. He'd spent most of the evening erasing every trace of Charlie's misdeeds, but he hadn't once thought about wiping Lucy's memory with a nice story of how her big sister got a tummy bug that's been going around the school.

"Charlie got sick." Finn tried to make his voice sound casual. "She puked a couple of times, but her fever had already started to go down when I got her in bed. I think it's something going around the school." Lucy started to cry harder and shook her head. Finn resisted the urge to snatch Lucy off Rachel's legs.

"How high?" Rachel looked at him with her piercing hazel eyes, still bent over to rub Lucy's shoulders.

His mouth went dry. "Pardon?"

"How high was her fever?"

"Oh." Finn breathed out and rubbed at his eyelids again. "Uh, I think the worst temp I got was 103—"

"Shit, Finn!" Rachel exclaimed. "Why didn't you text me?"

"I *did* text you."

"Not about Charlie being sick."

"You weren't responding to my texts or calls, so I figured we were bothering you, *Chief*." Finn gave her a bitter smile. He watched her nostrils flare ever so slightly and held on to the small victory of successfully tweaking her nerves. "It's fine, Rach. I know how to take care of a sick kid. I gave her a bath and some Tylenol. Threw some chicken soup at her. Like I said, her fever was gone by the time she hit the hay. There was no need to worry you."

"She's not right, Mommy." Lucy sobbed into Rachel's kneecaps. "There's something wrong with her."

"Lucy, I told you. Charlie just wasn't feeling well, honey. She's gonna be fine." Finn leaned forward and placed a warm hand on Lucy's back.

"Mommy, you've gotta fix her." Lucy looked up at Rachel, the whites of her eyes red from tears, her puffy face wet.

"I'll check in on her and make sure she's all right. There's nothing to worry about." Rachel ran her fingertips through Lucy's hair lightly. "We've gotta get you upstairs and into bed, missy. You can't sleep down here on the floor."

"NO!" Lucy screeched and grabbed hold of Finn's left calf for dear life, her legs still wrapped around Rachel's. "NO, PLEASE—please don't make me go upstairs! Please!"

"Lucy, honey, you're being a silly-billy." Rachel kept her voice light and airy, but Finn saw more irritation creeping into the lines on her face. "You're a big girl now, and big girls have to sleep in their own rooms."

"NOOOOO!" Lucy screamed so sharply Finn thought the whole town would hear. "Mommy, please! They'll get me. They'll take me away, too."

Finn glanced up at Rachel, trying to gauge how she would break on the matter. One day, she would lay down the law and force whoever was throwing the temper tantrum into their rightful place. The next, she could soften into putty and bend to the kids' pressure. He never knew which parenting technique Rachel decided to use from day to day; he got so tired of trying to fall in line with the Rachel of the day that he mostly delegated discipline and order to her when she was home.

"There's no one coming to get you. You've been watching too much television, kiddo. Don't you want to be a big girl for Mommy and Daddy?"

Lucy dug her nails into Rachel's and Finn's legs, shaking her head furiously.

"Well, you can't very well sleep on the floor down here." Rachel surveyed Finn's basement with an arched brow. "Would you come upstairs if you could sleep in Mommy and Daddy's bed? Daddy can sleep down here, and we'll snuggle up in the big bed upstairs."

Lucy hesitated, her sweaty little form shivering all over. She peeked over Finn's knee, and then looked at Rachel. "The whole night? You promise you won't move me once I've gone to sleep?"

"Lucy, what do you think is—?"

"The WHOLE night!" Lucy boomed at Rachel. "I'm not coming unless it's for the whole night."

"Nothing is going to get you upstairs, my lovely lady." Rachel lowered her voice and bent her forehead to touch Lucy's lightly. "But I won't leave you alone. Whatever has you spooked will have to get through me first, all right? And we both know that's not happening." She winked and tickled her fingers up the front of the girl's belly, which was framed between her parents' legs. Lucy instantly broke down into a fit of giggles and clutched at her tummy.

With that, Rachel took Lucy by the underarms and swooped her up onto her chest. Lucy wrapped her legs around Rachel's waist tightly and hugged herself against her mother's bosom.

"Oy, girl! You're getting so big! It's all those SpaghettiOs, isn't it?" Lucy continued to giggle as Rachel walked slowly toward the basement steps.

"Night, night, Daddy," Lucy sang out, opening and closing her fingers to wave good night.

"Night, baby. I'll see you in the morning." Finn mirrored the open-close hand wave.

A pang resembling remorse, regret, or rage lingered with Finn as his wife kicked the door shut with her boot, cutting him off from the rest of the family as she'd done since the night one-fifth of their life disappeared forever.

Fourteen

"Close the door, Mama," Lucy whispered from the pile of blankets and sheets she'd wrapped herself in.

"All right, all right."

Rachel threw one last glance over her shoulder toward Charlie's open bedroom door. She had checked on her a few minutes prior, Lucy hovering outside the door. Sure enough, Finn had been right: Charlie's fever was nonexistent now. If anything, she felt cold. So did the rest of the upstairs, for that matter.

With one nudge of her elbow, Rachel pushed her bedroom door shut. The room she and Finn had shared didn't look much different from when he'd been there with her, though she had taken down all the pictures of them that once graced those walls. His jumble of change, watches, and the couple of rings he owned were still in his father's old clay ashtray on his bedstand. Whatever pretentious book he had been reading before the night he'd destroyed their lives was still tucked under the rectangle alarm clock with huge glowing green numbers. Even his laundry still littered the floor from all the times he changed in there to keep up the show.

The more Rachel stared around at the room, the more she wanted to tear it all apart. Its one saving grace was the warm, glowing lights that wrapped around Rachel and Lucy now—

cozy, safe, comforting. For the first time in a year, her bedroom actually felt like a real home with Lucy inside.

"Tuck in, little girl. It's crazy late, or crazy early, depending on how you look at it. And you've got school in the morning."

Rachel fiddled with her belt and yanked down her stiff polyesters. Normally, she would shower off before even thinking about climbing in the bed. To do otherwise always made her skin crawl, but she wasn't crazy about the idea of her youngest staying up any later than she already had. She was positive Lucy would not fall asleep without her by her side.

"Mommy, can we keep the lights on? Just for tonight?" Lucy ducked three-quarters of her face under the green-and-white patchwork quilt.

"What's got you so worked up, kid? You're my brave little toaster." Rachel yanked a T-shirt out of the bottom dresser drawer. She'd already put it on before she realized it was one of Finn's old Nirvana tees. It would have to do since she was now devoid of fucks to give for the night.

Rachel climbed in the bed next to the pile of blankets that was her youngest child and tried to unmask her. "What happened tonight? Hmm? You can tell me, even if Daddy doesn't want you to." A spark of terror flickered in Lucy's crystal-blue eyes and Rachel felt her squirm under the blankets. "It'd be our little secret. I promise Daddy won't get in trouble."

"I don't believe you," Lucy whispered. "Daddy always gets in trouble."

"That's not true." Rachel wrinkled her brow and laid her head down on the pillow next to Lucy's face.

"It is," the girl insisted. "You think Daddy is bad."

"Whoa, kid." Rachel yawned. "I don't think your daddy is bad."

"Why don't you and Daddy sleep in the same room anymore?"

Rachel nearly choked on another yawn, though the question didn't entirely stun her. Lucy was always smarter than the average bear, and Charlie was likely to spew family secrets to her sister and anyone else who would listen at the slightest ruffle of her feathers.

"That's easy." Rachel recovered. "It's because I sleep like Aquaman with pneumonia."

Lucy burst into giggles so hard she drew the blankets up over her mouth and nose to cover her snorts. "That's not true, Mommy!"

"It *is* true! It's totally true. When's the last time you tried to sleep with me?" Rachel threw herself onto her back and comically stretched her arms and legs across the bed, mock-snoring as loud as her throat would allow, even as Lucy protested.

"Mommy!" Lucy cackled. "You don't sleep like that!"

"You don't know! Ask your Daddy! Poor fella." Rachel barely got the words out, even when they were in jest. She drew her arms and legs in on herself and snuggled up under the covers.

"Are you and Daddy gonna get a divorce?" Lucy asked quietly after Rachel had settled in.

"No," Rachel responded almost as soon as the words left the girl's lips. "You don't need to worry about it. Okay? I know things haven't been what they were—"

"—before Aidan went away?"

The words hit Rachel harder than a fist to the face, but she resisted recoiling. Aidan's name no longer conjured warmth. She wasn't even sure how Lucy or anyone else could speak it without feeling like they were chewing on glass. Lucy curled her body toward hers, their foreheads so close they nearly touched. At such close range, Rachel wouldn't have been surprised if Lucy could have read every one of her thoughts.

"Right." Rachel swallowed against a large lump in the back of her throat. "So . . . I mean . . . it makes sense, then, that *nothing* is the same as it was before, right? I mean . . . part of us is . . ."

"Gone," Lucy finished the sentence Rachel could not.

"Right. So, just like we've all been learning how to do things differently since Aidan went to heaven, your dad and I are still figuring out how . . . how to be . . ."

"Friends?"

"Yeah." Rachel forced a sleepy smile. "Yeah, we're learning how to be friends again."

"I hope you figure it out." Lucy reached out her warm, tiny hand and placed it on Rachel's arm. "You both need to be friends."

Rachel smirked and kissed Lucy's forehead. "Thanks, kiddo. We've gotta go to sleep now." She rolled over and snapped out her bedside light.

"Did you lock the door?"

"Of course I locked the door, silly." Rachel looked at her daughter, who was sitting upright in the bed once more.

"The bedroom door, too?"

"Lucy, I'm not locking the—"

"MOM! I won't sleep one second unless you lock the door!"

Rachel locked eyes with her six-year-old who possessed far more fortitude than she did in the moment. "Fine!" Rachel rolled out of bed.

"And I'm keeping my light on, too!" the girl barked.

All Rachel could muster was a shrug in response as she twisted the lock on the doorknob. A cold breeze nipped at her toes from underneath the door.

On the other side, Rachel heard the floorboards groan.

"What is it, Mommy?"

Rachel looked over her shoulder to see the blood had drained from Lucy's face, leaving her deathly white with fear.

"Nothing, baby." Rachel smiled. "The lock stuck for a second. That's all. Let's get some rest."

Fifteen

Finn awoke at precisely 7:11 a.m., mostly in confusion as the entire house seemed to be shaking with the bass of a Britney Spears song he had forgotten even existed. Someone was singing the song's lyrics at full volume, the floor creaking in time with its beat as they bounced around the kitchen. Groaning, he managed to push himself up from the couch on a mission to banish Ms. Spears from the home as quickly as possible.

Finn was the first member of the family to make his way into the kitchen. He stood barefoot on the freezing linoleum and reviewed the previous night, wondering for the first time in a long time if he had been too drunk to recall everything. As Finn stared at Charlie, however, he was confident *he* had not been the one drinking last night. Despite her now perfectly sleek brushed blonde hair, shimmering clean skin, and carefully coordinated cardigan and skirt, Finn distinctly remembered Charlie was the one who had been so wasted she had smeared a variety of bodily fluids on herself.

Charlie looked up from the mixing bowl in front of her and stopped singing. "Hi, Daddy!" she chirped.

All Finn could do was marvel. Once upon a time, he had been the comeback king himself, but he couldn't recall a time when he'd ever been quite *that* resilient.

The kitchen sparkled as if Charlie had been cleaning it half the night. Finn was sure the room hadn't been this clean the day the realtor showed them the place. Even as she zipped from counter to bar to sink, mixing bowl in hand and the griddle sizzling, it didn't appear as though she left any trace of debris in her wake.

"Well, aren't you going to sit down? I'm making breakfast!" she called over her shoulder.

"I can see that." Finn closed his mouth and swallowed several times to clear out the dryness. Stuffing his hands into his flannel sweatpants, Finn crept up to the breakfast bar quietly, throwing looks over his shoulder in case Rachel came racing down the stairs. "You feeling okay, Charlie?"

She finished flipping a pancake onto a plate from the griddle before turning to look at him. For a moment, the girl's stare was harsh and warning. Finn froze in his tracks, waiting for the head-spinning and projectile green vomit. But then Charlie's stern face broke into a warm smile, eyes dancing.

"Oh, I feel dandy, Daddy." Charlie set down a bottle of syrup and a plate with three stacked pancakes on the kitchen bar. "These are for you. The early bird gets the worm, as the old lads say."

Finn blinked hard as he slowly edged onto one of the barstools. The pancakes before him were perfectly round, perfectly golden, with perfectly even-spaced blueberries under the surface. He stared at them for what felt like forever, unsure as to how Charlie—a child whose last culinary attempt four years ago had resulted in nearly burning down the apartment building warming pre-packaged sugar cookies—could have slapped these babies together.

"What's wrong?" Charlie was still giving him a one-thousand-watt smile from the other side of the bar.

"Oh, um . . ." Finn cleared his throat and looked down at the pancakes once more. "Nothing's wrong. I, uh, I don't have a fork or—"

Finn nearly fell off his stool as Charlie brought a fork down next to his hand so hard the plate rattled.

"You think the music is loud enough?" Rachel yelled over the beat as she came into the kitchen from behind Finn.

"Mother!" Charlie threw her arms up in the air. "I've made breakfast! Take a look and see!" She wiggled a dance behind the bar before spinning around to flip another pancake over.

Finn looked over his shoulder at Rachel, and with one glance exchanged an entire befuddled conversation. He spied Lucy's frizzy bedhead hair peeking out from behind Rachel's legs, still too terrified to show her face in the bright light of day.

"Wow," Rachel began, nonplussed, "you've been busy."

"Uh-huh!" Charlie sang as she slid more steaming cakes onto a plate, then set it next to Finn's. "Take a seat!" She gestured toward the stool beside Finn. Rachel stood stuck to her spot with a suspicious look. "Oh, are you waiting for coffee?"

"Would you turn down the music? It's like waking up in a sorority house in 2002."

"Come on now, Mother. Don't be a drag. I *love* this song!" And Charlie began humming the words as she turned around to tend to the coffeepot.

"Volume down," Finn grumbled.

Rachel moved forward and around the bar, leaving behind Lucy, who refused to move any closer to her sister. The girl looked diminished and exposed in her mother's wake.

Finn motioned, beckoning her toward him with a soft smile.

"I've already made the coffee!" Charlie produced a cup from seemingly nowhere.

"Do you even know how to make coffee?"

"'Course I do!"

"Not how I like it, no way." Rachel arrived at the coffeepot and flipped open the top of the maker to check on the grounds.

"Your mother likes her coffee like she's a World War Two general who smoked four packs a day and drank bathtub gin throughout the blitz," Finn added while still waving Lucy to him. The little girl's eyes darted between him and Charlie's back. "It's more sludge than coffee."

"But I made you coffee already." Charlie yanked the pot away from the machine, just missing sloshing the hot contents onto Rachel's belly. Rachel stepped back with her hands up and reviewed the teenager as she poured light coffee into the cup. "See? Mother has to have her coffee!"

She turned on her heels, the cup jutting out toward Rachel, a gleeful expression on her face. Rachel failed to hide her annoyance at the uninvited perkiness she had been met with on such short notice. She slowly took the mug from her daughter's hand.

"Oh, come on, Mother! Turn that frown upside down!"

Charlie's hand shot out to Rachel's stomach with wiggling fingers, attempting to get a tickle in. Rachel reeled backward, sending coffee splattering across the kitchen floor. Her bare feet slid in a puddle of it on the linoleum, but she managed to stay upright.

"*Christ*, Charlie!" Rachel bellowed.

Charlie bent over with wild laughter. Finn fought to choke down cackles himself. Lucy, however, used the moment to find protection, and shot into his side like a linebacker. He gripped the bar's edge to steady himself before wrapping his free arm around Lucy. He could feel her shivering as Lucy buried her face into his T-shirt.

"It's okay, Luce," Finn murmured.

Rachel turned and stormed away, crashing the half-empty coffee mug down onto the breakfast bar.

The room suddenly fell silent. Charlie's laughter died as the pans on the stove ceased their sizzling. The refrigerator's constant low hum froze, as did the sound of water churning in the dishwasher. It took Finn another moment to realize that even the music that had been the soundtrack to their morning had abruptly silenced itself as well. It was as if the entire house was holding its breath to see what happened next, and though Finn didn't understand why, his heart skipped two beats as the unnatural quiet pressed in.

Charlie was on the other side of the bar, peering down at her sister with an unreadable face.

"Hey there, Lucy," Charlie began again in that chipper tone. "I made you pancakes, too, dear." She set the final plate at the end of the breakfast bar. It had two perfect blueberry pancakes on it with banana slices in the shape of a smiley face. "It's just for youuuuu."

Lucy closed her eyelids tightly. Her hold on Finn intensified threefold, and Finn couldn't blame her. Whatever had gotten into Charlie this morning now made Finn feel like slinking away into the basement and locking the door. He could hardly believe it, but he much preferred his angst-ridden teen to this bizarrely bubbly version.

Suddenly, Rachel thundered back into the room. She held a hefty Maglite in her right hand, thumb on the switch like it was a trigger. It wasn't until she rounded the corner of the breakfast bar that it became clear she was headed straight for Charlie.

"Well, hell's bells, Moth—" Charlie sputtered before Rachel had the girl pinned against the counter with her body, bending her backward with one arm across Charlie's chest while she shined the flashlight directly into Charlie's eyeballs with her free hand.

"Rachel! What the hell?" Finn tried to get to his feet, but Lucy hung onto him and began shrieking.

Charlie's eyelids had reflexively shut tight, which appeared to solidify Rachel's need to inspect her pupils closer. Their daughter was squirming against her hard, but Rachel wedged Charlie against the counter tighter.

"Charlie!" Rachel barked. "Open your eyes! Open your eyes right now!"

"What the hell are you doing?!" Finn yelled over Lucy's continued screams. He tried to stand up again, this time making it to his feet, though Lucy still anchored him to the spot. "Jesus Christ, Rach! Stop it!"

Whispers in the Dark

"OPEN YOUR EYES!"

"MAKE HER OPEN HER EYES, MOMMY!" Lucy shrieked, and Finn knew he had lost all control over the situation.

Charlie was bucking like a wild animal. Her legs flew up as she tried to back upward onto the counter. Her neat black tennis shoes knocked against the cabinets and sent an iron knob flying across the kitchen. Failing to get any traction, the teenager brought her one free hand against her mother's shoulder and pushed hard.

"OPEN YOUR EYES, CHARLIE!" Rachel boomed. "If you open your eyes right now, we can end this and go on with our day."

"What the hell is wrong with you?" Finn called out again miserably. "You're treating our kid like she's some perp you ran down."

"Get off me! GET OFF ME!"

Rachel ignored Finn, too focused on Charlie. "You wouldn't be fighting me if there wasn't something to hide!"

Finn rubbed at his face with his palms. Lucy collapsed against his right shin, holding on for dear life as she continued to scream: "*MAKE HER OPEN HER EYES!*"

Rachel managed to separate the lids of Charlie's left eye for a moment and caught nothing but the white of her eyeball rolling into the back of her head. That wasn't good enough. What Rachel was looking for, as Finn knew well, was the size and reactivity of Charlie's pupils.

Charlie's lids slipped out from under Rachel's forefinger and thumb and snapped shut again. By the looks of it, she was getting stronger instead of weaker as she fought against her mother. All Charlie needed to do was slip a limb loose from under Rachel's hold, and she could launch her mother into the refrigerator. Finn felt sick to his stomach as he watched Rachel throw her weight into Charlie against the counter and seize her lids once again.

Then Rachel fumbled. Charlie's eyelids slipped from her fingers again and shut tight as Rachel seemed to recoil, her face growing pale. She shook her head and took another deep breath. A foul, wet cold crept along Finn's spine. His wife didn't get startled. In all their years together, Finn couldn't even remember seeing her remotely surprised. Sometimes, he suspected she knew his next move before even he did. Watching Rachel's expression turn wild struck a fearful chord deep within Finn.

Just what had their Charlie gotten herself into?

In the next moment, however, Rachel recovered. Charlie's enraged screams and Lucy's incoherent wailing merely appeared to be background noise to Rachel, who continued trying to inspect Charlie's pupil reactivity as she pried their daughter's eyelids open again. Her own eyes widened. The next moment, she abruptly shut the light off and pulled away from the counter, Charlie dropping down to the floor. Any concern Finn had felt before instantly faded as their daughter landed with a thud.

"Did you see it?" Lucy was beyond consolation, clawing Finn's leg harder and wailing. "Mommy, did you see it?"

Rachel had already turned her back on Charlie. She stared at the Maglite as she walked away, avoiding Finn's glare.

"Your mother didn't find anything," he began loudly, "because there's nothing to find. Mommy's just a little overzealous about her line of work, Lucy-Loo. It's a cop thing these days, I guess." Finn watched Rachel seize the half-empty, mostly cold cup of coffee from the breakfast bar and beeline toward the stairs. His gaze then returned to Charlie, who remained on the floor.

The expression on her face was unearthly, filled with raw fury and a predatory gleam. Her eyes, while just as sober as they had been moments before, were narrowed and sunken further back in her head as if she had withered a little when Rachel released her. Charlie's mouth was twisted into a sneer, and though she didn't bare her teeth, Finn felt certain there were jagged fangs behind his daughter's lips. Worse still, Charlie's hungry gaze wasn't following the direction her mother had taken; it was fixed directly on the little girl who quaked against him.

He instinctively clutched Lucy to his leg.

A sudden loud rap at the front door made both Finn and Lucy jump. Finn scolded himself for being such a ninny ("Finny the Ninny" had been his brother's favorite nickname for him until the age of seventeen or so), and began moving for the door. Lucy gripped him harder and nearly made him fall into the refrigerator.

"Lucy! Come on now, kiddo."

Before he could break away, Charlie had flown past him, through the living room, and into the hall beyond. Finn moved several paces, Lucy still attached to his right leg, to glimpse the door. Charlie had opened it already and was staring out silently. Gemma and Sarah stood shoulder to shoulder in sweaters and skirts that, while they did not match, looked as though they had spent considerable time coordinating. The girls held hands and looked at Charlie with wide eyes and soft smiles. There was something vacant in their faces. Finn couldn't put his finger on it exactly, but something important simply wasn't there anymore.

Charlie bent her knees and picked up her backpack from the floor next to the door. Slinging it over her shoulder, she called to Finn without looking back.

"I'm going to school now. Father, I hope you have a very pleasant day. You as well, Lucy. I'll see you tonight." Charlie stepped out of the doorway, taking hold of Sarah's extended hand. Then, she closed the door gently behind her.

* * *

Their shoes didn't match. Black sneakers with sparkly laces, tan Mary Janes in the middle, and robin's-egg blue heels on the other end. The Charlie Thing threw a displeased glare across the front of Sarah to chide Gemma. The Gemma Thing looked right back at her and arched a brow as if daring Charlie to argue about the footwear.

Down the drive, the wild one stood swaying on her feet. The Kendall Thing still didn't look right, and it was evident even to the trio who marched into the street. She blinked hard in the sunshine and shivered every few moments. If the Kendall Thing was going to be in that kind of a state, they might as well have left her in the woods. Otherwise, she might scare people, and it was not yet time for them to be afraid.

Whispers in the Dark

The girl could have made it easier on herself, though they now understood Kendall had never been one to do things properly. If she'd only listened to the song, if she'd only relaxed into their embrace as the other girls had done, this thing standing before them would have been a beautiful addition. As it happened, Kendall had tried to fight back, and oh, dear—that had never gone well for anyone ever. Silly girl. Silly, useless, broken Kendall.

The Charlie Thing took Kendall's twitching hand in hers and squeezed hard. The Kendall Thing stared at the pavement resolutely. The Charlie Thing continued squeezing until Kendall's fingertips were white, then continued until the Charlie Thing finally felt a series of crackles and pops in Kendall's knuckles, the hand collapsing in on itself like an accordion. The Kendall Thing blinked several times and looked up at the Charlie Thing with understanding. She nodded her head once to the trio, and they silently returned the nod in unison. The Charlie Thing let go of Kendall's useless hand, and the broken creature followed a straight line to the woods beyond the Kennans' backyard, the right appendage dangling this way and that at her side.

The Charlie Thing took in a big, clean breath of mountain air and began swinging the arm locked with Sarah's. All three resumed their delighted grins and set off walking down the road toward Lee-Jackson Middle School. The thoughts burrowed in their minds were very serious indeed, but there was no reason to let a thing like that ruin a perfectly good, blessedly sunny day on the gods' green earth.

Sixteen

"You wanna tell me what that was about?" Finn's pulse pounded in his ears, and he felt his cheeks burning hot as he stood in the door of Rachel's bedroom. She didn't even pause to offer him a glare as she continued to dress for the day. Somehow that made Finn angrier.

"Daddy?" Lucy called from the bathroom where Finn had finally convinced her to brush her teeth alone.

"I'm right here, sweetie," Finn replied in a soothing tone. "Everything's okay, baby. Mommy and I are just chatting."

"Don't go anywhere," Lucy squeaked.

"We're right here." Finn swallowed an irritated sigh. Lucy had every right to be unnerved even if Finn didn't have time for it. "Rach." He redirected his frustration toward the woman he barely knew anymore as she buttoned her white blouse. "I asked you why you assaulted our daughter down there."

Rachel sputtered a laugh and shook her head, still unwilling to look at him. "Fuck off, Finn. Something is going on with Charlie. I know you see it; you're just not willing to do anything about it."

"Nothing is wrong with Charlie," Finn spat out and narrowed his eyes. "Our kid isn't one of your meth fiends."

"Yeah?" Rachel sighed as she tightened her belt. "That's what every parent thinks."

"Charlie isn't a druggie, Rachel. She was a little wound up and playing around—"

Rachel paused and met Finn's eyes. "You know what the difference between us is?"

Finn's throat tightened and his fingers twitched as he looked at her. "Uh, I'm not drunk on power like you and your brothers in blue? I'm not looking for excuses to beat the fuckin' shit out of innocent people? I don't know, Rach. I can think of many, many, *many* differences between—"

"Cute. Nice deflection, but no." Rachel pointed at him. "*You* prefer to bury your head in the sand when a problem arises. You hope that it'll disappear or fix itself if you ignore it long enough. Give it enough time and it'll just blow over. But *I—*"

"You smash everything to fuckin' bits to eradicate a problem, Rachel." Finn felt himself shaking, his jaw clenching while his molars ground together. He slowed his breathing, remembering the tools the therapist had taught him to quell the rage whenever it broke the surface.

"I tackle problems and fix them before they become bigger problems . . . before they destroy lives," Rachel spoke pointedly as she slid her Glock into its holster. "Maybe Charlie's not on meth, but she's not okay. The fact that she wouldn't let me even take a look at her only underscores that further."

"Take a look at her?" Finn raised his voice despite himself. "Rach, you threw her against the counter like she pulled a gun on you. You can't do that to our kids!"

"Mommy?" Lucy's voice sounded frightened now. "Daddy?"

Finn threw a look over his shoulder and saw Lucy standing at the edge of the bathroom, toothbrush in one hand.

"Lucy." Finn's fingers gripped the doorframe hard until his nails dug into the wood. "Please finish brushing your teeth. I have to get you to school."

"I'll take her," Rachel muttered as she swiped her wallet off the bed and stuffed it into her deep pockets.

"Don't worry about it. I don't want Lucy to end up with your boot on her neck."

"Watch it, mister." Rachel chuckled vitriolically and wiggled her finger at him. "If anyone should be worried about how to properly transport the kids . . . well, you get my point."

As Rachel ducked under one of his arms to slide out of the room, he caught the scent of her earthy conditioner. Memories socked him in the gut, and for the briefest moment, Finn wished his hands were buried in her hair as they made love in their tiny Richmond apartment again. The next second, Finn wanted to snatch her by the hair and throw her against the wall. Instead, Finn stood anchored to the spot as his wife slipped away.

"You ready to go, jellybean?"

Rachel was squatted down in front of Lucy. She touched her finger to the tip of their daughter's nose. Lucy's face transformed from scared to delighted in an instant as she giggled and booped Rachel's nose back. He wanted to scream at Lucy to stop smiling at Rachel like that. Tell her that Rachel wasn't nearly as funny or cute or warm as Lucy continued to think she was. That Rachel was a nightmare that couldn't be shaken off.

"Finish up, and we'll get on the road, okay? Your teacher will have my butt if I don't get you there in the next few minutes."

Rachel rose to her feet and kissed the top of Lucy's head as their daughter pranced back into the bathroom to finish up. A shadow passed over her face—sorrow overtaken by fury—as Rachel's eyes drifted to the door between her bedroom and Lucy's. The apples of her cheeks turned bright red, and her lips pressed into a straight line.

"What now?" Finn finally managed to break away from the frame.

"The door . . . the window. They're open. Who did that?"

Finn's chest tightened again as he saw Aidan's bedroom door yawning wide, swaying a little as a chilly breeze blew in through the window. From where Finn stood, he caught a glimpse of Aidan's long-abandoned bed. The covers were turned down like someone had climbed out of that bed just this morning and forgot to make it up again. Rachel, however, couldn't have seen that from her angle, and Finn decided to keep it to himself.

"I don't know, Rach." Finn sighed. "Maybe you can waterboard us at dinner to ferret out a confession."

Rachel glared and opened her mouth to respond, but at that precise moment, Lucy bounded out of the bathroom with a smile.

"I'm ready, s'ghetti!"

"All right!" Rachel gave Lucy a high five, any anger present on her face microseconds before evaporating in a flash. "Let's blow this joint."

"Bye, Daddy!" Lucy waved at Finn as Rachel avoided his stare.

Together, the pair jogged down the stairs, all giggles and sunshine. Finn, on the other hand, felt the darkness pressing in around him harder than it had in months.

"Love you," Finn remembered to yell down right before the front door shut.

A twinge of self-loathing flickered in his chest because he'd meant the statement for both of them . . . he really, truly had. It was dumb; it was foolish—maybe even pathetic. He hated her more than anyone he'd ever known. At the same time, he desperately longed for their life together to return to the messy, wonderful way it had once been. Finn would have given anything for his wife to once more smile at him without pretense; to lower the barbed-wire fences that shielded her emotions from everyone but him; to grip his hand as they held Aidan between them on the Sunday mornings he'd come to cuddle in bed.

Finn buried his face in his palms and gave himself permission to sob just once; one small cry out of self-pity was all he needed to release the pressure. It'd do for now, anyway.

Seventeen

"Where the hell have you been?" Jeremy yelled the moment Rachel stepped over the station door's threshold. "I've been trying to reach you for half an hour!"

Rachel fought to shake off the daze the morning had cast upon her. Finn's words had stung, but only because they were true. She had lost control, not just of her actions but even of her sanity, if only for a moment. When Rachel had pried Charlie's eyes open, all that shone back at her was a sea of inky black darker than the waters that had consumed Aidan. And reflected in the glimmering onyx that had seemingly swallowed Charlie's irises was a version of herself she never wanted to see again.

It was as if reality had snapped off like a light switch, the timeline of Rachel's life collapsing in on itself as every memory rushed into her mind all at once: sneaking out her bedroom window at fifteen to go get trashed with strangers; hanging up the phone when her mother tried to convince her to come home the last Christmas the woman drew breath; texting her now ex-girlfriend that she was swamped at work even as Finn lay naked beside her; tearing apart Michelle's Bible right in front of her the day that goddamn liar told her she was too pure to continue seeing Rachel.

The last thing she recalled before letting go of Charlie's slippery eyelids had been watching Finn down a tumbler of whiskey before grabbing his keys and heading off to pick up Aidan and Lucy. Even though Rachel hadn't been there that night, the scene had appeared as clear as day as the nasty little thought penetrated through the swirling imagery: *You knew, and you never stopped him. You killed your son, too.* And the hell of it was, Rachel hadn't even tried to push back on the indictment. Indeed, somewhere in the hidden corners of her mind, she agreed.

Finn had always thrown back drink after drink. He'd driven drunk many times. Not once had she confronted him about it. Most of the time, Rachel hadn't even thought about it despite seeing hundreds of deaths thanks to a few too many beverages. Finn had been different. He was the good guy—the funny, clever asshole who had somehow charmed his way into her life permanently. She trusted him even as empty bottles always cluttered their kitchen. How a cop, a mother, a goddamn force of nature could ever be so fucking dumb, Rachel would never understand. More than anything else, she would never be able to forgive herself just as much as Finn would forever be damned now. They were irredeemable, and whatever momentary fritz Rachel's brain had undergone as she looked into Charlie's eyes highlighted that with gut-wrenching clarity.

"RACHEL!" Jeremy shouted at her once more as he snapped his fingers.

She instantly returned to the present, eyeing Jeremy wordlessly. Much to her discomfort, the officer looked distressed.

Something had obviously concerned him, and that could only mean trouble.

"Chief," Rachel murmured.

"What?" Jeremy yelled, red-faced. The cell phone he held was trembling, though Rachel couldn't read if it was from sincere outrage or something worse. She moved toward her broom-closet office, juggling keys, sunglasses, and a coffee mug.

"It's *Chief* Kennan," Rachel grumbled, stuffing her growing anxiety down into the depths.

"Oh, come off that bullshit, Rach! I'll call you any damn thing you want, sweetheart, so long as we sort this shit out right now."

"I'll kick your balls right back up into your belly if you call me *sweetheart* again."

"Abby Grayson's missing," Jeremy blurted. "Ritchie and Florence's little girl. She's missing."

Rachel froze in the doorway to her office and turned halfway around to look at Jeremy. "For how long?"

"They aren't sure." Jeremy's voice softened. "Florence says she got up at seven or so to wake her up, and Abby was gone. I asked Florence if she thought Abby might have run off—"

"Four-year-olds don't just run off." Rachel threw her sunglasses and keys across her desk. Both went tumbling off the other side and into her desk chair. She marched toward the lockbox hanging on the far side wall that held the keys to the cruisers. "Is Marcus or Lou over there?" A quick glance into the lockbox answered her question before Jeremy could.

"No."

"And why the hell not?" Rachel snatched the keys for the Dodge as a cold anxiety swept over her. Time was ticking quickly, and something about this case was already gnawing at Rachel. First, a murder. Now, a missing child. Three years into her tenure as Dahlmouth's police chief, Rachel had yet to encounter either here . . . until now.

"Florence called at change of shift. We were waiting for you." Jeremy placed his hands on his hips.

"I don't give a damn whose shift it is." Rachel turned to him with a furrowed brow. "A kid goes missing, and one of you gets on it that fucking second. What's wrong with you?"

Jeremy grabbed his jacket from the back of his chair, ready to follow along with her. "No one is going to handle Florence as well as you. You know that," he finished in a low tone.

Rachel clenched her jaw and narrowed her eyes. "That's the excuse?" she seethed. "None of you could be bothered to go over there because I'm the woman of the gang? I'm the only one that can handle—"

"—a grieving mother?" Jeremy's brows knitted together as his eyes grew wide.

"Fuck you." Rachel wanted to shriek the words at him, but the admonishment felt dry on her tongue.

She had been around Dahlmouth long enough to recall when Abby Grayson was just a bundle of baby blankets cradled in Florence's arms at the town hall. The one-thousand-watt smile on Florence's face as she showed off her newborn to anyone who passed by now struck a nerve Rachel hadn't seen coming. Rachel didn't have to talk to Florence to know the frantic desperation and terror the woman was feeling as she wondered where her child had gone.

From the moment Rachel had gazed down into the churning waters of the James River the night Aidan was stolen from this world, Rachel hadn't stopped feeling that god-awful panic.

She wasn't going to say it, but she knew Jeremy was right. No one else would get the kind of information out of Florence they needed, and they certainly wouldn't serve as a voice of reason in the Graysons' darkest hour.

"C'mon, then," she muttered.

* * *

"Everything, everything was normal, you know? It was just a normal night. I put her to bed at eight like usual, I think. Right, Ritchie?" Florence Grayson looked over at her husband with eyes as red as the frizzy curls that hung around her pale, squishy face.

She sat on the family's couch, her fingernails digging into its fabric. Ritchie Grayson sat at the table several feet away in the kitchen. His hands were neatly pressed together, each finger meeting its partner on the opposite hand. The man's icy blue eyes stared down into the table, acting as though he couldn't hear a word anyone had spoken since Rachel and Jeremy had arrived. Ritchie made no response to Florence's question, and a cry shuddered through the woman's chest.

"He won't talk," Florence squeaked. "He's upset."

"I understand." Rachel nodded and looked over at Ritchie from the edge of the torn-up pleather recliner. Jeremy hovered by the door, alternating between fidgeting with his notepad and his hat. He kept eyeing up Ritchie from the side, suspicion plain on his stubbly face. Florence threw nervous glances at Jeremy and tucked her arms closer into her sides, her knees squeezing together every so often. Suddenly, Rachel wished she could throw Jeremy outside like a bad dog.

"It's okay. He doesn't have to talk right now." Rachel cleared her throat. "Right now, I'm talking to you, and *you* are going to help me find your little girl. We're going to do that together, okay? So, I need you to focus on what happened last night." Rachel scooted on the recliner seat to edge nearer Florence despite the long coffee table between them. "What time did you head off to bed?"

"I don't know." A whimper caught in Florence's throat, and she covered her eyes with her hands.

"It doesn't have to be precise."

"I guess about . . . maybe eleven. I watched an episode of that *Housewives* show, you know the one." Florence waved her hands in the air toward Rachel. "I *never* left the house, Chief. I would've known if something had happened before I went to bed."

"And what time did he come to bed?" Jeremy nodded at Ritchie. If looks could kill, Rachel's would have him spiked against the wall harder than their dead hiker.

"He was in bed before me. He did a double shift at the mill. He'd been awake twenty-six hours or somethin' between the drivin' and all. I think Ritchie was in bed not long after Abby."

"So, everyone was in bed before midnight." Rachel pressed her lips together. "Were the windows and doors locked?"

"Locked up good and tight, Chief. I heard there was some nonsense going on yesterday with them Wise boys again." Florence suddenly let out a tiny gasp and brought her fingers to her lips. "You think one of them did this?"

"Are you *sure* everything was locked up?" Jeremy cleared his throat. "We haven't found any broken glass or signs of forced entry."

"Oh God." Florence clutched at her chest and started to wail. "You really think one of them took her!"

"No, no, no." Rachel reached out a hand and placed it lightly on Florence's knee. She didn't need anyone else connecting the Wises, the dead hiker, and Abby's disappearance, no matter how suspicious the combo seemed. That kind of talk would create a firestorm of panic that would sweep across Dahlmouth and rip any vestige of control from Rachel. "We don't know what happened yet. That's why we're talking now. We're going to figure—"

"Oh God, if something happened to her"—huge tears slid down Florence's freckled cheeks—"I don't think I can survive it. I might as well lay down and die. I'm not like you, Chief. I can't take losin' my baby." The distraught mother grabbed hold of Rachel's hand atop her knee and squeezed.

Rachel fought the urge to yank her hand away from the woman. "Florence, we're going to find Abby. Let's focus on that."

"Ain't no Wise kid that snatched her," Ritchie suddenly announced from his trance with a strained voice. "She was following somethin'." His eyes refused to part ways with the tabletop even as he spoke to them. "And Chief . . . respectfully, take your goddamn hand off my wife's knee. I ain't got a problem with you doin' what you want on your own time, but when you're in my house, I'll thank you to leave your lifestyle at the door."

Rachel, Jeremy, and Florence sat stunned for a moment as they stared at the man. Biting down hard on the inside of her cheek, she slid her hand out of Florence's unrelenting grasp. Jeremy's nostrils flared and Rachel saw fire spark in his eyes. When he finally looked to her, Rachel shook her head once. She much preferred Ritchie's honesty over the rest of Dahlmouth's whispers regarding their wayward homosexual chief anyway.

"How do you know Abby was going after something?" Jeremy growled at Ritchie before taking a few steps toward the kitchen.

"That can't be true." Florence shook her head so hard Rachel thought her brain must have been taking a beating. "Abby's terrified of the dark. She wouldn't run out there on her own."

Rachel rose to her feet and spread her stance wide enough to block Jeremy from passing her. "You saw Abby leave the house?" she asked Ritchie.

"I din't see her leave the house ... no," Ritchie mumbled to Rachel. His eyes were wider, filling with tears but still anchored to the same spot on the table. "I woke up 'round three or four. I been gettin' up so damn early for these shifts at the mill, can't even sleep normal no more. So I's woke up when it was still dark out.

"When I roll over, I sees Abby up outta her bed 'cross the hall. She's lookin' out her window at somethin' real hard. I thought it musta been a deer or somethin'." Ritchie took a deep breath and shivered as if shaking off sorrow.

"I's just fallin' asleep again when I heard her little ... little feet tappin' on the floor. I looked up and saws her walkin' down the hallway real fast. She din't look at me. I figured she's gettin' water or somethin'... maybe sleepwalking again. Then I musta drifted back off. I din't come to until I heard Florence hollerin'."

"Did you hear the door open at all?" Rachel stepped toward Ritchie's spot slowly.

"No."

"Well, if there wasn't a struggle and the two of you were sleepin', you probably wouldn't have heard the door anyways. It coulda been someone Abby knew," Jeremy started out confidently. "Someone she'd feel comfortable opening the door to without making a fuss."

"Why don't we finish talking about what we know about the last time we saw Abby before we start theorizing? What do you think about that, Deputy Whitman?" Rachel muttered over her shoulder before turning back to Ritchie. "You said you thought she left willingly... that no one coerced her?"

"I don't think; I *know* she did." Ritchie sniffed and wiped his nose with the back of his hand.

"Why's that?" Rachel's voice grew softer.

"I din't think about it then. I shoulda." He shrugged. "I can't explain it proper now."

"Try for me."

"It was her face." Ritchie's voice cracked. "She looked... she looked like she'd somewhere to be. Abby in't brave or nothin'. She don't go lookin' for trouble. Her face, though... it was like she weren't seein' nothin' around her. She was in some kind of a trance."

The room was once more silent in the aftermath of Ritchie's words. Even Florence had quieted her cries.

Rachel inhaled deeply. "Does Abby sleepwalk a lot?"

"Only once before," Florence choked out.

"This weren't sleepwalkin'," Ritchie's voice fell to a low grumble, forcing anger to cover his fear. "I know that now. Somethin' called to her, an' she followed."

"If you had to guess, Ritchie, who do you think was calling her?" Rachel clicked the top of her pen in and out in quick succession at her side.

Ritchie blinked several times, severing his gaze from the table to look out the window instead. He brought his arm up to wipe at his nose and gave a humorless chuckle.

"I don't know. I sound dumb, don't I? Just another stupid hillbilly, as your man'd say." He shot an acidic stare toward Rachel from the corner of his eye. "Never mind, Chief. Weren't nothin' out there but a deer."

Eighteen

Rachel checked her phone every five minutes or so as she stomped through the underbrush, though she knew there wasn't any reception in this section of the woods. She needed Michelle to cough up the toxicology report on her faceless man. Mutilated strangers didn't just pop up in Dahlmouth. People didn't randomly go missing here either. The odds of both coincidentally happening in less than twenty-four hours were too great for Rachel to accept as plausible no matter how much Jeremy insisted little Abby simply walked off in her sleep. Rachel's gut screamed that whatever secrets their dead hiker held might unlock what had happened to Abby Grayson as well, and Rachel's instincts were rarely wrong.

Rachel had distributed walkies across the small band of searchers, which included her own officers, two elders from the church, and Florence. Ritchie decided to spend his day at the Grayson abode rather than trudge through the woods searching for Abby. The official reason for this decision was that someone needed to be there if Abby managed to wander home again. As Rachel headed out from the Grayson house, however, Ritchie had plopped himself down on the wooden porch steps, a bottle of Kentucky Gentleman in his hand, muttering.

"You ain't gonna find her, Chief. She ain't comin' back." He tipped the bottle up as he took in gulps. "An' you know it, too."

Rachel hadn't answered him because, in fact, some piece of her also believed they would never find Abby in time. Then Rachel reminded herself she would naturally be compromised when it came to cases like this—that her mind was still rattled from Aidan. Not everyone died; not every lost child disappeared into what seemed like nothingness. There were happy stories out there, too—ones where children were safely reunited with their loving parents, and they went on with their lives stronger than they had been before. Rachel had yet to witness any of those happy miracles, however, and her own loss made it difficult to hope against overwhelming odds.

Such irrational hope was often poisonous; it ensnared a person, dug its claws deep into the head and heart, and made them a slave to the past. Rachel would never entirely accept her son was gone, even though she knew Aidan couldn't have survived the crash. That was why she spent fourteen sleepless days scouring the crash site, river, and surrounding area as Jeremy trailed behind her. Why every couple of weeks, Rachel spent her entire shift walking along the banks still. She knew his body had been washed away and hidden by the James River like dozens of others before him. Yet, she still couldn't erase the foolish hope that Aidan would walk back in through the front door, sweaty and smelling of grass, tracking red mud all over the floor as always.

As she walked, Rachel tried to keep her mind from Route 6 at mile-marker ten; from the freshly repaired guardrail that had given way when Finn swerved straight into it and off the side of the small bridge; from the seat her son had slipped out of during the tumble into the churning river below; from the cross that marked the spot where the best part of her had died. It wasn't fair to say that, she knew. After all, Lucy had survived the crash by some miracle. Yet, that wasn't enough to keep a black hole from opening up inside Rachel. Lucy's smile, her giggle, her warm little hand inside Rachel's hand—all of it felt false now.

And with Charlie, things were so much worse. When she embraced Charlie, her eldest's muscles tightened like she was allergic to Rachel's touch. The coldness Aidan left behind only grew more frigid when Rachel tried (and inevitably failed) to bond with her teenager once more. All that remained between Rachel and Charlie was anger—Charlie's coming from the way Rachel handled Aidan's death; Rachel's coming from the way Charlie had been her entire young life. Directing too much effort into winning over or soothing Charlie was a fool's errand, and it always had been for Rachel. Charlie was undeniably her father's daughter.

There was a soft crackle on the walkie in Rachel's hand. She rubbed away the stinging in her eyes and lifted the radio up, ready to reply. It fell silent, and in that same moment, Rachel realized the rest of the woods had followed suit. Just as when she had found her faceless hiker, the quiet that had descended was unsettling. No breeze. No cracking. No scampering. Nothing but silence and Rachel.

Except that wasn't quite right. Rachel knew there had been more where her dead man rested tacked to a tree. Her ears perked; her skin prickled waiting for the strange and impossible sound of children in the depths of the forest, reminding Rachel how close she was to losing her mind entirely.

When the radio crackled with static again, Rachel let out a sigh of relief. She moved to the side, hoping to hit the antenna's sweet spot. She thought she could make out Jeremy's voice for a moment through the radio noise, but when she tried to buzz in for a response, the static only grew louder.

"Piece of shit," Rachel grumbled under her breath.

She had inherited the whole mess of these walkie radios from the prior chief. They must have been fifteen years old. Rachel turned it upside down and popped out the battery, blowing out dust from the inside. The moment she slid the cover back over the top of the battery, an unearthly howl erupted from the speaker, cranked to a volume Rachel didn't think the radios were capable of. Without thinking, she dropped the radio and covered her ears. Through it all, she could hear a mass of voices screaming a singular word through the static's roar:

MOMMY!

Nineteen

"She says she doesn't feel well," Mrs. Carrie Stockton, Dahlmouth Elementary's part-time nurse, explained through a thick southern drawl. She sighed into the handset. Parents usually didn't like to hear their children needed to be picked up, and she understood that. Heck, her Tammy and Peter faked being sick half of elementary school, too. Nevertheless, if a kid wasn't acting right—really, truly not acting right—it was her duty to notify the parents. This time she didn't doubt that decision at all.

Poor Lucy Kennan. The little thing was more resilient than Carrie ever knew a child could be. That said, it didn't go unnoticed the girl was a bit on the soft side. For the first few months after the crash, she had drawn countless pictures of the wreckage: her revolting father, herself, her older brother, that *thing*. Angel, was what the girl called it. The drawings had upset the other children in class right along with the kindergarten teacher. Lucy hid Aidan in her pictures—in trees, under bushes, inside the sinking car, under the water, in a closet, under a bed.

She told her teacher Aidan was hiding from the angel so he wouldn't be stolen again. When the principal asked Lucy why the angel had no eyes, the girl explained there absolutely were eyes; the angel's eyes were just nothing but massive black balls.

The principal had called Pastor Paul to the school for a chat with the girl, but the Kennans insisted Lucy would go to some fancy child psychiatrist in Roanoke instead.

Carrie couldn't have disagreed with their sodomite chief and her weasel more, but something about seeing the doctor must've worked. Those portraits stopped over the summer. When first grade began, Lucy seemed to have left the crash, her brother, and that demonic fiction with black eyes behind. But she was still an unusual child. Lucy preferred to play on her own, creating a whole gang of imaginary friends rather than engaging with the other children. She often giggled and waved to the trees that bordered the school, but immediately stopped the moment a teacher asked her about it. The girl hummed nursery songs no one had ever heard; shared make-believe stories that weren't quite right; posed questions no child should even think to ask. It wasn't unusual for teachers to quietly and uneasily exchange tales of Lucy's odd behavior. That was to be expected, though, with a pair of parents so boldly depraved. Everybody knew that was the real problem with the Kennan kids.

Poor Lucy.

Today was worse than Carrie had seen before, however, and that was counting just after the crash. The pale little girl had dark bags under her eyes. Miss Crowley sent Lucy to Carrie's office because she couldn't get the girl to stop bursting out into tears every few minutes. It distracted the other children, Miss Crowley said, and worse yet, Lucy kept jumping up from her seat to look outside, which prompted her classmates to do the same.

When Carrie finally got the girl to sit down on the cot in her office, she had taken Lucy's temperature and run through the list of common questions. The only real symptoms Carrie could see, however, was that no matter how many blankets she tucked around the girl, she was shaky and clammy. Carrie hated to call Lucy's father—hated hearing his smarmy voice on the other end of the line, knowing full well she could be the subject of his next blog entry—but there wasn't much anyone else could do for the poor thing unless she was going to be kept in Carrie's office all day. Carrie would have considered it except she got off early today for her hair appointment.

"What's going on?" Concern was plain in Mr. Kennan's voice when Carrie got out her first few words. She supposed even the damned could feel some kind of love for their own children.

Carrie looked over at Lucy, who stared outside the window again with bug eyes. Through the blankets piled up around Lucy's shoulders, Carrie could hear Lucy's breathing growing faster all the time.

"Well, I'm not quite sure, to be honest with you, Mr. Kennan. She's not running a fever, but I think it could be the start of a virus. Something's going around." That was what Carrie always said to parents if they gave her the business.

"Is that Daddy?" Lucy asked weakly from the cot.

"Sure is, sweetheart." Carrie gave the girl a reassuring smile from the corner of the room. "He's gonna come get you real soon."

"NO!" Lucy gasped. "Tell Daddy he's gotta go! He's gotta get out of here! There's no time. They're coming!"

"What did she say?" Carrie heard the anger Mr. Kennan kept tucked away in his basement wave hello, and she bristled. "Can you just put her on the line?"

"Mr. Kennan." Carrie spoke slowly and softly to avoid upsetting Lucy any further. "I think it's best if you head on over."

"No, no, no, no!" Lucy wiggled out of the blankets and tried to stand, though her eyes were still glued to something outside the window. "Daddy has to run. He still has time!"

Carrie ignored her. "We'll see you real soon, then."

"You're not listening to me!" Lucy's voice grew louder. Suddenly, she was running across the room, hands clawing for the phone at Carrie's ear. "Daddy! Daddy, you gotta run! Go, Daddy!"

"Mrs. Stockton, can you please put Lucy on the phone?" Mr. Kennan shouted into the phone, and Carrie held it away from her ear. "I'm on my way to the school; just put her on!"

"It's not too late for you, Daddy! You can still get out! Daddy, run!"

"Mr. Kennan." Carrie stood up to move the phone out of Lucy's reach. "We'll see you shortly."

"They're coming for us, Daddy!" Lucy shrieked as Carrie slammed the phone down onto the receiver.

* * *

Finn hissed several curses under his breath, most aimed at that bitch of a soccer mom who played nurse every Tuesday and Thursday at the school. It would shock him if Carrie Stockton had ever even taken a first-aid course. Though he couldn't make out all her words, Finn knew his daughter was in distress, and thought denying her reassurance from her own father was just about the shittiest thing that evil biddy could manage. He pulled on the front door so hard that it flew back and slammed into the wall again, this time sending Charlie's framed first-grade photo crashing to the ground.

"Dammit," Finn hissed and kicked broken glass away from the door to clean up later.

Then Finn heard the unmistakable low whir of Hot Wheels on a three-loop track. Every hair on the back of his neck stood up as he turned away from the open doorway and cast a long stare up the steps to the bedrooms. There was another bump and a roll, followed by what was once amongst the sweetest sounds Finn knew: his son's high-pitched laughter. It snatched the breath from Finn's chest. He wasn't sure if his heart was still pumping. Then again, Finn wasn't positive he cared.

"Hello?" Finn found words through a mouth full of cotton. Nothing but silence greeted him. Finn wanted to call out his son's name, but *Aidan* was a word that felt sacrilegious to speak aloud.

The quiet stretched out wide before him, filling every corner of the house, threatening to smother Finn. He chewed at the inside of his cheek for a moment, scanning his surroundings before deciding he would have to get on his hands and knees and beg the shrink for something more potent the next time he shambled into her office. Once again, Finn turned toward the open door and bounced his keys in his hand.

"Daddy..." A whisper floated on the air from upstairs and arrested Finn once more. His eyes and nose burned. There was no mistaking that voice, no matter how soft it echoed down from the top floor.

"Aidan?"

Before he could think, he was bounding up the stairs, the front door wide open behind him. When he reached the top step, Finn found the door to Aidan's room was ajar. The sight hit him in the breastbone, and his heart skipped a few beats.

"Aidan?" Finn cleared his throat and reminded himself to breathe.

Something was very wrong, and it didn't take a genius to riddle that out. This was the part in a horror film where Finn would scream at the main character to get his ass back down the stairs. He knew this even as he walked toward the cracked door, but he couldn't help himself. The room beyond the door was lit up with sunshine, a warm glow calling to Finn.

"Aidan, I heard you." Finn flinched and swallowed hard when he heard his own voice crack. "Little man, if you're up here . . . let me know." He drifted closer to the door, watching from outside of himself as if he were in a dream.

There was a light rustle from inside the room. That was the only cue Finn needed to plunge forward and push the door all the way open. Finn wasn't sure what he had expected on the other side, but what was waiting for him was beyond anything he'd dreamt in his persistent nightmares.

There were few things as gut-churning and horrific as seeing Aidan's sweet face disappear in the black water that night, but someone had managed to find a way.

Whispers in the Dark

From baseboard to baseboard, stretching across the ceiling and over the floor, the entire bedroom was wallpapered with twisted, mutilated photos of Aidan. Photos from all eight birthday parties he'd enjoyed, burnt along the edges with Aidan's face scorched. School portraits destroyed with a Sharpie that blacked out Aidan's eyes and turned his mouth into a dark, gaping hole. Aidan's baseball pictures, his first Christmas shots, his first Communion, his first visit to the beach—every single photograph had been desecrated, turning Aidan's image into something warped and wicked. The photos blurred together in front of Finn as bile sloshed up the back of his throat. He blinked again and again, but the photos remained.

His ears were ringing by the time his eyes dropped to the floor in the center of the room. There, not six feet away, lay the grotesque lost body of his son in all three dimensions. The boy was sopping wet, a puddle growing large beneath him. With red mud caked in his hair, Aidan's curled body rested in a heap on his snapped neck, dirty limp hands lying open to the sky. The broken body before him was turned away toward the window, hiding his son's face.

From somewhere deep in his mind, Finn could hear himself screaming to get the fuck out of that damned house, but his body seemed to move of its own accord now. He walked slowly around the twisted remains of his son, and the corpse remained rigid as Finn arrived at the front to stare into its face.

A scream caught in Finn's throat as he did.

This body had the vague face of his son with blond hair and round cheeks, but the eyes ... they were gone, cut out with nothing but black holes left behind. Finn could tell by then that this thing was, in fact, not his son—not *anyone's* son. Instead, it was a life-size, plastic doll with chopped hair in Aidan's clothing. Lucy's doll, as a matter of fact—Patty or Patsy or Penny or some shit like that. It was supposed to walk with her if held just the right way. A gift from one of the church ladies when the Kennans had first arrived in Dahlmouth, the doll was creepy as hell even on an average day. He stared at it right in its black holes, and it stared right back at him, unmoving.

Despite everything he knew to be true, Finn couldn't shake the feeling that this hunk of plastic was somehow alive—alive and laughing so very hard on the inside. And that was when Finn felt the precious few bits of his sanity crumbling to dust.

Twenty

"GODDAMMIT, JEREMY!"

Rachel burst through a tangle of oak and ivy at the edge of Johnnie Oldridge's dairy farm, where they had begun their search. She kept her pace quick to work out the shakes that had grabbed hold of her in the woods. "When I call you on the fucking radio—"

"When *you* call *me*?" Jeremy's face twisted sourly as he looked up from the pack of searchers congregated around him. "I've been buzzing you for the last hour. Hell, I was about ready to send out a search party for you."

"That stunt was real fucking cute," Rachel sneered as she held the walkie high. "When's the last time these damn batteries were changed anyways?" She chose to ignore the wide-eyed expressions of Abby Grayson's growing search party.

"We've got worse problems than our radios, Chief." Jeremy looked as though he wanted to crawl under the cruiser to escape the eager ears gathered around him.

Rachel inhaled sharply and held her breath. She wondered what state Abby's body would be in after an evening and most of the day in the woods, grabbed by god only knew what and dragged around all over the place. Her eyes searched from person to person to locate Florence.

"Where is she?" Rachel tucked her radio into her belt and drew her jacket closer around her.

"Which one?" Jeremy chuckled humorlessly and shook his head, folding up a map with pursed lips.

"Say what?"

"Travis Moreland ..." Jeremy's jaw tightened. "He's saying Kendall never came home last night. The school is saying she's nowhere to be found on their watch either."

"I'm sorry, Kendall Moreland?" Rachel's fingers suddenly felt numb as she stepped closer to look at the map Jeremy was crumpling in directions it was never meant to go.

"The one and only."

Of all Charlie's friends, Kendall was the one Rachel could best imagine thumbing her way out of Dahlmouth and into the big ol' world on a whim. Rachel could even see the young teen's long, multicolored locks blowing out of the side of a Ford pickup on the way out of town, fingers riding the currents of air as the truck zoomed toward the sunset. What Rachel couldn't accept, however, was Kendall choosing to hightail it out of Dahlmouth the same night an unrelated four-year-old went missing, less than twenty-four hours after a deformed corpse was found lounging in the woods.

Her hunch that Abby's disappearance and the dead hiker were connected was quickly becoming an unavoidable likelihood. If Kendall had also truly gone missing, Dahlmouth had a trend on its hands that would send the whole damn town into a spiral.

"All right," Rachel finally said. "We'll need to follow up with Travis and Jenna to pin down when they last saw—"

"They said they last saw her with Charlie." Jeremy quit trying to fold the map, balling it up in his fist instead before looking at Rachel with a rock-solid jaw.

"When?"

"'Round about three or four yesterday before Jenna headed out for her shift at Lem's Tavern. Kendall was hopping on her bike to follow after Charlie on their way to Gemma Thompson's place."

Rachel's chest tightened. "They're confused, then. Charlie was home all day yesterday." Head down, Rachel charged through the group toward the cars parked at the edge of the grass. She yanked her cell phone from her pocket and powered on the screen.

"Listen, Rach, there's still no trace of Abby." Jeremy trotted up next to Rachel as she made giant strides through the muddy grass. "And Florence . . ." Jeremy's voice darkened before he continued quietly, "She took off after saying something to Becky Foley over there . . ." He pointed the woman out, though Rachel hardly needed an ID on the town's PTA bake sale goddess and organizer of Dahlmouth's annual living Christmas nativity.

"Don't point," Rachel muttered. Finally, back in an area with reception, no less than fifteen missed calls from Finn were popping up on her phone all at one time. "What did Florence say?"

"Uh . . ." Jeremy took off his hat and ran his fingers through sweaty dark hair. "She said something about going to look for Abby by the river." Rachel froze, biting the inside of her cheek as she searched Jeremy's face. "Said she thought maybe Abby coulda slipped in or something. We haven't heard from Florence since."

A thousand responses rushed through Rachel's mind, each one nastier than the next. Instead, Rachel remained silent, back rigid as the image of the four-year-old little girl tumbling into the swollen waters forced its way into her head. Finally, Rachel took a deep breath and felt her senses return.

"Wish she would've said something about that sooner." Rachel could've spit fire as she looked up, then down at her phone.

You need to call me right now.

Finn's text scrubbed hard at Rachel's frayed nerves.

"I don't know, Rach. Maybe it's time we followed Florence's lead. We're striking out here."

"You planning on looking for Kendall by the river, too? Is that where all the dead kids go?" Her phone began buzzing in her hand wildly. Rachel hit reject.

"Rach!" Jeremy hissed and threw a wild stare over her shoulder to the crowd clustered a few dozen feet away. "You can't say shit like that in front of these people. Look, if you need to tap out on this one—"

She held her hand up, a razor-sharp glare cutting his words off. "I don't need to sit this one out. I just think you're wrong. Dahlmouth hasn't had a missing person case in decades. Now, we have two kids missing and a stranger dead in the woods within hours. The odds of Abby Grayson falling into the river, Kendall Moreland hightailing it out of town, and this hiker turning up spiked to a tree all being unrelated is . . . it'd be incredibly

Whispers in the Dark

naive to assume." Rachel's cell phone lit up again, buzzing like a hornet's nest before she rejected the call again.

"You think it's the same person doing all this?" Jeremy shifted uneasily and stared at her phone like it was a harbinger of doom. For all his swagger, the guy wasn't cut out for cases like this, and even he knew it.

"I think we need to get these people and their kids home until we know more. Word starts getting out that another girl is missing, and folks are going to get hysterical. I need them to stay out of my way."

"Rach"—Jeremy lowered his voice and drew close—"you try to shut these people up in their houses, you ain't gonna like the blowback. Trust me on this. It's only gonna make them try to hunt down whoever is responsible faster."

For yet another time, Rachel's phone sprang to life, vibrating in her cold hands as her least-favorite name flashed across the screen. "I gotta take this," Rachel groaned. "It's Finn. He's pinged me a million times. Can you just"—Rachel waved a hand toward the stalled search party—"keep them distracted somehow? Make sure they don't start a witch hunt or something."

Rachel trudged into the middle of the gravel road that bisected the Oldridge farm, feeling the gaze of each citizen that had spent the better part of their day looking for a lost girl, only to end up with two.

Using fingers that trembled regardless of how much Rachel demanded otherwise, she swiped the green phone symbol and whipped the cell up to her ear. "What do you want? I'm busy."

"You need to get home right now." Finn's voice shook like stretched wire. Rachel knew that tone; it was carved into her aural sense forever. To her knowledge, he had only ever sounded so quietly unhinged once before, and Rachel still had scars to commemorate the event.

"Tell me what's going on." Rachel swallowed against the rising anxiety that was quickly becoming a constant. Even if Finn believed he'd uncovered another one of her dirty secrets, she didn't have time to smooth over anyone's temper tantrum.

"You need to see it."

"Finn, honestly, the sky is kind of falling right now." Rachel lowered her voice further. "Two kids have gone missing overnight on top of the dead body no one else seems to give a shit about. I can't dip—"

"It's about Aidan."

The kick landed Rachel square in the gut and nearly bowled her over. She wanted to snatch the name right out of Finn's mouth.

"I'll be there in ten." Rachel dropped the call and stuffed the phone into her pocket. When she turned, she saw Jeremy had already wandered over to the search party congregated around a table Mrs. Oldridge had lined with coffee cups. For the moment, the gang seemed content chatting with the deputy as he put his southern charm to good use. As far as Rachel was concerned, no further explanation was needed. She hopped in the cruiser, turned on the engine, and smashed the gas pedal to the floor.

* * *

Rachel expected to see something impressive when she stepped into her house—bile spread across the entryway, trailing along the tile toward the kitchen, or up the carpeted stairs. Instead, everything was disturbingly tidy and quiet. She stood a moment, waiting for the disaster to become apparent. The only things out of place were a cracked, empty photo frame and her own muddy boots on the cream tile.

"Finn?" Rachel called into the unsettling calm.

"Up here." Finn's voice was still pulled tight with the same barely restrained rage she'd heard the night he caught her in Roanoke.

Rachel took to the steps with a bounce in her feet, chunks of mud smearing underneath her boots. It didn't take long to locate Finn. He sat at the top of the stairs against the wall between the bathroom and Lucy's bedroom in the darkened hallway. His knees were pulled up against his chest, arms wrapped around his shins casually. His face, though, was a hardened visage of fury.

"What happened?" Rachel scanned for the bottle she knew should be beside him. Finn nodded his head toward Aidan's room. She braced herself against the rail of the stairs. She hated even acknowledging the room existed, but the direction in which Finn was looking was unavoidable.

"Go take a look, Rach," Finn murmured, and now Rachel could hear the brokenness in his voice alongside anger.

Her feet went heavy, hands numb as she mounted the last of the steps to tower over Finn. Still, she honored his request and turned to face whatever wound he had ripped open again in their story. The door to Aidan's room was swung wide, but she couldn't see inside from where she stood. Rachel approached the bright glow timidly for a few paces. Then her body remembered the hate, the rage, the vitriol that had kept her moving forward since she had last felt her little boy's arms around her waist. Rachel suddenly grew several inches and felt strength surge through her arms like electricity. It carried her the rest of the way to the door of her son's abandoned bedroom.

And she saw everything.

Rachel couldn't understand how Finn had found it within himself to stay in the house, let alone summon her there. The chief's hazel eyes scanned the room several times over before stepping inside. She knew the images that lined the walls all too well; they were the only remaining glimpses of her son that would ever exist. What had been done to them, however—the burns, the crude markings, the slashes and cuts through sacred memories—sent an icy numbness through her core.

The trashed doll contorted on the floor was the worst part. It was twisted up in a heap, as if someone had modeled a crash dummy in the position Aidan had landed before the water tore him from the mangled SUV. When she rounded the distorted plastic body and saw the gashes where Lucy's doll had once had unblinking blue eyes, Rachel ran her tongue across the front of her teeth and sucked.

There was something wrong with her. She had known that for some time without anyone adding to the chorus. The most sensitive human pieces of Rachel's psyche shut down in the face of gore and suffering. It was simply the terrible way she was put together. In the moments when others averted their gaze or ran in the opposite direction, Rachel drew closer. It had served her well for years. Indeed, this morbid predominance in her personality had led her into criminal justice and risen her through the ranks in short order.

What it did not contribute to, however, was the relationship between herself and the rest of the world. Rachel took in what everyone else was too weak to digest. She, and only a few other twisted individuals of like minds, took the brunt of the ugliness humanity offered. That ugliness didn't disappear after the authorities cleaned it up. It danced around in Rachel's mind like wildfire and colored every decision she made. Most days, Rachel could turn off the tap and continue to take on whatever shit show the world handed down.

Some nights, though, the darkness overflowed and knocked Rachel off her feet. These were the moments when Rachel blew craters in the carefully crafted life she had built for herself. She felt one of those nights rolling in soon. Finn thought he had seen the worst of her, but as Rachel stared at the scene before her and felt absolutely nothing, she knew the abscess festering from her son's loss had yet to rupture.

"I want you to find the fucker that did this and grind them into powder." Finn stood in the doorway behind her, grasping both sides unsteadily.

Rachel quarter-turned and blinked at him. "You think I have time for this?"

"Are you fucking kidding me? Look at these." Finn grasped at images, taking fistfuls with each swipe and throwing them in her direction. "Someone took our son's memory and made a goddamn mockery of it. Somebody broke into our home—"

"Finn," she said, "I think you're getting a little ahead—"

"—rounded up all our precious fuckin' memories"—Finn spun in a circle with his hands held high—"and had a rip-roaring good time destroying each and every one."

"Finn—"

"I know these people hate me." His voice rose louder as he tapped at his temple with his forefinger. "I don't always get the local culture, shall we say? But I certainly didn't see this coming." Finn chuckled and shook his head, his chest rising and falling faster than usual.

"Finn, I don't think this was someone from Dahlmouth screwing with us." Rachel's cell buzzed in her back pocket. Without thinking, she pulled it free to check for a missed call from the coroner's office.

"Well, then explain to me, *dear*, how these ended up on our son's fucking bedroom walls!" Finn plucked the warped images of their son from the floor and hurled them at her face. She batted them away with a bored expression.

"Don't call me *dear*," Rachel muttered, beginning to text Jeremy for a status update.

"PUT DOWN THE FUCKING PHONE, RACHEL!" Finn's voice rose thunderously. He leapt forward to take away her cell.

"HEY! Give that back, asshole!"

Finn ripped the phone from its cover and yanked the battery out before throwing the pieces in different directions. Rachel's phone crashed against the wall next to Aidan's bed with a loud crack that signaled her screen was toast.

"JESUS CHRIST!" Rachel's mouth hung open. It was rare that Finn—or anyone else, for that matter—surprised her.

"Why are you not taking this seriously?" Finn looked as though he hovered between sobbing and exploding. "What the hell is wrong with you? What if Lucy found this sick fucking joke instead of me?"

"It's not meant to be a joke." Rachel's voice was empty as Finn looked up at her with a tight jaw.

"Did *you* do this?"

"Are you out of your mind?" Rachel chuckled. "You really think I'd do something like this?"

"I don't know." Finn let out a clap of humorless laughter. "Since Aidan died, you've done a lot of things I never saw coming."

Rachel stared at him for a long time, searching for the best answer that would end the conversation so she could be on her way. Try as she might, however, that perfect response wouldn't come to the forefront.

"Charlie did this. She's angry. She's bitter. She's going through a lot of changes right now." The words came out of Rachel's mouth in a quick, flat-toned flurry. She'd never dared to do something so horrific at thirteen, but it wasn't so hard to believe Charlie would, given her eldest's fiery disposition and recent angst. "She's looking for attention. She's looking to lash out at us, and so on and so forth."

"Are you kidding me?" Finn's eyes bugged out as he pointed around the room. "Charlie didn't do this. I know her—*I'm* the one that's around her every single day, and I know she wouldn't do something absolutely disgusting like this. That's not our daughter."

"Yeah, well, daughters change, and you can fuck right off with the nonsense about knowing the kids better."

"So, you're saying Charlie mutilated nearly every photo of Aidan we have, wallpapered his bedroom with them, then took Lucy's doll and knifed its fucking eyes out? Do you hear yourself right now?"

"Why don't you ask her about it? You two are so close, I'm sure she'll open right up to you." Rachel moved toward the bed to retrieve her smashed phone, but Finn ducked in front of her.

"This morning, you think she's a drug addict. This afternoon, you think she's a sociopath. How fucked up do you think Charlie is?"

"Actually, our kids *are* pretty fucked up right now. You did that, remember?" Rachel finally locked eyes with him again, staring him down as she felt the inevitable fight rolling in. Maybe this would be the final rumble at last. Perhaps they'd finally shred each other to bloody pieces, neither one able to walk away. The thought brought Rachel an odd comfort she hadn't known in quite some time.

"It's beyond disturbing you think our daughter is capable of this," Finn declared with a piety that ticked Rachel's blood pressure up a few notches. "And the fact you would just accept this parody of our son's death—"

"You mean, our son's *murder*," Rachel spat out. "It's called vehicular *homicide* for a reason."

Finn fell into silence, his face going lax. Rachel crossed her arms over her chest and shivered. The room was freezing again, even with the window shut.

"Jesus, Rach. How am I ever supposed to come back from that night?" he asked barely above a whisper.

"You can't."

"I would do anything to erase what—"

"Stop." She held up her hand as her eyes narrowed. "I don't care what you—"

"I'd give my life over and over and over again to bring him—"

"Oh, poor Finn. Poor *fucking* Finn." Her voice rose higher than she would've liked, knowing Finn would successfully keep pushing her until she erupted. She may have had the gun, but Finn always had words that caused more destruction than any weapon she ever carried.

"Every single day, I wish I had died in his place." Finn's voice cracked as the inferno in Rachel roared. "I cannot help it that a deer jumped—"

"It wasn't the goddamn deer, Finn." Rachel flexed her tingling fingers. "You couldn't put down a fucking liquor bottle long enough to pick up our—"

"I DIDN'T MURDER OUR SON!" Spittle flew from Finn's lips as tears sparkled in his eyes. "You act like I-I-I *wanted* to kill Aidan."

"I don't care whether or not you wanted to," Rachel sneered. "You did kill him, and there's nothing anyone can do to wipe that away—not you, not your touchy-feely therapist—"

"I wish you'd been behind the wheel of that car, Rach." Finn's voice grew sober and low. "I wish you could've saved the day with your superpowers. God knows, how can I ever live up to your—"

"Don't do this. Don't try to play the fucking martyr with me again."

"Why are we doing this?" Finn threw up his left hand to wiggle his ring finger in her direction. Once more, a visceral pang of rage throbbed in her chest. The asshole still wore the band that handcuffed them together. She had conveniently lost hers somewhere along the way.

"If I can never make things right," he continued with a wounded expression, "if I can never atone for what happened, why are we still doing this?"

Rachel paused, feeling her pulse pounding in her eardrums. "We're doing it for the kids."

Finn laughed miserably and rubbed at his stubble. "They know we're faking it."

"C'mon, Finn," Rachel hissed, "we've been faking it pretty successfully for fourteen years."

This jab hit Finn hard enough that Rachel saw him flinch and take a half-step back. He struggled to recover, forcing another chuckle and a nod to cover the pain. "Okay." Finn smiled bitterly. "Maybe you were faking it this whole time, but *I* loved you—silly, pathetic, fuckin' fool that I am—"

"My point is that precisely nothing has changed about how this marriage functions, so there's nothing for them to—"

"Really, Rach?!" Finn screeched, eyes widening. "Nothing? Then why am I sleeping downstairs on a fucking sectional instead of our bed? I don't remember that part prior to the crash."

"Ohhh!" Rachel feigned a sudden mock realization. "You mean the kids have noticed I'm done pretending to enjoy fucking you." She cackled in his face as his eyes turned wild. "Yeah, I honestly didn't think they were that astute. You're right. I never would've noticed that. It must be all that quality time you're spending with them—"

"*This* is what I mean. They feel how much you hate me, and they know I don't trust you."

"I don't think they give a shit whether or not you trust me, and quite frankly, neither do I."

"Of course you don't." Finn chuckled in the self-righteous, indignant way that made Rachel want to rip his eyes out. "You don't care about anything anymore. Not the kids, not me, not yourself. Where is the woman I married?"

"She never existed!" Rachel howled, throwing her hands in the air before clenching them into fists. "You fell in love with a character you created in your head, but it wasn't me."

"That's horseshit, Rachel, and you know it!" He thrust his pointer finger toward her chest.

"One minute, we're drinking buddies; the next, you've fuckin' twisted my arm until I had no choice but to consent to this bullshit marriage—"

"Bullshit marriage!" Finn cried in disbelief. "If it was such bullshit, why'd you want *two* more kids with me, Rach? Did I force you into that, too? 'Cause I specifically remember you were the one who dreamt up Lucy, and if memory serves me correctly, you were fairly enthusiastic about making Aidan—"

"Stop saying his name!" Rachel stepped closer, teeth gnashing together as she overflowed with rage. "You're so heartbroken about our perfect fuckin' marriage falling apart? Leave, then!"

"I'm not leaving without the kids." Finn shook his head. "You're not taking them from me."

Rachel felt herself losing control as her heart pounded. "If anyone should be worried about one of us taking the kids away, it's me. Which one are you going to drive off a—?"

"Don't do it, Rach! Don't you fucking go there."

"Or what?" Rachel advanced on him slowly once more, her tone dripping with venom. "You gonna fuck me up again?"

The bastard's face twisted from wounded to infuriated, and Rachel felt a little spark of pleasure. "No, you'd like that too much, you sick—"

"Get the hell out of my house!" Rachel shrieked, her chest heaving forward as her hands flew back.

"I'm getting a lawyer." He nodded and stepped away. "You might not be able to forgive me, but those kids know the truth. They know who is there for them—who loves them."

"Oh, fuck your truth, you cocky shit!" Rachel lunged forward and threw her weight against his shoulders, sending his back smacking against the wall and tearing down more photos. "GET OUT!" She thrust one hand against his breastbone and pointed to the door with the other.

Finn grabbed Rachel's wrist with an iron fist. She landed another blow against his shoulder with her free hand. Her head pulsed, and she felt an electric current sparking every nerve in her body awake. She was ready for this fight, craving it like a drug just as she had in that hotel room.

Finn closed his eyes and took deep breaths, though his grip on her wrist had grown tight enough to make her fingers tingle. His self-control, this self-righteous discipline he had cultivated over the past few months, enraged her unlike any other stunt he ever pulled. Rachel reeled back again and smacked him across the top of his head.

"Rachel," Finn breathed out as his cheeks reddened. "You crazy bitch—"

"Go ahead and hit me, asshole!" Rachel screamed and slammed him square in the middle of his chest once more. His eyes popped open as he caught the offending arm, clamping down on it, too. "Stop being a pussy and hit me—"

"Rachel," Finn began in a warning tone. "I'm not going to hit you. I know what you're doing." His grip on her wrists tightened to the point of pain, and she suddenly felt dizzy with adrenaline. "But I'm not that person. I'm not going to let you set me off—"

"You're a drunken little bitch, Finn . . . just like your daddy," Rachel seethed. "You've always been a little bitch, and you know what?"

"I swear to god—" Finn's voice shook as his breathing picked up pace.

"You're *my* bitch, Finn." Rachel leaned close to his face, writhing against his grip, ready and willing for the fight to end all fights. "*I'm* the one that holds your fucking balls in a vise, and everyone knows it, especially the kids. How does that feel, *bitch*?"

A sudden high-pitched tinkle of chimes filled the air. The sound interrupted Rachel's momentum, knocking Finn out of the pressure cooker as his eyes broke from hers. He let go of her arms suddenly to grip at his pocket.

Rachel fell to the floor after being held up by his resistance more than her own feet as she'd pressed in. When her ass hit the ground, she felt the blow ripple up her spine and rattle her skull. She heard a familiar beat joining the chorus from the direction of her own powerless cell, which was still lying untouched by Aidan's bed. How was that possible? She stared at it numbly before redirecting her eyes over to the closet door, where Finn had chucked her phone's battery.

"Jesus . . . dammit." Finn sucked in air and nearly dropped the phone as he moved it to his ear. "H-hey there, Mrs. Stockton. Yeah, I'm headed over now. We had a bit of a family . . . No, I understand." Finn's face fell as Rachel started to crawl toward her now-silent phone. "I'm sorry, what?"

Rachel paused abruptly and looked up at him from the floor.

"What's wrong?" Her sanity returned as her heartbeat slowed.

"I'll be right there . . . No, no, I'm coming. I'm on my way." Finn hung up the phone and stuffed it into his jeans before Mrs. Stockton could get out another word.

"What's going on?" Rachel jumped to her feet as she swiped her cell phone off the floor.

"Lucy's sick," Finn muttered as he turned on his heels and flew toward the stairs.

"Sick how?" He didn't respond as he sailed down the steps. "FINN! Tell me what's happening!"

He didn't bother to close the front door behind him, but Rachel heard the Dodge door slam shut, the engine rev, and tires crunch on gravel. Rachel stood still in the center of her son's quiet room for several minutes. Her wrists stung, and she knew bright magenta bruises were forming. Rachel felt rooted there, like it would be better to sit down and wait for something than to move ever again. Instead, she stepped toward Aidan's closet and picked up her cell phone's battery. She turned on her boot heel and shoved the battery into the back of the cell.

As she walked toward the door, however, something caught her eye. Or rather, the emptiness of the room caught it. She scanned the floor three times over before she felt the hair rising on her arms. She even spun around twice to check the area around her feet in case she had somehow kicked it while sparring with Finn.

But it was *gone*.

The doll that had been twisted up into a reflection of her son's corpse—the doll with its gaping black holes—was nowhere to be found.

Twenty-One

"She fell down," Finn repeated loudly for the third time. "Her eyes rolled back in her head ... and you didn't call nine-one-one?"

"I called *you*, Mr. Kennan." Mrs. Stockton smiled curtly with eyes narrowed into thin slits.

"Carrie, allow me." Mrs. Angelica Morris, assistant principal of Dahlmouth Elementary, placed a gentle hand on Mrs. Stockton's shoulder and squeezed. "Mr. Kennan, it's not uncommon for children to feel faint here and there, especially when they have a high fever—"

"Which she doesn't." Finn smiled but meant no goodwill.

"—or when under extreme stress."

"Which she isn't."

Mrs. Morris gave Finn a tight smile. "Children know more than we give them credit for."

"You people can't keep blaming Aidan's death for Lucy's issues. Do you know how many times I've gotten these ridiculous, loaded comments on her report card? How many parent-teacher conferences I've had over the past year? Hell, her music teacher wanted to talk about the way she doesn't play bells with the same enthusiasm as the other kids."

"Watch your language, Mr. Kennan." Mrs. Stockton rose as high as she could to stare him down. Finn couldn't even figure out which word he had used to put her out. "And we're not *only* referring to your son's passing when we discuss Lucy's ... abnormal behavior."

"It's like you don't even see Lucy anymore." Finn ignored the oblique shot. "You look at my daughter, and all you see is my dead son!"

Before Mrs. Stockton could fire back, Mrs. Morris raised her voice gently above Finn's. "I understand your concern, Mr. Kennan. We've all put in hard work to make sure Lucy readjusted properly after the tragedy your family suffered. However, sometimes children heal on a timetable that isn't the one we plan. Perhaps it would help if we saw Mrs. Kennan here more often to speed along little Lucy's reacclimatization, don't you think?"

"*Chief* Kennan," Finn seethed. "Rachel is Chief Kennan to you morons. She's the reason you can all sleep at night without some idiot high off his ass climbing—"

"Language!" Mrs. Stockton, again, looked as though she might have worked herself into enough of a tizzy to faint herself.

"—through your windows with him's damn huntin' rifle that's his god-given right." Finn's voice twisted into an ugly, exaggerated mockery of the local southern twang before reassuming his sharp, fast-paced cadence. "And lady, if I wanted to use some colorful language, believe you me, it'd be a whole lot more interesting than *ass*." Finn pushed past the two women.

"Be that as it may, Mr. Kennan"—Mrs. Morris wheeled around and followed through the school's reception office toward the nurse's office—"your wife—"

"The chief!" he yelled over his shoulder.

"*Chief* Kennan should really make an effort to collaborate with Lucy's teachers as well. Just a little bit of effort—"

"So, this is Rachel's fault now, as well? Lucy's fainting and your incompetence is Rachel's fault, in addition to our family tragedy, which you care oh so much about whenever it suits you?" Finn pushed open the thin door with yellow smiley face stickers covering it to find Lucy on a cot with the blankets pulled over her face.

"Mr. Kennan, you are a very rude man!" Mrs. Stockton scuttled in behind Mrs. Morris.

Mrs. Morris held up her hand to block the part-time nurse from rushing forward. "Mr. Kennan, now is probably not the time to address the matter, but someday soon, we'll need to discuss how to best help Lucy. That conversation will have to include her mother."

"You gonna call the pastor in for that conversation, too?" Finn snapped before his voice went soft. "Lucy, honey, we're going home. I'm here now."

He heard Lucy's tears as she wailed from under the covers, "We're all gonna die, Daddy!"

Finn looked back at the two women standing shoulder to shoulder at the doorway. His face flushed, but he lowered to his knees to come even with Lucy. "Why would you say that, baby?" He rested his chin on the cot next to her hidden face.

"You should've left, Daddy," Lucy choked out. "You could've gotten away."

He swallowed hard and reached out a hand that he wished was steadier to peel back the flimsy white blanket. Lucy's face was slick with snot and tears. Her hair was splayed out in every direction, some wild strands plastered to her cheeks. Her mouth fell open in a silent sob as he pulled the blankets down.

"You wanna tell me what's going on?"

"You won't believe me."

He forced a smile. "Lucy, your dad has an incredibly overactive imagination, which has gotten me into more trouble than I ever care to detail. I'm ripe to believe almost anything. Ask your mother."

"You'll be scared if you do believe me."

"Well . . . it's better not to be scared all alone, I think. Being scared and alone is one of the worst feelings I've ever had."

Lucy kept her mouth dipped under the edge of the blanket as she searched Finn's face. "Charlie's not right, Daddy," she whispered.

"Baby, I told you, she got sick." He tried not to show his irritation as he fought the urge to check if the looming hags were still listening in.

"Something got her in the woods."

"Lucy—"

"They got Gemma and Sarah and Kendall, too. They want all the kids."

The hair on the back of his neck rose as Lucy shrank into herself. He refused to believe she was wrestling with the same image burned into his mind because that image, that memory, was false, and it was Finn's alone.

"They take little boys and girls away." Lucy's whisper dropped even lower. "And we go somewhere else . . . somewhere you can never find us."

He remembered Lucy's terrified shrieks as she dangled in her car seat—the kind of scream one simply can't imitate. While Finn had fought with his seat belt, Lucy believed with all her heart she was going to die. And as she stared at her brother as water rushed in, there was no reason for her to believe otherwise. Finn would never know all the details of what Lucy saw— the child psychiatrist instructed them not to pry—but there was no doubt she saw what happened to Aidan in real time.

"Lucy, honey." Finn cleared his throat. "I think we need to talk to Dr.—"

"Charlie's not Charlie, Daddy. She's gone now; that thing only looks like her. It's gonna get you and Mommy. They're gonna get everybody." Lucy flung the blanket to her waist as her eyes widened.

"Not everybody goes away. After what happened to Aidan, I know it's hard to—"

"I knew you wouldn't believe me!" Lucy threw herself into despair once more.

"No, baby. I'm just trying to understand, okay? Daddy's trying to get it through his thick skull." Finn knocked on his head with his knuckles, but Lucy didn't even crack a smile.

"Daddy." Lucy squeezed his hand as her huge blue eyes glistened with tears. "I don't want to disappear."

Finn tried not to show how the words Lucy spoke exposed his worst fears and guilt. Maybe it exploited weaknesses in Finn and Rachel's relationship and cracked them in two; perhaps it sent Charlie into a quiet tailspin right as she was coming into her own; but for Lucy, the moment Finn stopped trying to pull Aidan from the wreckage, her innocence had shattered. Finn was responsible for obliterating Lucy's childhood just as much as he was for the death of his son.

For what may have been the thousandth time, Finn would've given anything to be back in the river that night. He should have kept trying, reaching, pleading with the gods to save Aidan no matter what he saw—no matter whether Aidan was already gone, no matter how dangerous the current had become.

He should've fought until he died, and he'd never forgive himself for having the gall to continue living.

"Baby, I will never let anything bad happen to you ever again." He rose from the floor to sit beside her on the cot. "The bad things are over, I promise. You believe me?"

"No." Lucy blew a snot bubble as she shook her little head.

Finn wasn't sure what to say, but he certainly didn't blame her for calling bullshit on Daddy's promises when they rang so hollow in his own ears. "That's okay," he whispered and gently rested his hand at Lucy's hairline. "You don't have to believe me 'cause I'ma prove it to you."

"Don't leave me alone."

"You'll never be alone again, sweetheart."

Twenty-Two

"All right, Travis, I need you to be one hundred percent honest with me." Rachel looked deeply into the big man's bloodshot brown eyes. "When was the last time you saw Kendall?"

"I told you." Huge teardrops ran out of his eyes and into his bushy brown beard in a steady stream. "She was headin' out with Charlie to go to Gem's yesterday afternoon."

"And what time was that?" Rachel clicked her pen three times in quick order.

"Rach, why we still goin' over this? Why aren't we out there searchin' for my daughter?"

"Because I know you're not being completely honest with me." Rachel cocked her head. "I'm leveling with you here. I know Kendall was not headed out with Charlie around three yesterday because Charlie was at home with her father at three."

"You know that, do you?" Kendall's mother, Jenna, was folded up into herself on the big squishy brown couch with a Virginia Slim in her hand. "From what I heard, you was out dealin' with that poor son o' bitch the Wise boys killed. So, how do you know for sure where Charlie was?" Her gravelly voice aged her by at least ten years. They were about the same age, but Rachel would have sworn otherwise if she didn't know Jenna's DOB from her prior record.

Rachel knew the Morelands well. When she'd dropped Charlie off for her first sleepover with Kendall, Travis and Jenna had insisted on sharing a beer with Rachel. After the little shits at the middle school had spread Rachel's old social media pictures around the town, the Morelands were the only parents who continued inviting her into their home. They were rough around the edges with almost indecipherable country accents, they were crazy enough to smoke weed right in front of the police chief, and they were even crazier for calling her a friend. Because of this, Rachel was confident she could get the full truth out of them, and not just about Kendall. The mounting desperation in her insisted that if she could shake something—*anything*—loose out of the Morelands, perhaps she could unravel Abby's disappearance as well.

"You're right, Jenna. You're right." Rachel licked her cracked lips and sat back in the torn bean bag chair they had offered her when she first arrived. "Tell me more, then."

"There's nothin' to tell I ain't already told you." Travis wheezed and wiped the tears away from his eyes with his massive hands. "Kendall left with Charlie, and I never saw her come home after that. I's at the shop last evenin'."

"Why were you at the shop so late, Travis?" Rachel clicked her pen again. She had yet to take any notes on the cases at all, but it felt right to have the pen and pad at the ready.

"He's been working on Mayor Jessup's ride." Jenna leaned forward. "Why you talkin' to us like we're suspects, Rachel? We're just tryin' to find our girl. You know we're not bad people."

"Of course you're not bad people." Rachel pushed a few of her rogue curls from her face. "Look, can I check out her room?"

"Sure, but hey—aren't ya gonna call the cops in to look for her? I mean, the real cops, the big guns from the county." Jenna swiveled around on the couch and made to grab her dolphin-shaped pipe off the counter that separated the living room from the kitchen.

"Not if you're toking up like that in front of little ol' *me*, Jenna. The hell do you think is gonna happen when the county rolls on up in here? You think they're more or less likely to believe you?" Rachel stood up on her feet and wobbled. "Besides, I've already called their sorry asses once in the last twenty-four hours, and they're hardly moved to our plight. We're gonna give this a couple of hours, but I'm telling you, you'd better straighten out your shit before they get here. Otherwise, they'll throw both of you in prison for distribution long before they find Kendall."

"Them Wises still walkin' free, ain't they?" Jenna croaked.

She handed off her cigarette to Travis and readied to light up her pipe. Rachel rolled her eyes and headed to Kendall's bedroom on her own.

"Where were you when Kendall left, Jenna?" Rachel yelled behind her as she flicked on the hall light that illuminated the small walk from the living room to the tiny bathroom and bedroom Kendall had made her haven. Rachel spied the tie-dyed shower curtain with a Hamsa hand in the center, along with a giant happy Buddha statue on the bathroom floor. She stepped one foot in, grabbed the curtain to check if it was wet from recent use. Rachel found it stiff and dry.

"I's at Lem's with them Mexicans!" Jenna hollered in her raspy voice. Rachel shook her head and inhaled deeply, just barely holding back a sigh. It was times like these when Finn's snide remarks about the town reverberated in her ears. "He had a bunch of 'em start up last week, so I's trainin' left and right. You know they don't know their way around a kitchen when they roll up here!" Jenna let out a fit of coughs to end her sentence.

Rolling her eyes once more, Rachel stuck her pointer finger through the rainbow bead curtain Kendall had hung over her doorway and stepped through. The windows had massive blackout curtains onto which she had painted a psychedelic flower-power garden that must've made her parents very proud. Rachel reached around the corner and flipped the light switch.

At once, Kendall's room lit up like a carnival. The vivacious teen had a black light in one corner, lighting up the teeth of her friends in the picture collage that hung directly underneath it. Charlie was in at least six different photos of varying sizes. Kendall's bed was covered with a pink mosquito-net canopy and was flanked by two bright lava lamps, the goo of which glowed at the bottom as the lamps began heating. Crisscrossing the room were multicolored LED Christmas lights Kendall had strung up that seemed to vibrate against the dark room.

Rachel moved into the center of the color wheel. Kendall kept her room clean enough to appreciate the decor she had proudly displayed, but anything that fell beneath that was fair game. Naturally, then, the floor was littered with notebook paper, mismatched pairs of shoes, charcoal drawing pencils, and discarded pieces of clothing.

"And you were at the restaurant until when?" Rachel called to Jenna.

"Oh hell, I'm not sure. Maybe eleven? Then I had to drive back from Lexington, and that took a while."

Travis coughed louder over Jenna's voice, and the couch groaned as he launched himself up to totter into the kitchen.

"I don't suppose you would've stopped anywhere else on the way home?"

"The hell does that mean, Rachel?" Jenna yelled as loud as her strained voice would allow.

Rachel scanned the room carefully now, trying to separate Kendall's natural mess from something that might have been truly out of place. "I don't give a shit if you were at the bar till dawn, Jenna. Just trying to pin down the last time someone saw Kendall. Stand down."

She refrained from telling the Morelands that little Abby Grayson had wandered off in the middle of the night, that she was trying to pin down if Kendall somehow left around the same time Abby did.

"And the sheriff is gonna wanna know, too, y'all, so you'd best nail down when the hell you were around."

"This weren't us, Rach—"

"*Chief*," Rachel grumbled too low for Travis to hear.

"We don't have nothin' to hide. This's the work of them Wise boys."

Rachel paused with her hands on her hips to listen closely to Travis's shouting. "You think Kendall was screwing around with meth?"

Please no. Please no. Please say no.

If Kendall was hitting up the Wises and their crystal candy, Charlie would be right at her side with eyes full of adoration that Rachel knew all too well. Finn may have missed it, Charlie may have tried to run from it, but Rachel had understood the way her daughter gazed at Kendall the very first time that girl graced their doorstep.

Rachel spied something on Kendall's bed looking glittery in the black light and made her way toward it. On her blanket was a dark, damp ring, and when she spread it out, a foul odor crashed over her. She nearly gagged as chunks of vomit rolled off the bedspread and onto her boot. At the same time, Rachel realized she was standing on a pile of sopping-wet clothes. When she leaned down, Rachel found they were drenched in urine.

"Shit," Rachel hissed and pulled her boot up from the clothing. It made a suction-slurp noise as she backed away. "Well, I can tell you she was here last night or early this morning unless one of you came in and upchucked all over her stuff."

Down the hallway, Rachel heard the screen door open and slam shut. She emerged from the beads, dragging her feet on the carpet in the hall to scrub off urine and stopped in the bathroom to wash her hands. Kendall had stuck photo-booth strips on the mirror there, too. Gemma, Charlie, Sarah, and Kendall had jammed themselves into one booth at the Greenview Mall and taken a series of silly shots over and over again. One with Charlie in the middle of the group flipping the bird with her tongue out caught Rachel's attention, and she couldn't help but smile. Her little hellion; her rebel without a cause.

"If you have a reason to believe Kendall was messing around with the Wises, you better tell me now," Rachel called to the Morelands as she flicked water from her fingers and turned the faucet knob with her elbow. "Look, y'all, I don't want to call the sheriff and his folks in on this again. They don't wanna hear from me either, but if the Wises are involved, we're gonna need some serious backup."

Neither Travis nor Jenna responded as Rachel caught a glance of herself in the mirror. The thick black circles under her eyes reminded her too much of the perpetual exhaustion that took her mother to an early grave. She shook her head and turned away.

"Otherwise, if I had to bet, Kendall probably ran off with somebody for a bit. I know you don't want to hear this, but it doesn't strike me as an odd thing for Kendall to do."

Rachel dried her hands on the powder-blue towel and finished the job on her pants. "I'm gonna talk to the girls about it. Much as I hope you're wrong about Charlie being out and about yesterday, I'll fess up and say it wouldn't entirely shock me if Finn missed her slipping out for a bit."

Rachel rounded the corner to arrive at an empty living room. The bowl Jenna had been smoking out of was abandoned on the coffee table along with the cigarette, which had burnt itself out in the ashtray. Rachel looked around the trailer and saw no sign of Travis or Jenna.

"Hello?" The chief strode over to the other side of the trailer and pushed the bedroom door wide. Rachel saw a queen-size waterbed, chest of drawers, scattered laundry, and an entire wall of a mirror, but no trace of the Morelands. She found the master bathroom's jacuzzi tub and double sink equally lonely.

She groaned. "Travis, I swear to Christ, if you ran off to confront those goddamn Wise boys, I'm gonna throw your ass in a cell overnight."

Rachel made her way to the front door, pushed it open, and stepped onto the wooden stairs that led down into the grass. Nearly everything around their trailer was open field. The land had once been Travis's granddaddy's farm. Now, it was just a big lot for one lonely double-wide and a couple of trucks. Those trucks were still parked where they had been when Rachel arrived. From end to end of the field, Rachel couldn't see anyone. She took a walk around the trailer and found it to be the same in all four directions.

A solid fifteen minutes passed before Rachel brought herself to reconcile with the inevitable.

It was time to pay the Wise family a visit.

Twenty-Three

The drive up to the Wise family's cluster of trailers wasn't an easy one. The dirt roads dated back to the mid-1800s and were well-worn death traps with ruts cut out from dozens of floods. It hadn't slowed the family business at all, though, and it wouldn't keep Jeremy's truck from rolling up either. Rachel and Jeremy bounced around on the bench seat as the truck rumbled along, kicking up a trail of red dust that the family would see long before they ever caught sight of the vehicle itself.

"I really hope you're onto something, Rach," Jeremy grumbled as he shook his head.

"Me too." Rachel checked to make sure she had an extra clip on her. "You remember what we've talked about before? One of us goes down, and the other falls back, okay? No heroics here. They've got us outgunned, outmanned. Leave the keys in the truck so either of us can get the hell out if things go to shit."

"You're not helping soothe me."

"Call your mama if you want reassurance and rainbows," Rachel muttered.

"This what it's like in the city?" Jeremy grimaced as his tires hit the fifth pothole.

"What?" Rachel looked up at him with a furrowed brow.

"Rolling up on drug busts all the time? All fuckin'... Rambo and shit?"

"No," Rachel scoffed. "If we were in the city, we'd have a trail of officers behind us, Kevlar vests, and a sniper team ready to go. And they... the Wises wouldn't have a goddamn arsenal in their shed. I didn't have to worry about a fuckin' grenade being lobbed at me in Richmond."

"So... we're more badass." Jeremy nodded, somehow more confident than before.

"No," Rachel hissed. "We're more fucked. And this isn't a drug bust. No matter what they're cooking up, no matter what shit you see them dispensing, we don't care about that right now. All we want is information. We just want to talk."

"Yeah." Jeremy laughed. "I'm sure they're just gonna want to chitchat, too."

The truck rounded another corner, and the cluster of trailers came into view. Ten singles and three double-wides crowded against one another around a large circular dirt yard. Vehicles cluttered the drive, most broken down and rusting, but still in better shape than half the trailers. The ruins of the family's old stone house, which had burned to the ground decades before on a particularly bad day in the lab, stood just beyond the edge of the woods, trees and vines now weaving through its cracks to return it to the earth. Any other family would have considered that a daily reminder to stop fucking around and finding out, but not the Wises.

Rachel tried to recount how many of them lived up there. How many Wise children would be running around, forcing

Jeremy and Rachel to hold their fire even as the Wises rained bullets on them? No more kids were dying or disappearing on Rachel's watch. She didn't think she could ever sleep again if even one more passed into the shadows.

"Where are they?" Jeremy murmured.

As Rachel looked around, the trailers seemed silent and still. None of the Wises were twitching about the perimeter—no gunfire exploded, no half-clothed children scampered across the burnt grass. No one moseyed out to greet them with goodies either, which meant they hadn't fooled anyone into thinking they were merely an average customer. Rachel's belly squirmed with what felt like a dozen snakes coiling tight.

"Something's not right," Rachel breathed out.

"No shit," Jeremy softly replied.

He parked the truck to the side of the dirt drive just before the circle of trailers began. If the Wises suddenly poured from their homes, Rachel and Jeremy would need some kind of cover. Then again, the Wises owned these woods. They could emerge from any direction with untold numbers of firearms. Cover from their fury was an illusion meant to soothe Jeremy's and Rachel's nerves, but both knew they were dead already if the family decided this was their last day.

The pair sat still for a few minutes, waiting for the family to make the first move, but the scene around them remained as still as it had been since they'd first arrived. The last time Rachel had laid eyes on the place, she'd been accompanied by state troopers and county police, and not one of them had parked before the Wises descended on their vehicles.

"What are you doing?" Jeremy's eyes grew wide as Rachel unbuckled her seat belt.

"What does it look like? I'm gonna go knock on the door."

"Uhhh, which death trap are you planning to start with?"

"The big one." She nodded toward the trailer at the head of the circle.

"You got a will ready, right?"

"Ha." She grabbed the door handle. "You gotta have something to give away to have a will. What do I look like to you?"

"An idiot." The color had drained from Jeremy's face as he stared at the double-wide trailer.

"Let's get this over with." Rachel swung open the truck door, fully expecting a firestorm of bullets and shrapnel to greet her. Nothing came, however. A silence had descended upon the Wises' property that was more jarring than the crack of gunfire.

Without another word, Rachel hopped out of the truck and marched toward the front door of the center trailer, doing her very best not to give any hint of anxiety—not to the Wises, and definitely not to Jeremy. Rachel leapt up the broken steps of the largest trailer in double time and pounded on the door.

"Police!" she shouted. "We just want to talk. We're not interested in arresting anyone today."

They wouldn't believe her. Hell, Rachel wouldn't either if she were in their shoes. She scanned the yard and surrounding trailers while listening intently for any sign of movement within the home. Jeremy reluctantly slid from the driver's side of his truck, his hand hovering over his holster. Rachel wanted to shout at him to move his damn fingers away from his weapon, but that would have only made things worse if the Wises were already spooked. Instead, Rachel clicked her tongue and rapped on the door again.

"This is Chief Kennan and Deputy Whitman. All we want to do is talk. I can get a warrant, but if you're smart, you won't make me do that. That'd end up going real poor for you folks; I can promise that."

She waited once more, her pulse throbbing in her ears with each passing second. Jeremy ambled to the bottom of the steps, still scanning the area as if a zombie horde could emerge at any moment.

"Rach, I don't think they're here."

"Of course they're here," Rachel grumbled. "You think they're going on family vacations? Christ." She pounded on the door again.

"Maybe we try a different trailer?" Her partner looked up at her, squinting from the bright sun overhead.

She suddenly heard shuffling inside the trailer beyond the door. Something metallic clinked and clattered to the ground, followed by the sound of hurried pounding. Her training told her to wait, to call for backup, to go obtain a warrant. After all, this wasn't a raid, and Rachel couldn't even point to clear evidence that the Wises were involved with her dead man or the missing children. Everything she'd ever been taught to do advised her to stand down, but in one foolish moment, she reared back and brought her boot crashing against the center of the flimsy trailer door. It crumpled on impact, the lock slipping from its latch as the door warped beyond repair.

"JESUS, RACH!" Jeremy howled and pulled his weapon to give her cover, ready for a showdown.

Beneath his alarm, however, Rachel heard a small yelp and more shuffling. A door on the far end of the trailer closed quietly. Without hesitation, Rachel stepped inside with her firearm raised and swinging in all directions. The dark trailer was littered with paraphernalia from spoons and lighters to pipes and needles. She was slapped with the smell of rotten eggs and swallowed hard against her gag reflex.

"I know you're here," Rachel called as she advanced into the trailer slowly. "All I'm asking for is ten minutes."

"Can you tell me the next time you're gonna do something so fucking dumb?" Jeremy hissed as he, too, stepped inside the front door.

Rachel ignored him and quietly moved toward the place she'd last heard rustling. Her vision narrowed in on the rear of the trailer and the small door, which she was certain had been closed moments before she'd stepped inside.

"We're not here to cause problems." Rachel knew that sounded like bullshit. No cop showed up at your front door and kicked it in unless they were looking for trouble. "Two kids are missing. One's only four years old. We just want to know if you've heard anything. The more you run from me, the more I start to think you had something to do with it."

Somewhere beyond the door, Rachel thought she heard stifled cries. She picked up her pace, Jeremy calling her name through clenched teeth. When she reached the door, she knew for certain someone was on the other side in distress. Soft, muffled sobs grew louder with each passing moment. Still, no one responded when she softly knocked on the door.

"Rachel!" Jeremy barked, no longer attempting to keep his voice quiet. "If they shoot through that fucking door—"

"I know you're in there," Rachel called. "Whatever is going on, I can help you."

"GO AWAY!" a girl shrieked in response.

Rachel threw a wild look at Jeremy, who stood frozen, unsure where to aim his gun. "We aren't here to cause problems. What's your name?" Her mind scanned through the Wise family tree. Each person who came to mind was more dangerous than the last, but older than this girl sounded. It was possible Rachel had never met this one, that this young woman had spent her entire life holed up on the property where her family kept her shielded from people like her.

"You don't have no reason for my name, bitch. Fuck off!"

That was precisely the kind of response Rachel expected from one of the Wises, but she wasn't sure what approach to take with one so young and unfamiliar. All the kid was doing was parroting what the rest of the Wises had told her her entire life.

Too soft a tone, and the kid might think her patronizing or weak. Too firm, and the girl might recoil and run. Instead, Rachel tried to keep her voice as neutral as possible. "Open the door so we can—"

"NO! Go away!" the girl screamed. "Get away from me!" Her sentence was punctuated by sobs that were no longer contained.

"Are you alone?"

The kid offered nothing but the sound of her despair. Rachel grabbed the flimsy brass doorknob and twisted, but the lock held. She let out a small huff.

Whispers in the Dark

"Kid, I can kick down this door a hell of a lot easier than I took out the front door. Don't make me trash this place. I don't want to do that." In truth, Rachel would have loved to burn the entire compound to the ground.

"No! Please no!" the girl shrieked. "Please don't break the doors. Please don't kill me."

Rachel looked to Jeremy, who shook his head uncertainly.

"Open up some of those drapes," she ordered Jeremy. "Throw some light in—"

"NO!" the girl howled. "Don't open the windows! They'll see me! They know I'm here."

"She's tripping out," Jeremy whispered.

"Fuck you, pig!"

"Why don't you open the door so we can talk?" Rachel called. "If someone is after you, we can help."

"Ain't no cop ever once helped me."

"Ain't no Wise ever asked," Jeremy retorted. At this, the girl fell back into her own despair, muttering to herself.

"I'm coming in," Rachel announced.

"Rach, don't," Jeremy protested, but by the time he did, Rachel had already kicked the knob off the door.

The girl inside the room shrieked louder as Rachel nudged open the door with her boot. Carefully, she holstered her gun and stepped inside the doorway with her hands high in the air, showing she wasn't out to harm anyone. The bedroom was tight and dark. The scent of cat urine stung her throat.

"I'm going to grab my flashlight from my belt, okay?" Rachel called, knowing better than to flick on the overhead light in a meth lab. "I am not reaching for my gun. I do not want to hurt you."

"Please go away," the girl sobbed.

When Rachel flicked on her Maglite and shone the beam across the room, it lit up a cluttered, filthy space filled with dirty laundry, mattresses propped against the walls, and dozens of overflowing trash bags scattered everywhere. In the far corner, tucked up tight against a wall, sat a teen barely older than Charlie. Dark, stringy hair hid most of her face as she hugged her knees.

"Careful," Jeremy whispered from behind as Rachel inched forward.

"What's your name?" she asked again softly. The girl shook her head and pressed her face further into her knees. "I'm—"

"I know who you are." The girl's voice turned sour. "You're the chief."

"Yeah," Rachel said softly. "You probably remember me—"

"—when you invaded our home with the rest of your fuckin' pigs," the girl spat.

"Where's your family?" Jeremy raised his voice from far behind Rachel. "We're not messin' around today. Little kids are missing, and we need to find them."

"They're not missing," the Wise girl whispered into her bare legs.

"Then where are they?"

"They're in the woods with the rest of them," the girl answered slowly. She shuddered. "All of them . . . they're gathering. They're getting ready to call us all in. They've been waiting."

"Christ. We don't have time for this bullshit." Jeremy rolled his eyes, standing in the doorway of the bedroom as Rachel crept closer to the girl. "Rach, she's high as a kite. You can't trust anything she's sayin'. The Wises are notorious for their colorful tales while trippin', which is pretty much all the time. Let's get out of—"

"I ain't crazy." The girl cut Jeremy's words short, her face still tucked into her knees. "I know what I's seen."

"Like your brother?" Rachel wagered. "Like Tommy?"

The girl stopped shivering and peeked her eyes out from behind her scrunched legs.

"Your brother, right?" Rachel continued as she crept closer.

The teen nodded slowly. "He was my bubba."

Jeremy shone his own light into the room from the doorway. "Where's Tommy hiding now?"

"Nowhere," the girl croaked. As Rachel crept closer, the girl tightened in on herself.

"His buddy said he was around just yesterday. They found that man out in the woods. Did he tell you about that?"

"That body don't mean nothin' now." The girl's hushed voice wavered somewhere between a laugh and a sob. "Just another dead man they's got tired of playin' with. But Tommy"—the Wise girl shifted suddenly, licking her lips with wide, panicked eyes as she tugged on her long hair—"Tommy shoulda run right then, right when he found 'em. He shoulda known the gates were open. That body wouldn't'a been there otherwise. No one . . . no one would've ever found that dead man 'less the door was open!"

"For fuck's sake." Jeremy groaned.

"Okay, okay," Rachel cooed as the girl edged closer to hyperventilating. "Tommy did eventually leave after finding the body, though? Right? Why?"

"They called, and he followed," she whispered, her dark eyes now meeting Rachel's. "Like everyone else."

"Your family . . . they followed Tommy?" Rachel crouched down a few feet in front of the girl who nodded slowly.

"Even the babies. My cousin . . . she carried her boy—he was only two—they went into them woods right after Tommy. She didn't even fight it. That's what them things do to people."

Rachel furrowed her brow. "What things?"

The Wise girl shook her head. "They always been around. You just weren't payin' attention. They slipped right past you and your piggies. Mama was the one keepin' everyone in this town safe—she knew. She knew this was a thin place . . . that they could break through here just like they's done elsewhere.

"But all y'all saw was white trash. That's all we've ever been to you. Now . . ." The girl's eyes suddenly turned dreamy as she swayed slightly on her sit bones. "You're all gon' die without us."

"Right. So, your whole family's up and gone now?" Jeremy huffed. "They just wandered off into them woods, never to be seen again 'cause they were called by angry leprechauns or some bullshit? That's what you're askin' us to believe?"

"Is your mom around? I'd like to talk to her, too." Rachel's thighs burned as she squatted, but she held firm, her gaze locked with the girl's who looked more feral than any wild animal she had ever seen.

The girl's bottom lip trembled before the rest of her face curled into mourning. "She followed, too, but before that, she knew ... She tied me here 'cause she knew long before they's started singing."

Rachel leaned back on her heels. Sure enough, a long, tangled rope was looped around the girl's waist, connecting her to the bedframe. "How long have you been tied up like this?"

"Last night," the girl gasped. "My mama loved me. She din't want me to follow her. She knew if I went into them woods, I'd be lost for good. There's nothin' they want more than the young'uns." Her voice dropped to a low whisper. "That's how it's always been. Wherever the door between this world and theirs is cracked, they take the little ones first. That's how they get stronger. That's why you gotta keep them happy ... or else." She ended with a bizarre squeak of laughter.

"They, them, their—who are you talking about?" Rachel blinked at the girl. "Who's in the woods?"

"Your boy." The girl's whisper turned into a hiss. "I seen him out there a long time now."

Rachel's face darkened and she sat back. "My son is dead," she stated flatly.

"Hasn't stopped him from wanderin' them woods with the others."

"Fuck this, Rach," Jeremy grumbled. "We ain't gettin' nowhere with this. Just junkie trash rattling off nonsense. If the Wises are creepin' all over the woods, we're bound to come across them."

"Yeah, that's what I'm afraid of." Rachel's eyes were still locked with the girl's. "Did your family tell you where they were going? Did they have anyone else with them? Maybe people who'd come here before looking to buy?"

"You're all so stupid you don't see it, but they sees you. They know everything, and now they're using your babies. They're stronger because of your girl."

Jeremy sighed heavily. "It's time to go, Rachel."

"My girl." Rachel raised her voice over Jeremy's. "You mean Charlie? Blonde, kinda scrawny . . . pink tips on her hair—she been around here?"

The Wise girl nodded slowly. "She's with them now. She was consumed."

Rachel scrunched her eyebrows together. "The fuck does that mean?"

"It doesn't mean anything because this kid's tripping balls right now," Jeremy growled. "We gotta go find the kids that can actually be saved, Rachel."

"How many times have you seen her? Charlie?"

The girl shrugged her shoulders. "Not many."

"But she's been here?" Rachel felt her heart sink simply asking the question.

"Her *and* your boy, too. He's always out there with them. Dancing . . . playing . . . singing. Mama left him more gifts than the rest. She felt bad for him, even if he weren't hisself no more."

"Okay." Rachel sniffed and steeled herself. "All right, your mama was leaving Aidan gifts in the woods—"

"Rach!" Jeremy scowled. "Are you kidding me?"

"Why was she doing that?" Once more, Rachel raised her voice over Jeremy's. Some part of her sensed she needed to keep asking questions.

"She been leaving 'em all gifts ever since she was a little girl," the kid whispered. "That's what you have to do to keep 'em happy . . . so's they don't take you or your babies for their own selves."

Rachel pressed her lips together, fighting the urge to smack the girl to her senses. "Doesn't seem to be working, does it?"

"It's 'cause Pastor Paul came up in here and started evangelizin'!" the teen screamed as rage flashed across her face. "He told Pa the ol' ways was wicked . . . that what Mama was doin' was the devil's work. An' Pa . . . he listened to that son o' bitch this time. He went right in them woods and smashed up everythin' Mama had left out. Then he told her she better not leave 'em nothin' else, or she's goin' to hell." The girl shook her head, eyes wide. "Mama tried to tell him, but he wouldn't listen this time. He don't know them the way Mama did."

Quiet hung in the air for a moment as Rachel stared the teenager down. "I'll ask you again, who are 'they'?"

"The Spirit Folk," the girl whispered, her eyes glittering in the darkness.

"Oh, for fuck's sake, Rachel!" Jeremy exploded. "Don't waste your time with this hillbilly mountain-magic bullshit."

"It ain't bullshit!" the teen shouted at him. "Just 'cause the rest o' you forgot the old ways—"

"Spirit Folk?" Rachel shook her head and pivoted to look at Jeremy. "Translation, please?"

Jeremy hesitated, shaking his head, but Rachel didn't miss the unease in his face. "She's goin' on about the same crap my great-gramma used to babble about: haints, boogers, unseelie—"

"Jeremy!" Rachel barked. "I don't know what the hell any of that means."

"Ain't everythin' easy to explain," the girl whispered and leaned toward Rachel though her eyes were trained on Jeremy. "But just 'cause you don't understand it don't mean you can ignore it."

"Shut it!" Jeremy ordered before continuing to Rachel. "Folks 'round here used to be a lot more superstitious and hung on to the garbage their people brought with them from whatever shithole country they came from. They were scared of the mountains and woods—"

"They weren't scared! They's respectful!" the girl screamed and writhed, pressing herself against the wall.

"—so they made up a bunch of stories about ghosts and monsters and faeries and—"

"It weren't made-up!"

"Shh!" Rachel held up a finger to silence the teen.

"To keep these stupid things happy, they left out a bunch of trash offerings and shit—marbles and cakes and dolls or whatever. Otherwise, the boogieman might come stomping through your door.

"Rach, these are the same people who piss in a jar and bury it to get rid of curses. It's nonsense and it's embarrassing. There's a reason people don't believe in that shit anymore, mostly 'cause it ain't real."

The girl laughed bitterly. "You're one dumb mother—"

"So, you're telling me ghosts in the woods are stealing children because they're pissed your mother stopped putting out Twinkies." Rachel turned back to glare at the kid.

"They ain't ghosts, and they ain't just hidin' in the mountains with the hillbillies," the girl murmured bitterly. "They're everywhere . . . right beneath the surface . . . waiting to push through. Here . . . we's just got a door. One day, they'll take the whole world."

Suddenly, her gaze shifted to Rachel and a strange fire burned inside her stare. "Wanna know what happened the last time Mama stopped givin' the Folk their dues?"

"Mothman swept down and snatched your dog?" Rachel scoffed.

The teenager broke out into a fit of giggles, but her expression turned vitriolic, setting Rachel on edge. "When you and your swine marched up in here and dragged everyone off to the county jail, there weren't no one here to keep 'em content. They ain't goin' stand for that. So's, they took what they wanted for themselves."

"Okay. We're done." Jeremy moved in and grabbed Rachel's forearm to pull her up.

"And what was it they wanted?" She resisted Jeremy's tug, her voice dipping low and warning, daring the girl to finish her tale.

"A little one." The teen smiled wide, her broken and rotting teeth visible through cracked lips. "Just so's happened your juiced-up old man was passin' through with your boy. Funny thing, ain't it? You're the reason Mama weren't around to leave them their dues, and they snagged your baby first. Seems fair to me."

"Fuck this." Jeremy yanked hard enough on Rachel's arm to knock her off balance. She stumbled to her feet and reluctantly allowed her deputy to pull her closer to the door as her blood boiled.

"You should run, Chief," the girl bellowed as she continued guffawing. "Get in your truck an' fly off back to the city where you belong 'fore you end up like that dead man my bubba found. Forget your girl, your boy. You ain't never gettin' them back. Run. Go run, little piggy!"

Rachel tore her arm from Jeremy's grip to stand firm. "Your folks responsible for that hiker in the woods?"

"Not *my* folks." The teen's broad blackened smile remained. "The Spirit Folk. I done told you already."

"Right." Rachel nodded, hands now planted firmly on her hips. "How could I forget?"

She chewed on her lip and began to walk away, but as she did, Rachel caught sight of where the girl's mother had looped the rope around the metal bedframe. She knelt down and jerked the long, fraying tether loose before tossing it into the girl's lap.

"Have a good evening." Rachel grunted and followed in Jeremy's footsteps.

"What? No!" the Wise girl shrieked. "Come back! Put it back like Mama tied it!"

The girl continued to wail as Rachel stormed out of the home-turned-lab and through the front door into the sunshine. Even as she jogged down the steps and across the yard to Jeremy's truck, Rachel could hear the teen's unearthly howls.

"What was that about the Wises being useful?" Jeremy jammed his dark sunglasses on as Rachel tore open the passenger-side door.

"She *was* useful." She drew a deep breath and climbed into the passenger seat. "Drop me off at the station, then get your ass back over to the search party and help Marcus figure out how to do his job."

"And where are you going?"

"I'm headed to the middle school," Rachel said lightly.

"Oh, come on, Rach." Jeremy threw the truck in reverse. "You can't possibly think what that trash kid said about Charlie was true. Ain't no way Charlie's been coming up here to buy the Wises' shit. You'd have been onto her the moment she tried it."

Rachel folded her hands together and squeezed to stop them from shaking. "I could've missed it."

"Okay, but think about what that little psycho said about Aidan." He shifted in his seat, clearly uncomfortable bringing up the subject even if he felt it was necessary. "Playing in the trees for the past year. Getting . . ." He sighed and squirmed in his seat before continuing. "Getting stolen by fuckin' . . . hobgoblins or whatever. That girl's fucked in the head!"

"In every lie, there's a kernel of truth," Rachel said, "and this is the second time today someone's connected the dots between Charlie and that family." She gazed at the trees rolling by as the truck bumped along the broken road from the Wises' compound.

"Should've known Finn would let the whole world go to hell."

Twenty-Four

Charlie rode to the station with a dazed smile on her face, peering out the window with wondrous glee as trees whizzed by. Rachel thought it was best not to start in on her daughter in the car; she wanted to look her right in the face when she pressed her about Kendall. Though Charlie had always been headstrong, Rachel knew her like the back of her own hand. There hadn't been a single instance where Rachel had not caught Charlie when she was telling a falsehood, and it wasn't because Charlie was a bad liar. Rachel could read it in the girl's expression—the twitch of her lips, the way her head cocked to the side, how her eyes grew wide with unjustified indignation.

"I want to thank you for picking me up from school so early, Mother," Charlie spoke dreamily. "I've been eager to talk with you."

Rachel glanced over at her daughter and resisted the urge to smack the high right out of her.

Moments later, Rachel led the way to the station's sad excuse for an interrogation room. She ushered Charlie in with a wave of her hand and closed the door behind them. Her daughter sat lightly down on the wooden chair closest to the door.

Rachel sat across from her. "All right, Charlie. I need your help."

"Anything for you, Chief," Charlie replied airily.

Whispers in the Dark

Rachel felt a growing unease as she watched her daughter's typically rigid body move in long, graceful motions. By now, she expected Charlie to have her arms crossed tightly, leaning back against the chair with a wicked glare in her blue eyes. This time, however, Charlie sat inclined toward her, hands folded neatly in her lap. And she wore the same serene expression, capped with a pleasant smile that welcomed her mother to continue. Rachel sniffed and laid out a notepad on the table, clicking her pen several times before writing down the date.

"Why are you anxious?" Charlie asked in an airy tone.

"I'm not anxious."

"Yes, you are. You always do that when you're anxious, clicking your pen like that." Her daughter let out a tiny giggle.

Rachel sat back in her chair. Meth made its victims jittery, eager to talk, nervous, delusional. What she had never seen a single addict display was superior serenity. Charlie's behavior should have made Rachel breathe easy, if for no other reason than the stark contrast between her child's current state and that of the dozens of druggies she'd questioned thanks to the Wises. It didn't. Instead, Rachel felt sudden, intense anger—maybe even fear—boiling within her. Perhaps she wasn't currently high on methamphetamine, but something was warping her brain bad enough to transform her into a complete stranger.

Rachel sucked her teeth before proceeding. "Where were you yesterday?"

"I was at school with the other children."

Rachel narrowed her eyes and plastered on an unfriendly smile. "Then what?"

"Father picked me up early—10:06 a.m., to be precise."

"Great, 10:06." Rachel wrote it down and underlined it sharply, not because it was helpful, but because she thought she might soon need to do something with her hands. "What did you do the rest of the day?"

"From 10:17 to 12:22, I sat in my bedroom and listened to music," Charlie began in a fast-paced but formal cadence. "Then, I began receiving text messages from my friends. We made plans to meet following school hours."

"Which friends?"

"Mother!" Charlie laughed too heartily. "You know the three. Thanks to you and Father, no one else—"

"What happened after they got out of school?" Rachel tilted her head, cutting off the nonsense that made her want to grab her child by the throat.

"I proceeded downstairs and discussed going to visit them with Father Finn. He initially did not agree. However, Father had been smoking cigarettes out on the porch earlier that morning when he thought no one would see."

Rachel arched her eyebrow and blinked several times over as Charlie continued, seemingly unfazed by her confessions.

"I, however, am very observant and determined he had been smoking cigarettes by locating the discarded butt, which he had carelessly flung into the yard below the porch. When I informed him of what I had discovered, Father allowed me to leave the house to visit my friends with the understanding that I should return home before dinner or before you, dearest Mother, indicated you would be returning yourself."

"So, you blackmailed your dad?" Rachel shifted in her chair, trying her best not to explode.

"Correct," Charlie continued, her body now awkward and stiff despite the flowery ease with which she spoke. "It's not terribly hard to do when he's petrified of a confrontation with you, Mother."

Rachel opened her mouth to respond, but before she could get a word in, Charlie pushed forward, talking louder and faster. "Following that exchange, I went to the home of Gemma Thompson, where I met Sarah Anderson and Kendall Moreland for a stroll in the woods to our secret place where we shared cannabis. My friends and I parted ways not long thereafter. I returned home at 5:47 in the evening and felt quite ill. Father helped me wash and put me to bed. Are there other details I may provide you, Mother?" Charlie fell silent as suddenly as she had begun, still smiling at Rachel, though an odd staccato twitch rippled across her shoulders.

That classic twitch was enough to renew her suspicion that Charlie was indeed on some new supersonic concoction the Wises had cooked up. Maybe the novel substance didn't produce quite the same familiar side effects, but it sure as hell twisted the user up. If the Wises' new product could turn Charlie into this ridiculous imitation of a proper lady, it could drive anyone toward madness.

Suddenly, a bizarre sense of relief and satisfaction washed over Rachel. She was vindicated, she was right, she had the key to unlocking the case—an explanation for all the horrific bullshit that had transpired over the past day. Control was safely clenched in her hands once more even if the mother in her was wailing for her baby's future. But Charlie would be okay now that Rachel had answers; she was certain.

"You're telling me you went to visit your friends so you could smoke weed?" Rachel picked the pen back up and tapped it against the notepad.

"That's correct." Charlie's odd smile remained in place.

"Right ... just some weed." Rachel smirked before taking a deep inhale. "And your dad allowed you to go because you found out he smoked a cigarette?"

"You're really put out with him, aren't you?" Charlie's smile grew into a wide, nasty grin that swallowed half her pale face. "You think he fell off the wagon, don't you? Maybe he was never fully on the wagon to begin with. That therapist was supposed to help him with his daddy issues, too, but it appears that famous Kennan temper stuck around, no?"

The deep unease that had been plaguing Rachel since they entered the station returned in full force. It was time to redirect.

"Where did Kendall go, Charlie?" Rachel leaned forward and assumed the sincere, wide-eyed stare that had convinced so many others she was simply there to help.

"Into the woods with the rest of us." She spread her arms far out on the tabletop and rested them there, leaning in toward Rachel with a serious expression as if mimicking her mother's well-practiced interrogation pose. Something strange flickered in her daughter's eyes—mischievous, menacing, even outright sinister.

"I mean after that. I stopped by her place earlier, and it looked like she'd had a little too much fun last night, same as you, except—"

Charlie broke into a quiet giggle, her nose scrunched and eyes closed.

"You think this is funny, Charlie?" Rachel set her pen down. "Your best friend is missing."

"She's not missing." Charlie sighed and opened her eyes again, reassuming her tranquil facade. "The Wise girl told you that already."

Rachel dug her pinkie nail underneath her thumb's to dig at the quick. Who did she know that would have also talked to the Wise girl since Rachel's visit?

Whatever Charlie was on was fast draining Rachel's composure. Enough was enough. "You know, I'm really glad you brought the Wises up. How about you tell me how long they've been supplying you?"

"Supplying me?" Charlie blinked and tilted her head a little too far to the right to be natural.

"With whatever you're hopped up on right now." Rachel used her pen to gesture a circle around Charlie's body. "C'mon, Charlie. You're damn near floating on the ceiling you're so high."

Her daughter burst into full-on belly laughter at this and bent forward to touch her forehead to the table for a moment. "Mother!" she exclaimed as she rose back up and flipped her long hair over her shoulder. "I don't do drugs! Well, except for the little indiscretion the other night, but otherwise . . . Ohhh."

Her bluebell eyes sparkled. "I see the look on your face, Chief Kennan. You don't believe your suspect."

"Yeah, I think you're full of shit, Charlotte." Rachel smiled, her chest tightening.

"Uh-oh ... you only use 'Charlotte' when you're very, very serious."

Suddenly, Rachel wanted to squirm under her daughter's gaze, though she couldn't explain why. She'd sat on the other side of the table from no less than twenty-seven murderers—probably more. Then again, none of those people had been her child. There was something about Charlie's eyes, though ... This was more than a bad high, more than conceit and provocation. A stray, wild thought suddenly raced through Rachel's mind—*Those are not Charlie's eyes*—but she quickly dismissed the ludicrous idea.

"Let's play truth or dare!" Charlie suddenly pounded her palms on the table, her face glowing with excitement.

"I don't do dares, Charlie."

"Oh, but I love this game!" Charlie whined and her shoulders dropped dramatically. "At least play truth! You love the truth, Chief." Her eyes flashed. "Ask me anything you want, and I must be honest with you. Then we switch. Let's play!"

She brought her hands down on the table again and she dragged her fingertips along its surface slowly until they reached the table's edge and hovered in the air. The wicked smirk tugged at the corners of her mouth, her lips oddly trembling at the same time.

"All right, Charlie." Rachel's jaw tightened. "Tell me where Kendall is."

Whispers in the Dark

"Kendall is nowhere." Charlie sat and stared at Rachel for a moment before breaking into a low, incredulous laugh. "Why'd you waste a question on something you already knew? My turn!"

"If you want me to play, you have to be honest with me." Rachel's face felt flushed as her daughter grinned from the criminal's side of the table. This was not her Charlie.

"I'm glad you agree to the rules! My turn!" She shot forward and pounded the table with her palms harder than before. The motion sent Rachel's pen bouncing into the air. "Do you ever miss her?"

Rachel furrowed her brow and searched Charlie's jovial face. "Who?"

"Michelle! You know! Or wait, was her name Melissa? Macie? Millie? No, you'd never go for a Millie. It was definitely Michelle. You called her 'Chelle,' right? That was cute."

Rachel grew rigid, her face turning to stone against Charlie's delight. She cleared her throat and tapped her boot's steel toe against the cement floor. "I don't know what you're talking about."

"Nah-uh." Charlie held up her pointer finger. "You're not playing the game fair, Mother!" Rachel considered ending the conversation then and there before locking her kid inside the room for a few hours to ride out this absurd high. "I asked you if you *missed* her. Do you ever miss Michelle?"

"No," Rachel snapped. "Tell me about nowhere. You say Kendall's there—"

"You didn't ask a question," Charlie whispered happily, her head tilted down. "And I don't think you're being entirely honest."

"Where can I find Abby Grayson?"

"You can't," Charlie said simply before continuing. "Do you miss *any* of them? Michelle was probably a poor example; there's a lot of negative emotion surrounding her, isn't there? She's the only one who's ever walked away from you. The rest of your ladies . . . you've enjoyed being the one to leave them jilted and alone. Michelle, on the other hand—hot damn, she bolted for the nearest holy man she could find."

"Did your dad tell you all this?" Rachel could feel her breath quickening, fingers itching to grab something and throttle it. If Finn had known about Michelle, he would have been the first to use it as a weapon. Still, Rachel couldn't think of any other way Charlie could have possibly learned about the illicit affair, the memory of which continued to sock Rachel right in the chest. This was perhaps the stealthiest and most effective tactic that son of a bitch had ever used.

"It's my turn to ask a question, Mother!" Charlie exploded, and for a moment, Rachel could've sworn there was actual fire in the girl's eyes. "And you didn't answer! There were lots of women before Father found you in that hotel. Do you ever miss *any* of them?"

"No," Rachel replied flatly as she shut down the bits of her that still smarted from Michelle's betrayal. "What do you mean when you say I can't find Kendall and Abby? I want a straight, plain English answer from you. Cut the cute bullshit."

"Well, the very plain response is that you simply cannot locate them because you are utterly unequipped to find them. They are Nowhere, and you are somewhere. The two most often do not intersect." Charlie blinked as the words tumbled from her quickly. "Do you think Father should have expected it from you? Your behavior?"

"Are you claiming Kendall and Abby are in another dimension or some shit, Charlie? Jesus Christ, when did you start using?" Rachel's forehead creased as reality hit her like a ton of bricks. She truly hadn't seen this coming, not even from Charlie. The line Rachel had given a dozen parents before was indeed true—you never thought it'd be your kid until it is. "Why would you screw with your future like this? You wanna stay strung out in Dahlmouth forever?"

"You're asking too many questions, and that's not how you play the game!" Charlie's balled-up fist hit the table, sending a rattle through the top down to the table's legs.

Rachel, however, remained still and quiet as she retreated behind the mental walls she'd long ago built to protect herself.

"I asked, do you think my father should have expected you would fall back into your slimy ways?" Charlie's chest rose and fell at an unnatural speed.

Rachel began tapping at the table with her pen once more. "You're saying being gay is slimy, Charlie?" Rachel raised her eyebrows. "Pastor Paul and his groupies have gotten into your head more than I real—"

"Not the queer part—I'm referring to your lying, your whoring, your infidelity. I have to say, *I* think he should have seen it coming." Charlie raised her finger in the air again and wiggled it with a song in her voice. "After all, you ran out on your girlfriend with him."

Rachel tried to refocus on the topic at hand—the whole damn reason she'd dragged her daughter from school to an interrogation room. She returned to the fanciful pieces of information Charlie had given. Warped as the answers were, Rachel's gut told her there was something to the idea of "nowhere." Thoughts of a basement or a cellar where Abby's and Kendall's bodies could be stored lingered in the back of her mind. Perhaps *nowhere* was the trunk of some stranger's car, or worse, a bedroom one of the Wise boys carried them to. Charlie had seen something, even if her drug-addled brain couldn't make sense of it.

"Tell me more about this 'nowhere' place you keep referring to. Is this something you saw while you were with the Wises?"

"You didn't answer my question, and I have answered every one of yours!" The smile on Charlie's face gave way to gnashing teeth and wide eyes as her pupils dilated. "This isn't how you play the game. Do you think Father—"

"Yes, I think he should have seen it coming," Rachel answered quickly. "Now, answer my question. How exactly do I find this place?"

Charlie's breathing was still too fast. Her chest puffed in and out, little gasps escaping with each exhale. Rachel would not be moved, however. Charlie could have thrown herself down onto the floor and cracked open her head at this point, and Rachel would have suspected it was for show.

"Nowhere finds you," Charlie spoke softly between gasps. "My turn. How much do you love Lucy?" The teen's chin tilted lower, her stare more menacing than before.

Rachel folded her arms against herself. "I love her—and you—with all my heart. You both mean everything to me."

"But not as much as Aidan did."

"It's my turn to ask a question, right?"

"It wasn't a question. You loved Aidan more than Charlie or Lucy. He meant more." Charlie's breathing slowed, but her eyes glossed over. Her voice dropped as her words became more vitriolic. "You didn't even want Charlie. You never wanted to be a wife or a mother. You were just sick of your girlfriend and how clingy she'd become.

"But it makes sense she was insecure, doesn't it? Because, in reality, you were getting hammered after work and screwing that annoying goddamn reporter who seemed to pop up at every crime scene. What a novel game that was . . . until Finn knocked you up. Whoops."

Rachel clenched her fists under the table, swallowing against the now nearly unbearable urge to clock her child. That blow needed to be properly redirected at Finn. He had really outdone himself this time.

"Was Kendall the one who got you mixed up with the Wises?" It was the first question Rachel could pull out from her fog of rage, and she knew before she asked that it was a useless question.

"No. How do you feel about Finn? Do you love him?" Charlie pressed, face locked in the same unmoving, threatening expression it had been for several minutes.

"Those are two separate questions."

"Now who's being cute?"

"I *feel* like he should hang for what he did, but the answer to your second question is yes, I love your dad." Rachel let out a long exhale. "If Nowhere finds you, how did Kendall and Abby get there? Who made them go to this place?"

Suddenly, the teen's shoulders drooped lower, and Charlie lolled forward. "They don't have names anymore."

Charlie seemed to be slipping away, the color in her face melting down inside her. Even her usually bright irises became dull like someone had switched off the light behind them. Charlie looked like a withered rose—thinner than ever, her spine curling in on itself as her eyelids fluttered.

"You're coming down, Charlie," Rachel murmured. "You're crash-landing from whatever nasty shit the Wises gave you. But you can still tell me what you've been doing with Kendall . . . what happened to her. You know I'll find out eventually anyways."

"Mother, dear." Charlie barely managed to shake her head while shivering. "You don't have that kind of time."

"Rach?" Jeremy knocked and opened the fishbowl door. "You ready to head back to the Oldridge farm? Could use some backup with the search party. There's a hell of a lot of people startin' to join in. Folks are spooked."

"They have no idea," Charlie whispered softly.

Rachel cast a long, cold stare over Charlie before looking up at Jeremy. "I'm coming. Hey, is Lou hanging around?"

"Nah, I left him and Marcus with the volunteers. I just stopped by to grab more of the tagging flags. Zeke's here, though. Fucker just woke up." Jeremy winced and covered his mouth for a second as he looked at Charlie. "Sorry. He just woke up and decided he'd come in to work for a change."

"How kind of him." Rachel smiled. "Can you ask him to keep an eye on Charlie here? She needs to sleep off a nasty high and think about what she'd like to pack for military school. Perhaps she can also notify her daddy he's gonna die once I finally make it home."

"Yikes. Poor bastard." Rachel shot Jeremy a glare. "I'll let Zeke know."

"Thanks." Her deputy stepped out. Then Rachel brought her eyes back level with Charlie's. "We're not done talking about this, you know."

Charlie's eyes were fixed on the wall behind Rachel as the girl's pupils appeared to pulse. The teen opened and closed her dry mouth, reminding Rachel of a fish out of water. Charlie abruptly paused this bizarre motion, her mouth yawning wide until the smallest string of spittle trickled from between her lips. She then snapped her jaw shut and sunk lower in the hard seat. Her whole body seemed slack now, and Rachel anticipated her daughter would soon take an impromptu nap on the tabletop.

"Try to rest, dear." Rachel stood up abruptly and marched toward the door. "I'll see you real soon."

"You surely will," Charlie whispered after the chief.

Twenty-Five

Lucy sobbed from the time Finn carried her out of Mrs. Stockton's office to when he laid her down in her rose-colored four-poster bed. There was nothing Finn could do or say to interrupt her heart-wrenching wails. It was as though Lucy was lost in mourning. And Finn thought maybe she was—maybe she had finally broken over Aidan; maybe they all were breaking at the exact same time. Nevertheless, he couldn't let her go on like that, so Finn lay beside his little girl, cracking jokes and putting on a play with Lucy's stuffed animals until they both quieted and fell asleep.

When Finn woke up, his shirt was plastered to him with cold sweat and tears and drool. He blinked to clear the hazy sleep from his eyes and saw that Lucy had rolled away from his chest to snuggle with her oversized tiger ("Striper," not to be confused with other similar titles, no matter how many times Lucy spelled it incorrectly). Finn leaned over to look at her sleeping face and found it peaceful, bathed in the waning rays of sunlight that shone between her curtains, a string of spit connecting her lips to the pillow beneath her.

Despite the sun and the heat radiating off Lucy, Finn shivered in his damp T-shirt. He slipped from her bed as quiet as could be, placing his feet down one at a time. She didn't so much as move a finger. He headed toward Rachel's bedroom to grab a fresh shirt from the drawers. As he passed Aidan's room, he saw Rachel had left the door open. When he grabbed the door handle, he spied the twisted doll's body, still staring out the window toward the trees. Finn tried not to slam the door, reminding himself of Lucy and her much-needed rest.

Despite her constant insistence otherwise, Rachel had evidently been able to take off enough time to rearrange her bedroom furniture that afternoon. Now, the bed and the nightstands faced the window, taking in the same view as Lucy's desecrated doll next door. Finn squirmed slightly at the reorientation. How Rachel could think such an arrangement would be comforting after finding that fucking doll was beyond Finn. Then again, he didn't understand most of what his wife did anymore.

The little ashtray that played host to his class ring, a Fitbit he never wore, and his dad's old wedding band were gone. A couple of drawers later, he confirmed his shirts and pants had been removed also, and it all made sense. This was what Rachel must have needed to do to cleanse the room of him completely, no matter how bizarre it seemed. Like they had agreed, the kids knew, so what was the point in pretending anymore?

Finn's eyes fell on the bed for a moment and lingered. The night they had locked horns in Roanoke, Rachel had walked away bruised and scratched up and sore from the inside out, but evidently happier than she had been in years. Finn, however, had left the hotel room and sobbed in the car for an hour. It wasn't until the drive home that he realized she had *wanted* him to catch her, that she *intended* for him to lose it when he did. It wasn't about her falling in love with someone else or even reclaiming her identity in the face of trauma. Finn was sure Rachel had fucked around to spite him and had left a trail of clues for him to follow. She wanted to push him over the edge. Still, Finn routinely tore himself to shreds for what he had done, for the monster he had turned into that night.

He almost hadn't stopped. Finn only ever admitted that once in a solo therapy session. The screaming between them had turned to bashing and scratching, which later turned to shrieking and biting, which then gave way to the rattle of Rachel's labored breath and the feeling of the fight leaving her body as he gripped her by the throat. In that moment, for the first time, Finn made a genuine connection with his father—instantly understanding, even sympathizing with the rage behind putting a harpy in her place. That was when he let go. Yet, the damage had already been done.

Finn had become something he never thought he would be, and because of it, he still averted his own gaze when he looked in the mirror. There was no doubt in his mind now that he was capable of doing horrific things just as grotesque and traumatizing as his sperm donor had. Worse still, Finn couldn't shake the thought that he'd *always* been like his father; the alcohol had simply kept the beast lurking within at bay. Next time, maybe he wouldn't let go of her. Perhaps he would choke the life out of Rachel, climb out of their wrecked bed, and put a pistol in his mouth.

Finn whirled around on his feet, trying to shake away the images of that night. He jogged out of Rachel's bedroom and past Aidan's door to whip around the banister and slip downstairs.

His eyes glossed over his son's door cracked open ever so slightly in its frame.

His socks slid on the slick wooden floor at the bottom of the steps, but Finn skated along with it toward the basement door. He wasn't going to get a lawyer. Rachel knew that was a bullshit line. That didn't mean he couldn't move out, though, maybe even with the kids, or at least with the kids most of the time. Finn had to figure out how to get the money to afford an apartment first. That likely meant moving on over to fucking Roanoke and taking a job that had nothing whatsoever to do with writing. Could he do it? Finn liked to think he could but knew somewhere deep down that playing with anything other than the written word would eventually kill him. He scratched his head as the ideas raced, speeding up his steps even faster so he could get back to Luce before she could stir.

A chirp came through the bluetooth speaker on the kitchen counter as Finn passed through, too soft to be intelligible but loud enough to catch his attention. He continued toward the basement door, his hand extended for the knob, when music roared into the air, boxing Finn right in the ears. In a knee-jerk reaction, Finn bent over and covered his ears before he looked around to find the source of his problems. But the kitchen was as empty as it had been before.

"Off," Finn commanded the pod loudly over the din. If Lucy didn't wake up to this, she could sleep through a hurricane. "OFF!" he yelled in a firm tone.

But if anything, the volume went higher, and though his ears had been clamped off, he could still hear an all-too-familiar melody rising to greet him.

"I once had a girl, or should I say, she once had me?"

Finn hated "Norwegian Wood" with a special kind of passion. He couldn't hear the damn song without seeing Rachel, drunk to the point of abandon, dancing barefoot along Richmond's riverfront in the dark, singing the song with everything she had. From that night forward, Rachel had him, her claws dug straight into his soul. He used to hum the song to Charlie when she was a baby; it was only fitting since they made her the night Rachel had been lost in this particular song. Now, the sound made him want to smash someone's nose in.

"OFF!" Finn barked.

The music didn't end, but the song changed without any transition right into a chorus he knew so very well:

"Oh, baby, baby, it's a wild world. It's hard to get by just upon a smile—"

Yeah, he'd screamed that one during the drive back from Roanoke, turning it into some kind of teary-eyed, pathetic, thrashing metal ditty over and over again.

"OFF! What the fuck?" Finn dropped his hands from his ears and started to march over to the pod when the song clicked yet again and dove headfirst into another melody.

"Now you don't talk so loud . . . Now you don't seem so proud . . ."

"All right, you piece of shit." Finn charged at the pod, took hold of the base, and yanked it as hard as he could, popping the cord out of the back. It kept on playing, smoothly transitioning to battery power to mock him.

"How does it feel? To be on your own . . ."

Whispers in the Dark

He flipped over the pod and tried to pull at the battery door, only to find that it was screwed in tight with one of those damn micro-screws he'd never be able to find a screwdriver to fit.

"Fuck me," Finn groaned, considering his options with increasing panic.

And still, the song played on.

There wasn't a damn thing Finn could do to fend off the sound of the skidding tires and crunching metal; Lucy's terrified wails; the ungodly silence that ushered forth from his son as his nose dipped beneath the water; then Finn's own sickening, useless cries into the darkness as he clawed through glass and metal to reach Aidan before the river killed them both; and this goddamn song serenading them all, fast becoming the soundtrack to Finn's worst nightmare as the engine drowned.

Finn closed his eyes and hit himself in the forehead with the pod several times, desperately trying to knock the noise out of his head. But the sounds would not die. They only grew louder with every rise and fall of his chest.

As the bridge of the song began, Finn brought the pod down onto the counter with both hands and felt the base pop in with the blow. He kept bashing the disobedient robot into pieces. Again and again, Finn smashed the cylinder against the faux-granite countertop, chunks of plastic cracking off and flying in all directions.

But the music didn't stop—it didn't even falter—and the sounds of the crash grew louder all around him in surround sound. Finn clawed at the mesh covering the speakers to rip the wires out of the interior. It was then that Finn realized the screeching, crushing, wailing, and worthless blubbering wasn't rolling around inside his head. It had fused with the music blasting out of the stereo.

"SHUT UP!" Finn shrieked as he crashed the speakers into the counter over and over.

When the stereo screen had caved in, and the music still had not ceased, a kind of madness swept over Finn. He dropped the device onto the counter and went headlong for the closet door in the hallway, rummaging around in the bottom to find the small tool kit they kept there. Finn returned with a hammer and began bashing the already smashed pod. Sharp plastic, pieces of wire, shards of the inner workings of the stereo all went flying into the air as he hammered it into oblivion.

Finn wasn't sure how long he'd been smashing when the noise finally died down, little more than a hum coming from the singular speaker piece miraculously left intact. He gasped for air, but held the hammer tight, ready for whatever might come out of the fucking heap of garbage next.

A haunting melody then reached Finn's ears, soft and steady, one he only vaguely knew this time. Teeth on edge, he realized it wasn't coming from the deformed pod, but from somewhere upstairs.

"Go to sleep, you little baby . . . your mama's gone away and your daddy's gonna stay . . ."

Finn's skin prickled, hair standing at attention up and down his forearms. He knew the singer's sweet voice like it was his own.

"Gonna need another lovin' baby . . ."

He gripped the hammer tighter and slowly drifted away from the wreckage of the speaker, through the kitchen and toward the staircase. Finn stood at the base of the steps, looking up and waiting for Lucy to cry out.

"Charlie," Finn called up, struggling to make his voice stern, "when did you get home, honey?" He bent to lay the hammer on the bottom step. "Your sister isn't feeling well. I think you should come down here to let her sleep."

Finn stood at the stairs and waited to hear Charlie's footsteps or Lucy calling for him, but neither noise made its way down the steps.

"Charlie!" His heart caught in his throat because, despite all the logical things he knew, something inside him screamed it was already too late to do anything but cry.

Finn bounded up the stairs two at a time until he landed at the top. The hair on his arms stood up as he looked around, head swiveling from Charlie's open bedroom door all the way around to Rachel's. Nothing was out of place except for Aidan's door.

Something pulled on him, demanding he make his way toward that room, but every cell in Finn's body resisted. The end was in that room; Finn was certain of it. Whatever awaited him there was the last thing he would ever be able to take.

"Charlie," Finn called out, his voice cracking on the second syllable. "Lucy, baby?"

Bright light beamed through Aidan's room. The same kind of ethereal light that glowed in Lucy's hair and illuminated the few short years Aidan had walked the earth radiated through the window.

When he came to the doorway, Finn saw the room had become more crowded than before, and his knees buckled. A tiny, cheap hunk of plastic with wiry blonde curls lay beside the first mutilated doll. No longer was the hellish imposter of his son curled at odd angles. Instead, it and this new baby doll were perfectly straight and parallel, laid out for burial with their arms flat at the sides of their bodies.

It was the baby doll Lucy had received from a nurse when she was discharged from the hospital after the accident. Lucy named the thing Caitlin, hugged it to her chest on the ride home, then threw it into the back of her closet and never touched it again. But here it was, lying in repose next to the wrecked body of another doll Lucy had once loved. Just like its mate, the baby doll's eyes had been hollowed out, the sunlight streaming through the windows setting the orange plastic around the empty sockets aglow.

"Lucy," Finn tried to call out, but his voice failed.

He distantly heard the front door open and close, but it took several more beats before Finn's feet would consent to move. When they did, Finn fell into the door on a clumsy spin. Righting himself once more, he charged into Lucy's bedroom. The sight of her empty bed didn't even surprise him. Still, Finn rushed forward and ripped the blankets and sheets from the mattress. He ducked down to his knees to peek under the bed and found only more dolls and stuffed animals staring back at him with empty eye sockets. One glance in the closet, and Finn began to acknowledge the terror consuming him was justified. It felt like someone was watching him.

"Lucy," he called out. "Daddy needs you to come out now."

A rustling from inside Rachel's room caught his attention, and he ran toward it, only to find that the rustling wasn't Lucy.

Rachel. She was sprawled out across the bed. Her head lolled to the side as Aidan's had, hazel eyes wide open and glassy. His wife was naked with nothing but a sheet haphazardly covering a thin strip of her thighs. Dark black-and-blue marks coiled around her neck. Finn didn't need to move closer to see that Rachel was gone, and he didn't need her accusing dead eyes to remind him of the villain he was. Her body was the evidence.

And then there was the creature sitting with his back to Finn. Or was it Finn who was sitting with his back to himself? His hair, his clothes, his poor posture, even—Finn couldn't deny the man's identity.

This was what insanity looked like. After years of claiming he was going there, Finn had finally arrived. The mirror image of himself was holding something in his lap, bouncing his leg up and down. Whatever it was, Finn most definitely would not stick around to see it. He wanted to leave immediately and run as fast as he could until he made it home to DC. That's what he should have done years ago: taken the kids and ran like hell back to his mother and where he grew up. It was too late now. Finn remained anchored to the spot, with only his hands free to grip the edges of the doorway.

Finn opened his mouth to speak but couldn't force out sound. The man on the bed suddenly seemed to realize that he, too, was being watched. Finn stared in frozen horror as his unwelcome reflection swiveled slowly on the bed to face him. This copycat may have appropriated Finn's body, but there was nothing left of

Finn in his eyes. They were vacant despite the familiar gray color and an unearthly reflective glow.

The thing cocked its head and reviewed Finn for several moments. Goosebumps sprang up and down his arms. Now more than ever, he had to get out. Lucy needed him, and he needed her. He knew his fight-or-flight instincts should have kicked into gear by now. Indeed, his brain had sent white-hot panic coursing through every muscle in his extremities. His body, however, would simply not respond.

The other Finn slowly brought forward what he had been cradling in his lap. The barrel of the .22-caliber pistol shimmered in the long shadows the late afternoon cast.

"You're not real." Finn was finally permitted to speak. "And I didn't kill my wife."

But the thing before him didn't care to argue back. Instead, this unnatural version of himself opened his mouth wide and began to shove the gun far into the back of his throat. Beads of sweat emerged on Finn's neck, chest, and underarms. Their eyes locked, and Finn felt a cold numbness sweep through his body from head to toe. His vision began to narrow into a tight tunnel with this creature as the focal point. A swirl of screams encircled him. From Rachel's barrages of insults to his own pathetic wails of despair—every miserable sound amped up to 120 decibels and drowned out any lingering thoughts Finn had to hold on to his own sanity. He could feel his finger on the trigger of the Glock as if he and this creature shared the same hand.

Suddenly, a small flicker of movement outside the window wrenched Finn's eyes out of the deadlock stare. Charlie wore a strange white dress he'd never once seen her wear. Lucy flopped in her sister's arms, the fabric of her princess dress shimmering in the sunlight. It was only a moment before the image of his daughter approaching the forest edge disappeared from view, but the brief sighting had been enough.

"Luce," Finn gasped and fell away from the door.

The eyes of the wrong version of him grew wide as the pupils expanded to push the gray from his irises. Soon, an uninterrupted pool of black consumed the thing's eyes entirely. Its lips widened beyond the range of any human mouth as it swallowed the barrel of the gun. But it was too late. Finn was already in motion.

As Finn took off for the stairs, he realized he'd been gripping the handle of Rachel's pistol. He shivered and dropped the weapon on the steps as he flew downward.

Finn ran full speed into the kitchen. The back door was his quickest route to intercepting that critical flicker that had jarred him free from the cruelty of his own mind. Lucy was there. She was right there. All Finn had to do was pick up the pace, and she would be safe in his arms once more. It didn't matter what else waited for him at the edge of those woods, so long as Lucy was there, too.

With the door in sight, Finn raced faster. His foot caught on the edge of tangled plastic, and he faltered, corrected. He tried to kick off the Hot Wheels racetrack that hadn't left Aidan's room since his son had passed. Finn crashed against the kitchen counter, cursing and ripping the twisted plastic from around his ankles. His eyes then lifted to the counter where he had smashed apart his smart radio only minutes before.

There, instead of the broken radio, lay Rachel's pistol once more, a clip loaded and the safety off. It was waiting for him ever so patiently. Finn pushed himself away from the counter with disgust. His job wasn't done yet. No matter what anyone thought of him, Finn was not a quitter, at least not when there was any ray of hope still glimmering.

But there isn't any hope left.

"Shut up!" Finn screeched at the voice inside his mind. He hit himself in the forehead with the palm of his hand frantically.

Lucy's gone, and they're going to say it was your fault.

Finn let out a howl and bent over, squeezing his eyes shut and trying to sort through his racing thoughts.

And it is *your fault, just like last time. You left her alone. She told you they were coming.*

"FUCK YOU!" he shrieked. He couldn't reorient himself. The kitchen, the gun, the voice echoing in his head dominated.

Take the gun and put it to your temple.

"Where the FUCK were you going, Finn? THINK!" Finn screamed over the voice as it grew louder.

Aidan's gone. Lucy's gone. Charlie is gone.

"Charlie's not gone!" Finn yelled reflexively. "Charlie's *not* gone!"

Take the gun—

Suddenly, the memory of Lucy's blue *Little Mermaid* dress sparkling bright while Charlie—or something that looked very much like her—carried the little girl toward the woods broke through the madness. Electrified by panic, Finn tore off for the back door with his hand outstretched.

Twenty-Six

Finn spotted his daughters near the edge of the thick line of trees. Charlie's back was turned to him, but his teenager clutched Lucy in her arms as the little girl's head and feet flopped without resistance.

Finn wrenched the back door open and lunged onto the porch.

"CHARLIE!" He gripped the porch railing, leaning far over as he screamed.

They were so close to the trees. Too close to them, and so very far away from him.

"Charlie, baby, talk to me! Stop!"

Suddenly, Charlie froze in place, swaying gently on the balls of her feet.

"Charlie! It's Daddy." Finn took advantage of the pause and launched himself down the porch stairs. "Honey, talk to me."

He began a soft jog toward the girls, careful not to startle Charlie. When only a few dozen feet were between him and his daughters, Finn slowed his pace to a trot. Whatever bad trip Charlie was on, whatever trouble she had gotten into, it could still be corrected. All she had to do was hand Lucy over to Finn, and the family would work through it. He would quit his perpetual pity party and suck it up once again. He was man enough to do that for Charlie's sake, Finn reassured himself. Once Lucy was safe in his arms again, he could worry about saving Charlie from herself.

"Sweetheart, I need you to give me Lucy. You can't take your sister with you. Whatever is going on, honey, I'm gonna help you. I just need you to put your sister down first."

Charlie tilted her head as if slowly processing Finn's words through her drugged haze. Then, she shuddered. Finn stilled. The noise of nature around them died, as if every critter and the wind itself had scuttled into hiding. All that was left was Finn's heavy breathing as Charlie began to turn on her heels to face him.

This thing, however, wasn't his Charlie—not even a strung-out version of his Charlie. This abomination might have been the offspring of the creature lurking in Rachel's bedroom, but it was in no way a reflection of his own child. The Charlie Thing's face was lax, as if fronting human nature had become too difficult for it after twenty-four hours. Its jaw hung limp while the bags under its eyes were dark and heavy. The color was gone from its cheeks and lips. Her eyes were black pits, sucking all of the light and life from the rest of her face. No trace of her beautiful blue eyes or fiery spirit remained. Finn couldn't bear to lock eyes with the creature; this perverse replica of Charlie was only a vessel for something hungrier inside.

The thing lowered its chin to look down at Lucy. Finn's first reaction was to charge it and rip Lucy from its grasp, no matter if that meant tearing this creature to pieces. Lucy was the only thing he had left. She was the one thing worth living for, which meant she was every bit worth dying for. Then again, what if it destroyed Lucy in the seconds before Finn reached it? Until she was safe in his arms, this monstrosity held his youngest's life in its hands. Finn held up his hands to show they were empty, that he meant no harm. The Charlie Thing remained still.

"Give her back. She's just a little girl. If you need somebody or something to take with you, take me. Put her down, and I'll come with you." Finn inched closer to it, his heart pounding in his ears.

The thing lifted its head to look at him full-on. Charlie was gone. He averted his gaze from her eyes and paused his slow advance.

"Just put her down."

The Charlie Thing abruptly released Lucy from its arms, and she hit the ground with a hard thud. Finn flinched but breathed out a small sigh of relief. He started toward them once more as alarm bells began ringing in his ears. Lucy wasn't moving.

"Luce, sweetie, Daddy's here. You're okay now, honey."

"Daddy? Daddy! Over here!"

Finn froze once again. The voice belonged to Lucy, but it hadn't come from the tiny figure that lay before him. Over the thing's shoulder, just beyond the edge of the trees, Finn saw another small form flit between branches and trunks. It was more shadow than shape, but he could make out enough detail to know that it was a weak duplication of his Lucy.

"Daddy," it called to him playfully, "I'm in here, silly-billy!"

Finn looked at the Charlie Thing and shook his head, refusing to play along even if the choice was no longer his.

"I'm not buying your bullshit. Do you understand me? Get the fuck away from my daughter."

The thing blinked and flinched as if something inside its skin was struggling for release. Then, without any change in its expression, the Charlie Thing reached down and snatched Lucy's long blonde hair, lifting the little girl halfway from the earth. Finn lunged toward the creature as it dragged his youngest child into the forest like a rag doll.

"Kennan? What in the hell is happening over there?" a deep voice called out from behind.

Finn gripped the back of the Charlie Thing's dress and pulled it backward with all his might, but the thing didn't slow.

"I said, what the hell are you doing to your daughters, you fancy fuck?" the voice shouted, louder this time.

Finn tripped as the thing pulled Lucy forward. He fell to the ground and scrambled to recover quickly. Lucy was only a few short steps from disappearing into the woods, and somehow he knew, once his baby girl was enveloped by the trees, he would never get her back. He grabbed onto his little girl's tennis shoe and held tight, screaming like a madman in a bizarre tug-of-war as he dug his toes into the grass.

He heard a shotgun cock, and it suddenly registered that someone had been screaming at him.

"Stop right there!" The voice boomed over Finn's desperate cries and the faint whispers, which multiplied with every inch Finn was pulled toward the forest. "Hey! Do you hear me, girl?"

The thing halted, and Finn gasped into the grass. He tightened his grip around Lucy's ankle and shook her leg gently.

The imposing voice of the Kennans' neighbor, Darryl Tucker, grew closer and louder. "Look, I don't know what kind of horseshit y'all have gotten into this time, but I've had it. This is my line, Kennan. You and your freaky little family can do whatever the hell you want inside your own house, but I don't want to see it, and it sure ain't happening in my backyard. Take your crazed kids and get the hell on outta here."

Finn rolled onto his side, still holding on to Lucy for dear life as he stared up at Darryl. The thick man's double-barrel was pointed directly at his chest with only a few feet separating the two. Finn blinked at his neighbor and shook his head, lost for words entirely.

"I said, get off my property, or I'm gonna blow a hole in your candy ass right in front of your kids. I ain't playin' with your nonsense no more."

"Are you shitting me, Darryl?" Finn looked back at the Charlie Thing, still frozen like a statue facing the trees.

"What the hell is wrong with her?" Darryl motioned with the barrel of his gun.

Finn opened his mouth, unsure of what he could possibly offer the man that wouldn't end with him getting his ass beaten or blown away. As he did, he felt the Charlie Thing turn, twisting Lucy to the side with her. This was either the end of Finn, or the one thing that could win him a temporary ally. He wasn't banking on the latter, but he didn't expect Darryl's next move either.

The Charlie Thing faced Darryl, its face just as blank and lifeless as before. Its eyes, black and unblinking, met the big man's. A wave of voices, too hushed and overlapping for Finn to decipher clearly, floated on the wind from beyond the trees. Darryl stiffened and his face dropped, gaze still locked with the creature's. Finn's breath picked up and he inched backward from the man, shaking Lucy's leg harder now.

"Lucy," Finn whimpered. "It's time to get up now. Daddy needs you to get up." He kept his eyes trained on Darryl's bizarre, dazed expression.

"That ain't the way it happened," Darryl shakily murmured underneath his breath.

In the next moment, Darryl raised the shotgun and fired into the woods over Charlie's shoulder. The thing didn't react as the slugs whizzed past. Finn, however, recoiled and grabbed hold of Lucy's dress. He attempted to pull the girl from the ground and into his chest, but the thing made one abrupt jerk of its wrist and sent Finn flying back down onto the ground.

He heard the gun cock yet again. One look over his shoulder told him there would be no more warnings or last chances. His neighbor redirected his aim. Instinctively, Finn rolled to cover Lucy as the bullet blew chunks of grass into the air where he had been only moments before.

"DARRYL!" Finn shrieked. "It's not real! Whatever you're seeing, it's not real! Listen to me!"

Cocking the gun once more, Darryl remained fixed on Finn and Lucy. Finn jumped to his feet, barricading his daughter as well as the thing that gripped her. He threw his hands into the air again with wide eyes and prepared for the next round.

"Darryl? What on earth are you doing?"

Darryl paused as he stared down Finn. Mrs. Lizzy Tucker's voice seemed a million miles away on their deck, but at the very least, he was glad someone else was there to witness the end. Finn raised his hands higher for Lizzy to get a good look. Suddenly, he felt the thing he shielded begin to move once again. Finn twisted to look over his shoulder as the shots rang out, and a white-hot sensation spread out across his right ribs. He heard Lizzy's high-pitched shriek underneath the concussion still ringing in his ears. He gripped at his side and felt sticky warmth through his T-shirt.

His sight began to go hazy as he watched the Charlie Thing finally pull Lucy's body into the trees, his girl's sparkly shoelaces untied and trailing behind. In another moment, the pair was gone, fading into the brush seamlessly.

Finn realized he had been shot, perhaps even killed. For all he knew, Darryl was seconds from unloading another volley into him.

"Darryl, no!" Lizzy screamed as Finn turned back to face his neighbor.

The big man had turned away from him and was walking toward his house in a steady, calm stride, shoving slugs into the shotgun barrel as Lizzy spun and smacked into the door she had already closed. Finn took a deep breath and peeled up his T-shirt to inspect the wound. His fingers shook as he traced his ribs to find the hole left behind by Darryl's bullet. After writing dozens of articles on homicides, Finn was numbly amused that he wouldn't get to report on the most interesting one of all.

Finn heard another blast of gunfire and a window shattering. Dark blood covered his fingertips when he pulled them away from the hole that skirted his side. The scoop from his skin was maybe the size of a Ping-Pong ball just under his ribs to the outside. In and out—not even straight on, or the wound would have been larger. It was little more than a nasty graze. Finn chuckled to himself as he began to shake from head to toe. He was bleeding like a son of a bitch, but he was one lucky son of a bitch.

Another blast of gunfire followed by screams shook Finn out of his daze. Darryl had reached inside the shattered window of their back door to unlock it. Finn could make out Lizzy farther inside their living room with a handgun leveled at her husband's face. There wasn't anything that he could do for Lizzy that she couldn't do herself, or so Finn told himself in that moment.

Finn looked behind him at the trail of beaten-down grass that led straight into an overgrown tangle of trees and brambles. If Lucy was gone, there was nothing left, and he may as well ask Darryl to fire on him one more time. But how far could he be behind them? Even if the girls were beyond his reach, what good did it do to stand around and stare? If he caved now and played it safe on the sidelines, he would definitely lose Lucy, and then he'd truly be a dead man walking.

He didn't need any more prompting, even as the gunshots grew more rapid. Without another glance over his shoulder, Finn was sprinting into the trees. By god, he wasn't a quitter.

Twenty-Seven

The sun was sinking below the treetops at a rate faster than Rachel believed possible. She stood over the patrol car's hood with the marked-up map of Dahlmouth and its surrounding woods, a cigarette in one hand and a red marker in the other. Marcus hung over her shoulder, glancing down at the sheet as she drew Xs here and there.

"Ain't it time to call the sheriff in?" Marcus said lightly. For a split second, she fantasized putting her cigarette out in the kid's cheek. She tilted her head from side to side, trying to crack the tension out of her neck.

"That's a neat idea. Why don't you give them a call, Marcus? See how that goes for you." Rachel whipped the map off the hood and stuffed it into the cruiser. "Hell, maybe they'll listen to you since you've got a dick hanging between your legs."

"Has Jeremy tried putting a call in?" Marcus cocked his head to the side and scratched at his stubble.

"It was a joke, Marcus. They're not fucking coming," Rachel growled. "Odell made it clear they're not gonna sail in to rescue us."

"Rachel! Rachel!" There were pounding footsteps from behind. She spun around to see Jeremy coming at her in a full-on run.

"What is it? What did we find?" She was ready to take off sprinting into the woods herself if he would point her in the right direction. But Jeremy's face was dark when he drew nearer, and Rachel knew at once he was the bearer of bad news.

"Rach, I think you need to come with me." Jeremy's voice trembled at the end of his sentence.

The radio at Jeremy's hip began squawking, but he reached down and twisted it off at once. At the same time, her own radio was firing up with chatter inside the cruiser. She looked toward the car door and started to reach in, but Jeremy slid in front of her.

"What's going on?" Rachel tried to push past him. "Don't tell me someone else has gone missing."

The look on Jeremy's face told her that whatever secret he was holding on to was worse than another missing citizen, no matter how young and vulnerable they might be. The crackling voices over the radio were muffled by Jeremy's body, but they had grown loud enough for Rachel to make out a handful of words:

"... *shots fired ... not breathing ... attempted CPR ... Croatoa Drive ...*"

Rachel's eyes met Jeremy's, and her breath stopped. Just then, she could hear the distant siren of an ambulance tearing down Route 6.

"Get out of my way," Rachel demanded as she threw the cigarette behind her.

"Rachel—" Jeremy grabbed hold of her shoulders, but she smacked his hands away.

"I said, get the fuck out of my way!" In a flash, she swung herself into the driver's seat and put the car into gear.

Jeremy stumbled back and out of the way as Rachel took off.

* * *

Rachel's patrol car spun into their front yard, tires flinging chunks of grass and mud high into the air. She didn't bother to turn the sirens off before she stumbled out of the front seat and bolted for the door. Two ambulances were parked in the driveway already and a fire truck rolled in behind them.

Rachel threw a wild look around the yard before she heard voices and clattering coming from the Tuckers' garage next door. A young man in an EMS vest emerged from the Kennans' front door and began jogging toward the Tuckers'.

"HEY!" Rachel called out and trotted over to meet him. "What's going on?"

"You the local chief? What took you so long to get here? We hightailed it from Amherst faster than y'all. What kind of a shitshow are you running out here?"

"Why don't you focus on your own job, kid?" Rachel growled, hands shaking while her adrenaline pumped harder. "Tell me what's going on."

The young man rolled his eyes and picked up his pace but answered her dutifully along the way. "Got a call from the wife that shots were being fired. Sounded like a neighbor dispute. On the call, the wife said her husband shot the guy next door. Then we get here, and it's the husband that's dead on the floor."

"Darryl? Darryl Tucker?" Rachel tried to keep her breath steady as they moved faster. "What about the other gunshot victim? The neighbor?" She glanced over her shoulder as a second set of swirling red-and-blue lights tore tracks in her front yard.

"Can't find him." The paramedic shook his head. "We thought he might have been in the house next door, but no sign of him. The dead guy's wife says she didn't see exactly where he went once her husband broke down the door."

"Broke down the door?" Rachel tried to meet the EMT's eyes, but he was laser-focused on the Tucker's front door.

"Husband went apeshit and blew the back window out with a shotgun. When we got here, she was in the front screaming she only shot him 'cause she had to."

"Why the hell would Darryl come after Lizzy?" The Tuckers were all about fitting in; a double homicide didn't exactly help one's image in the community.

"Isn't questioning the suspect your job, Chief? I'm just trying to focus on mine, remember?" A muscle in the paramedic's jaw spasmed. "We're going into the woods. The lady is saying there's a hurt kid in there, too."

"Whoa, wait a sec." Rachel grabbed his arm to slow him down. "A hurt kid? What did they look like?"

"Says it was the neighbor kid." The EMT sighed. "She says that's why the vic shot the neighbor before the kid went running off into the woods."

Rachel felt a breeze behind her, and a hand landed heavily on her shoulder.

"Rachel, come on," Jeremy ordered, his patrol car now parked in the yard next to hers.

"I'm fine." She stepped forward to stay even with the paramedic, pulling away from Jeremy's tight grasp.

The EMT shifted his gaze from Rachel to Jeremy with an arched brow.

"The neighbor kid you were talking about, what's the description?" She drew closer to the paramedic's side as they hustled.

"Rachel—"

"Small kid. Blonde hair, blue eyes, *Little Mermaid* dress," the EMT rattled off, ignoring Jeremy as much as Rachel was. "Maybe you can get a picture or something from next door? Might help us when we go trampling through the woods."

"Rach!" Jeremy belted out as he drew close to her again. "Hold up a goddamn second!"

"The kid." Rachel cleared her throat to keep herself from yelling. "How bad was she hurt?"

"Wife said she was unconscious."

Rachel's heart skipped a beat. "How'd the kid run off into the woods if she was unconscious?"

The paramedic chuckled and shook his head as they ducked through the Tuckers' front door and into their wrecked living room. "She says the kid was dragged in there by someone else—yet *another* girl. Look, this lady's clearly off her rocker or hopped up on something. The description she's giving us is—"

"Chief!" Lizzy sat at the kitchen table, her eyes red and her cheeks wet. "Oh, Chief, I'm so sorry." Mascara trails smeared down her face as she sobbed.

"Go ahead and ask her." The paramedic shrugged as he bent down to pick up his bag beside the body of Darryl Tucker spread wide across the living room floor in a drying dark brown pool. "Gonna be a long night."

"Jesus." Jeremy sucked in air through his teeth as he caught sight of Darryl.

"Chief, something is terribly wrong," Lizzy gasped from her seat at the table.

"Bit of an understatement," Jeremy murmured under his breath and crouched down beside the man's corpse.

"My Darryl . . ." Lizzy shook her head and swallowed back tears. "Darryl saw something funny happening out back. He got his gun when he saw Finn grabbing at Charlie. Looked like he was gonna hurt her, but she . . . she was dragging little Lucy by her *hair*. And Lucy . . . Lucy wasn't moving," Lizzy squeaked.

Rachel swallowed hard against her growing panic. "Finn was trying to hurt Charlie, you said? Was he acting violent, maybe under the influence?" Rachel fought to keep her tone even, but to her deep embarrassment, she knew everyone could hear the trembling in her voice as well. Dahlmouth's residents were well aware of Finn's drinking problem thanks to the crash, but not a single one of them knew what Finn was capable of doing in a rage . . . except Rachel.

"I-I don't know. It all happened so fast. Darryl went out there, and something . . . something was wrong with Charlie."

"What was wrong with Charlie?" Rachel's volume continued to rise.

Jeremy hopped to his feet and grabbed at Rachel's elbow. "You know you can't be here now, Rach." She pulled her arm away from him and focused on Lizzy's words.

"Charlie ... she turned to look at Darryl, and that's when he ... he went crazy." Lizzy fell back into tears. "Her eyes ... there was something wrong with her eyes. They were black ... just all black, all the way, Chief.

"I didn't look too long 'cause ... 'cause somehow, I knew if I did, bad things would happen. When she turned around"—the woman's voice had dropped to a whisper—"you could hear voices ... coming from the trees. I think it was the voices that made Darryl shoot your husband."

"Your husband?" The paramedic paused to examine Rachel with alarm.

Rachel's tongue grew heavy in her mouth. "Do you think Darryl got a good enough shot in to take Finn down? Maybe he made it to the woods, but do you think he was wounded enough that he wouldn't chase after the girls? I need to know what we're looking for, Lizzy."

"Is she the mother?" The paramedic turned to Jeremy.

"Yes." This time, Jeremy seized Rachel around the waist and picked her up off her feet.

"NO!" She clawed at his fingers. "I'm fine. I can do this! Put me down, asshole!"

When they reached the Tuckers' lawn, Jeremy's hands slipped loose to try to grab her by the upper arm, but Rachel was too quick and veered toward the Kennan abode on a mission. Every nerve in her body was alive and tingling with adrenaline. Tonight, she was going to watch the light fade from Finn's eyes, and she was going to be the one standing over his body with the smoking gun in her hand.

Twenty-Eight

"Where is he? We need to find Finn." She pulled the Glock out of her holster as she stepped through the front door. "I don't care how high she might be, the only reason Charlie would've dragged Lucy off like that is if Finn did something to hurt them . . . if she was trying to protect Lucy."

"Chief! Put down your weapon!" Jeremy roared from behind, but Rachel kept moving deeper into the house, looking each room over from floor to ceiling while her neck burned as though she still laid beneath Finn on that fateful hotel bed in Roanoke.

"The Dodge is in the driveway. Chances are the fucker is still lurking in those woods."

She held the gun steady with both hands. If Finn popped up around the corner, Rachel would unload the clip without hesitation. He didn't deserve a chance to explain himself; he hadn't deserved it the night Aidan died, and he certainly didn't now. The image of Finn's bare hands wrapped around Lucy's neck as their little girl's face turned purple sent electric shocks through Rachel, and she sped up her search.

"Rachel, I will disarm you by force if I have to!" Jeremy's deep voice echoed through the empty house. "I'm not gonna let you do something stupid. You *will* put your weapon down NOW!"

The kitchen was empty. Rachel even rounded the breakfast bar to be sure Finn wasn't cowering behind it. She headed toward the basement door—perhaps Finn was hiding down there like the little troll he was. When Rachel pivoted, however, she saw Jeremy standing in the open space between the kitchen and the living room, gun raised and pointed at her, poised to take a shot.

"Rachel," he started in a low growl, "put down your weapon."

"You're gonna shoot me?" She laughed and gripped the Glock harder. "That's a shit-ton of paperwork, shooting your boss and all."

"I'm not gonna let you kill him, Rach."

"You have no idea what that bastard is capable of doing. He's lucky I didn't put a bullet in his head before now."

Jeremy held his gun higher. "Set the gun down on the floor and push it toward me with your foot, Rach."

"*Chief*. It's chief to you. I am the motherfucking chief in this town whether or not anyone likes it."

"Put your weapon down on the floor, *Chief*."

Rachel stared at Jeremy in disbelief. The paramedics' shouts in the backyard took up all the room in Rachel's head for any other noises. She wouldn't have heard Finn if he was blubbering in the basement directly below her. Impotent fury surged through her as she thought of the paramedics traipsing through those woods to find Lucy and Charlie lying lifeless while Finn drunkenly powered his way through a gunshot wound.

For a wild moment, she wanted to shoot them all, anyone who happened to get in her way. She would take every last person down and finish herself off in the end. Then Rachel took a deep breath and recaptured a fraction of her sanity. Ever so slowly, she crouched down and slid the gun across the linoleum, glaring at Jeremy the entire time.

Rachel felt her power draining away. Jeremy bent down and snatched the gun off the floor, immediately putting the safety back on.

"We need to find Finn," she repeated, this time through gritted teeth. "If he's still breathing, he could hurt Charlie. He killed Aidan; somehow, he knocked Luce out or worse—he could hurt Charlie just as bad. You don't understand. She's only a kid; she can't fight him off."

"You don't know that Finn did this." Jeremy clenched his jaw.

"He has taken EVERYTHING from me!" Rachel screamed wildly as she bent forward, clutching her midsection. For a moment, Rachel remembered what it was like to run her hand over that same belly and feel her little ones kicking peacefully, safely, protected from the world by their mother no matter how inadequate she was otherwise. Her knees locked and her legs nearly gave way.

"Rachel." Jeremy's voice softened. He still clutched his own loaded Glock in one hand, though he had lowered it to his side. "Lizzy said it over and over—something's not right with Charlie. *Charlie*, not Finn."

Rachel shivered as a cool breeze hit her sweaty skin. "Lizzy was nearly murdered by her husband an hour ago. She isn't thinking straight—"

"Yeah, she ain't the only one," Jeremy muttered. "We need to talk about what's happening right now."

"We need to get our asses into those woods and look for my children!" Rachel just barely contained what she knew was a hysterical shriek. "We don't have time for this bullshit." She pressed her palms against her temples to ease the mounting pressure.

"You were questioning Charlie earlier today," Jeremy said, pushing forward. "Kendall disappeared right after being with Charlie. We've got little Abby Grayson disappearing into the forest at the same time. Now Charlie was seen dragging Lucy off into the woods lookin' high as a goddamn kite."

Rachel's eyes flashed. "Are you accusing Charlie of something?"

"I don't know, but this shit don't look good." A pained expression overtook the humor that usually lived on Jeremy's ruddy face. "You can't have your fingerprints all over these cases if it turns out Charlie was involved. They'll take everything from you—your badge, your title, everything. I'm not asking anymore, Rach. You have to step back from this."

"Don't tell me what I can and can't do here," she warned through gritted teeth. "This is my town, and I will—"

"We both know that's not true. Dahlmouth is anything but your town, and it never will be." Jeremy shook his head, more somber than Rachel had ever seen him. "Just because you got in good with some out-of-town higher-ups and landed here, that don't mean nothing to these people. You're an outsider, and thanks to that shit on the internet, you and your family always will be. They won't ever forget."

"I don't give a shit about whether or not Finn and I meet Dahlmouth's standards," Rachel scoffed.

"Yeah? Well, you should. They've started to think you're responsible for everything that's gone wrong these past couple years. The Wises, all the drugs that have been dumped around here and the terrible shit they've done; breaking into folks' homes, killing cattle, burning down one of Oldridge's barns. It wasn't like this before y'all showed up.

"And now things are spinning completely out of control." Jeremy's voice cracked. "All of this at one time? Who do you think they're gonna blame, Rachel?

"Listen, I don't understand what's going on, but I have this terrible feeling, like . . . like when there's a storm rolling in over the mountains, and you know there ain't nothing you can do but run for cover. I can't stop thinking . . . maybe we're not gonna be okay when whatever this is—"

The radio on Jeremy's hip suddenly roared to life with what sounded like twenty different voices buzzing in all at once. He jumped before snatching it from his side and cranking the volume knob. As the crackling, urgent voices became clearer through the radio, more frantic movements and screaming pierced the air. Edging closer to the back door, Rachel gazed across her porch and down onto the lawn. The sun had now sunk below the horizon, sending all search parties across Dahlmouth into darkness. Rachel could see tiny white pinpricks from flashlights dodging in and out from behind trees. Some swayed back and forth while others blinked in chaotic patterns like fireflies.

"I can't understand you. Repeat," Jeremy shouted into the radio receiver.

Rachel leaned closer to the window and narrowed her eyes. The lights were clustering together, more and more of them joining in one location, growing brighter as each new ball of light joined with the rest.

"They found something," Rachel murmured.

"I repeat," Jeremy called into the radio, "I could not understand you."

She yanked the door open and stepped out onto the porch. She could hear them in the distance, though she couldn't make out the words. Boots thundered through brush as several voices shouted in deep, commanding tones. If she was very, very lucky, they had found Finn dead as a doornail on the forest floor. At last, there would be no more cover for Finn's failures, no further bailouts. After fourteen years, the mad charade would be finished.

"... a body ... located a body..." a stranger's voice relayed through the static, and Rachel shivered.

Jeremy stepped closer to the porch, and the signal began to strengthen further.

"... a girl ... blonde hair, blue eyes. Looks six or seven. Fits the description the wife reported."

"No." Rachel shook her head and pushed herself away from the porch railing. "No, no, no—it's not Lucy. She's a baby."

Jeremy made a weak attempt to grab her by the shoulder, but she bumped past him and stumbled through the kitchen.

"Do you copy?" The paramedic's voice echoed over the radio behind her.

"Copy," Jeremy muttered into the radio. "I'll be on scene shortly. Is anyone else out there?"

This wasn't real. It was a ridiculous misunderstanding—another one of Finn's fuck-ups. Hell itself couldn't steal another child from her, and Finn certainly would not. Lucy had hidden from him somehow. That was it. Charlie must've dragged Lucy into the woods to get away from Finn on a psychotic, drunken binge. Then, Lucy would have doubled back home. She was just hiding—hiding like a frightened little girl would. Rachel knew it, and she would prove it to them all when she carried her baby out of the house to show them Lucy was safe, sound, whole.

Rachel rounded the bottom of the stairs and began charging her way up, her hands trembling against the banister. Something akin to anger twinged in her chest, though Rachel couldn't quite peg the emotion. It was sucking the air from her lungs as she climbed each step, and by the time she crested the top, she felt weak.

The lights were out upstairs. Rachel unsteadily put one foot in front of the other as she fought to make it to Lucy's bedroom.

Lucy. Her baby.

From the moment she first held her daughter in the NICU, Rachel was mystified as to how she and Finn could have produced something so beautifully fragile. Lucy was delicate and sensitive in every way—only the best bits of Finn and almost nothing of Rachel at all. She tried with Lucy. She really did. It could never have been enough.

Rachel flicked the light on in Lucy's room and surveyed the mess Finn had left behind from his rampage. The bedding had been torn off. Dolls and stuffed animals were flung this way and that. The folding doors on her closet were off the tracks and crooked. Rachel's eyes hovered over the empty bed where her daughter had made a small indent on the mattress through the years.

She should have seen this coming. From Finn's recent reengagement with Rachel to the disgusting stunt with the dolls he likely orchestrated himself, Rachel should have realized Finn had been teetering on the edge of another dangerous meltdown. She should have tried harder to protect her girls, but, once again, Rachel had been too preoccupied to see the looming disaster in her own home.

She gasped and gripped the wall as her vision darkened a shade. "Lucy," she cried weakly. "Come out, baby."

A small click behind her sent Rachel spinning around. She expected Jeremy to be there, coming to deliver more bad news. The hall was empty, however, except for the light that now streamed out of Aidan's bedroom door.

"Jeremy?" Rachel called out as she left Lucy's room and inched toward Aidan's door.

As Rachel arrived at her son's room, her chest grew painfully tight. She opened her mouth to pull in a full breath but couldn't quite fill her lungs. The goddamn doll had found its way to the center of Aidan's room once more. Now, a small, blonde-haired baby doll sat beside the mutilated doll meant to represent her son. The Aidan doll dwarfed this little one, but they made quite the pair sitting there together, upright and gazing out of the window at the black woods. It was a grotesque scene Rachel couldn't swallow anymore, particularly with the growing suspicion that Finn had been behind it all on his spiral into violent lunacy.

Whispers in the Dark

Rachel charged at the dolls before she realized the maroon wallpaper of her son's bedroom had once again been papered over with photos. Finn had torn down many of the defaced images when he threw them in her face, but the bare patches of wall space that should have been left behind were covered up once again. Indeed, every last inch of Aidan's walls were layered with photographs, one overlapping the next.

Rachel's throat seized like Finn was strangling her again as she made a slow circle around the room. The desecrated pictures of her son had been rehung, but there were others now, too. Lucy—bright-eyed, sweet, lovely little Lucy—had joined the collage. Photos from her infancy to the image of Luce dressed in a princess costume that Rachel had snapped just last week were scribbled over and shredded. In the most recent school picture, cruel Xs had been drawn over her daughter's eyes as if she were a dead cartoon character.

Amongst these were still more terrible images—ones with which Rachel was too familiar. Every time Rachel had discovered one of Lucy's horrendous drawings over the past year, she'd immediately torn it up and thrown it in the garbage. Rachel had instructed Finn and Lucy's teachers to do the same even if the shrink said the pictures might help them better understand Lucy's state of mind. If these were the kinds of scenes playing in her little girl's mind every day, Rachel didn't want to know about it.

Now, as the crudely drawn pictures peeked from between the mutilated photos of her children, Rachel couldn't ignore them. It seemed Lucy had scribbled every angle of the crash onto notebook paper with fat Crayolas, the thick lines making the sinking SUV pop off the page. In one scene, Finn prepared to dive while Lucy cried on the riverbank. In another, Aidan hung upside down in the car staring blankly as dark blue squiggles showed the rising waters. Still others showed Aidan peering out from the tree line, his hand extended to wave. In all of them, Lucy had inserted that goddamn figure dressed in white with massive black eyes—crawling over rocks in the river, swinging from its legs in the tree branches, hovering on the other side of the SUV's shattered windshield.

Rachel's eyes rejected the images no matter how many times she circled the room until she yanked one down from the wall and held it close to her face. Ice coursed through her veins and cold sweat blossomed on the back of her neck. Lucy had taken a black marker and scribbled over the scene several times. Yet, the attempted redaction couldn't entirely blot out the girl's original drawing—colored pencil had left pronounced indentations that still revealed Lucy's work. Two tall figures were front and center, their heads cocked to the side as they dangled from long strings in the trees, feet hanging far above the ground. Behind them, three smaller individuals stood holding hands, letters scrawled above the crowns of their heads—C, A, and L.

Rachel's hands shook so furiously that she dropped the drawing. Her vision darkened another shade as she caught sight of a different set of pictures lining the upper wall: Charlie as a toddler on a carousel, her eyes poked out while her mouth had been blotted out to mimic an open, dark mouth silently screaming. Charlie alongside Sarah, Gemma, and Kendall—all four girls' heads cut out and glued back onto the photo upside down upon their necks.

Rachel tried to inhale. Her chest was locked, however, and her lungs refused to cooperate. Now, she couldn't even gather enough air to call for Jeremy. Rachel slid past the littered walls and out into the hall. Something shifted behind her—footsteps on groaning wood floors—but Rachel refused to look back into her son's forever wrecked room.

Rachel still couldn't loosen her airways, and the world before her began to blur. She knew what it was like to be ambushed from the shadows, but this was coming from all directions. A dark figure inside Charlie's room zigzagged from one side of the doorway to the other. From behind her, Rachel heard a twisted, warped giggle that sounded like something Mattel programmed into one of their best lifelike baby dolls. Beneath the bizarre laughter, that unholy lullaby, sung by a chorus of unseen children, began to rise.

It's not Finn, Rachel realized as her eyesight went black. *Jesus Christ, Finn didn't do this.*

Her knees finally gave in to gravity, pulling the rest of Rachel down into the depths.

Twenty-Nine

"Hey, Rossi!" Adam Krenshaw shouted as his flashlight hovered over something he hoped he'd never have to see. His stomach gave a lurch, sending hot bile up into the back of his throat, and the EMT turned his head away from the corpse splayed out on the ground. "Rossi! I think I found her."

"Which one?" his partner yelled from a few dozen feet away. As Krenshaw knelt to feel for a pulse, he could only make out Bobby Rossi's shadow against the backdrop of bouncing lights scanning the trees.

"The girl . . . the little one," Krenshaw finished miserably as he stood to full height as his partner drew near.

"Ah, shit," Rossi muttered. Next to his partner, he cast his own beam across the tiny blonde's lifeless body, spread-eagled with glassy blue eyes staring at the night sky. "You sure she's gone?"

"I'm sure." Krenshaw nodded, his stomach growing sourer with every word. He rubbed his dripping nose on his jacket cuff. "I checked for a pulse. She's cold as ice. Kid's only six years old. Now, you tell me how God is good."

Rossi sniffed. "Looks like she's the cops' problem now."

"Not these cops," Krenshaw muttered. "The chief is this one's mom. Didn't know it until her partner said something. Shit luck."

"These cops couldn't tell the difference between their assholes and their elbows anyway." Rossi grunted. "Probably better to call in the county even if it wasn't the chief's kid. Throw a flag down, radio it in, and let's keep moving. With any luck, we can find the teenager and dad before the guy bleeds out."

"I'm not holding out hope." Krenshaw grimaced at Lucy's remains. "Don't know what the hell is going on out here, but I've got a bad feeling."

"Well, she didn't just fall over. Someone laid her out that way . . . like a little angel," Rossi murmured. "C'mon . . . we've got other people to find."

Krenshaw took a deep breath and turned toward where the rest of their colleagues trudged through the woods. He tugged the radio from his belt and pressed the push-to-talk button: "This is emergency personnel calling over. We located a body on the northwest end of Dahlmouth, inside the trees."

The radio buzzed with static, garbled voices chattering inside white noise. Krenshaw groaned and hit the button again: "I repeat, we've located a body."

"Emily?" Rossi asked from behind, surprised hope elevating his voice.

"What?" Krenshaw paused and glanced at his partner.

A voice broke through the static: "I can't understand you. Repeat."

Krenshaw's brow furrowed as Rossi's face relaxed in the dim light, eyes fixed on something beyond the girl's body. "Hey, Rossi," Krenshaw yelled before the radio buzzed again:

"I repeat, I could not understand you."

"Goddammit," Krenshaw hissed before raising the radio closer to his mouth and shouting. "Located a body. It's a girl. Blonde hair, blue eyes. Looks six or seven. Fits the description the wife reported. We need law enforcement assistance for search-and-rescue operations. Still haven't located the teenager and father." He let go of the button as his neck tingled. Rossi still hadn't moved from his spot, though his head now lolled to one side.

"Rossi, what the fuck?" Krenshaw barked. "Throw the flag down, and let's keep moving!" But Rossi failed again to respond. From Krenshaw's position, he could make out the tears beginning to form in his partner's eyes as the man's fingers twitched. "Hey, I'm not messing around."

When Rossi remained frozen, Krenshaw wheeled around to follow his partner's locked gaze. His eyes trailed along Rossi's beam of light as it washed over Lucy Kennan's unmoving form. Krenshaw flinched as he looked at her. Though still quite dead, he could swear the child's body gave off the slightest glow of its own.

"Fuck me," he muttered to himself and tried to shake off the persistent dread that plagued him.

He swung his light around to join with Rossi's as his partner swayed slightly on his feet. The beams fused and Krenshaw followed the light just beyond the little girl's body. When he did, Krenshaw shrieked and jumped backward, tumbling to the ground. His radio rolled out of his grasp and roared with the voices of a hundred children singing a lullaby Krenshaw had never heard before. Heart thundering in his chest, the paramedic blinked hard, hoping he could erase the image before him.

Krenshaw opened his mouth to call for the others. He'd found her—the other girl.

Charlotte Kennan stood only a few steps behind her sister's body, her long blonde hair wet and tumbling over her shoulders. The girl wore a thin white gown, the bottom fringe of which was torn and soaked with what may have been Virginian red clay or the blood of god only knew who. Her hands hung limp at her sides, shoulders tensed to her ears.

Though her mouth yawned wide with thick cords of bloody saliva stretching from her lips, it was her eyes that troubled Krenshaw the most. The girl's pupils had swallowed her reportedly bluebell irises along with the white sclera. He quietly scolded himself as a wimp, knowing Rossi would have called him just that were he not stunned by the sight himself. Maybe the teen was blitzed or fucking around, but whatever it was, Krenshaw's job was to help.

He tried to call for the others, but his voice caught in his throat. Looking in the direction of the rest of the crew, Krenshaw watched the beams from their flashlights go wild. Some bounced around as if his colleagues were running while others grew bright white until they then appeared to pop out of existence. The screams, though ... It was their horrendous, sickening shrieks that might echo in Krenshaw's ears forever. Wails to mothers, gods, and saints filled the air until they curdled and warped into fits of rage. Flesh beat against flesh, bones cracked on tree trunks, gun blasts tore through the night.

Krenshaw knew at once he should run. With any luck, his preoccupied colleagues would never see him go. He didn't know where he'd end up, but anywhere was better than right there.

A twig snapped by his left side, so close to his fingers that Krenshaw pulled his hand onto himself for fear of being trampled. Instinctively, the paramedic turned to identify the sound.

What he saw could've halted a freight train.

Sweet little Lucy Kennan, the angelic victim still in repose at the feet of her sister, now somehow also stood by his side. Glowing in her own ethereal light, the smiling child was close enough for Krenshaw to embrace if he wanted. That was the very last thing on his mind, however, as the girl bent down to gaze into his eyes with her own shimmering black orbs.

"Come play with us." She giggled.

Before Krenshaw could scream, the girl's small hands locked around his face, crushing its bones until the only thing Krenshaw knew was eternal darkness and the haunted songs of children in the void.

Thirty

"Pastor Paul!" Jake McNeil called out as the group of teens started to trickle into the sanctuary for Dahlmouth's First Calvary Baptist's Friday night youth service. "Do you need any help moving in the amplifiers?" The boy jogged toward him, his shaggy brown hair falling into his eyes.

"Ah, no, Jake. I already lugged 'em on in." Paul pointed over at the massive boxes to the side of the pulpit with a wide smile. "I just gotta push 'em over to either side of the steps."

"I got it!" Jake bounced a little in his sneakers and headed off toward them.

Jake was a good kid—much better than Paul had been at thirteen before he'd found the Lord Jesus Christ, but that was no surprise. All the kids in youth group were awesome young'uns for the Almighty. He took a lot of pride in that. The youth group had tripled in size since Paul arrived in Dahlmouth three years before. The Lord was doing mighty things in this place.

"Thanks, Jake!" Pastor Paul threw the guitar strap over his shoulder and grabbed the sheet music from his black guitar case. He didn't really need the sheets in front of him anymore; he knew all the tunes by heart, but it never hurt to have a reminder here and there.

Pastor Paul set the papers on the pulpit and took a good look around the room. To his disappointment, he saw there were fewer kids there than usual on a Pizza and Praise night. Food usually brought out a sizable crowd, sometimes as many as twenty or so. That night, however, maybe twelve kids were taking seats in the pews. Excited as they were, giggling and hollering at one another, it still struck Paul as wrong.

"Is something going on tonight? A basketball game I didn't know about?" Paul called over to Jake, who had just finished pushing the last amp into place across the platform.

"Not that I know of, but sometimes I'm outta the loop. You know how that goes," Jake said without a shred of bitterness in his tone and shrugged. "Some weird stuff has been going on, though."

"What kind of weird stuff?" Pastor Paul furrowed his brow but continued smiling. How could he have missed something going on in Dahlmouth? He was usually the first person to be called upon in a sticky situation.

"Well, Kendall Moreland got up to some trouble, apparently. Her parents can't find her, so they've been searching the woods and stuff half the day. Oh, and the Graysons' little girl . . . she wandered off, too."

Pastor Paul's heart sank. His broad smile faded. Why *hadn't* he been called? It was Paul's job to be there to minister to the hurting families, especially those of the young men and women of Dahlmouth. Florence Grayson attended nearly every service, and while the Morelands tended to shy away from the Lord's grace, he'd happily counseled Kendall more than once at the middle school's request.

"What on earth happened, I wonder?"

"Don't know, but lots of people have been out tryin' to help Chief Kennan and the police look for 'em."

For a moment, Paul considered whether the group ought to abandon their post and head off to help with the search. But then he thought about the kids getting lost in the woods themselves. Then what would he tell their parents? What would that do to attendance from there on? While Chief Kennan was doing her best to reject Jesus Christ's love, Paul was confident the Lord wouldn't allow Kendall or little Abby to suffer for the chief's sins. He'd guide her wayward hand toward those little ones if it was His will. The best thing he and the youth congregated here could do, the most important thing *anyone* could do, was to pray.

Pastor Paul flicked on the microphone, though he didn't really need it for such a small gathering.

"Hey there, guys and gals." He strummed his guitar gently. "You know, I'd love to get started, sendin' up our love and worship to the Prince of Peace tonight, but I think we've got a bit of work cut out for us first. I heard from Jake here that Kendall Moreland and Abby Grayson have gone missin'. Did any y'all hear about this?" Several heads in the crowd nodded with somber faces, though a few were still quieting down from their joking around a few moments before.

"Well, I think we oughta spend some time on this. You see, bein' called to God's purpose is about more than bathin' in the glory, ain't it? Sometimes … well, sometimes we're called to battle. Sometimes, we gotta be prayer warriors for our hurtin' brothers and sisters. Now, tonight I imagine there's a lot of fear and worry and pain those parents are goin' through. I pray to the Lord above that Kendall and Abby aren't afraid right now themselves, but maybe that's the case. We don't know.

"What we do know is, we ain't gonna sit around and act like nothin's goin' on, or like we can't do nothin' about it. Nah, we ain't the police; we ain't out there stompin' through the woods with them. We're in here. Here, before the Lord Almighty, we take our stand and we raise our hands up to Jehovah Jireh, the Perfect Lamb, because we know He's in control of this situation, ain't He?"

"Amen!" a few of the youngsters cried out in response. From somewhere far outside the church's stained-glass windows, Paul could hear excited shouting. His heart fluttered. Perhaps the search party had located the girls; perhaps Jesus was once more demonstrating in real time just how good He is when the faithful pray.

"Hallelujah, Jesus!" Pastor Paul nodded his head and held up a hand high, a placid smile resting on his lips. The rest of the kids in the pews slowly raised theirs and lifted their faces toward the arched ceiling. "Lord Jesus"—he closed his eyes tight—"Lord Jesus, we come to you tonight with our hearts wide open, searchin' for your mercy. We know, Father, that You are in control—not the police; not Chief Kennan; not anybody out there lookin' for those girls; not even anyone that would seek to do harm to those precious daughters of Christ." Pastor Paul heard a thud on his right and a reverberation in the amplifier. He hoped Jake hadn't stubbed his toe too hard.

"Jesus, we come before You to ask that You bring those girls home safely accordin' to Your will, dear Lord. We know we ain't worthy to be askin' You for nothin', but we throw ourselves at Your holy feet, Heavenly Father, to beg that You, in Your divine grace, will guide the eyes and feet of those officers straight to Kendall and Abby. We ask that You lay upon the Moreland and the Grayson families peace beyond all earthly understandin', Almighty Savior. Can we all say *amen*?!"

Pastor Paul shouted out into the microphone, excitement bubbling up into his chest as it always did when he felt the fire of the Lord upon him. But there was no response from the audience. His eyes fluttered open, and suddenly, the prayer stuck in his throat. Before him, twelve sets of eyes stared at him unblinkingly. They all stood, shoulder to shoulder across the pews, hands clasped together tightly. Any trace of emotion had fallen off their faces. Now they looked at Pastor Paul blankly, like robots awaiting a command.

"I said amen," Paul repeated weakly, almost as if it were a question. Once again, he was met with an ungodly silence. He tried to clear the tightness from his throat. "Now, I know we are all a little shocked by . . ."

Paul's voice trailed away as he watched them break hands and turn in unison to face the back of the chapel. One by one, they began to shuffle down the aisle in an orderly line. At the front, Jake, who must've scuttled down from the podium to join the others during the prayer, opened the church door wide and held it open, at rigid attention, while the rest of the teenagers wordlessly exited. In the distance, Paul suddenly heard the unmistakable cracks of rapid gunfire.

"Now, hold on there, y'all!"

Paul took a step forward but froze. Jake had turned to him, and Pastor Paul could see from where he stood that the boy's eyes had turned to black glass. They weren't empty, however. On the contrary, Paul discovered they were jam-packed with secrets—his, to be precise.

Paul was transported back in time to when he was a boy himself—not so far from Jake's age, in fact—laughing as he aimed his pellet gun up toward a bird's nest again and watched the feathers float down until the mass of twigs eventually gave way from the branches. Paul suddenly remembered Julia Kacey struggling in the back seat of his daddy's Mustang, hitting him in the shoulders and crying for him to stop. He hadn't, though. Paul never seemed able to stop anything once he started. Julia never returned to school after that.

His tiny son's brow was once more soaked with sweat beneath his fingers as the doctors implored him to consent to the treatment they said would save the boy's life. The frightened expression on his ex-wife's face floated before him as she pointed a rifle at Paul, demanding he get out of the house before he could perform the exorcism the good Lord had said would save their son instead. Paul had told First Calvary's elders that his wife had lost her mind long before he arrived in Dahlmouth—that the divorce and restraining order was due to her backsliding, but all this time, he'd known that wasn't quite true.

It suddenly occurred to him as he remained locked in a stare with this black-eyed boy that Paul was a very wicked man. He, in fact, was irredeemable, no matter what the pastors at Bible college told him—no matter how the chaplain in Afghanistan said the Lord spared his life for a reason. Paul was the exception to the rule. God hadn't intended to use him for good or to cleanse him. Paul simply won the lottery, and evil men win all day, every day.

That was when Pastor Paul remembered the keys to the maintenance shed hung in the prep kitchen between the cabinets and the door. In that maintenance shed, next to the riding lawn mower, the groundskeeper always kept containers of gasoline. Pastor Paul reached into the pulpit and withdrew the small pack of matches kept there to light the candles before each service. As the last of the youth wandered out of the church, Pastor Paul turned on his heel, retrieved the keys for the shed, and headed out where he did indeed find two large jugs of gasoline awaiting him. Then, Pastor Paul began to take his last holy bath and Jehovah graciously cleansed him with fire.

Thirty-One

Rachel woke to screams echoing off the trees behind the Kennans' home. She turned her head to the side and saw Aidan's bedroom door was open, the world beyond it darker than her dreams. There was nothing after that door, she was sure now. That door led to Nowhere.

She sat up slowly, still in a haze, but sharp enough to know danger was still close by. Did Jeremy know yet, or was it already too late? Panic surged as thoughts of an unknowable force chasing him down broke through her foggy mind. Rachel's skin prickled under the stare of unseen black eyes from inside each bedroom. Clutching the wall for support, Rachel rose to unsteady feet and wavered. She cast one last look into the void of Aidan's room before stumbling down the steps.

"Jeremy," she called weakly.

Gunshots rang out in the distance—thunderous, deep blasts that shattered the night.

"Jeremy!" Rachel fell into the front doorway to see Jeremy silhouetted by the lights of emergency vehicles idling abandoned in the front lawn, sirens still wailing without anyone to operate them. He spun around, hand to holster, when he heard his name. She held up her hands instinctively to show they were empty. "What happened?"

"Rachel!" Jeremy gasped with relief before panic reclaimed his expression.

He raced toward her, reached inside the doorway, and flipped the porch lights off. Then, he shoved her back inside and hurriedly flicked off the interior lights as well. Rachel could hear his unsteady breathing, and even in the dark, she saw his eyes were wide with fear.

"Remember how I said things were spinning out of control?" Jeremy hissed as gunfire rattled through the night. Rachel didn't have to answer. "Well, they done spun out completely. The whole goddamn town has gone insane."

"What happened to the EMTs?" Rachel propped herself against the wall and ignored a sudden rumbling from upstairs. "Was it . . ." She took a deep breath and reluctantly gripped at reality. "Was the body really Lucy? Are we sure it wasn't Abby Grayson?"

"They found someone, but I don't think it was Lucy *or* Abby." Jeremy's eyes darted from the ceiling to the front door and back to meet Rachel's. "None of them have come out to tell me."

Rachel furrowed her brow. "Where did they go?"

"Same place everyone's going, I imagine." Jeremy choked out a sound somewhere between a laugh and a sob. "While you were out, calls started coming in over the radio fast and furious. The kids . . . there's something wrong with the kids. They're taking off into the woods, acting like they can't hear anybody around them, like they can't even stop themselves from doing it."

"This has got to be some kind of joke. It's some prank they're all in on." Rachel tried to strangle the panic rising in her voice. Her head still swam, and cold sweat lingered on her brow. "Right?"

Please say yes. Please shake me awake. Please make it stop.

"Rach, listen to me; this ain't a fucking prank." Jeremy ran an unsteady hand through his hair. "First call came in seconds after you hit the floor—Alice Henn disappeared into the woods, dead-eyed, in some kind of trance or something. Kimmy and Dennis—they tried to stop their girl from runnin' off, but she just dragged 'em right along with her. Ten minutes later, Dennis comes stumbling out of the woods again, walks straight into the barn, grabs ahold of his axe, and buries the bitch right between his eyes.

"Next call was a fire at the church. Tonight was youth group—"

"Shit." Rachel fell back against the wall, planting her hand into her sweaty hair. Her breath still couldn't return to normal.

"I'd say the kids are all fine; they certainly made it out. Doris Gill said she watched all of 'em walk in a straight line right into the trees. That's when she saw Pastor Paul."

"He chase after them, too?"

"Not at all. Our saintly reverend dumped several cans of gasoline over his head and set himself on fuckin' fire. Didn't move an inch while it happened, neither."

"Jesus Christ," Rachel hissed.

"The same kind of shit kept flooding the radio." Jeremy's voice shook. "Kids takin' off and parents and grandparents and anybody around chasin' after them into those woods. Most of the time, nobody comes back out again, but when they do, they're all . . . fucked. The last thing was about Johnnie—"

"Oldridge? We were just with him, and he was fine." Rachel's head began to clear as her adrenaline ratcheted up.

"He went in them trees to find everybody who'd been helping search for Abby and Kendall. I don't know what he found, but he came back out with his huntin' rifle and started blowing away the first people he saw, screaming something about the goddamn war."

"What?" Rachel recoiled, thinking of the sage old man with happy, fluffy white eyebrows and a cotton-ball beard.

"He took down at least five people before he turned the gun on himself and blew off the back of his head." Jeremy licked his lips and pointed out the front window as shots continued to echo. "So, I don't know whose gun that is that's fired up right now, but I know it ain't good."

"But you said Johnnie was the last call that came in. Someone would've called in if there were more—"

"That's the thing." Jeremy laughed to hide the terror creeping in. "That was the last one because then the radios went dead. All the channels are static. I can't get anything tuned in. Nothing coming in, and nothing going out.

"Phones ain't working, neither." He took his phone out of his pocket and tossed it onto the floor. "I tried to text my ex to make sure the kids are all right . . . that this bullshit hasn't spread to Roanoke, too. Can't get a signal to save my life, and it ain't just me. Those EMTs' radios cut out all of a sudden in them woods, and it wasn't long after that they started screaming to high heaven. We're cut off, Rachel."

Rachel ran her palm across her forehead, stretching the muscles across her wrinkled brow. "Take the cruiser and head on over to Roanoke for backup. Go make sure your boys *are* okay."

"No way in hell I'm leaving Dahlmouth right now. You need me. Ain't nobody else gonna have your back now."

She closed her eyes and listened to the steady *pop, pop, pop* now coming from the opposite direction. "Do we know where the rest of us are? Louis? Zeke? Marcus?"

"Last I knew, Marcus was at the Oldridge farm. I don't know what's happened since then. Maybe he's still there? I haven't heard from Zeke since we left him with Charlie." Jeremy's voice faltered when her name left his lips. "And Lou . . . I never got a call back since he found Zeke's car off Route 6."

Rachel scratched her scalp hard, clamping her eyelids tighter. "He found Zeke's car?"

"Abandoned on the side of the road, yeah . . ." Jeremy rubbed at the stubble of his chin, looking as if the words forming on his tongue were painful. "Route 6, right past the bridge."

Rachel's eyes popped open to shoot a glare at Jeremy that he didn't deserve. "So, what was Lou's plan from there? Did he tell you where he was going?"

Jeremy shook his head. "All Lou said was that he saw something he was gonna follow up on. Didn't tell me if it was Zeke or something else. He just hung up."

"And we haven't heard from him since?" She cleared her throat and pushed herself away from the wall.

"No, not from him directly."

Rachel peered at Jeremy, eyes narrowed to slits. "Someone else heard from him?"

Jeremy hesitated. Rachel saw a muscle in his jaw twitch as he turned from her to scoop up the phone from the floor. He swiped through a few screens before he slowly handed the phone over to Rachel. She looked down at the bright words in a bubble beneath Finn's name:

Tell Rach that Lou saw him. By the road with Charlie and Luce. They're not right.

She'll listen to you.

"Him who?" Rachel's voice quivered. "Who did Lou see?" She looked up at Jeremy, begging him to tell her anything other than what she already knew was true. Her deputy simply shook his head and looked away.

Rachel took one last look at Finn's message. There were no texts from Finn before or after that. The time on the text said 6:07 p.m., while the phone's current clock read 7:15 p.m. She inhaled sharply and tossed the cell back to Jeremy.

"I have to go. I have to find Charlie. Luce, too. Sounds like those EMTs didn't know what they were looking at, and if that's true—"

"You're out of your mind if you think I'm gonna let you run off into those woods after them. Not with whatever happened to those EMTs in there. Not to mention you took a major hit to the head when you passed out upstairs with those ... fucking pictures all over Aidan's room."

"My daughters are out there!"

"No, your daughters..." Jeremy struggled to find words, sputtering as he choked out what he could, irrational as it sounded. "Even if they're in them woods, there's ... there's something evil in there with them, Rach."

"It's nothing we can't handle, Jeremy," Rachel muttered under her breath, but it was weak now. No matter how hard she tried to shake off the thought, she couldn't dismiss that something greater than them was stirring in the forest that surrounded Dahlmouth.

"Listen to me, please. Lucy ... Rachel, something bad happened to—"

"Shut up."

"I know you know, Rachel! Lucy is—"

"SHUT UP!"

"And if something bad has happened to Lucy, that means ... that means there's some truth to what Lizzy Tucker was sayin' about Charlie. Something is very wrong with Charlie, and it ain't a bad batch of meth as much as that answer would make you feel better."

Rachel busied herself fishing around in her pockets for keys. "You think I'd feel better knowing my kid is addicted? As opposed to what?" When she finally wrapped her fingers around the keys, Rachel looked up at Jeremy with a warning expression. "You think she's some kind of homicidal maniac now? You think she killed her sister, yeah?"

"That ain't at all what I said." Jeremy crossed his arms tightly as his voice dropped low. "I'm not so sure Charlie is Charlie anymore."

Rachel froze for a moment, her face twisted into an expression that held both fury and befuddlement. "The hell does that mean?"

Jeremy hesitated. She could almost see the internal argument taking place between the overly confident Jeremy and the one that wanted to curl up and hide. He ran his rough thumb over his lips.

Enough of this. Rachel headed toward the front door.

"When I was a little kid," Jeremy spoke up loudly, stopping Rachel in her tracks, "my great-grammy was still around—ancient, but still around. We all said she'd lost it back then, but . . . you're gonna think I'm crazy. Hell, *I* think I'm crazy."

"Jeremy! Just say it."

"Look, Grammy rambled on about the same nonsense as that Wise kid earlier today. Told us all kinds a' stories about creatures in them woods . . . all up and down the Appalachians and even further . . . Things older than us, smarter than us, *angrier* than us."

Rachel gritted her teeth and stuffed her hands into her pockets once more. A sudden chill ran down the back of her neck before spreading across her shoulders, down her arms, and all the way to her feet. Still, she tried to remain stone-faced, desperate to get to the forest and her children. Jeremy clucked his tongue and shifted uneasily, but pushed ahead.

"There was always one story she came back to. It scared the piss outta me till Mama told me Grammy was just tryin' to keep me in line. Thing is, now I'm not so sure it was just a story. I don't know if she meant to scare me into behaving, or . . . maybe she was tryin' to warn me, to protect me.

"Grammy used to say those things in the woods, if ever I was bad enough, they might come and get me. They'd carry me off to their world where I'd be stuck forever—never growing old, never dying, never seeing my friends or family ever again. I'd be their plaything until they got bored of me. An' then, even Grammy didn't know what happened to a person.

"And the worst part was, no one would come lookin' for me 'cause they wouldn't even know I's gone . . . for a while, at least. Those things would leave behind something that looked exactly like me—one of them, but no one would be able to tell until . . . until bad things started happening."

"What kind of bad things?"

He licked his lips and looked down at the floor. "People would start to notice little things at first . . . the thing that looked like me acting a little off, doing things I'd never do—talkin' weird, dressing different, a little more rowdy—that kind of stuff. Then, it'd start causing real trouble.

"Grammy said it happened to one of the families where she came from. Normal kid one day; the next week, the same kid killed off a bunch of livestock and ate it raw. She said that boy tried to make her follow him into the woods, but she knew somethin' weren't right about him . . . that if she followed, Grammy wouldn't come back again—not really."

"Come on, man." Rachel dropped her head and squeezed at the bridge of her nose, exasperated even as fear welled up stronger. "Something is wrong, okay? Very, very wrong. And I don't know what it is, but I *do* know my daughter isn't some sort of goblin, or—"

"But that's what I'm saying, Rach!" His voice cracked as his eyes grew wider. "What if Charlie... Look." Jeremy took a deep breath and steadied himself. "Grammy said that when she saw that boy, when he tried to get her to come with him, his eyes were what kept her from going. He looked normal to everyone else, but when Grammy saw him in the trees, the kid's eyes were shiny black, like a beetle—she couldn't even see the whites of his eyes anymore, just like Lizzy Tucker was sayin'."

"So, what happened then?" Rachel asked through the fingers pressed to her lips. "What happened after your grammy ran away from him? Where did the little boy go?"

Jeremy's shoulders drooped before he began shaking his head. "I don't know," he answered softly. "Grammy said she ran home and told her folks what she saw. Quick as lightning, they grabbed her up and got the hell outta town. Ended up runnin' till they were an ocean away from that place."

Rachel cleared her throat and tried to ignore the hair rising on her arms. "So, you think Charlie has become one of these... things your great-grandmother talked about—"

"No, I'm sayin' maybe Charlie ain't here at all. Maybe the kid you've been seeing lately... maybe that ain't the real Charlie. They just want you to think it is."

Unavoidable terror swelled in Rachel's chest. Charlie was no monster even if she had somehow done monstrous things. Her teen was sick with whatever mind-bending substance the

Wises had fed her. No doorways to other worlds would convince her otherwise, even if every other child in Dahlmouth was warped by its call. Charlie wasn't like everyone else. Rachel had to believe that.

Rachel needed to get into those woods, to wrap her arms around her daughters, to get Charlie to a safe place where she could recover—where Dahlmouth's rumors couldn't hurt them anymore, where all the madness of the night would fade away. First and foremost, Rachel needed to keep Charlie alive before someone could hurt her, drunk on whatever fear and darkness emanated from the forest around them.

"And if that's not Charlie anymore," Jeremy continued, "chasing after her into the woods ain't gonna help."

"I'm not just chasing after Charlie," Rachel spoke sharply as the heap of keys jingled in her hand. "I have to find Finn, too." She turned for the door. "Lucy . . . she became his everything after the crash. If . . . if there's any truth to what Lizzy Tucker said, Lucy is hurt." Rachel fought to ignore the pitiful look Jeremy gave her, one that screamed the truth Rachel still couldn't fully accept without Lucy's body in front of her. "And Charlie could very well be responsible if she's on a bad trip."

"Finn would never hurt the kids intentionally." Rachel's mouth went dry as an image of their mangled SUV lodged in the river flashed through her mind. It was quickly replaced by the memory of Finn pinning her down on the cheap hotel mattress, eyes ablaze with fury. "But he has that Kennan temper, and if Finn thinks Charlie did something to Luce—"

"Honestly, I think he's in more danger than that thing Charlie is right now."

"Right—because my daughter is a shell for some demon now." Rachel narrowed her eyes.

"Listen." Jeremy scrubbed at the back of his head nervously. "I'm not only talking about Charlie. That hiker showin' up, those girls goin' missing, the way all the kids are acting all of a sudden, how everybody suddenly lost their goddamn minds? It's everywhere, Rachel. It's got to everyone in Dahlmouth.

"I don't know what this is exactly. I have no goddamn idea how to fix it, to make it stop." He pointed out the window with a forlorn stare. "But what I do know is that runnin' headlong into that forest ain't nothing but suicide. I know I'm asking for a miracle, but I need you to use your head, Rachel, even if you are a fired-up mama bear right now. We need to slow down and think this through before we make any more moves. Otherwise, we're just as fucked as everybody else out there now."

Unbridled fear mixed with rage made Rachel's body tremble. Maybe Jeremy wasn't completely wrong, but he wasn't offering solutions either. "Okay, well, I'm not going to stand around and wait for your Grammy's ghost to tell us what to do. We're the ones responsible for keeping this place safe, and if that means..." Rachel nearly choked on her words but she spoke them all the same: "If that means stopping Charlie along with whoever else is out there, then so be it.

"But I'm not gonna throw up my hands and surrender my daughters to the fuckin' forest while the whole damn town rips itself apart. And I'm not gonna let Finn or some other idiot armed to the teeth take matters into their own hands either. My kids are going to make it out of this fuckin' hellhole in one piece even if no one else does. Dahlmouth isn't taking everyone from me.

"So, are you coming with me or not?" Jeremy shifted uncomfortably as Rachel threw open the front door. "I'm going after my family either way."

Thirty-Two

At first, Michelle tried to keep her pace steady and cool as if there was no reason to cause a stir. Five minutes later, however, she decided she didn't give a damn and broke into a full-on run from the elevator bank toward the door with ROANOKE SHERIFF etched on the frosted-glass window. By the time she skidded from the white-tile hallway onto the red carpet in the lobby outside Odell's office, Michelle was panting. Odell and two of his officers turned to stare at her, all with baffled but amused expressions.

"You okay there, Doc?" Odell asked, thumbs resting in his belt loops.

Michelle didn't have time to bullshit tonight. "No," she gasped. "I need to talk to you right now."

To Michelle's relief, Odell's face shifted from amused to concerned in an instant. She didn't have a reputation for making waves or causing trouble. Sometimes, she was convinced the only reason people remembered her at all was because of her pretty face and fancy title. Her meek disposition and quiet nature lent one advantage, however: when Michelle *did* get riled up, people tended to listen.

"What's going on?"

Michelle struggled with the words she knew Odell wouldn't like at all, but there wasn't time to be timid anymore. "It's . . . it's about the dead hiker they found in Dahlmouth."

"Christ." Odell rolled his eyes and bounced on his heels. "Doc, I'm headed out for the day. Let's put a pin in this until to—"

"No!" Michelle shouted, startling the three officers and herself as well. "I need you to listen to me. Something is very wrong, and it requires your immediate attention." She raised the file she'd been hugging to her chest high, her hands trembling. "I identified the body. Please . . . just give me a few minutes of your time."

Odell looked her over with pursed lips. He didn't want to help her; Michelle already knew that much. Yet, here was the city's respected junior medical examiner at his doorstep demanding an audience with a file full of information ready for his review. She wasn't leaving him much choice.

"Fine," he groaned. He leaned back to twist the doorknob on his interior office. "You got ten minutes."

Michelle rushed past him and into the office, laying the file open on his desk.

He plopped down in his oversized leather chair.

"The hiker . . ." Michelle sorted through photos, her fingers shaking as if she had been dunked in a tank of ice water. "The man that Rachel—*Chief Kennan*." Michelle quickly corrected herself and hoped Odell didn't notice the pink flush on her cheeks. "The man Chief Kennan found was a twenty-four-year-old Caucasian male from Marquette, Michigan, named Brian Clark—"

"Great work, Doc. Now—"

"LISTEN!" Michelle snapped and threw a glossy photo of Mr. Clark at him. "Does that image look a little funny to you?"

Odell held the picture close. As much as the man wanted to brush her off, Michelle saw the discomfort creeping into his expression. "I don't know what I'm supposed to be looking at, Doc."

"It's a little dated, no? That's because that picture was taken in 1974 . . . right before Mr. Clark went missing." Odell arched an eyebrow as he looked up at her. Michelle shoved away her self-doubt and pressed on. "I took the liberty of calling Marquette's police department. It's a cold case. They never found any trace of the guy. His parents reported him missing after he'd set out on a hunting trip and didn't come home. They were particularly worried because Mr. Clark hadn't been himself for some time.

"He, um . . . There was a terrible car crash." Michelle felt perspiration suddenly bloom on her upper lip. "Apparently Mr. Clark had been driving under the influence. He ran the vehicle off the road into the forest going some ungodly speed. His little brother died in the accident, though he was thrown so far from the car they never found his body in the woods. It was a miracle Mr. Clark survived himself.

"After that, his parents said he'd spiraled, eventually developing a preoccupation with a series of unusual cases."

"Unusual how?" Odell handed back the photo of the smiling young man with crooked front teeth.

Michelle licked her lips before she continued uneasily, "Missing children . . . specifically some disappearances involving little girls." Odell raised both brows now, giving Michelle a suspicious look. "I know. That's what the local police thought, too. So much so that they actually arrested him at one point when a young girl disappeared two towns away." She laid a yellow-tinged photo of a little girl in a frilly blue-and-white dress atop a rocking horse before Odell.

"Her name was Angela Simmons. She was only five. Went missing while on a camping trip with her parents. The mother told the police the whole family went to sleep in their tent around ten. When they woke up, Angela was gone, and the flap of the tent was wide open. They never heard her get up and couldn't understand why she'd wander off. Said she was terrified of the woods from the moment they arrived. They never found her."

Odell held the image close to his face, brow furrowed, until he let out a sigh and set the photo down on his desk again. "That's a real tragedy."

"Sure is." Michelle placed her hands on the edge of Odell's desk and leaned forward. "Not twenty-four hours later, both parents were found in their car a mile from the campsite. The father shot the mom before tearing his eyes out of his head and bashing his skull on the dashboard."

The sheriff's eyes grew wide even as Michelle watched him try to maintain a blasé expression. "Sounds like they figured out who the culprit was, then. The father was clearly unstable."

"Which is why they released Mr. Clark. By that time, they'd already booked and fingerprinted him, though. That's how I know this is the same guy as Dahlmouth's dead man.

"Before he left, Mr. Clark reportedly told friends he was looking for something . . . for a place he said these kids were all going. He told them he was headed out to find it . . . a gateway to this . . . this world that he believed swallowed the children. He said this place . . . it opened in thin places."

"The hell does that mean, Doc?"

"I don't know!" Michelle nearly exploded before composing herself again. "But I think . . . I think he may have been onto something, even if the guy was a little disturbed. At least six kids went missing that year within a ten-mile radius of the place Angela Simmons disappeared. Each of them was gone without a trace. Most of them were under the age of ten and had last been seen near the woods.

"In every single case, the caregivers . . . well, bad things happened not long after the kids disappeared. Six of them died within a couple days—five of those were brutal suicides and the other was so torn up that no one knows how they ended up that way. Two more went missing only to be found six months later washed up on the beach of Lake Superior. The last four . . . well, they vanished as bizarrely as the children—no note; all of their wallets, keys, even shoes left behind. It's like they just stopped whatever they were doing, walked off into the forest, and fell into a black hole. None of them were ever found."

"Doc, people go missing in the woods all the time. These folks were likely so distraught they went looking for their children and—"

"—and the ones that maimed themselves?" Michelle shook her head. "I suppose five people with no history of violence or mental illness went completely insane at the loss of their kids."

"Grief does funny things to people."

"Bullshit." Michelle nearly stunned herself into silence with the vulgarity, but when Odell looked up at her in surprise, she decided to push on. For once, the son of a bitch was paying attention. "I don't know exactly what he was looking for, but I think Mr. Clark found it. No one saw him after he went searching for those kids until Chief Kennan found him pinned to that tree like he'd walked out the door yesterday."

Odell gave a chuckle that set Michelle's teeth on edge. "Seems like he was a little worse for wear than when he left his mom and dad's."

"I don't think you understand me." Michelle swallowed hard. "I'm not just saying a missing man showed up nailed to a tree in Dahlmouth nearly fifty years after he disappeared. I'm telling you, after all these decades, this man hadn't aged at all when Chief Kennan found him. The Brian Clark of 1974 is by and large the same Brian Clark today. It's like he marched into the Michigan woods and something spit him out on the other side in Dahlmouth as if no time had passed at all."

Odell stared at Michelle for a long while, his index finger tapping against the desk. She stood tall, mustering every ounce of strength she possessed to keep from shaking under the weight of his gaze. At last, Odell cracked a smile and rapped his knuckles against the polished wood.

"Wowza." He nodded. "That's a hell of a medical mystery. Thanks for sharing, Doc. I'm sure Chief Kennan will find this absolutely thrilling. Now, if you'll excuse me—"

"That's the problem!" Michelle exclaimed. "I tried contacting Dahlmouth straightaway. First, the station; then Chief Kennan directly. None of the calls would go through. I even tried her personal cell phone. I don't even get a dial tone, sir."

"Her personal cell phone?" Odell wiggled his eyebrows. "I had no idea you and the chief were such good friends."

Michelle flushed again but carried on. "So, I started calling other places in Dahlmouth . . . businesses, the church, the schools, private residences. Not a single call registers."

"Must have some bad weather out their way. The surprise snowstorms this time of year can be pretty nasty in the country—"

"A call came in from Dahlmouth a couple hours ago." Michelle's voice cracked as she shouted over Odell's dismissal. She folded her arms tight across her chest, her sweaty palms slipping against her forearms. "Some kind of shooting. Amherst dispatched two teams of medics to assist."

"Oh, yeah?"

Michelle swallowed hard and nodded at the sheriff. "They lost contact with the entire group about an hour ago. Their radios are dead. I had one of our dispatchers give it a go as well. Nothing. There's nothing going in or coming out of Dahlmouth at all."

Odell sat forward and laced his fingers together. He scanned Michelle's open file wordlessly, and once again, Michelle found herself struggling to remain still. After another few seconds passed, she gave up.

"Aren't you going to do something?" Michelle yelled at the big man, who looked up at her as if she'd lost her mind.

"Doc, I'm struggling to see how this dead hiker and some phone lines being down connect."

"Maybe they don't connect at all, but it's concerning to say the least. We know there was a shooting. We know medical assistance was dispatched. Now we know the entire town is cut off. And it's *not* just the phone lines." Michelle raised a quivering finger to him. "Cell towers... their *radios*?"

"Okay," he began softly. "I can see how you're worried for your friend—"

"This isn't about Rachel!" Michelle felt woozy as the air in Sheriff Odell's office suddenly grew thick. "There are hundreds of people there who may be in danger, including emergency personnel from an entirely different town that has nothing to do with Chief Kennan. I know you can't stand her, but for God's sake—"

"I'll see what I can do," Odell croaked.

Michelle stood, wobbling slightly on her feet as she looked Sheriff Odell over. "I need you to promise me—"

"I will take care of this," he cut her off with a firm tone. "I'll send out some people."

Michelle hugged herself tighter as she met the sheriff's gaze. Finally, she nodded and broke her stance. "Thank you," she murmured and reached out for the file she'd spread out for him.

Before she could gather its contents, Odell's massive hand flew down onto the folder, pinning it to his desk. "Doc, I'm gonna hold on to this. It's evidence."

"But I—"

"And I'll have to ask you to keep this quiet for now as well." He pursed his lips again and dragged the file across the desk toward himself.

Michelle's mouth hung open as she searched for words to argue against Odell. Such things weren't exactly her forte, however, and she could feel herself shrink several inches as her confidence slipped away. In the end, all Michelle could manage was a single nod before turning on her heels.

"Hey, Doc?" Odell called from behind just as Michelle reached the door. "What happened after Mr. Clark went missing?"

Michelle spun around, head reeling. "What do you mean?"

The sheriff rapped his knuckles on the closed folder atop his desk. "The kids—did more of them go missing after Mr. Clark skipped town?"

"No." Michelle's voice grew even smaller, quieter as she always did when scolded. "It stopped as suddenly as it started."

"Well." Odell smiled at her with a syrupy-sweet grin. "I think you have that answer, at least. Those Yankee cops may not have been able to pin shit on Mr. Clark, but there ain't no doubt the guy was guilty. Listen, don't worry your pretty little head about all this." Odell winked. "I've no doubt that Chief Kennan has everything under control."

* * *

Michelle jammed her keys into the ignition of her Kia and tried to steady her breathing as the engine came to life. A praise song suddenly blared over the radio twenty times too loud for Michelle's worn nerves. She shrieked her second obscenity for the night before gripping the steering wheel and closing her eyes. This was dumb and dangerous in more ways than Michelle could properly explain. Nevertheless, she wouldn't be able to sleep tonight unless she was sure Rachel—with all her swagger and false confidence—was safe with her little ones and that dipshit husband.

Michelle flinched at her own nasty thoughts. What a lost little lamb she was. The pastor would be so very disappointed. And yet . . .

"Fuck it," Michelle muttered under her breath as she threw the car in reverse and set out for the tiny town of Dahlmouth and the woman who just might send her to Hell.

Thirty-Three

"Rachel ... Rachel, you're going too fast." Jeremy sank into the passenger seat of the patrol car, his elbow resting against the door, chewing on the skin around his forefinger's nail. On either side of the road, a wall of trees whizzed past them. Their headlights lit up Route 6 as Rachel pressed her foot against the accelerator and watched the speedometer tick higher.

"You tear up and down this stretch all the time."

"Not like this." He shook his head once. "Not with everything falling apart."

"You scared a stampede of gremlins is gonna come rushing out of the trees?"

"Maybe. Why are you smirking like that's a dumb-ass fear? Like I'm an idiot for even thinkin' it? It's not the craziest thing that's happened today. I don't think you should be behind the wheel right now anyways; not with what's going on tonight, not on *this* road." His words wiped the dismissive smirk off Rachel's face with one broad stroke. "We keep going. That's what we need to do. Keep driving until we get all the way to Roanoke to rally the troops."

"I'm not doing that," Rachel growled.

"Why? You're determined to run headlong into these ... fucking ... death woods?"

"Death woods?" Rachel sputtered out a laugh.

"Don't laugh at me. You wouldn't be flying out here like you're goddamn Speed Racer if you weren't scared, too."

"I'm not scared," Rachel lied.

"Don't act like this is normal. I see through your act on an average day, let alone—"

"What act?" She gripped the steering wheel harder.

"Oh." Jeremy raised his eyebrows as he looked into the woods flying by. "You're just as soft and scared and fucked up as all the rest of us, Rachel. Maybe even more so, what with Aidan—"

"Oh, my kid dies, and now I'm broken forever?" Rachel exploded. "Certainly it can't be that I keep my shit together better than the rest of you, right? I mean, I'm a mother—no, *a woman*!" She gave a mock gasp. "I'm far more fragile than you big, tough boys—"

"You never stopped!" Jeremy screamed. "You were right back at the station the day after the crash!"

"I was looking for my child's body! What else was I supposed to do?" Rachel took her eyes off the road for a split second to shoot Jeremy a deadly glance. "Fall apart? You think that would've been the proper response? I didn't collapse into depression like Finn, so I did it wrong?"

"I'm not digging into the shit between you and Finn, and I'm not telling you how you should mourn—"

"Here it comes, here it comes—"

"—but—"

"*There* it is!" she boomed.

"BUT." Jeremy raised his voice over hers. "Look, I know Finn fell apart like a pussy, but there's a middle in there, right? I mean, did you even cry about it?"

"Fuck you," Rachel sneered. "Did I cry? That's none of your goddamn business."

"All I'm saying is . . ." He sighed and clucked his tongue. "No one would have blamed you for taking some time. You didn't have to pretend nothing happened."

Rachel cleared her throat and glanced over once more. "You done? We all good here?"

Jeremy sat up in his seat and leaned forward. "Rachel, is that—?"

"There it is!" Rachel pressed hard on the gas, and the engine shuddered. Half a mile up the road, Lou's cruiser was pulled off to the side right behind Zeke's rusted Chevy, dark and empty.

"Listen to me," Jeremy said, his voice tense. "We check out the cars, we check out the surroundings, then we figure out our next move together. Do *not* take off into those woods without me. Do you hear me?"

"Lucy is in there and needs medical attention. Charlie might, too, and if she—"

"Whatever Charlie you find in there is the same one that dragged Lucy and god only knows who else in there with her."

"You don't know that!" Rachel brought the car screeching to a stop behind Lou's cruiser.

"If you go in those woods right now"—Jeremy's hand shot out and gripped Rachel's wrist, keeping her from lunging from the car—"I don't think you're coming back. Now repeat back to me, you will not—"

Rachel wrenched her hand free of Jeremy's grasp and catapulted out of the car. Jeremy was out on the other side in the same breath. He flicked on his Maglite and started in the direction of Lou's lonely patrol car.

The dark wall of trees stretched out before Rachel, no hint of light escaping between the branches. She watched them sway, moved by a breeze Rachel couldn't feel. The leaves should have rustled, the evergreens should have groaned with the motion, but something had hit the mute button on the entire forest. She heard Jeremy's boots on the gravel shoulder as he circled Zeke's car while her own pulse thundered in her ears.

Suddenly, Rachel realized there was a constant hum—not of insects or tree frogs but composed of innumerable whispers moving too fast to be deciphered. Somewhere in that tangle of words, Rachel picked up the faint traces of voices she knew better than her own. They were the same ones she spent years listening for in the night, watching home videos on loop just to hear one more time, both dreading and craving their slightest peep.

"You got the spare keys?" Rachel asked over her shoulder, her breath coming out in small white puffs.

Jeremy looked up from Zeke's car to Rachel. "Don't." He lowered the flashlight. "Don't make me come in there after you."

"Take mine." She flung the heavy key ring at Jeremy's feet and took off for the mouth of the forest.

"RACHEL! GODDAMMIT!" Jeremy scooped the keys from the gravel and stumbled into a run after her. Rachel was already ducking between dangling branches and tree trunks. Brambles caught around her pant legs and slowed her down enough for

Jeremy to catch up, bringing a bright beam of light along with him as the darkness swallowed them whole.

* * *

"FINN!" Rachel tore at the brambles. "LUCY! CHARLIE!"

Jeremy swore to himself. He swung the flashlight's beam back and forth wildly, waiting to catch sight of whatever lurked in the eerie stillness. "You don't even know where you're going! They could be anywhere!"

"Shh!" Rachel halted without warning, and Jeremy stopped short of crashing into the back of her. "Did you hear that?"

He strained his ears. He heard nothing, saw nothing but the thick brush and crowded trees that his light fell upon in every direction. His pulse raced as it occurred to him they could easily lose track of their way out, and without any cell signal, operating radio, or search gear, he and Rachel would be royally fucked. He slowed his breathing to listen, but there was nothing—nothing at all.

"I don't hear anything, Rach," Jeremy panted, nose quickly becoming numb from the cold.

"FINN!" Rachel shrieked into the night. "Don't you fucking touch Charlie! She's sick! She doesn't know what she's doing!"

"Rachel, shut—" Jeremy was cut short, however, by the distinct sound of a deep voice, muttering beyond their line of sight. A chill crept from Jeremy's toes, up his legs and out his fingertips. The hair on the back of his neck stood on end. "This isn't right. We need to get out of here."

"But I told you," a miserable voice sobbed ahead. "I didn't mean to. I never would have said that to you if I knew you'd go and do that, Angeline. Why won't you forgive me?"

"That's Lou!" Rachel gasped. "You heard him, right?"

"Back to the car right now!" Jeremy hissed through the darkness.

And yet she plunged forward. Though Lou sounded so close, she couldn't spot him anywhere, no matter how hard she strained her eyes in the dark. His unsettling voice continued, serving as their only beacon through the silence.

"LOU! It's Rachel and Jeremy. Keep talking! We're coming to you." Rachel broke into a sprint, dodging branches that whipped and clawed at her cheeks. Jeremy struggled to keep on her heels, cracking chunks of dead wood beneath his boots as he ran.

"Aww, Angeline, I wish you wouldn't look at me like that." Louis broke into loud, rattling sobs beyond their sight. "You know I didn't mean for nothing to happen to you, girl. I was just a kid, like you was."

Rachel crested a small hill and slid down the other side, evening her steps out into a trot instead of landing on her ass. "I don't see him! I don't see him anywhere. Do you?"

Jeremy skidded down behind Rachel, his boots sliding in wet leaves and red mud.

"No, and I don't think we should—" Rachel sped off into a wild run, cutting Jeremy's words short. "Dammit, Rachel."

He gripped the flashlight harder and prepared to run after her. Face hot with frustration, Jeremy blew out a puff of air and took two steps forward. As his foot landed a third time, something darted in the corner of his eye, and without thinking, Jeremy swung the light in its direction.

He wasn't sure how long he and the figure caught in the beam of his flashlight stood there before he realized he should have already fled. Time had run out by then; he knew that because what the little girl standing in his light showed him was impossible.

Her tiny glowing fingers wrapped around swirls of color that blossomed into images Jeremy had fought very hard to forget. The longer he stared, the larger the figures within her hands became, and soon it was almost possible to forget Lucy was on the other side of the vision. The voice of his stepfather grew clearer and louder until it, and the sound of his mother screaming for mercy, became the only things he could hear. He was ten years old again, cowering beneath the kitchen table, watching his stepfather beat the life out of the woman Jeremy was too scared to save. All the while, Lucy's black eyes shimmered like volcanic glass as Jeremy descended into the hell he'd spent his entire life running from.

Thirty-Four

Michelle's foot pressed down on the gas pedal harder even as the trees grew thicker and the roads wound tighter. This was madness, but it didn't stop her from speeding up. Every few minutes, she screamed at her car's smart system to call Rachel; each time, the call couldn't be completed. Michelle howled curses in the darkness she'd never heard come out of anyone else's mouth other than Rachel's.

Twenty miles outside of Roanoke, Michelle finally saw DAHLMOUTH—10 MILES reflecting in white against a green road sign. She let out something between a moan and a relieved cry. Whatever she was driving into, she was sure she wouldn't like it. Nevertheless, she was anxious to get it over with, to see Rachel and her shit-eating smirk at the sight of Michelle running toward her in tears. After that kind of spectacle, it wouldn't be long before Rachel showed up at her apartment door, whisking Michelle to the bedroom again and straight into eternal condemnation.

"SHUT UP!" Michelle shrieked to herself. It didn't matter what happened after this—not right now anyway. The Kia sped up even faster.

Another road sign came into view, promising Michelle her current troubles were nearly through. Dahlmouth was only five miles out. Her stomach clenched at the thought of driving over that bridge and knowing what happened there ... knowing she'd compromised all her professional morals when she edited her report to protect a man she'd never met because of that godforsaken bridge.

"Rachel," Michelle hissed under her breath. "I'm gonna kill you when I find you." But even when she tried to sound tough, it came out desperate.

Mile markers whizzed by along Route 6. Michelle gripped the steering wheel and bounced a little in her seat.

Almost there. Almost there. Almost there.

She thought of Rachel marching through the forest that closed in around the car, discovering that inexplicable man nailed to a tree. Then, she saw Rachel leaning over the desk at the morgue, flashing that ridiculous smile that made Michelle's skin prickle. The memory of Rachel lifting Michelle's dress up and over her head sent an unwanted thrill through her chest, and now Michelle was tapping on her dashboard as if that might bring Dahlmouth into view faster. She watched the miles fly by on her odometer.

Four.

Three.

Two.

One.

But still there was nothing.

A lump coiled in the back of Michelle's throat as she flew along the country road. She drove another five miles past where Dahlmouth should have been, then another five miles. When signs for Amherst began appearing, Michelle's heart skipped a beat. She'd lived in Roanoke all her life, and while tiny Dahlmouth had never been a place she went out of her way to find, it was impossible to miss. Route 6 cut straight through it.

Convinced she was losing her mind, Michelle pulled over to the side of the road and then turned around, still going far too fast for such a maneuver. Her tires slipped and squealed as Michelle whipped the car around and drove back toward Dahlmouth. Ten miles later, Michelle felt a strange desperation swell.

There was no worn WELCOME TO DAHLMOUTH sign, and no dented twenty-five miles per hour sign as you zoomed through the town's center either. No dilapidated storefronts lined the main road, and the church steeple that loomed over everything else in Dahlmouth was absent from the scenery. Even the dreaded bridge and the chipping cross memorial that would be forever linked to it were gone.

Michelle repeated this trek at least six times, driving a few miles beyond where Dahlmouth always had been before turning around and driving back. Sometimes, she putted along slowly, searching for the place as if it could have been hiding. Other times, Michelle drove faster as her heart rate ticked upward.

The last time, Michelle drove all the way to Amherst before circling back, but it made no difference. The darkness along the highway only deepened the more times she drove by. Her fingers grew numb as a wave of cold nausea swept over her. Two miles past where Dahlmouth should have been, Michelle brought the car to a screeching halt. She scrambled out of the car and over to the ditch before falling to her knees and vomiting.

Whispers in the Dark

When her retching finally ceased, Michelle held her breath and her thick blonde hair away from her ears to listen. She longed to hear something—*anything*. It didn't matter if the noise was a gunshot in the distance, Michelle would run like hell after it. She'd scream for Rachel until her voice gave out. God wouldn't smile on her now, she knew, but Michelle prayed anyway. Yet even the trees failed to rustle as Michelle waited on her knees.

Suddenly, Michelle was sure the unnatural silence would drive her mad faster than the missing town and all its inhabitants. She pushed herself to standing and stumbled as she looked around. Cold sweat ran down her spine as goosebumps spread along her limbs. Something was watching her—she didn't have to see it to know. Whatever that something was, it wasn't anyone from Dahlmouth.

She spit one last time onto the ground to clear her mouth of the bile. As if in the sights of a predator, Michelle moved slowly and carefully to the Kia. The unseen gaze upon her multiplied and pressed in from all directions. Her skin crawled with the unnerving sensation, and a sob caught in her chest. There was no choice—Michelle had to leave, or else.

They didn't want her here.

A shiver rolled down her spine as the thought came and went.

Michelle clutched the car door with a trembling hand and cast one more look around her. The cry that had been stuck inside her finally broke free as she was suddenly racked with tears.

"RACHEL!" Michelle howled into the black night, bending over as the shriek tore through her chest. "RACHEL, WHERE ARE YOU?"

Michelle didn't stop screaming until she pulled into her home's small driveway, and the cold shivers persisted for hours after that. That unbearable sensation, however—the one that warned her she was being hunted by something she couldn't comprehend—that feeling would never entirely leave Michelle.

Thirty-Five

"LOU! I'm coming to you!" Rachel screamed. Jeremy's steps slowed behind her, but she continued her mad dash, focusing on little other than the growing sounds of Lou blubbering. "FINN!" Rachel's throat burned from shouting and the cold. She found herself rushing up another slope, using her bloody stinging hands to push herself up when suddenly she spilled forward into the frosty underbrush.

"FINN! Listen to me!" The image of Finn carefully steadying a seven-year-old Charlie on her bike before she tore off down a sidewalk like a stuntman flashed through Rachel's mind, and suddenly, a moan rose in the back of her throat. "Finn, *please*, Charlie doesn't know what she's doing! Whatever happened, she didn't mean to do it!"

Rachel wanted to proclaim Charlie's complete innocence ... that their daughter would never hurt her little sister or anyone else, for that matter. But she couldn't bring herself to offer that reassurance to Finn, wherever he lurked. He'd know that was bullshit by now just as much as she did. Something was wrong—wrong with the woods, wrong with the town, wrong with this night. Terribly wrong with Charlie. Nevertheless, Rachel was convinced she could fix it. Finn had to stay calm, though how

Rachel would persuade him to do so, she didn't know yet. The best she could do was stop him in his tracks before he got ahold of their eldest and did something unspeakable in a blind rage.

That old familiar tightness around her throat returned as if Finn's hands were cutting off her oxygen once more, growing tighter and tighter all the time. Not Charlie . . . Finn would never do that to Charlie. No matter how fucked up or angry Finn was, he wouldn't murder a child. That wasn't the man she knew still existed beneath the shell of hatred that had formed between them.

Finn's mischievous smile, backlit by streetlights the night he finally convinced her to go home with him, danced before her.

A stray branch snagged her cheek.

Happy tears sliding down his nose as he cradled newborn Charlie for the first time flooded her.

A gnarled tree root caught the tip of her boot.

His hushed laughter in the darkness of their bedroom, watching some terrible monster movie from the eighties, echoed in Rachel's ears.

A thorny vine tangled around her calf.

The broken expression in his guilty gray eyes as he sat in the back of an ambulance, their son already swept away by the river . . .

His sickening wails as he shriveled on the basement floor, hands clasped over his ears like a child while Rachel unloaded her fury onto him . . .

The smell of his sweat as Finn's fingertips dug into her throat, her grip on his biceps growing weaker as consciousness began to slip away . . .

She broke out into a stilted run again, powered by sheer adrenaline. Her speed accelerated in the impenetrable shadows, but in the next moment, Rachel felt as though she had run headlong into a fleshy wall. She stumbled backward, sliding on decaying leaves. A hand shot out of the darkness and grabbed her by the back of the head, steadying her and pulling her close. A sharp scream started out of her mouth before another hand flew over it and clamped down. Her eyes struggled to adjust to make out the features of the shape she had tackled.

Finn.

"Don't look, Rachel," he instructed, barely audible even though his face was centimeters from her own. "Don't take your eyes off me, okay?" His voice shook with fear in a way Rachel had never heard from him before—not even when he struggled against terror to ask the doctor questions as they rushed newborn Lucy into the NICU six years ago.

Her eyes slowly adjusted, and Finn came more clearly into focus. The hand he kept tight over her mouth was trembling and dewy. Rachel could taste the faint metallic tang of blood on his fingertips. His other hand coiled in her hair and tensed to keep her head perfectly positioned to face him and nothing else.

"Rachel," Finn shakily breathed out. "Stay still."

She tried to nod, but his grip was too tight to manage even that. Finn released the hand from her mouth and brought his finger to his lips, miming for her to stay quiet. Any bravado Rachel had felt as she stormed through the woods gave way to terror when she saw the speckles of blood dried on his long fingers.

"You know I can't do that, Angeline," Lou yelled angrily somewhere off to Rachel's right. "But I'll tell you what this old son of a bitch *is* gonna do!"

Rachel's gaze instinctively flitted toward Lou's voice, but Finn gripped her hair harder and jerked her head to force her eyes back on him. Another shockwave of fear rippled through Rachel at the thought of Finn's unmasked aggression unleashed on their daughter. Yet, his panicked expression insisted he was the one being hunted.

"Don't look," Finn repeated firmer than before. "They're gonna try to make you look, but you can't. Please. Don't look at them. Don't talk to them. Don't touch them. Do you understand me?"

"I ain't no wussy!" Lou cried out, his voice crackling with laughter and cries. "I ain't scared of you, girl! I'm right here facing you down, ain't I?"

"Who's he talking to?" Rachel whispered.

"Definitely not whoever he thinks it is."

Finn's face looked paler and wilder than moments before. Blood stained almost all of him, flaking from his face and arms. Rachel's gaze wandered down and caught the scarlet stain that had bloomed against his T-shirt from the gunshot on his right side.

"How much blood have you lost?" she whispered.

"I'm not crazy, Rach, and I'm not in shock." Finn's fear lessened for a breath as his aggravation broke through.

"Finn, what's happen—?" Finn brought his cupped hand over Rachel's mouth again and pulled her closer, their eyes unavoidably locked as their noses touched.

"You keep askin' for more an' more an' more," Lou shrieked to the specter neither Finn nor Rachel could hear. "Who the hell do you think you are, Angeline? I's already given you what your friends wanted! He ain't good enough for you?"

"Is he talking about Zeke?" Rachel jerked away from Finn's grip over her mouth. She tried to squirm from Finn's grip entirely, feeling an undeniable need to bring the situation under control, to stop whatever madness was eating Lou alive. Finn held her tighter and shook her by the back of her head once again. She clenched her jaw to stop herself from gasping.

"I will never ask you for anything else, Rachel, but just for tonight, please trust me. Please." Finn touched his forehead to hers, and she felt the cold sweat from his brow mingle with her own. "Listen, that man fucking destroyed Zeke with his bare hands, and I don't even think he realizes he did it. There are things running around these woods—"

Lou howled with all the power he possessed, "You think you're so gotdamn clever, don't ya, Angeline? You think you's got me o'rer a barrel, don't ya just?"

"Rachel, we gotta go. There's no time to fuck around and investigate. They're going to come for us, too."

"Well, I's got one up on you! You ain't even seen it comin'. I'm gonna give you somethin' special, Angeline."

"I don't know what they are, but none of them are children." Finn squeezed hard at the base of her skull. "And they are definitely not *our* children. You have to remember that, Rach, because when they come for us, they're going to try to get in your head—"

"What's happening? Where—" *Our children*, she wanted to moan. *Where are they?*

Finn ignored her question. "When those things come for us, you're going to want to look at them. You're going to want to talk to them, but you can't." His voice cracked. "If you start to listen to them, we will never make it out of here, and I very, very much do not want to die out here like this. So, we are going to run like hell—"

Rachel flinched as Lou let out a deranged cry, somewhere between agony and delight.

"Go on, then, Angeline! TAKE 'EM!" Lou was overcome with cackles. "Can't push me around no more, cans ya? Didn't think o' that one, did ya? Nows I can't see ya, ya can't look at me that way no more, Angeline! Nothin' but two black holes lookin' right back at you! You take them eyeballs with ya, an' tell 'em all good ol' Lou done outsmarted ya."

"Jesus!" Rachel yelped in horror. "Did he really just tear his fuckin' eyeballs out of his head? LOU!"

"HONEY!" Finn screamed in her face as she began to turn toward Lou. She snapped her eyelids shut and clenched her teeth. A stitch of pain twinged in her chest as Rachel faintly realized he hadn't called her that since before the crash.

"Focus!" Finn spoke quicker and at full volume now. "Charlie isn't here. Lucy isn't here. Aidan . . ." Finn's voice faltered before he pushed on. "He isn't here. These things are imitating the people we love, but they're not real. Do you understand me?

"They're going to call for you, okay? Just like they called for Lou, and you're going to want to believe it's them, but it's not, Rach. It's not—"

"Mommy?" A high-pitched voice pierced through Finn's words and snuffed them out. Rachel's eyes popped open, and she stared into Finn's.

"Lucy," Rachel breathed, tears suddenly flooding her eyes as hope swelled in her chest.

"It's not her, Rach." Finn pressed his forehead against hers tightly. "Lucy is gone. Don't listen to—"

"Mommy! I'm over here." Lucy's voice sang sweetly from far beyond Finn's shoulders.

"She's not gone," Rachel tried to shout, but her voice was weak as the EMT's radio message echoed in her head. "Lucy's not gone. Don't say that—"

"Honey, I saw her body," Finn forced out, tears streaming down his face now, too. "They left her there for me to find in the brambles like she was trash. I picked her up and I held her. Baby, Lucy was already cold." He gasped and shuddered as a sob rattled through him. Rachel could taste his salty tears on her lips, could feel his legs trembling, threatening to give way. Their baby—their miracle who'd defied death's grasp too many times to be fair in the few years she'd walked the earth . . . "She's gone, Rach."

"SHUT UP!" Rachel screamed into Finn's face and half-heartedly struggled against his grip, already knowing what Finn said was true and hating them both for it. Yet again, they'd let the most precious parts of themselves slip through their fingers.

Rachel landed a weak blow against his shoulder as a deep rumble of sorrow shook her body. "Not Lucy—no. Finn, take it back! FINN!" she shrieked, and his name echoed off the trees surrounding them. Finn's hands tremored as he tried to hold her close, gasping for air as he wept silently. "Finn, our babies—"

"Mommy," Lucy's sweet voice rang out, fearful and hurt. "Daddy left me alone. I was so scared. Take me home, Mommy."

With that, Rachel went wild, bucking against Finn as he fought to keep her in his arms.

"RACHEL!" Finn bellowed. "It's not her!"

Rachel clawed at Finn's hands, ripping deep scratches in his skin. "This is crazy! She's right there!"

"Mommy!"

"Rachel!" Finn pulled her against his chest, wrapping his arms around her in a bear hug as she kicked. "Listen to me! I'm going to tell you something, and I need you to listen to me. The night of the crash—"

The words slowed Rachel's fight, tempering her struggle as the memory of wreckage scraping over boulders down the river when she arrived on scene overtook her. Finn seized the moment, taking her chin in one hand while the other continued to grip her from behind. She tried to look anywhere but into his eyes, yet Finn refused to let go.

"The night of the crash, I saw something, okay?" His words rushed out over Rachel's cries. "I saw something, and I thought I was just drunk—I told myself that's all it was, that my brain created this . . . this fucked-up image to wipe out what happened to Aidan, but now I know—I wasn't hallucinating, Rachel. It wasn't the alcohol. It wasn't something I made up.

"There was a girl, okay? A little girl." Rachel ceased her squirming altogether as she stared into Finn's face and saw his sober sincerity. "She was standing right in the middle of the road, right on the bridge. She ... she came out of nowhere. Aidan dropped his baseball in the back seat; I looked back at him for just a second. Right away, I turned around and there she was. I swerved. I didn't even think about it—"

"It was a deer," Rachel choked out. "You said it was a deer."

"I know what I said, but it wasn't a deer, Rachel. It was a little girl." Finn took a deep breath before he quickly pressed on. "And I swerved, and I fucking ... That's when we flipped off the bridge."

"No." Rachel shook her head. "That's not true."

But they hadn't found a deer. They hadn't found blood or hair in the car's grille either. Finn had said he must've missed it, and it had nearly ripped Rachel in two that he'd exchanged their son's life for a deer's. She chose to believe he swerved for that deer because of his outrageous blood alcohol level, even though she knew Finn drank so much through the years that his tolerance was rock solid, that he could down a fifth of whiskey on his own and still flawlessly change a diaper or bang out an article right in time to meet the morning deadline. No matter how much of a drunken city boy he was, deep down, Rachel never thought his judgment had been all that impaired. It was why she loathed him, why she barely tolerated his existence. All along, there had been a small voice in the back of her head whispering that Finn had killed their son for no reason at all.

He wouldn't have swerved for a wild animal. Finn would have taken his chances and slammed on the brakes, and maybe that would have sent them skidding into the guardrail, but never, ever would it have ended in the merciless, devastating way that it had. What *would* have moved Finn's hand—the thing he wouldn't have risked plowing into—would've been a child, just like his own. He instinctively ran them off the road and over the side of the bridge at sixty miles per hour to avoid a little girl, no matter how improbable it was or how dark her eyes might have been.

"In the water"—Finn swallowed hard, closing his eyes and grimacing as if the words he was trying to get out were about to kill him—"when I was trying to get Aidan out—"

"Stop it, Finn!" Rachel wanted the nightmare to end, to stuff the story back down into Finn's chest and forget he'd ever started his confession.

"I was trying to get Aidan out!" He raised his voice as Rachel continued protesting. "I kept going under. I was doing everything I could to grab him out of that fucking car, but the last time . . . the last time I tried—Rachel, the girl . . ." Rachel froze entirely in his arms as a cold chill crept up her spine. "The girl was there again. She was *in* the car sitting right where Aidan had been. He was gone, and she was there in his place. And—and she looked at me—"

Rachel opened her mouth to cut him off, but her vocal cords failed. Before Finn could finish, Lucy's drawings fluttered through Rachel's memory again. Every image the doctor said Lucy had invented—all the revolting depictions of the angel with black orbs for eyes stalking their son—sprung to life like a film reel.

"She looked at me, and her eyes were . . . they were black—not missing, not dilated, not anything even remotely rational.

They were solid black eyes. And when I ... When she saw me, she opened her mouth and screamed under the water—this ... this howl from hell. And I ..." His voice trailed off for a moment as he scanned Rachel's teary eyes.

"I gave up," he whispered at last. "I gave up because I was scared. I've never been more scared in all my life. And I let our son ..." Finn's voice gave out. His face twisted in agony as he reached his breaking point. "I let him go, Rach. I let her take him."

Rachel stared in shock as Finn's shoulders heaved, and suddenly, there was nowhere else to run from the truth. She felt it all around her in the very air she breathed. Her pulse quickened as her thoughts began to race faster, puzzle pieces falling into place that had seemed senseless moments before. She shook her head furiously even as this horrendous reality wrapped around her.

"Everything Lucy drew and screamed about at night and tried to tell us," she choked out. "The children in the woods—it's true." Finn nodded as cries rattled in his chest.

"Why didn't you tell me?" Rachel whispered slowly in horror.

"Would you have believed him, Mom?" the thing that had stolen Charlie's voice suddenly spoke from behind Rachel. Without thinking, Rachel began to turn to grab her Charlie and pull her close, to protect her from the nightmare closing in all around. Her teen was the entire reason she'd run into the goddamn forest to begin with, and here she was. Finn let out a sharp howl as he tightened his hold on Rachel to the point of pain, desperate to hold her still.

"RACHEL! It's not her!" As Finn shrieked and held her head against his, Rachel couldn't tell whose tears were whose anymore.

"With as much as he'd had to drink? Does it matter anyways?" Charlie's voice warped again, dipping low and twisting into something unholy. "He gave up on saving Aidan because he was *scared*."

It was then that Rachel realized Lucy's heart-wrenching cries had morphed into a high-pitched giggle. "Just like when he left me, Mommy!"

"Finny the Ninny got spooked again and left sweet lil' Lucy all alone. That's when I broke her neck, Mom," the Charlie Thing chirped happily. "She clawed and clawed, but I didn't stop. It was so easy. Now I know what it feels like to be a murderer like Daddy."

Rachel felt Finn's hand ball up into a fist in her hair, shame shaking him like a leaf. She let go of his arm and placed both hands on either side of his face.

"Remember what you said—that's not our Charlie, Finn," Rachel whispered. "It's not real."

"Daddy almost killed you, too, Mom. And that was very real," the Charlie Thing continued. "He knows what it's like to hurt someone and mean it. *Monster*."

"Why'd you want Daddy to kill you, Mommy?" the Lucy Thing piped up once more. "You wanted him to make you die at that hotel. You got so sad when he didn't."

"When he chickened out," the Charlie Thing's voice hissed into their ears, but there was no breath against their cheeks. "Like always."

"You wanted him to strangle you, Mommy—"

"But all he could do was knock you around, and even then, you got the better shots in, didn't you, Mom?" The Charlie

Thing's voice distorted like a worn-out cassette. "Same as always. You wanted him to put you out of your misery—"

"Down like a sick dog, Mommy."

"—but you wound up letting him screw you in that hotel room instead to try and knock out the pain the only way you know how, you filthy—"

"Why did you hurt Mommy like that, Daddy?" The sound of Lucy's voice suddenly came from the right of Rachel, as if their Lucy-Loo was hugging their waists. "You hurt her real bad, Daddy."

"But he didn't have the balls to off you, right, Mom?" Charlie's twisted voice dripped with venom. "He just ended up crying like a little—"

"You're a bad man, Daddy."

"You gave up your life for this piece of shit, and all you got in return is your son washed into a fuckin' sewage pipe somewhere."

"Finn, you listen to me." Rachel opened her eyes to look at him point-blank as they shared the same air. "You and me—we're fucked up, and dumb, and we make the worst decisions sometimes, but we are not whatever these things say we are. You know that, and I know that."

"They throw men in jail for the bad things you did, Daddy." Lucy's voice was growing louder as if someone had turned the volume dial up until she was impossible to ignore.

"I'm so sorry, Rachel," Finn panted.

"Don't apologize to her, Dad. She had it coming. She lured you into it, didn't you, Mom?" the Charlie Thing snarled. "Aidan hadn't even been in the ground for two weeks before she got herself a lady friend. She kept telling you she was working late after busting the Wises with the sheriff and the troopers, but really, she was hunting down pussy and leaving your pathetic, weepy ass to deal with us all alone." Rachel pressed her lips together and waited for Finn to release her as Charlie's words twisted the knife. "You couldn't even look at us, could you, Mom?"

"Just like now, Mommy," Lucy cooed.

"Because now all we remind you of is everything you ever lost."

"We've gotta get out of here," Finn said. "It's going to get worse."

"You should finish the job, Dad." The Charlie Thing laughed. "She deserves it, and you know that better than anyone."

"Come sit down with me, Mommy!" Lucy chirped. Rachel felt a light tug on her jacket and jumped. "Let Daddy put you to sleep."

"It's not hard, Dad. Just put your hands around her neck like before and look at me. I'll help you." The Charlie Thing hovered close to Finn's shoulder, and Rachel felt a numbing coldness sweep over him.

"Finn, I'm going to hold your hand," Rachel breathed out shakily, whispering as if the things flanking them could not hear. She started to feel her way down from Finn's face, over his shoulder, and down the shaking arm that held her in place. "You shouldn't ... shouldn't run with that wound. So, we're going to turn and walk slowly with our eyes shut and go directly back from the direction I came from. We walk until we find the road again."

"Then what?" Finn loosened his grip on Rachel's hair as her hand slipped over his wrist and her fingers laced with his.

"I don't know that part yet." Rachel swallowed hard. "But we're getting the fuck out of here. We've got to get you medical attention."

"Mom? Dad? You're going to leave me?"

His voice was like a gust of spring wind, blowing away the bitter cold and reminding them life was about playtime and sun and laughter and hope. It was the same as when he had said goodbye to Rachel that morning as he slid out of the car's back seat when she dropped him off at school, his baseball T-shirt clutched in one hand: *Go save the day, Mom. I love you.* She had forgotten just how beautiful the sound was.

Rachel let out a full-bodied cry but held firm as salty tears slipped into her open mouth.

"Don't leave me, Mommy," Aidan cried. "I'm scared."

Rachel fought against the wails shaking her. "Make it stop."

"Daddy, why'd you let them take me?" Aidan's voice drew closer. "They stole me away, Daddy, and you didn't even try to stop them. Mommy, it hurts."

"We have to go, Rachel. Right *now*," Finn shouted. Rachel blinked a thick curtain of tears from her eyes to look into Finn's once more. To her left, she could see the faint outline of Charlie's slim form. To the right, two small children meant to be Aidan and Lucy huddled close by. She clamped her eyes shut again as Finn continued unsteadily. "Fuck walking—we're running, Rachel. I can do it."

She nodded her head and began taking in shaky, labored breaths. "Don't let go of me," Rachel commanded, "and if you start to feel faint—"

A sudden breeze rustled the leaves overhead, surging stronger with each moment. Finn and Rachel hesitantly raised their eyes to the black sky, and as they did, a song swept through the trees. A jumbled chorus supported by hundreds of children's voices resonated off branches, rocks, dried creek beds, and the river itself. Soon enough, the three creatures gathered nearby also joined the indistinguishable throng with voices that sounded more like echoes in a cave than anything human.

"NOW! We go right fuckin' now!" Finn screamed.

Rachel stumbled with lowered eyes and turned as Finn yanked her around whatever had been standing beside them. The things that might have been her children once were blurs as they took off at full speed, hands clasped for dear life as they ran into the black wild with nothing to guide them but panic.

"Don't go!" Aidan's voice broke out into a miserable wail, but it fell behind them faster than Rachel expected. Fear twisted her stomach. Nothing so dangerous would give up that easily.

Thirty-Six

The song receded like the tide, but both knew it would return soon if they didn't get out of the woods. Finn and Rachel ran headlong into sharp branches and trunks, slipping and sliding into jagged bushes that ripped open their skin and halted them one at a time. Still, they did not break hands. Rachel and Finn kept their eyes glued to the ground searching for safe terrain, but it was as though the sky had swallowed the moon and the stars. The only shapes they caught sight of were ones from the corners of their eyes—the ones that weren't supposed to be there at all.

The fifth time a branch struck a blow into their outstretched arms, taking bits of their skin with it, Rachel tugged Finn backward into herself.

"We can't keep doing this," Rachel shouted. "We're going nowhere. We have to stop and figure out how the hell to get out of here."

"Absolutely not."

"One of us is going to end up with a broken ankle or a gouged eye. How fucked do you think we'll be then, Finn?" Rachel began fumbling around her belt with her free hand. "I have my flashlight."

"Rachel, you are not going to try and guide us out of here swinging that around, looking every goddamn which way." Finn's voice rose until it cracked. "You're gonna lock eyes with one of them, and—"

"Don't let go of my hand. Ignore whatever else you see or hear or feel except me, okay?" Her voice wavered, but Rachel slowly began to regain some measure of calm.

"I don't want to do this. This is stupid, Rach. This is really fucking stupid—"

"You keep your eyes on the ground, okay?" Rachel swallowed hard. "I'm going to count down, and then we'll keep going."

"If something happens to you, I can't just take off. You know that, right?" The panic in Finn's voice threatened to set Rachel's teeth on edge. They didn't have time for anxiety now.

"On three," she began carefully.

"If you start looking at them, if you stop and start listening to them—"

"One . . ."

"We may have had a lot of shit times, you and me, but I'm not abandoning you to die in fuckin' Dahlmouth."

"Two . . ."

"Rachel, promise me!"

"Three!"

Rachel's eyes fluttered upward as she switched the flashlight on and bathed the trees before them in white light. In the very next moment, she snapped her eyes back to her boots, plastered with mud and leaves like papier-mâché. She sucked in gulps of air and squeezed Finn's hand. He squeezed back.

"You still there?" she asked.

"Yes, I'm still fucking here. What's wrong?"

Rachel glanced over toward him and saw the faint profile of something standing in the woods beyond Finn's shoulders and fixed her eyes on the ground again. "We need to move." She flicked the light off once more.

"What did you see?"

Rachel ignored him, forcing herself to focus on the task at hand as she always did. "Big steps now. No running this time. If you think you see something, just close your eyes again, okay? I'll guide you."

"Rachel." Finn swallowed. "I'm a grown-ass man in the middle of a complete breakdown, and it seems very likely that I've lost more blood than a person really should in a day, so I don't think I can take much more bullshit. Just tell me what the hell you saw."

Rachel licked her lips and blinked hard, searching for words that wouldn't scare the shit out of Finn. Nothing fit the bill. "There's something ahead of us."

"What kind of something?"

"Well, I'd have to be looking at it to tell you exactly what it is, wouldn't I?" Rachel shouted.

"You couldn't even make out a shape?" Finn yelled, incredulous.

A voice suddenly rang out with crisp clarity, "I told you not to run into these woods. I told you that wasn't the right Charlie."

"Why didn't you tell me you brought Jeremy with you?" Finn whispered.

The answer stuck in Rachel's throat. She'd simply forgotten, and there was no good excuse for that.

"She told me what you done," Jeremy continued miserably. "She told me all about you coverin' for him ... shielding his dirty little lies so's he can keep walkin' a free man."

"Jeremy ... who's been talking to you?" Rachel tried to look up, but her courage crumpled at the sight of swarming, shifting shadows around Jeremy's figure. "Was it Charlie?"

"Whoever's been talking to you, it's not who you think it is, man," Finn began.

"You shut the fuck up, Finn!" Jeremy exploded, and Rachel heard the unmistakable sound of a gun cocking. "I know what you did!"

"Jeremy," Rachel started again gingerly. "You had this place and everything that's happening pegged right. I should have listened—"

"That thing"—Jeremy vacillated between fear and bluster—"the thing pretending to be Charlie ... it brought little Lucy here. And now, now Lucy's explaining it all. Now, she's free, and we're all gonna listen."

"Jeremy, you listen to me, all right? Whatever she's telling you, she's just the same as the thing using Charlie. That's not my Lucy."

"No, no—I know the truth now, and there ain't no goin' back," Jeremy bellowed. He marched closer to them in the darkness, and Rachel could smell his sweat mixed with thick cologne. "This son of a bitch here—he murdered her! This sick fuck held a pillow over her face so she'd stop crying."

"I didn't—"

"You callin' your little girl a liar?" Jeremy shrieked and pounded toward Finn through the forest brush.

"Jeremy, no!" Rachel begged. A fresh wave of terror washed over her as she saw her partner's gun butt against the flesh of Finn's forehead from the corner of her eye.

"This man here," Jeremy shouted, his spittle sprinkling across Rachel's cheek, "he's a drunk, a wife beater, a low-life slacker feeding off his family." Rachel felt Finn's sweaty fingers slip a little and she tightened her grip. "He's a fucking baby killer, and a waste of space, takin' up oxygen that ain't his to breathe." Jeremy leaned in close and muttered into Finn's ear, and he flinched in return: "People like you aren't welcome here."

"Listen to *me*, Jeremy, not that thing pretending to be Lucy." Rachel kept her voice gentle. "They're trying to trick you like they've done to everyone else, but you're smarter than that." Rachel pulled on Finn's hand, easing over toward him by millimeters. "You're too smart to be conned by these things."

"I trusted you," Jeremy groaned, his rage evident even through tears. "When everyone else was talking shit about you, I backed you up. I put my neck on the line for you."

Rachel took a deep breath. "I know. Since the moment I got here, you've been the only person I knew I could rely on. We're a hell of a good team, right?"

"You lied to me." His voice broke. He began sobbing. "You lied to me so's you could protect this piece of shit. He shoulda gone to jail for what he done to Aidan, but you covered it up. Now he's killed Luce, too."

Rachel licked her lips as her mind raced for answers. She wanted to scream it wasn't true, that her whole life had been dedicated to ferreting out the truth, not hiding it. That would have been a lie, though, and it seemed all the falsehoods she'd ever told were unraveling. If she tried to sidestep reality now, these creatures could steer Jeremy's wrath toward her. Should Rachel confess, however, she had no doubt that Jeremy would empty a clip into Finn's head.

"How 'bout you put the gun down, and we head to the station to talk?"

"You're tryin' to worm your way out of this," Jeremy said. "I can't let you do that. I'm doing this for Lucy. I'm making it right for her."

"I didn't kill Lucy!" Finn managed a strangled cry.

"Finn, stay calm," Rachel spoke quickly. "Jeremy, you take us back to the station, and I promise you, Finn will get what he deserves. The troopers will run every test on him possible—"

"You gonna fuck one of them so's they'll hide those results, too?"

"What's he talking about?" Finn risked a glance in Rachel's direction, but she didn't return one.

"How much better would it be for Finn to rot in prison?" Rachel raised her voice again. "You keep your hands clean, and Finn lives in hell. You know what they'll do to a baby killer in jail. C'mon, now. They'll take care of him for you, and it won't be as kind as a bullet to the head, will it?"

"I don't want to hurt you," Jeremy whined before descending into muttering, "I don't want to do it. *Please* don't make me do it. Don't make me hurt her."

Jeremy pulled away from Finn and started pacing. She saw his dark outline moving frantically back and forth while another entity gave off an unearthly glow a few feet behind him.

"You talking to Luce?" Rachel swallowed hard. "Is she with you now?"

"I know your mama's games," Jeremy murmured to the thing in the distance. "I won't fall for her smooth talk, little one. Don't you worry none."

"Do you hear her?" Finn whispered.

"Not at all," Rachel replied quickly before resuming her careful negotiation with Jeremy. "Hey, if that's Lucy, can you tell her I'm sorry? Can you talk to Lucy for me?"

Jeremy fell into whimpers again. Rachel heard the gun rattling and something thumping as he paced faster.

"I know she's runnin' a game for him again. I ain't stupid. Why can't you trust me? Don't make me hurt your mama."

"Rachel, get out of here," Finn murmured. "He's about to kill you."

"No, he's gonna kill us both. Let me handle this."

"Would you two shut up?!" Jeremy screamed in their direction. "They're all talking so loud! Jesus Christ, I can't hear *me* anymore!"

"Jeremy, you're a good man," Rachel called. "You know hauling our asses to the troopers is the right thing to do."

"She won't let me do that, Rachel."

"You're gonna be bossed around by a *six*-year-old? You know better than that. Take us in. Drive us to Roanoke and tell them what we've done—tell them I'm a dirty cop who tampered with evidence to shield a bastard. Odell will fuckin' love that. We can walk out of here together and straight to the punishment we deserve. Me and Finn ... we won't even fight you. We'll get in the back of the cruiser without a fuss. Hell, cuff us right here.

"Be the hero. They'll probably promote you to chief after this, won't they? They're not bringing in some outsider like me again. That wasn't right. We can fix that now, can't we?"

"Why can't everyone just shut up?!" Jeremy cried into the darkness. "It's so loud!"

"You kill us right now," Rachel shouted over his growing hysteria, competing with voices she couldn't hear, "and nobody knows what we did. Make us tell the world what we've done."

"I don't want to do this." Jeremy suddenly fell on Rachel, grabbing her by the shoulders and howling into her hair. He held the gun against the side of her cheek, the end of the barrel pressing into her skin. She heard Finn yell out her name. Rachel's breath snagged as she tried to shut down her own panic to bargain their way out of a death sentence.

"I don't want to do this, but they won't stop unless I do. They want their mommy." Jeremy rocked with Rachel clutched in his embrace. "The kids ... they want their mommy back. They're lonely."

If Rachel let go of Finn's hand, she could make a break for the gun and possibly rip it out of Jeremy's hand. That meant breaking her solid connection and possibly losing Finn in the darkness. It also very well meant finding the Lucy that had bent Jeremy's mind.

"I'll stay! I'll stay with them. Leave me here and take Finn."

"RACHEL!" Rachel ignored Finn's protest, speaking faster as time began running out.

"Can you do that? No blood on your hands tonight. I'll stay, and you save the day."

"I'm not doing that." Jeremy backed away, removing the weapon from her face. His voice was suddenly clear and calm, more unnerving to Rachel than the madness that had overtaken him moments before. "They won't stop. They're *never* going to stop. They want you and Finn and me, and all of us. That's what they really want, and I'm not giving it to them."

"Jeremy, what are you doing?" Rachel fought against the urge to lunge forward and seize hold of him. "Talk to me."

"They're here to make us pay for what we've done in this life," he spoke darkly. "But I ain't doing their dirty work for 'em. Fight like hell, Rach. You always do."

"Rach, he's gonna—"

The blast rang out like a clap of thunder and cut off Finn's words. Rachel screamed and fell to her hands and knees, scuttling forward toward the dark outline of a body that had crumpled to the ground several feet away.

"RACHEL!" Finn screeched the moment she let go of his hand. "You come back here right now!"

"No, no, no, no." Rachel reached Jeremy's limp body and rolled it over. In the glow of some unholy light, she saw his eyes were still wide open despite half his skull being splattered across the forest floor. "Jesus Christ, Jeremy! No! Why'd you do that?" she wailed over his corpse. "I'm so sorry."

Thirty-Seven

"UP! NOW! We've gotta go!"

Finn nearly wrenched her arm from its socket as he grabbed Rachel, pulling her to her feet. Out of her peripheral vision, she saw shapes moving, some well-formed and solid, others like translucent shadows against the backdrop of the forest trees. Rachel stumbled, began running, then let out a tiny shriek that froze her in place.

"The keys!"

"What?" Finn turned and shouted into her face as if she were yards away from him.

"Jeremy—I gave him the keys!" Rachel tumbled backward over her feet as she said it, scrambling away from Finn. She fell on top of Jeremy's body and desperately dug through his pants pockets.

"Fuck the keys! We gotta get out of these woods. We'll walk the road if we have to."

"Are you crazy? It's over twenty-five miles to Roanoke. When's the last time you pulled a marathon, Finn? With a gunshot wound?"

At the base of Jeremy's head, she saw a pair of tiny little feet with pale toes—ones she had counted and wiggled and sang to from the time they'd been removed from an incubator. Every instinct in her begged to look up, to grab her little girl and hold her tight. But her Lucy didn't radiate this kind of coldness, nor did she flicker like the light of a dying firefly. Rachel stared as red clay welled up between the Lucy Thing's glowing toes as a lullaby began to rise from the trees all around them. The creature wiggled her daughter's digits, and to Rachel's horror, she realized the rust-red color caked upon its feet was not Virginian clay but the contents of Jeremy's skull.

As tiny clumps of gray matter gathered in the ridges of Lucy's toenails, the creature began to giggle with her child's stolen voice. Rachel swallowed a wail as her fingers grasped around jagged metal teeth and a steel ring deep in Jeremy's left hip pocket. She tore her eyes from the creature's feet as she pulled the keys loose from Jeremy's body.

"I've got them! I've got the keys!"

"Let's go!" Finn seized her around the waist and almost yanked her off the ground as they began running once more, no longer bothering to keep their eyes toward the ground or carefully maneuver around trees and branches. The stares that bore into them from all sides spurred them on faster and faster. Rachel narrowed her eyes into slits that could easily snap shut if one of them dove in her path. Still, they were open wide enough to see the little figures dotting the woods around them on all sides.

The trees did not part or grow thinner. They simply stopped like a heavy stage curtain at the side of the road. Rachel and Finn broke free of the forest, nearly in lockstep, and kept running until they slammed into the side of the patrol car. Rachel fumbled with the keys, hands shaking, panting. Lou's cruiser and Zeke's Chevy were still parked empty in front of them, small handprints scattered across the condensation on the windows.

Rachel's thumb hit the remote and popped up the locks on both front doors. She dashed to the driver's side as Finn slid into the passenger seat.

"Go south! Go south!" Finn slammed his palm against the dash, leaving smears of his own blood behind. Rachel turned the ignition and the car roared to life. "We can't go back to Dahlmouth. We can't ever fucking go back there, Rach."

Rachel jammed her foot down on the accelerator and quickly brought the car to the highest speed it could go. Finn deflated against the side of the passenger-side door, taking his head in his hands and allowing himself to cry softly for a moment. The car zoomed past a familiar white wooden cross with a small boy standing beside it, the breeze catching strands of his dirty-blond hair and whipping them across his forehead. A mud-caked teddy bear from the makeshift memorial hung limp in Aidan's fingers and his mouth was wide open as their son turned to look at them with onyx eyes.

Finn's eyes snapped shut. A miserable wail left him while Rachel screamed, her eyes back on the road.

"What is happening?!" she shrieked to no one in particular, smacking the steering wheel with an open palm.

"I told you to go south toward Roanoke!" Finn squirmed beside her.

"I AM going south, Finn!"

"Then why did we just go by Aidan's marker?" He turned in his seat, though the cross and their child's imposter was long behind them. "It's on the northbound side of the road."

"I'm going south! I started driving south! YOU SAW ME!"

At the same moment, the car sped by a green-and-white road sign that lit up in their headlights. Dahlmouth was five miles ahead.

"RACH!"

She slammed on the brakes and the car came to a screeching halt, throwing both Finn and Rachel forward in their seats. She threw the car into reverse, then looked into the rearview mirror. The brake lights illuminated the faint outline of small bodies wandering onto the road hand in hand, slowly stretching out in a dark line bathed in the red glow. Wasting no time, Rachel ripped the mirror from the windshield and tossed it onto Finn's lap.

She spun the car in the opposite direction and hit the gas pedal all the way to the floor as the engine protested. The headlights caught a rainbow of colors as they fell on children's shirts, pants, and dresses.

"CLOSE YOUR EYES!" Rachel bellowed, accelerating straight into the precious row stretched across Route 6. Finn squeezed his eyelids tight and braced for impact, but none came. After several seconds passed that should have brought the sickening crunch of bodies against the cruiser's tires, hood, and windshield, Rachel saw Finn cautiously open his eyes to find an empty road whizzing by. Rachel's hands shook on the wheel, but she clamped down with white knuckles and sat forward, never taking her foot from the bottom of the floor.

"Where'd they go? Where the fuck did they go?"

"Nowhere," she wheezed. "They disappeared into Nowhere."

Not two minutes had gone by before the car flew past the tilted white cross on the right-hand side of the road once more. The Aidan Thing had abandoned his post there. Very soon after that, another sign: DAHLMOUTH, FIVE MILES. Rachel broke into a manic scream and bounced in her seat.

"Fucking hell, Rachel!" Finn shrieked. "What do we do now?"

"I'm gonna turn the car around again."

"And how is that going to help?"

"What else do you want me to do?" Rachel screamed.

"How fast are you going?" Finn gasped, clinging to the grip handle with one hand while he clutched the hole in his side with the other.

Rachel slid her hands down the steering wheel and craned her head. "'Round about ninety."

Rachel saw Finn wince, his fingers slick with blood from the wound. "That means we hit Dahlmouth in less than two minutes. Slow down." He pressed back into the headrest.

"I'm gonna turn the car around."

"Those kids aren't gone. If I had to guess, they'll be right back there again when we turn around."

"And I'll mow them down again."

"Unless they get in your head and fuck with your brains, and then you end up careening off the road and the car bursts into flames or some shit."

"Wouldn't that be poetic justice?" Rachel's voice shook with terror.

"Really?" Finn shouted, turning to her with wide eyes. "After what you saw and heard back there, you're still gonna take shots at me for—"

"It's not a shot. I'm trying to say," she began tightly, gripping the steering wheel harder, "that it appears all our dirty deeds are being repaid threefold in one night . . . *everyone's* all at once."

"Dirty deeds . . ." Finn's nostrils flared. "Is that what Jeremy was talking about?"

"Jeremy said a lot of things." Rachel's voice dropped. "Called you a baby killer multiple times, if I'm not mistaken. Just because he rattled something off doesn't make it true—"

"You fucked with the toxicology report—"

"You knew that." Rachel clenched her jaw, eyes focused on the road despite the imminent threat of what awaited in the shadows.

"—or you fucked *someone* to alter the toxicology report for you?"

Once more, Rachel struggled to find the right words, her mouth opening and closing as she shook her head. "Does it really matter now?" she finally managed.

"It matters, Rachel." Finn grimaced. "Because that would mean you were fucking around long before I ever found you in that hotel."

"Oh, come on, Finn; you knew I was having affairs *way* before that night." Rachel gripped the wheel until it hurt.

"Before Aidan died?" Finn asked, clearly wounded before she could answer.

"No." Rachel's face twisted in outrage.

"I thought we had a good thing, that we were living a pretty good life together, y'know? I thought you were happy with me and our family—"

"Are you blind?" Now Rachel turned her attention from the road to Finn, eyes flashing. "I loved you. I love the kids, but this—this *Brady Bunch* bullshit was never me.

"I tried to be what you wanted me to be—what *everyone* wanted me to be—but I'm not that person. You knew that. I told you that as soon as I knew I was pregnant, but you asked me to play house anyways because that's what *you* wanted."

"So, you're saying what?" Finn flung a hand in the air as his eyes narrowed. "You wish you'd aborted Charlie? That you'd skipped right over our life together?"

"I wish I'd never pretended to be straight!" Rachel slapped the wheel. "I wish I'd said no when you asked me to marry you—not because I don't love you, but because it nearly killed me. I don't regret the kids or you." Rachel tried to swallow tears and failed. "I regret lying to myself. I regret shoving who I am aside over and over and over again to hang on to a dream that was never mine in the first place."

They both fell silent for a few beats, the sound of the tires zooming over potholed pavement filling in the void their argument left. Rachel braced herself for another jab—something about her leading him on, her self-imposed imprisonment, her selfish promiscuity while Finn waited at home like a saint. Instead, Finn slowly reached his bloodied hand over the console and placed it on her leg.

"You were my best friend," he murmured at last. "You were the only person that believed in me, and I believed in you. I didn't want to lose that . . . but I did anyway. It wasn't fair."

For the first time since Rachel had shown up on the side of Route 6 to find Finn soaking wet and clutching Lucy tight, she felt her soul stir with something other than outrage. The edges of the black hole within stung, raw and bloody, as it lay bare at last. The warmth of his hand on her leg and the words that lingered between them recalled memories of a thousand moments they'd shared that were more than shards of pain.

Rachel could see all the knowing glances they'd exchanged as Dahlmouth's residents hurled religious advisories at them—sharing in the private joke that they'd never really belong there and never cared to. She remembered his low wisecracks at Aidan's baseball games that no one else heard but her, and she allowed them to bring a smile to her face once more. The stories they shared in bed, staying up far too late to be responsible adults; the times they hid on the balcony of their Richmond apartment to sneak a cigarette away from the kids; the way he kept joking with Rachel as they hurriedly moved her shit out of her girlfriend's place to his, even under the angry glare of Rachel's former friends; the god-awful pickup lines he used the night he unsuccessfully tried to weasel a story out of her fourteen years prior. The memories of her best friend Rachel had buried finally broke through as the gates to Nowhere hung wide.

"You didn't lose me," Rachel whispered. "We just lost our way for a bit. There's no point in worrying about that now, is there?

Right now, we're all the other one's got. That's gonna have to do for tonight."

She reached down and laid her hand atop his, giving a quick squeeze. No matter how damaged Finn was, there had never been a time since they first met that he wasn't her best friend, and Rachel knew she was his. The world would never understand the bond that laced them together, and for once, Rachel was at peace with that.

"They won't let us out." Rachel licked her dry lips and swallowed.

"I know," Finn murmured.

Rachel slowed the car to the mandated fifty-mile-per-hour speed limit just as she fought to slow her thoughts. No matter how hard she tried, however, no good solution came to mind. There was really only ever one option, and that was to continue on to the quaint little town of Dahlmouth.

Thirty-Eight

Dahlmouth was not a particularly bright town, especially at night. Rachel doubted there was much of anything you could see from an airplane. However, on any given evening, there were at least some lights that filled home windows and illuminated Main Street. Nearly every house had a floodlight flickering on and off through the night as deer scuttled through country yards, but as Rachel and Finn roared into the heart of Dahlmouth, there was nothing but darkness.

"Where is everyone?"

"I don't know," Rachel replied softly. "But we're going to the station."

"What?" Finn whipped his head around to look at Rachel. "No. We keep driving. I don't care if we drive through Dahlmouth a thousand times, I don't want this car to stop rolling."

"There's a generator there, and some first-aid supplies, and that'll be the first place the sheriff and EMS come."

"Did you not hear me? We don't get out of this car."

"We'll run out of gas eventually or lose our minds." Her eyes darted toward him for a moment before returning to the fast-approaching town center. "I don't think either one is very far off. We lock the station down like it's the apocalypse. No one even has to know we're there. I need to figure out what to do about the goddamn bullet hole in your side. It's probably infected already, and the very last thing I need is for you to go septic if we have to hole up here for days."

"This is a bad idea, Rach."

"Would you rather go back into the woods?"

"Obviously not, but . . ." Finn's voice trailed off as several small beams of light appeared in the road straight ahead of them.

Rachel slowed the car and leaned forward over the wheel. Despite first appearances, they were not alone in Dahlmouth.

Rachel felt herself go numb as she hit the brakes and rolled the car to a stop. The couple sat in complete silence, taking in the sight. Twenty or so faces awaited them. They clustered together with screwed-up sneers and wrathful eyes, huddling close around Officer Marcus Blevins, who stood front and center with arms crossed.

Several citizens held torches while others held flashlights—lights that not so long ago had illuminated the woods in search of two missing girls. One of the beams shone over steel rifle barrels that glimmered as black as the eyes of the Kennan children. Rachel noticed another beam lighting up a ratty brown rope coiled around Joseph Stockton's forearm and shoulder.

"Rachel," Finn began slowly as he surveyed the scene, "I want you to know I love you . . . very, very much. I haven't said that in a while, but—"

"I love you, too," Rachel whispered.

Marcus broke from the pack and strode toward the car with pep in his step. Rachel fumbled for the door handle, prepared to meet the kid on equal footing.

"Rachel, don't." Finn offered a weak protest, but defeat was already in his tone.

Rachel swung open the door, managing to get to her feet and hold steady as Marcus came even with her. "What's going on here?" she asked gruffly.

"Where are they?" Marcus's shoulders hunched to his ears. "What have you done with them?"

"What have I done with who?"

"The kids, Rachel. Where are the children?"

Rachel looked over Marcus's face and was met with rage that blocked out all reason. "What do you mean?"

"They're all gone. Every single child in Dahlmouth is gone. But you knew that already, didn't you?"

"All of them?" Rachel's eyes grew wide. "They *all* went into the woods?"

"Yeah, including the babies—*my* baby, to be exact. Maisie Louise is gone right along with Jennifer. My whole family went into those fucking trees, and ain't nobody coming out again."

"I don't know what's going on any more than you do."

"Don't give me that horseshit." Marcus grabbed hold of Rachel's chin and squeezed. "All of this started with Charlie, didn't it? I know you questioned her. Everyone that's been around her in the last twenty-four hours went faster than everybody else."

Rachel shoved Marcus's hand away from her face. "Something happened to Charlie, but it's not what you think—"

"Then we trekked on over to y'all's place and found that room you've been keeping. Those photos of your kids ... them poor EMTs from Amherst propped against the walls like fuckin' dolls ... Lucy's body laid out on the bed all dressed up and pretty like it's Easter Sunday ... All that your work, or his, or'd you do it together for fun?" Marcus's eyes flitted behind Rachel. She quarter-turned to see Larry Simmons and Bob Jessup prying Finn out of his seat and slamming him against the side of the car.

"I don't know what you're talking about," she whispered, a shiver creeping up her spine before she turned back to face Marcus.

"Where's Jeremy?" he asked sharply. Rachel opened her mouth to reply but the image of Jeremy on the forest floor, brown eyes shining as his body grew cold blotted out her words. "Lou? Zeke?" Marcus pressed. Rachel still couldn't offer him a better answer other than to shake her head and look away.

"You know, bad things like this didn't happen to good people like us before you came strolling on in here."

"Oldridge had to shut down his outer pasture. All them cows over there turnin' up cut all to pieces," Ronnie Morris shouted from the left flank of the group.

"We had that bout of—what was it?" Mrs. Brady pushed her way past Miss Crowley to hiss. "Swine flu? The virus cooked up in a lab? Ain't nobody in this town out picking up exotic diseases."

Finn let out a high-pitched chuckle—a nervous defense mechanism Rachel knew would only serve to confirm Dahlmouth's worst fears.

"And then the children ... the holiest of God's creation," Mrs. Stockton bellowed from the right. "You came for them from the start, didn't you? Corrupting them with your perversion. Don't think we didn't see it in your Charlie, too." The woman's voice dropped to a dangerous whisper, her eyes sparkling with righteous venom. "Your wickedness . . . it's like an infection that spreads until it gobbles the righteous whole."

"They've been in the forest," Finn called to Rachel as Larry and Bob clamped his hands behind his back with cuffs from inside the cruiser. "They're messed up from those things in the woods."

Rachel wasn't so sure. These accusations seemed too familiar.

"Woe be to us for failing to cut out the blight sooner," Mrs. Brady proclaimed. "We're paying for it now with the lives of our children."

Rachel looked over her shoulder once more and saw the men jerking Finn away from the car and pushing him forward toward the crowd. Larry kicked him in the back of his knees, and he fell on his face with a thud. Someone let out a righteous hoot as Finn spit a mouthful of blood onto the pavement with a groan. Panic seized Rachel as she felt her control slipping away.

"Awww." Marcus twisted his head to the side to watch Finn struggle to rise to his knees, the trail of blood beneath him quickly becoming a pool. "You okay over there? Hey, I think you should know—we've all read your nifty articles online, Mr. Kennan. They're real cute and all.

"You think you're smarter than all the rest of us? You think you're so much better than us country bumpkins, don't you? Just like you wrote that fancy article sayin' them folks out in the Kentucky sticks was responsible for all you city folks' problems? We don't understand the news; we're too simple; we need some smart-ass bitch like you to come on in and educate us on the way things are out there, right?"

Rachel flinched. That goddamn exposé may have won Finn a dozen awards, but it wasn't going to save him now. Right as Finn managed to get back onto his knees, Larry landed his boot directly between Finn's shoulder blades and sent him crashing face-first onto the pavement again. Rachel bit back a wild scream; it'd only make things worse for Finn if they saw Rachel react.

"And you"—Marcus's eyes fixed back on Rachel—"we knew what you was right from the start. We didn't need no damn pictures of your womanizin' to tell us, and you ain't foolin' nobody just 'cause you got him to give you cover. We know what kind of lifestyle you prefer, and I'm here to tell you, it ain't nothin' to be proud of, no matter how many flags you wanna fly.

"The two of you brought near every sin in the whole Bible up into this town, so no, it ain't so crazy to think you'd turn on your own children . . . or that one of your brood turned to worship the forces of evil. That hiker in the woods? That hiker was being called here by something. Ain't no other reason for him being here. And I'm willing to bet everything I ever had he was being called by your demonic little bitch."

Rachel watched the men drag Finn off the ground and pull him closer toward the group. A few steps further and he'd be completely enveloped by them, a wall of Dahlmouth citizens standing between Rachel and Finn. She knew she would never take down all the gunmen in front of her, but if they gave one squat about Marcus, they would turn Finn over when she had her gun against Marcus's temple. She would have to be quick about it, fluid in her movements, bringing the Glock against his temple with the same speed she would throw him in front of her chest. Anything less than perfect, and Rachel could get her head blown off in the blink of an eye.

Her hand hovered near her belt as she ran her wrist along the edge of her pants to feel the grip of her weapon and prayed Marcus was too busy on his soapbox to notice. The trouble was that Rachel's gun wasn't in its usual place. Then it hit her. The gun was still a half a mile away in the Kennans' empty house where Jeremy had disarmed her what felt like centuries ago. When the memory rushed through Rachel's mind, all hope fell away.

"We turned our heads and pretended we didn't see ... and that's on us!" Marcus yelled to the crowd. "But we're gonna make things right starting now."

"You know the sheriff's gonna come and take you down," Rachel murmured flatly. "This isn't going to just go away."

He snorted. "Half our town's missing, and you think they're going to wonder what *we* did to *you*? No, ma'am. We're gonna stuff your bodies so deep in that fuckin' forest, they won't find you till kingdom come."

"I hope you do that." Rachel managed a chuckle despite Marcus's sneer. "I really hope you do carry your pathetic ass into those woods, you sad little man, you."

Marcus snatched Rachel by the back of her neck and sent her flying forward onto the pavement. The impact rippled through Rachel's outstretched arms and rattled her teeth. Her palms stung as gravel bit into the skin, lighting up her fight-or-flight instincts. She moved to push herself up to swat Marcus's legs out from under him. Instead, she was swept up by Marcus on one side and Barret Lorry on the other, her feet dangling far enough from the ground to prevent her from dragging them.

"Get off me, shitheads!"

Rachel twisted and turned, but their hold was steadfast. Before she knew it, the men had carried her into the crowd, which opened like a gate to let them pass. The squeals and jeers that flew at her as they passed blended together, until she could no longer pick out the individual indictments against her.

"Rachel!" One voice rose above all the others and her heart leapt into her throat.

"Finn!" she screamed, looking frantically above the heads around her.

The crowd fell away, and she saw him thrown into the square before them, stumbling to stay on his feet. It was only as Joe Stockton threw a rope over the bend in one of the massive branches of the maple tree that Rachel truly understood.

"NO!" she shrieked and fought at the hands that held her with renewed intensity. "Let him go! He didn't do anything!" Someone smacked her hard in the back of the head. "This is crazy!"

"Come on, now. Where's the big brave *chief* now?" Marcus pressed his mouth against her sweaty ear. "Don't you worry—you're gonna swing right there next to him, sweetheart. We're sending you both back to hell together."

Someone had brought out two of their finest dining room chairs and propped them under the tree. Larry and Bob descended on Finn and jerked him up to attention as Joe fastened the end of the rope to his Ford pickup.

"Oh, my god, no." Rachel broke down as she watched them force Finn up onto the chair with the noose around his neck. At the same time, she watched Shane Bowler throw another thick rope over the same branch, a noose dangling there, too. "We didn't do anything to you!" she shrieked.

"You opened the gates of Hell!" a woman shouted from behind her.

As she watched Finn's panic set in while death drew ever nearer, Rachel was rendered completely helpless. "This isn't going to bring your children back!"

"Maybe not, but it sure will get rid of you," Barrett growled and twisted her arm at a sharp angle.

Rachel arrived at the base of the maple tree and the polished dining room chair that waited for her. Marcus threw her against the tree trunk, knocking the wind out of her before he cuffed her hands together. At the same time, a noose fell over the top of her head and the scratchy rope tightened against her throat. Barrett's and Shane's arms hoisted her onto the chair where she stood facing the crowd beside Finn. The faces reflecting unintelligible rage looked warped as Rachel faintly heard the truck's engine gearing up behind them.

"Finn," Rachel choked out as the crowd's frenzy grew, "I'm sorry. I'm so, so sorry. I tried to keep you and the kids safe. I didn't know it would end like this. I shouldn't have brought you all here. I should've known—"

"Don't apologize," Finn responded with the voice of a dead man. He'd already stopped fighting the cuffs around his wrists. "You did the best you could . . . and so did I. We fucked up every single day, but there's no one else I would've rather tried with. I love you, Rachel."

"I love you, too," Rachel gasped through tears. "You were the best mistake I ever made."

Finn released a short laugh and closed his eyes.

Just then, the wind, smelling of pine, must, and honeysuckle, shifted and brought an electric chill. A strange creeping sensation made its way up Rachel's bound arms as if a hundred small fingers had reached out to brush her skin. Even with her vision blurred by tears, what she saw from her vantage point high above the mob sent a shiver down her spine—from terror, yes, but also . . . elation.

A black tide pushed forward from the tree line, slow and steady like a tsunami gathering power from the warm waters beneath. As the parade drew near, the features grew clearer—tiny hands clasped together, figures dressed in a patchwork of different clothing, hair glittering in the moonlight as their onyx eyes shined like glass. Their advance was fluid as if they floated rather than stepped over uneven fields and broken pavement. The children were silent as they approached, untroubled by the mass of furious adults raging at Finn's and Rachel's feet.

Rachel's voice was hoarse as she said to Finn, "Do you see them? The children . . . they've come back for us . . . all of us."

Thirty-Nine

The crowd remained drunk on their fury as the truck behind Rachel and Finn revved its engine. At any moment, Finn expected the driver to tear off, jerking their bodies backward to snap their necks. Yet, the tide of children continued to roll in, and Finn now knew beyond a doubt this was the last night *anyone* in Dahlmouth would see. He thought to shout at the people gathered before them, to tell them to run before these creatures masquerading as their offspring reflected their nightmares back onto them, but hell—who would listen to him anyways?

Rachel began laughing like a madwoman as the shadows approached. Their bodies stole the light from the sky and the flames from the torches of Dahlmouth's last citizens, taking on their own glow as they began to file in from between houses and streets.

"They came back like you prayed they would! Praise the Lord!" Rachel screamed out at the mass before her. "Welcome your babies home, you holy fucks!"

Some turned in the direction of Rachel's eyes, and broken shrieks rose as neighbors jostled into one another. Several women on the edge of the crowd—ones who had been content to watch as the rest of the town bloodied their hands—went slack; their shoulders drooped and their hands fell limp at their sides as they watched little ones draw near with palms now wide open. Finn couldn't see what the children before them offered, the wicked memories they spun from stardust and blew back into their mothers' faces, but he didn't have to. In unison, the women fell into states of bedlam.

On Finn's far left, Becky Foley swiveled, grabbed her husband by his thick brown hair, and sank her teeth into his throat. Almost effortlessly, she tore his larynx from his body, the severed jugular spurting dark red blood into the air long after the man collapsed at her feet. Off to Finn's right, Miss Crowley took a knee as if in prayer before the tiny girl who gently approached. Finn first thought the teacher was begging or perhaps crying in the creature's presence. But when the woman reared up, arching her back to face the sky, he saw she had clawed her eyes raw, a white mash of flesh in dark eye sockets as blood began to pour down her cheeks. She held her hands out to her sides, palms up as if to praise the heavens as stringy red gore dripped from her fingernails. From the fringes of the crowd, rising high into the night, there was that odd lullaby sang in tones unnatural to the human race.

Chaos broke loose. Blasts of gunfire erupted from within the tight group and Finn watched as Mrs. Brady happily leapt into a swarm of youngsters. The children encircled her with outstretched hands, placing them on the woman's head—and his imagination painted the rest of the picture for him.

Finn felt a cold wave crash over him as the children continued to pour from the forest. He couldn't count their precise numbers as they pressed in from every angle, but Finn knew there were more children gathering than had ever lived in Dahlmouth's boundaries. As citizens turned and hurtled into one another, Finn watched a small girl wearing a decaying bonnet and a long, torn, dirty dress slowly turn on her heels to survey the scene with a smile. Another child ambled between neighbors tearing each other apart, his pristine white collar and newsboy cap dapper as ever.

At the furthest edge of the swarm, Finn caught sight of a girl dressed in a white gown, wet unraveled lace from its hem dragging along the ground. Her long dark hair, drenched in river water, clung to the sides of her pale face. It was the child, from that awful night.

Though her expression was neutral, Finn remembered how impossibly wide her mouth could open, how thunderous the girl's scream sounded even beneath churning whitecaps. Her eyes were just as dark as they'd been when Finn's high beams first illuminated them—as dangerous and deep as when she stared back at him from the seat where Aidan should have been in the twisted SUV. That's when he understood. As the streets filled with these misplaced beings, Finn knew these were not just the children of Dahlmouth, but all those who had ever slipped into Nowhere.

Suddenly, Marcus peeled off from the group, twitching and rubbing at the back of his neck as if something rested on his shoulders. Without so much as a glance toward the pair he had been so intent on exorcising moments before, he stormed past them toward the window of the library. In one smooth motion, Marcus bashed his fist through the glass window where an array of Dr. Seuss books had been displayed for as long as the Kennans had resided in Dahlmouth. When he pulled his hand out, he grasped hold of one of the massive shards of glass and buried it deep into his right temple. The officer spasmed on his feet, his arms twitching before his body dropped to the ground, his head landing squarely on the glass shank.

Finn's knees almost gave out before he remembered his precarious situation atop the chair. Through his dry throat, Finn croaked, "Rach, what do we do?"

* * *

The crowd thinned as some walked silently with the children, hand in hand, toward the dark fringes of town while others had fallen where they stood, shrieking or praying or begging at the feet of the tiny gods.

Rachel blinked and turned her attention away from the scene unfolding before her and back to Finn. His lips were moving, but the words failed to penetrate the rising song of the children flooding the streets. The lullaby expanded inside her head until it began to push out even her own thoughts.

This wasn't the first time she'd heard the melody, but each time before, the tune had brought with it a sense of dread. Now, Rachel felt a strange calm wash over her despite the bedlam unfolding. Part of her knew this feeling was far more dangerous than the terror that had accompanied the song before. The rest of her, however, longed to relax into the lullaby and let it carry her away. Nothing felt easier than to close her eyes and drift into the music.

The words, which had been so muddled amidst the tree branches and leaves, now began to untangle. Voices separated out from the throng of children bringing the lyrics into relief, first in a language Rachel couldn't identify. Then, they slowly transitioned in crisp harmony to English:

Come along,
We've opened the door,
To the Kingdom,
To Nowhere,
Where we'll stay forevermore.

The longer the song played, the louder it became, the clearer Rachel could understand the words. More than that, Rachel swore she knew the voices carrying the tune.

"They're coming," she murmured, though she could barely hear herself. "Oh god, they're almost here."

And the music grew even louder.

* * *

"Rachel? Rachel, are you okay?" Finn's heart raced as his wife suddenly appeared faint. He instinctively tried to reach for her but was held in place by the handcuffs and noose around his neck. "Rach! Talk to me!"

"Can't you hear them?" Rachel called out, a sudden odd distance in her hazel eyes.

"Hear what?" The world was tearing itself apart at their feet. There was so much to hear, but Finn had the nasty suspicion Rachel was referring to something far different. "What are you talking about?"

Finn twisted in his restraints frantically again, his fingers slick. He threw a quick glance over his shoulder. The driver's-side door of Joe's pickup truck was open now, and through the glare of the headlights, Finn saw the man trying to scurry inside. Unadulterated fear seized Finn's heartbeat for a moment. Joe was preparing to hightail it out of Dahlmouth like any halfway sane person would, but his retreat would take Finn and Rachel's heads with it.

"RACHEL!" Finn screeched as he tugged harder at the cuffs. "We've gotta—"

"The song," Rachel shouted, pulling Finn's attention away from Joe's impending departure and back to his wife. "God, Finn! Can't you hear them?" She squeezed her eyes shut and trembled.

"Honey, open your eyes! Look at me," Finn commanded as she swayed on the chair. "Listen to my voice, baby," Finn pleaded with her as she squirmed in sudden agony to a sound he could not hear no matter how hard he tried.

Rachel let out a piercing scream that echoed off the branches above them, rising over the chaos that surrounded the pair. "They're so loud," she sobbed. "I feel like . . . my brain . . . it's on fire."

Rachel bent to rub her ear against her jacket, scrubbing away the fluid that had begun trickling from the canal. Finn stared at the dark smear of blood she left behind, powerless to comfort her. The truck door behind them slammed, jolting Finn, who gasped and craned his head around to see how little sand was left in their hourglass.

Joe's faint outline was visible through the windshield. In his mind, Finn saw the man throwing the gearshift into reverse with his boot on the pedal so clearly it was as if he sat beside Joe. A sickening whimper escaped Finn as nausea swept through him. Rachel's shrieks grew louder by the second. He flinched as she began screaming his name, wailing for help that he couldn't give. Soon, Finn heard her coughing and sputtering, her cries muffled by fluid. When he threw a glance in her direction, Rachel sent a mouthful of blood spraying into the air, strings of it hanging from her lips as she continued to screech.

"Make it stop!" she howled. "Finn! Make them stop!"

And suddenly, Finn would've given anything for Joe to move faster. Once again, he twisted in the chair to look over his shoulder. Joe still idled in the truck, his dark shape motionless behind the glass.

"WHAT ARE YOU WAITING FOR?!" Finn bellowed at the man. "DO IT!"

The shadow inside the truck leaned forward, and Finn took a deep breath. He hoped it wouldn't take long, that Joe would hit the gas pedal so hard, Finn and Rachel would die within seconds—that the inevitable blow to the neck as they were launched into the tree would end Rachel's suffering instantly. Joe was the only one who could do that for them, and in the most bizarre turn Finn could've dreamt up, he'd be forever grateful to the hulking man.

But as Joe's dark form shifted in the truck, a sinking feeling in Finn's gut began to weigh him down. The man straightened without moving the vehicle. The engine remained steady as Finn saw a long, thin shadow emerge from within the cab. Joe pulled it closer until it merged with his own silhouette, and suddenly Finn understood. As he opened his mouth to scream at the man, an orange flash pierced through the darkness of the truck's interior followed by an explosion that rattled Finn's ears. Blood splattered against the back windshield as the rifle's bullet cracked through Joe's skull and the window behind him, leaving only a small hole behind.

Forty

Rachel gasped as she felt something pop behind her eyes, instantly relieving the pressure of the children's lullaby in her head. She opened her eyes to find the world a hazy red. Hot tears began running down her cheeks. Finn's screams were just audible through her ruptured eardrums as the song began to grow quiet. Her eyelids felt heavier than they ever had before, and Rachel could think of little else other than sleep.

"Finn," she murmured, tasting metallic blood on her lips. "I'm dying."

"No, you're not!"

Rachel heard the fear in his voice and felt a twinge of sadness through her brain's fog. Despite the suffering they'd put one another through, Finn didn't deserve to die afraid. Few people did. There was no doubt in her mind, however, that he most certainly would because the children were coming. The music may have quieted as her mind melted away, but that didn't change the fact that Charlie, Aidan, and Lucy were near. Finn simply didn't know it yet.

Finn teetered on his chair, desperate to get over to Rachel even as she felt the twin streams of blood flowing down her cheeks grow wider.

"You're all right, Rach," Finn screamed at her, though it remained muffled in Rachel's damaged ears. "We're getting down from here, and I'm going to get you somewhere safe, and we're going to be okay, right? Say it back to me, Rach!" His gray eyes were wide, and Rachel sleepily wondered if he was now scared of her dying or just scared of her. She supposed both could be true at once.

"Mommy?" A voice cut through the haze, through the blood that flooded her ears, and sank directly into her heart.

The terror she'd felt moments before evaporated. As if someone had thrown the curtains wide to a bright spring day, Rachel felt sunshine on her face and smelled freshly cut grass. Aidan's voice was crystal clear—no more distant than the sound of her own heartbeat. There was no menace to it, like the nightmares that had been brought about by the other forest creatures' voices. It was real and warm, and it was as perfect as the moment she'd last held him in her arms. The darkness that had long ago burrowed into her core was washed away by the light. Now she could breathe again; Rachel could live again.

"Baby." Rachel sighed dreamily and closed her eyes.

"I missed you, Mom."

"I missed you, too," she whispered. "I'm glad you came."

* * *

"Rach," Finn spoke slowly as Rachel swayed on her feet, eyes closed with a soft smile on her bloody face. "Are you talking to Aidan, baby?"

"Can't you hear him?" Rachel breathed out with her eyes still closed as her smile broadened.

"No. No, I don't hear anything, baby."

As he watched Rachel sway, bliss sweeping over her, Finn considered how to shimmy from his chair to hers, how to wrap her in his arms and hold her until the madness faded. The thought of watching her die mere inches from him was too horrific for him to even consider.

Rachel and their children were the only home Finn could ever say was his—the one place he knew he belonged even when he didn't want to be there. But as this realization struck him, Finn considered whether that home, that sacred space in time, could exist anymore at all. Even if he and Rachel somehow clawed their way out of Dahlmouth physically intact, what world would remain for them? How would they revive a life that didn't include the reasons why they'd built one together in the first place?

As Rachel softly rocked back and forth on the strange breeze, chattering quietly with their son, Finn knew the answer.

"Aidan!" Finn called out over the gentle hum of Rachel's quiet voice. "Aidan! It's Daddy. I want you to talk to me, too, big guy!"

Finn's breath picked up as he waited for Aidan's voice. He gazed up into the tree branches to look away from Rachel's bloody tears. Still, his son's voice didn't come through.

"Aidan!" Finn bellowed as loud as he could manage, throat raw. "Charlie! Lucy! Please, god, someone answer me."

Instead, silence pressed in. Dahlmouth's chaos had quieted. The citizens so eager to destroy Finn and Rachel now lay at their feet, on the pavement, down the sidewalks. He didn't know where the other children had gone, nor did he care. All Finn wanted was to be swept up in the same illusion that held Rachel tight, even if it was just a fantasy . . . even if it ended the way Finn was certain it would.

"Rachel," Finn whimpered as the fear of surviving this night gripped him. "Don't leave me like this."

"Finn." Rachel's voice took on a measure of serenity he'd never heard before. He shifted his gaze from the heaps of bodies scattered around Dahlmouth's town center back onto his mate. Blood streaked down her face, her neck, her blouse. It clouded her eyes, turning the whites to a deep shade of scarlet at the same time it dried in the corners of her mouth. Yet, Rachel hadn't appeared so peaceful in all of the fourteen years they'd known one another.

His wife leaned closer to him, wrists still bound behind her. "You're not listening," she whispered sweetly and smiled, watery blood smeared across her teeth. "They're here. They've come home."

"Daddy!" Finn heard his little boy from behind the tree, beyond the truck that anchored their ropes. Rachel's blood-filled eyes met Finn's, and they stared at one another for a few short moments.

"See?" Rachel raised her eyebrows, her face aglow. "They came back for us."

"Mommy! Daddy!" Lucy called playfully. "Come play!"

"Dad!" the confident voice of the bold young woman Charlie was becoming rang out. "Come on, Dad! We're gonna be late!"

"It's time to go home, Finn," Rachel whispered.

She gave him the smile that had snagged Finn's heart the first time they sat beside one another at a run-down bar in Richmond. It was the same one Rachel wore when she'd looked into his face from a hospital bed, newborn Charlie resting against her chest—the dreamy smile his best friend flashed as they lay beside one another their first night in Dahlmouth after the kids had fallen asleep. He finally saw it again, in that moment beneath the maple tree.

Rachel broke her gaze with Finn first, but his eyes trailed effortlessly behind to greet their children.

It didn't take long—a few otherwise meaningless seconds—and contrary to what they had once expected, there was no fear left inside either one of them. Suddenly, they both remembered how the world was supposed to spin. For the first time in such a very long time, it all made sense. Finn and Rachel Kennan exhaled in relief and stepped off their chairs in perfect harmony as the things that had become Charlie, Lucy, and Aidan waited patiently for their feet to cease twitching.

Epilogue

"Drive," Officer Jack Carlyle commanded as Officer Danny Boyd threw the mouthpiece of the radio back into the patrol car.

"Where the fuck do a few hundred people go without telling anyone?"

"I don't know, and I don't want to know," Jack grumbled and swung the passenger-side door closed.

"People don't just disappear without a trace—not hundreds of them. And these fucking symbols everywhere ... This isn't right."

"Shut up and drive."

Danny didn't have to be told again. He slammed the car door shut and hit the gas pedal north up Route 6 toward Roanoke, a thick corridor of trees lining the way. They would need to discuss the report, how they were going to handle delivering this kind of news to Sheriff Odell, how crazy they would both sound. Then again, it couldn't get much crazier than what the junior medical examiner was going on about. Jack thought she must've cracked—an ageless hiker, a whole town missing from the map—but now that he saw what remained of Dahlmouth in the light of day, Michelle's story wasn't so unbelievable. Odell would have to send out more people. There was no getting around it this time.

One thing was for damn sure, though—Jack wouldn't be one of them. He'd shoot himself in the foot before they made him traipse through those woods.

"SHIT!" Danny gasped and slammed on the brakes, throwing Jack forward and scaring the hell out of him to boot.

What waited for him when Jack looked up, however, was far more concerning than the unexpected stop. A small girl—maybe six or so—stood dead center in the middle of Route 6, her light blonde hair matted with leaves and small twigs. Looking as if she was in a daze, the girl clutched a muddy teddy bear to her chest as she stared at the police car that had nearly plowed right into her.

"The fuck?" Jack murmured, almost numb with fear.

"She came outta nowhere," Danny panted, red-faced and still bracing for impact. "Jesus Christ—I thought I was gonna run right into her."

Jack swung open the cruiser's door and stepped out, though that was the very last thing he wanted to do. Danny began radioing the situation in as Jack slowly approached the little girl, still standing firm only a few feet from where the car had skidded to a stop. She swayed a bit now, hugging the bear tightly and humming a tune Jack didn't know.

Something about her made his skin crawl. His first instinct was to unholster his gun, but Jack mercifully regained his senses before doing so. Instead, he carefully knelt in front of her, coming even with her bright blue eyes. A few scratches were laced across her cheek, but otherwise, the girl seemed physically unharmed.

"Hi there, sweetheart," Jack said, forcing gentleness into his tone as he looked her over. "What are you doing out here? It's dangerous to be in the road."

The little girl shrugged in response and began humming again, though she never broke eye contact with the officer.

"You from Dahlmouth?" Jack tried again.

The girl nodded once before smiling a big, toothy grin.

"What's your name?"

"Lucy!" the girl said. "Lucy Kennan. Do you know my mommy?"

Jack felt as if all the blood drained from his face. "I think so." He nodded but couldn't manage a smile. "She's the police chief around here, right?"

"That's her!" Lucy rocked faster with her muddy bear.

Jack continued nodding while pushing down the urge to get in the car and drive off as fast as possible. "Where is your mommy? We were just looking for her."

"Nowhere." Lucy shrugged before returning to humming yet again. Jack leaned back onto his heels, once more trying to shake the terrible unease closing around him.

"You look like you've been outside awhile. Where were you?"

"Nowhere," the girl sang in between humming before she paused to give her ratty stuffed animal a quick kiss on the head.

Jack led the child to the car, held the back door open for her to climb inside, still holding her bear close. As much as he knew he should be ashamed, Jack was thankful for the bars that separated him and Danny from the girl in the back.

"Should we keep looking around?" Danny mumbled to Jack, his eyes pleading for the answer to be a no. "I mean, if the little kid's here—"

"You can look around, sir, but you're not gonna find anybody else," Lucy offered from the back with sunshine in her voice. She placed her teddy bear in the seat behind Jack and buckled him in before obediently buckling her own seat belt.

They should have asked her why or questioned where everyone else had gone, but Jack imagined the answer would be about as helpful as the ones Lucy had already given.

"Let's just get back to Roanoke, get the kid checked out, and call over CPS."

Danny nodded eagerly and put the car in drive. The little girl's continued humming grated on Jack's nerves, but he couldn't bring himself to command her to stop. Jack saw Danny press his lips together and shift uncomfortably as they approached the bridge where Chief Kennan's husband had careened right over the edge with two of her kids in tow—perhaps even this one. He ran a hand over the back of his neck to brush away the crawling sensation.

Jack knew he should be thinking, *Poor kid*. He should be hoping Chief Kennan and the rest of her family would be found so this little girl wasn't facing down another tragedy for the second time in her short life. Yet, all Jack could think of was the moment they could pull up to the station and get her out of the vehicle.

"You can hit the siren. It'll clear everybody out so we can get there faster." Jack cleared his throat to loosen fear's grip on his vocal cords.

"There's nobody on the road."

"Do it anyways."

With a short sigh, Danny reached down and flipped the switch on the car's siren and swirling lights. As he did, Jack's eyes caught movement in the backseat through the rearview mirror. Her small legs swinging, a tune still on her lips, Lucy Kennan was excitedly waving goodbye out of the back window toward the small roadside memorial marking the place where her brother had lost his life. Beyond that crooked white cross, Jack could've sworn he saw a small boy waving back at her from the tree line.

The little girl dropped her hand and swiveled in her seat to face forward. Panic seized Jack's heart as for just one moment, the Kennan girl stared at him with sparkling black eyes. He blinked hard as his vision blurred. When Jack looked again, however, there was nothing in the mirror other than the blue-eyed little girl smiling with unnerving serenity.

No impending danger. No black eyes. No lost boy hovering beside his own memorial.

Nothing at all.

The boy and every other citizen of Dahlmouth were forever nowhere to be found.

Acknowledgements

From its inauspicious beginnings as a few paragraphs on my cell phone, to the moment in which you are reading it now, a small army of incredible people helped *Whispers in the Dark* come to life.

First, I cannot thank my agent, Logan Harper, enough. Your enthusiasm, patience, creativity, and—most importantly—kindness have bolstered me. A big thank-you to everyone at the Jane Rotrosen Agency who sent along fresh ideas to make the story pop, especially Rebecca Scherer. Many thanks to Allison Hufford at JRA as well for her continued international outreach.

My deepest gratitude to my editor, Loan Le, whose keen eye and love of twisted tales makes every horror novel she touches sparkle. Without your vision, the world would never have known the tenderness that once existed between Finn and Rachel, the memories haunting Charlie, or Pastor Paul's glorious last bath.

Many thanks to everyone at Atria whose tireless work made all the difference for *Whispers in the Dark*: Elizabeth Hitti, Dana Sloan, Shelby Pumphrey, Paige Lytle, Aleaha Reneé, Sonja Singleton, Debbie Norflus, Nicole Bond, Sara Bowne, Rebecca Justiniano, Kelli McAdams, and Jimmy Iacobelli.

Thank you to the troop of beta readers who provided invaluable feedback. Cheers especially to my critique partner E.W. Doc

Parris. Sticky notes with your words of encouragement still wallpaper my workspace.

Mom, you gifted me with the tenacity and zest to keep moving forward. Despite our differences, you still support and love me. I promise I'll write you something happier one day. Dad, your fearless evolution encourages me to never stop growing. Thank you for reading this novel long before I ever dared to give it to the world. To my sister, Jamie, your humor and courage carried me through much of my childhood. Your love of literature and horror shaped me into the writer I am today. Thank you all for joining me on this wild ride.

To my dearest friend, Julie McVey, you were there the moment I decided to finally publish, and you haven't stopped rooting for me since. Thank you and Jon Musser for allowing me to camp in your basement to finish multiple drafts of *Whispers in the Dark*, periodically reminding me to eat or take a walk. To Katie Labor, you are my perpetual cheerleader and a font of joy in the face of turmoil. My heart overflows with gratitude to you all. The four of us are more than friends; we are family.

Devon, thank you for challenging me with kindness. You can finally hold the book I rambled about over countless glasses of wine. I love you.

Finally, to my daughters: Carys, your ferocity, passion, loyalty, and unmatched wit not only served as the inspiration for Charlie, they inspire your mother every single day. Lennon, you grew up faster than Lucy while I wrote this book, but your everlasting sweetness, love, and gentleness shaped her character and still shines through the pages. You both saved my life, and no words will ever fully convey how grateful I am to be your mom.

Author's Note

"Hit me!" he screamed in my face with his hand reared back. "Go ahead and hit me!" I knew the neighbors could hear the latest battle unfolding. The kids had left moments before. I was late for work with my best friend waiting outside. Panicked and embarrassed, I slipped under his arm and ran out with my heart pounding.

Within a week, Finn and Rachel Kennan were on the page standing in place of my former spouse and me, wrestling with truths I'd hid even from myself. *Whispers in the Dark* was born.

The foundation of *Whispers in the Dark* was laid long before that day, however. Growing up the daughter of a fundamentalist pastor in the rural South, I ingested the prejudices and anxiety of the believers surrounding me. I learned every fire-and-brimstone verse my teachers assigned. I dog-eared pages of my Bible to remember how to guide others to Christ. Most of all, I hated myself for the "sin" growing in me—the inescapable knowledge that I possessed a one-way ticket to hell: I was queer, and no amount of "praying the gay away" seemed to help. The subsequent self-loathing and fear would color every decision I made for the next twenty-five years, leading me into the depths of depression, destructive behavior, and poisonous relationships on a desperate path toward some sort of redemption.

Whispers in the Dark grew out of those bleak moments, lacing together the shame of my childhood with the beautiful shock of motherhood and the horror of a toxic marriage. This novel served as a break between the old and new versions of me, the moment in time when I finally confronted the demons that had long chased me in the night. It marked the death of an era filled with hurt and trauma.

But *Whispers in the Dark* isn't just about suffering. Writing the novel allowed me to treat wounds left by years of burying my identity beneath dogma. It gave me the strength to own my mistakes, forgive myself and others for being human, and finally embrace authenticity. This book contains pieces of the person I once was, glimpses of the person I am now, and love for the person I will become.

My hope is that the novel challenges readers to reflect on their own lives, interrogating the past through a new lens with an open heart. For those whose journey includes similar themes—religious oppression, stigmatization, isolation, grief—may you find comfort knowing you are not alone, for even in the darkest forest amidst seemingly insurmountable foes, you are strong enough to escape your own darkness.

About the Author

Allison Gunn is a professional researcher, writer, and tarot reader with a penchant for all things whimsical and strange. She received her master's degrees in history as well as library science from the University of Maryland in 2016. She has previously published in the fields of public policy and digital librarianship. *Whispers in the Dark* is her debut fiction novel.

She currently resides in the wonderfully weird land of West Virginia with her twin daughters, precocious pup, and one seriously troubled tabby.

About Embla Books

Embla Books is a digital-first publisher of standout commercial adult fiction. Passionate about storytelling, the team at Embla believe our lives are built on stories – and publish books that will make you 'laugh, love, look over your shoulder and lose sleep'. Launched by Bonnier Books UK in 2021, the imprint is named after the first woman from the creation myth in Norse mythology. Embla was carved by the gods from a tree trunk found on the seashore; an image of the kind of creative work and crafting that writers do, and a symbol of how stories shape our lives.

Find out about some of our other books and stay in touch:

X, Facebook, Instagram: @emblabooks
Newsletter: https://bit.ly/emblanewsletter